Every Time a Bell Rings

CARMEL HARRINGTON

Harper impulse
we've got the love

Harper*Impulse* an imprint of
HarperCollins*Publishers*
1 London Bridge Street
London SE1 9GF

www.harpercollins.co.uk

A Paperback Original 2015

First published in Great Britain in ebook format by Harper*Impulse* 2015

A catalogue record for this book
is available from the British Library

ISBN: 978-0-00-815656-5

Set in Minion by Born Group using Atomik ePublisher from Easypress

Printed and bound in Great Britain by
Clays Ltd, St Ives plc

MIX
Paper from
responsible sources

FSC
www.fsc.org   **FSC® C007454**

Carmel Harrington

'Will make you see life in a different way'
Woman's Way

'Heartwrenching and heartwarming'
Evening Herald

'Guaranteed to brighten your day'
Novelicious

'Carmel Harrington has done it again! Brilliantly
written … it surpasses all expectations'
Chicklit Club

'A bittersweet, quietly brilliant novel that will make you
cry, laugh and cry all over again'
Female First

'Funny, poignant and bursting with heartfelt humour'
I Heart … Chick Lit

'Completely stunning'
Reviewed the Book

'It will stay with you well after you have turned the last page'

Carmel Harrington lives with her husband, Roger, and children, Amelia and Nate, in a small coastal village in Wexford. She credits the idyllic setting as a constant source of inspiration to her. She has won several international awards including Kindle Book of Year and Romantic eBook of Year at the Festival of Romance in 2013 for her debut novel, *Beyond Grace's Rainbow*.

Carmel is a regular on Irish TV as one of the panelists on TV3's *Midday* show, as well as being interviewed on RTE1's *Today* show, TV3's *IrelandAM* and *The Morning Show*. She has also been interviewed on US TV – Indiana's WNDU. A regular guest on radio stations nationally, including BBC Radio 1 Ulster, RTE Radio 1, Newstalk, SouthEastRadio, Artyfacts and many more regional stations. A popular freelance writer, she has written features for the *Irish Independent*, *Daily Mail*, *Evening Herald*, *Woman's Way* and acclaimed online blog, *Mothering In The Middle*.

Carmel is also a popular motivational keynote speaker at events in Ireland, UK and US.

To find out more about Carmel, go to www.carmelharrington. com.

For my family – the H's,
Roger, Amelia, Nate & Eva.

Your children are not your children.
They are the sons and daughters of Life's longing for itself.
They come through you but not from you,
And though they are with you yet they belong not to you.

Khalil Gibran

Prologue

Blessed is the season which engages the whole world in a conspiracy of love.

Hamilton Wright Mabie

Christmas Eve, 2005

'Happiness is …' I exhale a long, deep, satisfied sigh, and the cold breath of winter floats out of my mouth up into the air.

'*This* is the best Christmas street lighting yet.'

I know I say the same thing every year, in this very same spot, at this very same time. I'll probably say it again next year too.

In this moment, I've never seen anything more perfect. The Victorian-inspired decorations are from a bygone era that shine with goodwill to all men. I know, I know, that sounds all cheese on toast, but when it comes to Christmas, that's allowed. With extra parmesan on top, as far as I'm concerned.

My city, my beloved Dublin, is sparkling in a festive glow. And its inhabitants are collectively holding their breaths, because Christmas is almost here.

And this year, I've been delivered an early Christmas present. The fact that it's the same one I received when I was eight years old isn't lost on me. Coincidence, fate, magic, I don't know what forces are at play to make this happen, but I'm grateful.

Just two weeks ago, I was single, happily so too, living my best life, teaching kids in St Colmcille's. I honest to goodness didn't wake up each day lamenting the lack of love in my life. Because I had a *good* life, boyfriends coming and going. I figured that one day I would meet Mr Right. But now that he is here, I cannot believe that I ever got through each day without him by my side.

Here I am, at the foot of Grafton Street with Jim Looney of all people. If you would have suggested such a thing to me a mere few weeks ago, the words 'look up' and 'flying pigs' would have been uttered.

Jim Looney.

I sigh again as I take him in, standing beside the statue of Molly Malone, laughing at the tinsel that someone has draped over her cleavage.

An image of Jim strutting down a runway pops into my head and I giggle at the thought. He could give any male model a run for their money, but I think he'd rather pull his nails out one by one than do that.

I grab my phone and take a photo of him. I've already taken at least a dozen this evening. He could be modelling a new line in men's winter clothing, he looks so good. I mean, not many could get away with that multi-coloured Dr Who-inspired scarf wrapped around his neck over and over. But on him it looks quirky and cool.

And, this is the bit that I still can't quite believe.

He's my boyfriend. All mine.

Don't go getting too used to this, Belle. It never lasts.

I quickly banish the little voice inside my head. Go away nasty mean voice.

I know full well that I'm punching above my weight. I mean, for goodness sake, he's even got a chiselled jawline. Seriously, I'm telling you, he's fecking gorgeous. I can't find ways to describe him to you without sounding like a big sap. But trust me when I say this. He's, as we are want to say in Dublin about a good-looking man, a 'ride'.

When I look into his big blue eyes, I'm done for. I keep forgetting what I'm about to say when he directs those baby blues at me.

And don't get me started on his hair. That's always been my Achilles heel. It makes me feel all protective and full of love. You see, it has this habit of just flopping over his right eye. I'm sure most would say it's red or ginger, maybe even auburn. But I like to call it foxy.

Jim McFoxy Looney.

When it does that flopping thing, it's as if my hands have a mind of their own and they involuntarily reach up to brush it back off his forehead. But there again, I'm not complaining about that, because I don't need any excuse to touch Jim. And I've realised that when I do touch him, it seems to have a delicious knock-on effect. One minute I'm lightly touching his forearm, then the next we're kissing.

A shiver ripples through me as I remember what happened only this morning when I brushed past him on my way into the bathroom.

Twice.

Who would have thought that Jim Looney had *that* in him? I'm telling you, it's ridiculous how sexy he is.

He is, no other word for it, but a fecking ride.

You'll notice that I'll find any excuse to say that.

Jim Looney, the big ride, my boyfriend.

I feel a bit giddy with it all, to be honest. It's like it's five o'clock all the time and I'm half drunk. The mad thing is, I've not had much to drink in weeks. Jim's not a big drinker and that in itself is charming, because all the guys I've dated recently seem to be more in love with a pint of lager than me. Kind of refreshing to be with a guy who gets that there are more things to do in life than prop up a bar.

'What are you thinking about?' Jim asks, with a raised eyebrow.

'Ah, that would be telling,' I say with a grin.

Thank goodness he can't read thoughts. If I tell him what I've just been thinking, we'll be in a taxi and on our way back to my apartment before the words are out of my mouth. And as tempting as that thought is, it will have to wait.

Because it's Christmas Eve and we're on Grafton Street, where its festive delights await us.

'So, tell me about this tradition of yours, the one you do every Christmas Eve?' Jim asks.

'This is my tenth year. Started because of Joyce O'Connor,' I say.

'Why do I get the feeling there's a story there?' Jim remarks.

'Oh yes, there's a story alright. She asked me to go into the city with her one Christmas Eve, when I was fifteen,' I say.

I wonder what Joyce is up to now. We lost touch a long time ago. But she's wrapped up in this particular tradition and standing here usually sparks a memory of her.

She wasn't even a close friend. In fact, if I'm calling a spade a spade, she was a bit of a bitch. I don't know why I said yes in the first place when she asked me to go with her. I mean, she'd been one of those passive aggressive wagons for years. The queen of making snide comments behind my back, giving inverted compliments that everyone knows is really an insult.

I spent half my childhood trying to dodge Joyce and her cronies in the hallways at school. Anything to avoid one of her 'chats'.

'I remember her. At least I think I'm remembering the right one. Blonde, small girl? Touch of the mean girls about her? She was one of the gang who used to give you a hard time,' Jim says.

I laugh, yep, he's got her number. 'Good memory. She had her moments, for sure. And the only reason she asked me to go with her on that day was because she had no other options. Her usual cronies were busy and she needed a decoy. Her parents would never have let her go off to meet a boy on her own. But a nice innocent trip into town with a friend, well, that was different.'

'Oh, I get it. You got to be a big, fat, green, hairy gooseberry,' Jim says.

I nod. 'I'd nothing better to do, so thought, why not? And it made Tess happy when I told her I was off gallivanting. She was always worrying about me being such a loner.'

'Did you have fun in the end?' Jim says. 'Maybe she wasn't as bad as you thought?'

'No, we didn't bond over hot chocolate or anything. She was true to form and remained a wagon. But despite that, I did have fun,' I say.

The 16B bus had been jammers with lots of people with the same idea, to head into the city to soak up the festive atmosphere.

'Joyce didn't even bother keeping up a pretence that we were together for more than a few minutes. Once we jumped on board the bus she ran upstairs to the upper deck and within seconds was doing a round of tonsil hockey with a pimply, horny boy called Billy Doyle. I swear her arse hadn't even hit the seat he'd saved for her before his tongue was down her throat,' I say.

'You can't buy class.' Jim says shaking his head.

'A right dirt bird.' I say and he laughs with me. 'You know, they hadn't even bothered to save a seat for me. As the upper deck was so full, I had no choice but to retreat back downstairs, tail between my legs and stand. Joyce didn't give me a backwards glance, the cheeky mare,' I say.

I marvel that I ever allowed myself to be treated like that.

'Once we arrived at O'Connell Street, the two love birds headed to McDonalds to share a strawberry shake. It was clear I wasn't included in their romantic date, so I left them to it. I suppose I should have been annoyed with her, but I didn't mind in the slightest.'

Jim throws a sympathetic glance my way, but I'm quick to reassure him, 'I was used to my own company back then, preferred it a lot of the time.'

It baffled me as to why they wanted to sit on plastic seats in a noisy fast-food restaurant, when they could be out, soaking up the Christmassy atmosphere in the city.

'It was their loss. I got to explore Dublin, on my own. It was almost dusk and the city changes in that light. Everything seemed so magical.'

I pause, feeling embarrassed, 'This probably sounds silly but, to me, it felt like I was looking at my city with new eyes.'

'Not silly at all.' Jim replies. 'You know what I thought when we got to O'Connell Street? There's a touch of Bedford Falls about it all now. You know, the town in *It's a Wonderful Life*.'

I smile and nod in agreement. I've always thought the same. 'I love that movie.'

I jump as a badly dressed Santa roars in our direction. 'Merry Christmas. Ho ho ho.' He rings his bell and rattles a box loudly, collecting change for charity. He seems intent on frightening passers-by and is clearly delighted with himself when everyone jumps in shock.

I throw a few euro into his box and then Jim says, 'So fill me in on how this tradition of yours works.'

'Well, ever since that year, I've come back each Christmas Eve. I start off in O'Connell Street, then walk over the

7

Liffey, past Trinity College, say hello to the Molly Malone statue in all her glory, stroll up Grafton Street, then head over to the Ha'penny Bridge, before going home,' I say.

'You ever mix it up and change the route?' Jim asks.

'Oh, God no. Has to be in that order,' I say. 'Oh, I nearly forgot to say, I do have a quick pit stop in Captain America's for hot chocolate and a slice of their, quite frankly, decadent Mississippi Mud Pie. Just to keep the energy levels up.' I grin like a four-year-old.

'Sounds like quite a nice tradition to keep.' Jim says. 'I'm glad I'm here to share it with you this year.'

'I'm glad you're here too. You know, I've had years of strolling up and down this cobbled street with boyfriends, girlfriends, school friends and, yes, I'll even admit it – the shame – on my own a few times.' I look at him, feeling a little shy. 'But this feels special, more than any other year. That's because of you, Jim.'

He grabs my hand and laughs, 'I'm honoured. Come on then, Ms Bailey, show me what this great city of ours has to offer.'

My eyes greedily take in the view ahead of us, down Grafton Street. Red, flickering lights coil around luscious green garlands, which drape from one side of the street to the other. In the centre of each garland is a large red Victorian lantern and the light casts a warm glow over the busy cobbled street. Each shop window is alight with Christmas lights and resplendent baubles in rich jewel colours.

There's something about the energy here … well, it is breathtaking.

I'm not the only one who feels that. I can see it on the faces of people as they rush by too, with their pre-Christmas festive highs.

Okay, maybe not so much on that guy's face, I giggle, as a harassed man in his forties rushes by. Last-minute shopper, I decide. Poor sap. I've mine all done and dusted since October. I wouldn't dream of leaving it to now. But aside from the odd scowling face, the street is awash with a sea of shiny, happy people.

'Look over there,' I shout in excitement as I spy a window display with a group of reindeers nibbling on fake grass in the snow. Then another scene catches my eyes and I'm darting over to the other side of the street, pulling Jim behind me.

'Earlier, when you said happiness is ...' Jim waves his hand around the Christmas-card view in front of us, 'is all of this what you meant by happiness?'

'Well, obviously lots of things make me happy. But this, well, it's up there with the best of them. I love everything about Christmas. You must feel it too? Doesn't it feel like we're in a Christmas movie right now?' I exclaim.

'Oh, a blockbuster for sure.' He drawls. 'Aside from twinkling lights, which I know you're a sucker for, what else makes you happy?'

I reckon the feel of my hand in his, as we walk through the frenzied crowds, is top of my happy list right now. But a girl has to hold some cards to herself, so I remain silent.

'I want to know. Come on, Belle. What else makes you happy?' Jim persists.

'Oh, a lot of different things. Not having to set the alarm on Saturdays and Sundays. Peanut butter on hot toast. But don't be giving me cold toast. I can't be doing with rubbery cold toast,' I say.

'A shootable offence that?' He asks and when I nod, he says, 'I'm taking notes here. This is good intel.'

'Well, while you're at it, add to the list that not spreading said peanut butter to all corners of the toast is equally damnable. I can't be doing with someone who just smears it on willy nilly, not giving due consideration to all parts of the bread,' I tell him.

'Got it. Take care when smearing peanut butter – evenly – on piping-hot toast. What else makes your ladyship happy?' He says, tipping his hat in mock salute.

'I love starting a new book and then realising that it's one of the good ones. The kind that I am not going to want to finish,' I say.

I think some more and add, 'Oh and dancing. Any kind, but preferably one that involves a lot of bum-shaking is guaranteed to make me smile.'

Jim raises his eyebrow so I reward him with a little shake of my bum.

'See. Look how happy my dancing makes you too.' I tease, and he bursts into laughter.

'Oh, you can be assured that your bum makes me happy,' he declares, giving it a pat, and I thank the stars that I stuck at the squats this summer in the gym.

'You've not mentioned swinging,' Jim states.

'How very dare you! I'm a respectable lady, I'll have

you know. I've never left my key ring in anyone's fruit bowl.' I feign outrage. I know what he's referring to, but it's still fun teasing him.

He starts to splutter an explanation, then he realises my game.

'Yes, Jim Looney, I still love swings. I can't pass by a park without seeing how high I can go.' I admit. 'And I do some of my best thinking when I'm up there chasing the clouds.'

'You were always the same,' he remembers. 'I was more of a slide man myself.'

I remember him always trying to climb up the slide, rather than use the ladder and me begging him to push me higher and higher on the swings. That was a long time ago, though.

He pulls me to the side of the street, out of the lane of traffic and looks searchingly into my eyes.' What about me? Do I make you happy?'

I'm surprised to see that my confident, laid-back boyfriend looks like a ten-year-old boy, suddenly unsure of himself.

Without hesitation, I take his hands between my own and tell him, with the utmost sincerity, 'You, Jim Looney, make me happiest most of all.'

My friends would be horrified that I've laid my heart bare so early on in our relationship. I know that I probably should play a little harder to get. But I've never been any good at hiding how I feel.

'You get what you see with my Belle.' Tess always says. Heart-on-sleeve territory.

Well, he's getting a complete, hopelessly devoted to you, kind of lovestruck feeling from me right now.

He gives me the strangest look. Damn it, I've frightened him off.

'You're full of surprises,' he says after a moment of tortured silence and you'd swear he was just seeing me for the first time.

'You okay?' I ask and my stomach flips. That strange look is back on his face. It worries me.

'So much has changed since I left, but then, some things are just as they were when I said goodbye.' He murmurs. 'It's disconcerting.'

'You're getting all reflective in your old age.' I poke him in his side. 'Now enough of that, come on admit it, Brown Thomas gives Macy's a run for its money, doesn't it?'

'Absolutely, it's not half-bad.' He acknowledges in his slow half-Midwestern, half-Irish drawl, and we pause to take in the decadent window displays.

'I really think it's the most beautiful street in the world.' I murmur. 'When I stand here, I feel like a child again.'

As we move from window to window of the department store I have the most wonderful sensation that I've been engulfed in a big Christmas hug. Mannequins draped in Victorian clothing, bejewelled with pearls and glittering gems, stand and sit in displays, dressed with snow, fairy lights and dazzling Christmas trees. I lean back into Jim's embrace and nuzzle my head into the crook of his neck.

Oh, I love how he smells. I've spent some time on this subject and have decided that it's a mix of spice and cinnamon and oaky leathers. He actually smells a bit Christmassy.

And then his arms wrap around my body and I think he's just so … I struggle to find the right word and then giggle when it comes to me. He's just so manly, yes that's the word.

I catch a glimpse of us in the reflection of the window display, me giggling and him smiling in response, even though he has no idea why I'm doing so and I don't think I've ever felt luckier.

I notice a few people looking at us. I'm used to that, the gawping, that is. The foxy-haired Irishman with a Midwestern US drawl and the caramel-skinned Amazonian woman, with black afro hair and Dublin accent. An unlikely pair maybe, but we somehow fit perfectly.

When I stand by his side, he makes me feel prettier than I've ever felt with any other man. It doesn't hurt that at six foot four he can make my five foot ten-inch tall frame look almost petite. Well, maybe not petite, that's probably a stretch.

And never mind how he looks, it's how he makes me feel that has me undone. Ever since our amazing first kiss, I crave him, there's no other way to describe how it feels than that.

I mean, I was doing very nicely without him for the past ten years, thank you very much. Now I cannot be without him.

Is this what true love feels like? Did Cinderella feel like this when she met her Prince Charming? I hope so.

What happens when he goes home to Indiana after Christmas, though?

There's that nasty inner voice again. Shut up. I refuse to even think about anything more than this moment right now. And to prove that point I turn to face him and kiss him passionately, with every fibre of my being. I don't care who is watching and it appears, as his tongue makes its way towards mine, that he doesn't either.

'Ahem.' A voice coughs and we pull apart to see who is trying to get our attention. It's the dapper concierge of Brown Thomas. He's wagging his finger at us, but he's smiling, there's no sting to his rebuke. He just wants us to move away from the front of his store.

'Sorry about that.' Jim tips his head towards him and we start to move away. 'Let's go get some of that mud pie you keep going on about. I think I'm going to need to keep my strength up with you.'

I wave happily to the concierge and he waves his top hat to me, shouting, 'Merry Christmas, lovebirds.'

The chocolate pie tastes as good as I remember. Jim suggests sharing a slice, but I put that notion to bed straight away.

'I'll add the "no sharing of chocolate treats" to my list,' he jokes.

When we leave Captain America's, sated and giddy with sugar, we stop, listening to the sounds that tinkle in the air.

We walk slowly up to Stephen's Green and take a stroll around the park. It's quiet there and we walk in comfortable silence.

'Where to next?' Jim asks when we have done a full loop of the park.

'I told you, we head to the Ha'penny Bridge then to O'Connell Street, finally back to Tess's,' I say.

'And I really have to sleep in her spare room tonight?' Jim moans.

'Yes. Don't you dare try to do any bedroom flits. You'll give her a coronary,' I say.

Before we have a chance to debate sleeping arrangements any further, the sound of a girl singing floats towards us. 'That's so pretty.' I point towards the Ha'penny Bridge. 'It's coming from over there.'

'She's singing your favourite Christmas song,' he says.

His knowing this, remembering that fact, overwhelms me. He sees this and lightly touches my cheek. 'I keep telling you, Belle. I remember everything.'

We move towards the sound of her voice. It is so pure and beautiful, it makes harried shoppers stop in their tracks, one by one. We push our way through the crowds and I half expect to see a CD deck. But to my surprise, I see that the owner of the voice is in fact a young girl, standing in the middle of the bridge.

'She's no more than ten or eleven,' I say, unable to take my eyes off her.

'She's so cute,' a woman remarks and we both nod in agreement. The girl is wearing a double-breasted red woollen coat. She has bobbed, black shiny hair that bounces off her black-velvet collar. The lights on the bridge bounce off the still water below and back up around her, creating a soft glow.

It's the most beautiful moment I've ever experienced. There is something so pure about the voice, the girl, the bridge.

'Can you believe that voice?' Jim says in amazement as she belts out *O Holy Night* like a pro.

'She has the voice of an angel,' I whisper and feel emotion swell inside of me. Tears threaten to fall and that won't do at all, not on Christmas Eve.

'*A thrill of hope, the weary world rejoices. …*' I sing along with her, reaching for Jim's hand. He clasps it tight. The words touch my heart in a way they've never done before. I realise that I felt exactly like that, weary, only three weeks ago. Then Jim walked into my life and, in an instant, everything changed.

I feel my whole body shudder as another wave of emotion overtakes me and I have to pinch myself hard to stop myself falling to the ground weeping. Is it just me, or is Jim as affected? I pull my eyes away from the girl and take a peek at him. Thank goodness, I can see he's not immune to her voice either. His eyes glisten in the crisp night air and I lean in towards him once more.

And then something hits me with a jolt. I've finally come home. Right here, in this man's arms. I'm home.

It's only been three weeks, though.

But it feels like a lifetime. How can that be?

I know why. He's my destiny. I wished for him. And he arrived all but wrapped up in a bow.

I look around at the gathered audience standing around this young girl. Families, couples and groups of friends, all captivated by a beatific voice.

I decide there and then that I must never forget this moment. There aren't many times in life that are so perfect and pure that they can make your heart explode in joy. This is one of them.

As the young girl builds up to the last line, her voice hits the high note with ease. And all at once the busy thoroughfare is silent, spellbound, by her pure voice.

How long do we stand in wondrous silence? It seems to stay that way for ages, but it can only be for a few seconds.

Then the hush is interrupted by a joyful jingle as the crowd moves forward, one by one, to drop coins into a red-velvet hat that is by her feet. As the coins hit each other, they chime and tinkle, casting magical notes high up into the night air.

'It's like the bells are ringing.' I say in wonder.

'Bells ringing for *you*, Belle,' Jim says.

I take my turn to throw a handful of euros into the red cap and the girl looks right into my eyes, a big smile across her face. And you know what? The weirdest sensation overcomes me. I swear I know this girl. I have this ridiculous urge to hug her.

As her parents are most likely watching right now and would think I'm a crazy lady, I resist.

'If Simon Cowell were to rock by right now, he'd have euro signs shining in his eyes. That's a Christmas number one right there, that song,' I turn to tell Jim, expecting to see him behind me. Where's he got to? I scan the bridge right and left, kicking myself for moving forward, away from him. The crowds are thick as everyone moves to continue their evening, and I can't see him anywhere.

But then, I feel his hand grab mine and I smile in relief, feeling silly for my dramatic panic.

'There you are!' I exclaim. Now what the hell is he doing? I watch in complete shock as he drops to one knee, right here, in the middle of the Ha'penny Bridge.

'Have you lost something?' I ask, thinking he must have dropped his wallet or something. I start scouring the cobblestones around me.

'Look. That man is going to propose,' someone shouts from behind me, and my stomach starts to flip, even though I know that it's impossible. Jim's not going to propose.

I turn to them to say, 'Don't be so ridiculous, there's no way that's happening.'

Sure I've only known Jim three weeks. People don't propose that quickly. That only happens in books or movies. Not in Dublin. And certainly not to me, Belle Bailey.

But when I look down, he's not laughing, he's looking at me intently. He doesn't look like he's lost anything. Nor does he look terrified. In fact, if I had to call it, I'd say he looks downright happy. A little bit goofier than normal, with a strange look on his usually cocky face.

'I've not lost anything, Belle. On the contrary, I would say that I've found something pretty wonderful.' I can hear an audible gasp from someone behind me. I look around at the sea of faces who a moment ago were united in emotion at the young girl's song. And now they are united in expectation, as delicious real-life drama unfolds in front of them. They'll have plenty to chat about over their mince pies later on.

'I want my happy-ever-after to be with you, Belle. I want to grow old with you. I never want to let you go. I want to love you so much that you never look sad again,' Jim states.

Did I just dream that?

I mean, it does sound like a proposal, but there again he hasn't actually asked me. I purse my lips tight. There's no way I am going to jump in and say 'yes' to a declaration as opposed to a question.

But, even so, something that feels a lot like excitement starts to course its way through my body.

'I want to marry you. I want to marry my best friend.' His voice is strong, unfaltering.

Oh boy. No room for misunderstanding now.

The crowd who were about to disperse moments before have now made a circle around us. In an unspoken movement, they are now protecting us from jostling shoppers. I hear them gasp and shush each other as Jim's words echo through the crisp night air.

'I didn't plan this, which is silly, because it's all I've thought about for days. I don't even have a ring.' He says, and looks forlorn.

I've spent my whole life dreaming of happy-ever-afters, where the prince drops to one knee, diamond ring in one hand as he pleads his devotion. But now, in this moment, I realise that I don't care one jolt about a ring. I smile in an attempt to reassure him of my non-materialistic self.

'But I do have this,' he continues, his face breaking out into a big smile again, and he reaches into the inside pocket of his jacket.

What on earth is he going to pull out? He's got a square box in his hand, wrapped in red paper, with a brilliant white bow on top.

'That's one fancy-pants wrapping job there,' I say to him.

'I bought this earlier for you. It's only one small part of your Christmas present. Don't worry, there's more. I was going to put it under the tree at Tess's. But I think it might just work quite well now.' He hands the box to me.

My hands are shaking so much I can hardly peel off the wrapping paper. I hold my breath as I unclasp the hook at the front of the box. I know it's not a ring, he's made that clear, but I have no idea what delights might be hidden inside.

A tiny silver bell. Nestled on red-velvet fabric within the box, with a red-velvet ribbon attached to it, I don't think I've ever seen anything more perfect.

'Oh, Jim.' I sigh and, I swear, the crowd sighs with me.

'A silver bell for my Belle,' he says.

I take it out and shake it once, twice and it rings out into the night air. The group around me all sigh again, louder this time, in unison.

I don't blame them. For goodness sake, I'm about to faint with the beauty of the moment. I've read about moments like these, watched them in Christmas specials and now I'm actually part of one. Me.

He takes the bell from my shaking hands and unties the red ribbon.

'It's not a ring, but it can be a promise of one if you say yes,' he says.

'Appleby Jewellers is still open, love,' a voice shouts out from behind me and the crowd laughs in appreciation of typical quick Dublin wit.

My head races around and around, like a spinning top, and I feel faint as blood rushes to my brain. I reach back to clasp the wrought-iron railing on the bridge.

For someone who has spent twenty-five years never ever feeling faint, I've been doing a good job of it lately, I realise. I close my eyes and take three consecutive deep breaths, until I feel steady once more.

Maybe I just imagined all of that. I look down, expecting to see nothing there, but a red cobbled street.

Instead, there's Jim, my ride of a boyfriend, still on one knee looking up at me. And I can see only love in his eyes.

'We've only known each other three weeks,' I splutter to him. It has to be said. One of us needs to be responsible here. This elicits delicious and shocked gasps from our ever-growing audience.

He stands up and grabs my hands in his. 'My darling, beautiful, courageous Belle. You know that's not true. We've known each other all of our lives.'

PART ONE

1

Isn't it funny that at Christmas something in you gets so lonely for — I don't know what exactly, but it's something that you don't mind so much not having at other times.

Kate L. Bosher

December 1988

'She's not said a word. It's not normal. Maybe it's time you had her tested. You know, to see if there's anything wrong with her.' Mrs Gately, my about-to-be ex-foster carer, sniffs as she taps the side of her head.

'She's done this before. Stopped talking, I mean,' Mrs O'Reilly replies, and sniffs in solidarity.

Mrs O'Reilly is my social worker, for as long as I can remember. She doesn't look happy with me right now, either. I don't want to make her cross. I never mean to upset anyone, but it keeps happening all the same. I made my mother angry a lot.

I hold my doll Dee-Dee close to me and stroke her black hair, trying to block out memories of my mother.

'Have a good Christmas, Belle,' Mrs Gately says loudly as she moves towards me. She almost hugs me, then seems to change her mind at the last minute. She ends up just patting my head instead.

I think I got off lightly because she smells weird. She wears this perfume that makes my nose itch and sneeze. I can see she's delighted to see the back of me. I heard her telling her husband earlier that no money was worth it. Even though I'm only eight, I've worked out that *it* must be me.

'Put your seat belt on, Belle,' Mrs O'Reilly snaps over her shoulder. She's definitely cross with me too. But then her face softens a little as she looks at me in the rear-view mirror. Her voice goes all high and strained as she tells me, 'You'll like this house, you wait and see. Tess is a good woman and this time it's a permanent placement. That will be good, won't it? Settling into a new home and unpacking your things.'

I look down at the small backpack that lies at my feet, which holds everything I own.

'Belle,' she snaps again and I realise she's waiting for me to say something in return.

I nod and attempt a smile, even though I don't feel much like it.

It seems to satisfy her, because she stops staring at me in the rear-view mirror and returns her eyes to the road in front of us.

What do you think Dee-Dee? Will this home be a forever one? Dee-Dee always tells me the truth. I think she's the only person in the whole world who does.

She looks at me with her big brown eyes and says, 'Well, Joan and Daniel's house was supposed to be a forever home too.'

True, in fact Mrs O'Reilly has said that very same line to me loads of times now.

As always, whenever I think of Joan and Daniel, I feel scared all over again. All I want to do is go back to Dun Laoghaire, back to that house I've lived in for the past few years. Problem is, Joan and Daniel are not there any more. The house is for sale and locked up. My old foster parents are now somewhere called the Silicone Valley. I don't know where that is, but I know it must be far away, because they had to go on an aeroplane to get there.

Why did they have to leave me behind, Dee-Dee? My stomach starts to flip.

Dee-Dee looks at me with her big sad eyes and I know what she's thinking.

Everyone leaves. In the end, they all leave me behind.

'It's just you and me, kiddo, stick with me and we'll be fine,' Dee-Dee says.

I kiss her forehead and nod. Yes, we'll be just fine.

Mrs Reilly starts to chatter on about how much fun I'm going to have in this new house in Drumcondra. It will be a new adventure, she keeps saying. And even though I don't need to go on an aeroplane to get to this new place, I know it's a long way away from everything I know.

'Tess, your new foster mum, has been fostering for over thirty years. She has a room ready for you. All to yourself, too. Won't that be nice? And you can walk to your new school every day, just like you did at Joan and Daniel's.' She smiles in the rear-view mirror.

I look at her eyes. The smile doesn't reach them. Whenever

people smile at me, I check out to see if the eyes crinkle up at the corners. I know it's a real smile if that happens. I've noticed that there are a lot of people who fake-smile all the time. Mrs Reilly is a prime example.

The car stops and starts in splutters as she hits the usual rush-hour traffic. I feel a little bit sick, so I decide I'd better close my eyes in an attempt to stop the nausea.

'It's almost the Christmas holidays, so we all agree that it's best you start your new school in January. That gives you a few weeks to settle in. New Year, new beginning. I think that's best all round. Isn't that exciting? You'll love it there, trust me, you wait and see,' she states in that high, strangled voice of hers.

Thing is, I don't trust her. I'm only eight years old, but I already know that it's safer if you don't trust anyone. People lie all the time.

Dee-Dee nods in total agreement.

'The traffic is heavy this evening,' Mrs Reilly complains, looking at her watch.

I wipe the condensation from the car window and peek outside. We're not moving, we've stopped at another red light. I know that it has to change to green to move. I learnt that in school. I can't remember what amber means, that one always confuses me. Is it prepare to go or prepare to stop?

Oh, here we go again. We move forward a little bit, but just as quickly we're at a standstill again.

As my stomach heaves, Dee-Dee says, 'You better not get sick in Mrs Reilly's car.' I feel a little bit of vomit jump into my throat and my stomach flips again. Mrs Reilly will get so cross if I get sick. She might change her mind and not take us to this new house. And then where will we go?

I try to think of something else, anything, to take my mind off the possibility of being sick.

A red car inches up beside us and to distract myself, I count the people in it. One, two, three, four. Easy. I'm good at counting. I can count to one thousand and twenty-nine. I'm sure I could have passed two thousand, but I got distracted and lost my spot. Maybe I'll try beat my record now.

A little girl stares at me through her car window and waves. I wave back and look at her family properly. At least, I think they must be a family. The daddy is driving the car and the mammy is beside him, but she's looking back at her two children, a boy and a girl. And whatever the mammy is saying to them, they are all laughing.

I look at the mammy's face. It's soft and joyful and happy.

Why are you so stupid? Get out of my fucking way, you little brat.

Tears spring into my eyes as a memory pierces through my thoughts. I feel a pain in my side. It hurts like a stitch when I run too fast in the park. I blow on the window to make it steamy again, so that I can erase that happy, smiling family away.

I don't feel much like counting any more.

'Don't cry,' Dee-Dee tells me when she sees that I'm getting upset. 'The grown-ups get cross when you cry.'

I sigh, pinch myself and look back down again, stroking Dee-Dee's hair.

'What are you getting from Santa this year?' Mrs Reilly asks me, making me jump.

I shrug. Who cares? I mean, Santa won't even know where I live. For the past two years he came to Joan and Daniel's. And before that, well, I don't think he came at all.

'Santa is magic, he'll find you,' Dee-Dee reassures me. 'Remember that.' I kiss her head. She always knows what to say to me to make me feel better.

'Now, let's try to find a parking spot,' Mrs Reilly says. We're on a street with red-bricked houses on either side. It's almost dark and the big trees are making shadows on the path. Some windows are already filled with Christmas trees, and fairy lights twinkle on the driveways.

'Look, Belle, see that lovely red door? That's your new house.' Mrs Reilly points to the other side of the road.

There's no Christmas tree in the window.

The house in front of us, well, it looks dark and menacing and I don't think I'm going to like it here.

'Remember you're not to cry,' Dee-Dee warns again, as we walk up the drive towards the door. When Mrs Reilly rings the doorbell, I hold my breath and Dee-Dee even tighter, as I watch a shadow coming towards the door, through the opaque glass panels.

'You're shivering,' Mrs Reilly says, pulling me in close to her. 'You'll be inside soon, nice and warm.'

The door opens and I gasp and take a step backwards. Standing right in front of us is the big bad wolf dressed in a really bright-yellow dress.

The wolf looks like she's ready to eat me.

'She's fat,' Dee-Dee says.

That's not nice, I admonish her. She always says it like it is. Thing is, I don't think I've ever seen anyone that size before.

'She's probably so fat because of all the children she eats,' Dee-Dee continues.

That's not helpful, Dee-Dee, and I look back towards Mrs Reilly's car and wonder if I should make a run for it now.

But before I get the chance to make my getaway, the wolf smiles at me and I can see that she doesn't have any fangs at all. Just slightly yellow teeth. And even Dee-Dee has to agree that she looks happy to see me as she ushers me in, telling me she has lots of treats waiting.

'This could be okay,' Dee-Dee says agreeably. We both like treats.

I sit down at a long rectangular kitchen table, which is covered in a bright-orange and red-patterned oil-skin tablecloth. The lady, Tess, has placed a glass of milk and some Penguin bars in front of me.

'Tuck into these, pet,' she says, smiling her big yellow teeth at me. But she doesn't look so scary any more. And I quite like her yellow dress. It's pretty. Then she disappears into the hall with Mrs Reilly to whisper about me.

'Listen up,' Dee-Dee tells me. 'See what they have to say.'

'She's still not talking. It's been weeks now since she uttered a word,' Mrs Reilly sighs. 'I'm at my wits ends with it all.'

'Sure, is that any wonder? The poor thing must be scared out of her mind. How many times has she been shoved around from pillar to post?' Tess asks. 'She'll talk when she's good and ready, not a moment before.'

Mrs Reilly doesn't answer her question, but I could. I've been to four foster homes since I left my mother's. But I'm only eight and don't really remember everything so good yet. So I suppose it could actually be more than that. And I've learned already that grown-ups don't really like to talk to me about my past. If I mention my mother, they start to get real jittery.

'I've tried everything. I'm on my last nerve trying to make her speak.' Mrs Reilly moans. 'I hope you've got the patience of a saint, Tess. You'll need it.'

'You know, you can chase a butterfly all over the fields and you'll never catch it. But if you just sit still, he might just come over and sit on your shoulder,' Tess says.

I don't understand what that means. I look at Dee-Dee and she tells me she doesn't know either. But she likes her, and I trust her opinion.

'There was some bullying in her last school, so maybe it's as well she's moved from there,' Mrs Reilly says. 'Racial slurs, that kind of thing.'

I don't know exactly what 'racial slurs' mean. But I have a fair idea. Children were mean to me, on and off, calling me names. They kept saying I should go back home to Africa and other such things.

Both Dee-Dee and me always get confused by those remarks, because I've never been to Africa before. I've never left Ireland. Dublin is my home. So technically I am home already. It's just so complicated.

'Oh, God love her. That's awful,' Tess replies. 'You'd think in this day and age we'd be a bit more tolerant. It's 1988, for goodness sake.'

'She still sticks out, though. Not that many black kids in our schools yet over here. Maybe in the UK …' Mrs Reilly says.

Black. There they go again, Dee-Dee. Always going on about me being black.

'Oh and she has nightmares too. She won't say what they are about, but don't be surprised if you hear her screaming in the night,' Mrs Reilly continues.

My stomach flips again and I start to worry that Tess will tell Mrs Reilly to take me away. She's not saying very nice things about me.

I can't hear what they say next, because they start to whisper really low. But after a moment or two, Mrs Reilly sticks her head into the door of the kitchen, fake smile on again.

'I'll be back next week to check in on you, Belle.' And then, like that, she's gone.

'We can't wait,' Dee-Dee says, 'we miss you already, Mrs Reilly.'

I giggle, Dee-Dee is so funny.

'So this Dee-Dee, is she your favourite doll?' Tess asks, making me jump when she walks back into the room. She walks over to me and picks her up. 'Isn't she a beauty? What a lovely dress she's wearing too. Mrs Reilly told me all about her, that you don't like to go anywhere without Dee-Dee.'

I nod and I'm happy that she knows the lie of the land.

'Would you and Dee-Dee like to see your bedroom?' Tess asks and without waiting for me to answer, she beckons me to follow her as she huffs and puffs her way upstairs.

A white wooden door opens to a small room with a single bed in it. It has a pink duvet cover on it and lots of little pink and purple cushions piled up high over the pillows. A pine bedside locker has a pink lampshade on it and Tess shows me how to switch it on and off.

I really like the walls. They have little pink roses on them with green leaves and there's a wardrobe in the corner that looks a bit like the one from *The Chronicles of Narnia*.

Tess opens the double doors, but there's no fur coats in there. Instead there are a couple of outfits hanging up and a row of shelves, with items folded neatly on them.

'I popped into town earlier and went into Penny's to get a few bits for you. Underwear, socks, pyjamas, a few tops and a pair of jeans. But we'll get some more things when we work out what you need.' Tess tells me. 'I never know what a child will have until they walk through the door. And I think I've got your size all wrong. Look at those lovely long legs you have. I might have to get a bigger size in the jeans.'

I peek at her, expecting to see irritation on her face, but she doesn't look upset at all by the length of my legs. She's smiling as she pulls out a dressing gown and a plastic pack with a pair of brand-new pyjamas in it. They are fluffy pink ones with big red hearts on them. I decide I like them a lot.

'I'm pretty sure these are your size, though. Would you like to get all comfy and put them on?' Tess asks me. 'I like to do that of an evening. You know, when there's nobody due

34

to visit, nothing nicer than to get cosy in a pair of pyjamas. Then we can put on the TV and have our tea on our laps. As a special treat to celebrate you arriving here.' She smiles at me expectantly.

I blink twice and nod, feeling overwhelmed. She's being so kind and I don't know how to respond. I want to cry, but I know without Dee-Dee telling me that I shouldn't do that. Don't frighten Tess, she seems really nice. But I can't find any words to say either. They're all stuck in my throat.

'Come here,' Tess says and leads me to the bed. She pats the spot beside her so I sit down on the edge.

'I know you're scared, Belle. Good Lord, I would be too, if I was in your shoes. But I promise that if you give me a chance we can be happy here. You'll be safe in this house, I give you my word on that and we might even have some fun together, you wait and see.' She looks at me and smiles and I am overjoyed. Her smile reaches all the way up to the crinkles in the corners of her sockets. I've not seen one of those in a long, long time.

'I like her,' Dee-Dee whispers to me.

Me too.

2

Don't let the past steal your present. This is the message of Christmas. We are never alone.

Taylor Caldwell

December 1988

We've been putting decorations up for the past four hours, all over Tess's house. There's not a single spot in the hall, kitchen, living room, even the bathroom, that doesn't have something Christmassy pinned to the walls.

Tess has a lot of stories. Every time she picks up a new decoration, she starts a new tale, all about how she bought it, who she was with, what she was doing. She insisted that we both wear a Santa hat while we hang them all up. Tess sings along to all the Christmas songs which are on a tape deck, on loop over and over, in the kitchen. She's so funny because she keeps making up her own words to them, getting them wrong all the time.

Her good sitting room now contains rows upon rows of Christmas music boxes and toys. Snow globes, which when you shake them, reveal little figurines skating on a blue lake, with the soft snowflakes falling at their feet. A Rudolph the reindeer cuddly toy that sings about red noses when you touch his antler. Music boxes that play every Christmas jingle and song I've ever heard, over and over.

My favourite, though, is Santa Claus, sitting on a wooden rocking chair. He's wearing a green plaid shirt and bright-red trousers with black boots. His long white beard is like snow and he has little glasses that are perched on his nose. There's these little books and when you clip them into his right hand, his chair starts to rock and he begins to read *The Night Before Christmas.*

I could listen to his voice all day. If I had a grandfather, I would want him to talk exactly like that and have him read me a bed-time story every time I visited. But I didn't. I only had my mother.

My parents don't want to know me. Disowned me. And you want to know why? Because of you, Belle. My life is ruined because of you.

My mother's voice is never far from my thoughts. She keeps popping up, catching me unawares. There's no grand-father for me and that's my fault. I feel shame and guilt.

I turn my eyes back to the decorations, I start to turn on all the musical boxes, all at once, to try and delete her cruel voice.

'Do you fancy helping me make my Christmas pudding?' Tess asks, making me jump. She's standing in the doorway, watching me. I wait for her to give out to me about the noise. But she holds her hand out to me and when I clasp it, she pulls me in for a hug, kissing my head. She keeps doing that. Hugging me for no reason.

I like baking, so I follow her into the kitchen.

Lined up on the table are bowls filled with raisins, currants, eggs, breadcrumbs, flour, sugar, treacle, loads of jars of spices and even a bottle of Guinness.

'I'm a little bit late in getting this done this year but I was waiting for you to arrive, to help me stir it all together,' she says. 'Now some bakers, of course, prefer a lighter pudding, but for me, I like it dark and rich.'

I help her add all the ingredients one by one into a large ceramic mixing bowl. We take turns to stir them all together and she tuts and aahs as she adjusts the taste.

'We have to get the right balance, or it could be a complete disaster on Christmas Day,' she tells me. 'Now time to add Mr Arthur himself.' She giggles and I join in, even though I'm not sure who Mr Arthur is. She pours a large bottle of dark stout into the mixture.

One last dip of her little finger into the batter and she licks it and declares the batter to be just perfect. She then takes out her purse and pulls out a coin.

'Can you wrap that up for me in a bit of foil?' she asks.

I don't know why it feels like such an honour to do this, but it does. She's given me a job of grave importance so I make sure that the coin is completely covered, folding the corners of the foil carefully.

'Now stir it into the bowl and make a wish as you do,' she orders me, smiling and nodding in encouragement.

I close my eyes and wish with all my might.

'I'm gasping for a cuppa now. That's been a busy day hasn't it?' Tess says, putting the kettle on. 'I think it's time for the first mince pie of the season too. I made a batch last night when you were asleep. I'll just give them a little heat in the microwave and we'll have one with a dollop of cream.'

A few minutes later, with my mouth full of sugary mincemeat and shortcrust pastry, I look up to see Tess watching me intently.

'Would you do something else for me, Belle?' she asks.

I nod quickly. I would do anything for her right now. I've had more fun today than I can remember ever having. I like Tess and I want her to like me too.

'Can you write a letter to Santa for me? I've asked you a few times, but you've not done it. I'd really like you to do it for me, even if you don't want to. I know that Santa is always happy to make a guess as to what you want, but he prefers a letter, you know, if it's at all possible. I happen to know that he enjoys reading every single one of them,' Tess says.

She hands me a piece of paper and a pen and moves her chair closer to me at the table.

'I can write it for you, if you tell me what to say,' she says kindly.

I shake my head at this suggestion. I can write it by myself. I've written lots of letters to my mother. She just doesn't ever answer me.

It's just, I don't know what to ask for. Joan and Daniel always said that we couldn't ask for anything too big, that Santa didn't have much money. So I used to just tell them that I wanted a surprise from him and they seemed to like that.

But Tess seems to think that Santa wants me to have a say about what I get. I look at Dee-Dee and ask her for advice on what I should write down.

Another doll? I tease her. She doesn't find that one bit funny.

'You know what you want,' Dee-Dee tells me.

But I can't ask for that, silly.

'Why not?' she replies. 'Santa is magic, he can get anything you want. Everyone knows that.'

I start to write and concentrate so hard to make sure my writing is in a straight line. Sometimes I make my letters too big and it looks all wrong. I hate making a mess of it. But I'm determined to make this the most perfect letter ever. Because this letter is very important.

There, I'm done.

I fold it up and push it across the table to Tess, feeling shy and unsure of myself.

'Can I read it?' she asks me. I shrug and I suppose she takes that as a yes, because she unfolds it carefully.

'Let's see, what do we have here?' She sticks on a pair of her glasses and exclaims, 'Oh, look how neat your writing is.'

I'm chuffed with her praise and am so pleased I tried my hardest. She starts to read the letter aloud and I mouth along with her. I know it off by heart.

Dear Santa,
My name is Belle and I am eight years old. I live in a
new house now with a lady called Tess. I don't live with
Joan and Daniel any more, they are a long way away

*now. I like Tess, she's nice and gives me biscuits. Do you
like biscuits too? I can ask Tess for some to give you on
Christmas Eve.*

*This year, I would like to have a best friend for my
Christmas present, someone to play with me. I don't mind
if it's a girl or a boy, but I'd prefer a girl. Dee-Dee says
she would love a new dress too, her favourite colour is
gold.*

Thank you,
Belle Bailey

I watch Tess's face as she reads my letter and my stomach
flips in disappointment. Oh no Dee-Dee I've done something wrong. Tess looks upset with me.

'You shouldn't have asked for a dress for me,' Dee-Dee
scolds me. 'That was too much.'

'Is that all you want, Belle?' Tess asks me, looking down
at my letter again, then back up to my face.

I nod. She picks up a magazine from the table and starts to
fan herself with it and then blots her face with a tea towel too.

'Well now. If this isn't the nicest letter I've ever seen in my
life … I have no doubt that you'll find a best friend when
you start school after the holidays. No doubt in my mind
about that fact at all, a lovely, kind girl like you. But I'm
going to have a word with Santa and ask him to put a few
surprises in your stocking too. Maybe a few toys and games,
what do you think? Because I know you've been a very good
girl and you deserve to have a stocking full of presents.
And I'm sure that he can find some nice new clothes for

Dee-Dee and for you too. Oh and we can't forget about some chocolate. A stocking wouldn't be complete without some chocolate now, would it?' Tess asks and when I smile at this, she looks happy and not upset any more.

She stands up and walks to the press and pulls out a plate. It has a picture of Santa on it and he's smiling, his big blue eyes twinkling, just like the talking Santa in her good sitting room.

'This is my special plate that I keep just for biscuits for Santa on Christmas Eve,' she tells me. 'You can put as many as you like on it this year.'

I trace my finger over Santa's white beard and the smile on my face just gets bigger and bigger.

'Ho, ho, ho,' Dee-Dee says.

If Tess can talk to Santa about adding all of those things onto my list, well then she'll make sure he knows where we live now too. All my worries about him not finding me vanish.

Maybe this Christmas is going to be special after all.

3

It came without ribbons. It came without tags. It came without packages, boxes or bags. Then the Grinch thought of something he hadn't before. 'Maybe Christmas,' he thought, 'doesn't come from a store. Maybe Christmas … perhaps … means a little bit more.'

Dr Seuss

Christmas Eve, 1988

'You know there's only one thing that I really want for Christmas?' Tess says to me.

We've been busy all morning already, making sausage rolls and mince pies. The kitchen smells like a bakery and it's making me so hungry. A ham is bubbling away on her range cooker too and the turkey is defrosting in the sink.

She places a plate of sausages and toast in front of me at the kitchen table and my stomach rumbles hello to them.

I lick my lips in anticipation, but then as Tess's words sink in, I look at Dee-Dee in panic. What are we going to do? We don't have any money. We can't buy Tess a present. And I have to get her something good. She's so nice, she deserves something special. I reckon I've no more than forty pence in my savings, which would not buy much. I suppose I could get her a bar of chocolate.

'She loves chocolate, that's for sure,' Dee-Dee says. 'You have that picture you drew too.'

I did take ages and ages to make sure I coloured it all in. But I'm not that good at drawing Christmas trees, I think it looks a bit wonky and more like a Christmas cracker.

'I'll let you in on a little secret, Belle. All I want this year is to hear your voice,' Tess says. 'I bet it's just as pretty as you are.'

Oh.

'You should say something,' Dee-Dee says.

And I nod. I want to, but I can't seem to make my mouth co-operate. I don't want to upset Tess, though.

Yesterday, when we were watching that movie, I wanted to say something to her. I was so cross with Jack Frost trying to take over Christmas, but I couldn't get the words out.

'Maybe she'll throw us out, if you don't talk,' Dee-Dee tells me and I start shivering at the thought. Where would we sleep, Dee-Dee? She doesn't have an answer for that and I hold her in close to me again.

'Don't be getting upset,' Tess says, reading my mind. 'I have lots of patience for you, my little butterfly. You speak when you are good and ready. I can wait.' She kisses my head and goes back to the frying pan to plate her own breakfast.

Maybe it's going to be okay. I think I'll draw a butterfly on her picture, though. With lots of bright colours on its wings. Because she's always calling me that. She must really like them.

'Who's that on the phone at this ridiculous hour?' Tess says when the phone rings out, filling the house with its shrill sound. She shuffles in her slippers out to the hall, to answer it.

These sausies are good. I ask Dee-Dee if she wants some, putting one up to her face so she can have a nibble.

When Tess comes back a few minutes later, she's singing in her off-key voice, '*Have yourself a merry little Christmas*' and I start to hum along with her. I like that song a lot.

'Well, it appears that you really have been a good girl this year, Belle. Santa has arranged it so that one of your presents will arrive early. This very afternoon, in fact. So eat up your sausages, we've lots to do. I have to go down to Tesco to get a few last bits for our special surprise.' Tess is beaming at me and I feel a thrill of excitement.

I've never had an early present before. I beam back at her.

'I bet it's my dress,' Dee-Dee says. 'A big, gold sparkly one.'

'Answer the door, there's a good girl,' Tess tells me, when it buzzes. She jumps up and quickly stubs her cigarette out. Then she starts waving her magazine around the place to disperse the smoke. As I walk out the door, she's sticking the ashtray under the sink to hide all the evidence.

'What Mrs Reilly don't know, won't kill her.' She winks at me.

I wonder, is this my present at the door? I've waited all day for Tess to give it to me. But what has Mrs Reilly got to do with it? Why is she talking about her? I get my answer and see her standing on the porch.

The problem is that I've come to realise that whenever Mrs Reilly arrives, so does bad news.

Oh no, Dee-Dee, she's come to take us away. I move backwards towards Tess, and I want to scream at her, let me stay, I like it here. Tess is smiling, though, and nodding towards the door, telling me to look in that direction. She doesn't have that look that I've come to recognise on grown-up faces that they all get when they are about to tell you that it's time to go.

She places her hands on my shoulders and directs my eyes towards the door again. And then I notice that standing just behind Mrs Reilly is a boy.

A tall, lanky, thin boy with hair the colour of a fox. It's wavy and it's falling over his eyes. He's got his head looking down, though, and I notice his fists are clenched by his sides. He doesn't look very happy, I realise. My heart contracts. I know that feeling.

'Hello, Jim.' Tess says, moving towards him. She welcomes them both inside and closes the door behind them. 'Belle, will you come over and say hello to Jim. He's coming to stay with us for a while. And he's eight years old, too, just like you are. Imagine that.'

She gives me a triumphant look and I get it. Even before Dee-Dee screams at me, 'this must be Santa's present,' I get it.

'He's not a girl, though,' she laments. I agree that's a pity, but he looks okay, for a boy, that is.

He looks up through his hair and I see the bluest eyes I've ever seen before. Freckles are scattered densely across his nose too.

Then he looks up and shoots me a dirty look, as if to say, what you looking at? He looks me up and down and sneers.

'He looks a bit cross,' Dee-Dee says, stating the obvious.

'There's not a pick on you,' Tess declares, taking him in too and I sneak another glance at him.

Yeah, he's skinny alright.

'Well, there's a challenge for me. How quick can I sort that out for you, young man? I reckon I can put some meat on those bones, quick smart. I've enough food in to last us a lifetime in there,' Tess jokes, thumbing the kitchen.

'I've a boy at home the same way. All legs and not an ounce of fat. He eats me out of house and home,' Mrs Reilly says to Tess and they both tut at the misfortune of it.

'Sure I only have to look at a bun …' Tess says and I giggle.

'She does more than look at buns,' Dee-Dee jokes.

'Do you want to put your bag up in your bedroom?' Tess asks the boy. 'You'll be sleeping in the room at the top of the stairs, first door on the left.'

He looks upwards and suddenly his face doesn't look cross any more, instead he just looks scared.

I recognise that look. Something in my heart contracts again in sympathy and I feel myself moving forward towards him.

I don't think about it or plan it, but somehow or other, the words tumble out of my mouth with ease. 'I'll show you where your room is if you want me to.'

Before he has a chance to answer, Tess rushes over to me and pulls me into her, so that I'm squished into her big boobs. It feels nice, even though I can't really breathe. I take in her smell, her Tess smell, which I reckon is the not-unpleasant concoction of onions, sausages, chocolate and tobacco.

'I knew your voice would be pretty, my little butterfly,' she says. I think about pulling away from her, but it feels nice and safe here. So I put my arms around her waist, as far as I can make them go and think that I could stay here like this a long time.

'You do like it here,' Mrs Reilly says in approval. 'I told you so.'

'I like it a lot,' I say to her and turn to Jim, who looks a bit bewildered by the scene that just unfolded.

I want to show him that I understand how he feels right now, that I know that he's scared. I want him to know that I feel the same way, most of the time too. But even though it's scary, it's going to be okay here. Tess is okay. More than okay. I've worked out that she's kind of wonderful.

'I know how you feel,' I whisper to him. I stare into his eyes and he looks at me, our eyes locking. Neither of us moves a muscle and it feels like he gets that I'm trying to tell him something important.

'Okay,' he says and smiles for a second. I run up the stairs and can hear him running up behind me, two steps at a time.

When we get to the top, I say to him. 'You're my Christmas present, you know. I asked Santa for you. And look, here you are.'

And even though he must think I am barmy, he doesn't say anything, he just looks away. I can tell that he's all embarrassed by my declaration. But I don't care.

'I'm in there.' I point to my bedroom on the other side of the landing, then open the door to his room. Tess was up in here for ages earlier, I didn't know what she was doing. But I can see that she was getting the room ready for Jim. It's like mine, but it has a blue duvet on the bed instead of pink. There aren't any cushions, but there is a mat on the floor in the shape of a car. And the wallpaper has blue stripes on it.

I thinks it's pretty cool.

'It's a boy's room,' I tell him and he sits down on the bed, trying it out for size. 'Mine is a girl's room. In pink.'

He looks at me, head cocked to one side, as if he's trying to work me out. 'Do you have to stay here too?' he finally asks.

'Yes,' I say, 'I suppose I do.'

'For how long?' he asks.

I shrug. I don't know the answer to that. But then I surprise myself by saying, 'I hope it's forever.'

He doesn't like that answer, though. He's starts to shake his head and the angry look is back on his face again. I didn't mean to upset him. I'm not sure what I said wrong.

'I'm going home soon. I won't be here for more than a day or two, you wait and see. My mam says she will come get me when she feels better and gets herself sorted. It will be any day now.'

'Oh, you're a temporary.' I say. I've seen lots of them over the years. Boys and girls who come for a few days, sometimes as short as one night, until some family member comes by to take them home.

I haven't met as many like me, who stay for a long time.

'You're lucky so. I don't have a mam,' I tell him.

'Everyone has a mam,' he replies, looking doubtful at my statement.

'Not me,' I say, as my mother's face jumps into my thoughts, making me a liar.

I'll be back later. Don't you dare leave this house. And don't break anything.

Don't go, mam. Don't leave me here on my own. I'm scared. I want you.

I don't want to talk about mothers any more. 'Do you like biscuits? Tess has lots of them,' I say.

He nods and I'm relieved that he looks happy enough to drop the subject. So we run downstairs to get some. I know Tess will already have the tin out.

I'll be back soon, Dee-Dee, I shout to my friend, as I run out the door. She smiles happily to me, telling me to have fun.

'Simon's a computer, Simon has a brain, you either do what Simon says or else go down the drain.'

Jim and I are both in stitches as we chant the song over and over, each taking turns on my new computer game.

Out of all the things Santa put in my pillowcase last night while we were sleeping, this is my favourite. Jim is still marvelling at how Santa knew where to find him at such short notice. He even got the exact same Lego set he'd asked for.

Santa is magic, I keep telling him. I wish I could see Santa right now to give him a big hug. I hope he liked the biscuits I left out for him. He sure ate lots of them.

We've been playing Simon for most of the day, only stopping for a little bit to have dinner. I'm the best at remembering and I keep beating Jim's best score, which is driving him mad.

'Have a go, Tess,' I shout to her. She looks like she's almost asleep, her head bobbing up and down to her chin.

'I wouldn't know what to do,' she splutters.

'It's easy. It has four different-colour panels. And all you have to do is touch them quickly to copy whatever pattern that Simon sets. Easy peasy.' I show off my skills and give her a quick demo.

She gives it a go and Jim and I giggle when she's out after only a few seconds.

Then, she throws the game back to me, sitting up with excitement in her chair.

A movie is starting, it's in black and white and the song *Buffalo Gals* fills the room.

'It's not Christmas till I watch this. *It's a Wonderful Life*. My absolute favourite movie of all time. What I wouldn't do to George Bailey if he came a knocking on this door looking for refuge. I'd not turn him away,' she sighs. 'You will both love it …'

But before she can finish, Jim jumps up, knocking his juice to the ground as he runs out of the room.

'Jim?' I call after him and he shouts back, 'I don't want to play any more.'

What did I do? I can hear him tearing up the stairs, so I scramble to my feet to follow him.

'I'll go,' Tess says, placing her hand gently on my shoulders. I can't understand what's happened.

Tess is gone for ages and I don't feel much like playing any more. I half-watch the movie, but I can't concentrate on it. I flick though my new Bunty annual, but even that can't keep my interest.

After an age, Tess comes back down. 'He'll join us in a bit. Nothing to worry about, I promised you. He's just a bit lonely for his mam, that's all. *It's A Wonderful Life* is her favourite Christmas movie too, it appears. They always watched it together. So I'm afraid it made him a little homesick.'

'Where is his mam?' I ask. 'What's wrong with her?' The way Jim talks about her, she's the perfect mother. So why isn't she here with him right now?

'She's not well,' Tess lowers her voice to a whisper and says, 'She suffers from her nerves, God love her. She'll be grand soon enough.' Tess sighs and starts to mop up the spilled juice with her ever-present tea towel.

'Tell you what, why don't we open up those chocolates? See if we can take that frown off your little face.' She says to me.

I decide that I'll save some chocolates for Jim too. As I nibble on my favourite soft caramel, I wonder what is worse: having no mother at all or having one, then losing her.

I don't have an answer to that.

4

If you live to be a hundred, I want to live to be a hundred minus one day, so I never have to live without you.

Winnie the Pooh

May 1988

'You're the only black person I've ever known,' Jim says, hoisting himself up on his pillow. We're in our den, eating chocolate that we've nicked from Tess's secret stash.

'Well, you're the only red-haired boy I know,' I say, sticking my tongue out at him and he laughs in response.

'What's it like being black?' he asks.

'What's it like being an eejit?' I reply and throw a packet of cheese-and-onion Tayto crisps his way.

But I don't mind his questions in the slightest. Within a few weeks of arriving, Jim became my very best friend. Just like I asked Santa for Christmas.

'Thanks for today,' I say to him.

He shrugs off my praise. 'Shut them up anyhow.'

'Sure did,' I say.

Joyce O'Connor and her cronies had shoved past me

so I fell down and then started pointing and laughing at me. I've got one of those faces, it seems.

'What you looking at?' Jim shouted at them, standing on his feet.

'What are you looking at?' Joyce mimicked and her friends laughed some more.

'Not much, from where I'm standing,' Jim replied.

'Where's your friend from? Bongo-bongo land?' she shouted.

'I told you, I'm from Dublin, just like you,' I said and started to pick up my lunch stuff. I just wanted to get away. I could feel myself getting angry and when that happens, I usually end up in a fight and that never ends well for me.

'Liar,' Another one shouted at me and then they all started to chant 'Bongo, Bongo, Bongo,' over and over.

'Take that back. She is not a liar and that's not nice.' Jim clenched his fists and walked towards them.

'Oh. I'm shaking,' Joyce, the obvious ringleader, said.

'Wagons the lot of them. If they weren't girls, I'd give them a slap,' Jim said.

'It's no big deal,' I replied. I pretended to yawn and hoped he didn't look too closely at my eyes, which I knew must be shiny with unshed tears.

Then Jim stood up and sauntered over to them, his hands in his pockets. 'You know who she is? That girl over there, that you're picking on?' He pointed in my direction.

'Who?' Joyce sneered. 'The Queen of Sheba.'

'You know who Paul McGrath is?' He said, and of course they all nodded. Everyone in Ireland knows who he is.

He's our most famous footballer and a hero to practically the whole nation.

'Well, Belle is his niece. I'd be nice to her if I were you. Because I don't think he'd like it if he heard kids were picking on his favourite girl.' He walked away, leaving them all gawping at me with their mouths wide open.

'Jim,' I said. 'I'm not. ...'

He winked at me as he replied, 'Sure, how do you know? You could be. You said yourself that you don't know who your father is.'

'You know, I didn't know I *was* black until I was four.' I tell him. 'I hadn't noticed that I was any different to anyone else.'

'What do mean?' he asks. 'Surely you'd looked in the mirror? Sure you couldn't miss that ugly mug.'

I look around for something else to throw at him, but as he's tucking into my crisps now, I realise that he's only deliberately baiting me, just to rob my treats.

'I know your game,' I tell him and slowly open my bar of Cadbury's Tiffin. I know it's his favourite and pop a piece in my mouth. That will teach him. I was going to share it with him, but now I won't.

'What I mean is that I'd never heard that term before. Black. As in, used to describe someone, that is. Not until I moved into my last foster house, Joan and Daniel's. They had this big house out in Dun Laoghaire, three stories high,' I tell him.

I'm pleased to see that he looks impressed at that nugget of information.

'It had a basement too and they had it made into a playroom for all the children they fostered.'

'Deadly,' he replies.

Yeah, it was deadly, I agree.

'There was more than just you living there with them, then?' he asks.

'They had loads of kids. There was always someone coming or going. Some came for a day or two only, others for weeks or months. I was there the longest, though,' I tell him.

'Did you call them mam and dad, then? Seeing as you were there for ages?' he asks.

'No. Never.' I answer quickly.

'Why not?' he asks.

'Because they weren't my mam and dad, stupid,' I say. He's so dumb sometimes.

But what I don't tell him is that they never asked me to call them mam or dad either.

'I'd love a playroom,' Jim says. 'When I'm grown up, I'm going to have the biggest one ever in my house.'

'With a slide,' I say. Jim is always sliding down things.

'Natch,' Jim replies. 'And I'll put in a swing for you.'

'Natch,' I say. That's our new favourite word. Followed closely by 'deadly'. We say them a lot.

'You'd have loved their basement, though. It was cool. It had shelves painted in every colour you can think of. It looked kind of like a rainbow. And all the shelves were stacked with lots of cool stuff.' I say.

'Like what?' he asks.

'Well, Lego, books, puzzles, dolls, cars. Kind of like a toy shop. Everything,' I boast.

'Wow,' he's well jealous now.

'Yeah.' The first time I saw the playroom I gasped. I was overwhelmed by the size of the house, my new home, which looked strange and scary to me.

I look at Jim and decide to tell him something. 'Sometimes I don't feel like talking.'

He stops munching his crisps and gives me his full attention.

'And on that first day at Joan's, I was having one of my non-talking spells' I say.

I'm expecting Jim to make a smart comment here, but he doesn't.

'Why don't you talk? Why go all quiet?' he asks.

'I don't know. Sometimes I've just got nothing to say.' I reply. I don't tell him that I learned very young that sometimes it's safer not to talk.

Shut up with all your constant whingeing. I'm sick to death listening to you. SHUT UP.

'Fair enough,' Jim says, satisfied with my answer and I try not to think about *her* any more.

'Joan was nice. She made me smile and laugh. Pretty soon I was chattering away to her and the other kids who lived there.' I close my eyes, remembering those early days.

'There was a shelf full of dolls there,' I tell Jim.

'Is that where you got your doll Dee-Dee, then?' Jim asks.

I nod and in an instant I'm back in the moment we found each other.

Joan bends down and pulls out a white basket from the bottom shelf and as she does a lone doll falls forward. It is a Barbie doll too, but this one looks different. She has a brown face. And short, black curly hair with long red earrings that dangle from each ear. Her dress is long and bright red with a gold necklace attached to the front of it. She looks exotic and beautiful and I can't take my eyes off her.

I hold Dee-Dee in my hands for the first time and know that I'll never let her go.

'She looks a little like you,' Joan says to me. She looks down to the doll and back up to me again.

I look back up to Jim. 'Joan said to me that I was black just like Dee-Dee.' He doesn't say a word and I'm glad.

Black. I don't understand what she means. That word panics me. I don't want to get into trouble. The whole way over to Joan's house, my social worker warned me not to get dirty. I'd been so careful.

I must have gotten messed up somewhere along the way to their house. I look down at my hands and fingers, but they are spotless, even my nails. I'm a good girl. I stayed clean. I don't know what she is talking about.

'She's so beautiful, isn't she? Daniel got her on one of his trips to the US. Her name is Dee-Dee.' Joan tells me. 'You should keep her.'

I look at Dee-Dee and cannot believe that she is mine. I pull her in close to me and I smile my thanks to Joan.

Later that night, I can hear my foster carers whispering outside my bedroom door.

'It's probably the first black doll she's ever seen. Nice for her to have a doll that looks like herself.' Daniel tells Joan.

Dee-Dee looks like me?

Do you Dee-Dee?

I pull the red dress off Dee-Dee's plastic body and then lift up the sleeves of my pyjama top. Are we alike? I can't understand why they call us 'black'.

'You're brown,' I realise suddenly. And Dee-Dee smiles back, agreeing with me. 'So are you,' she says. 'We're both brown.'

I worked it out eventually, what they meant.

'After that day, I'd hear people call me black all the time. I used to look at the other kids in school or on our street, searching to see if anyone else had the same colour skin as mine.'

'And is your mother black, then?' Jim asks me.

I shake my head and sigh. No. She's not. Blonde and white. She couldn't be more different to me if you tried.

'I have one picture of her,' I tell Jim. 'Do you want to see her? My mother?'

Jim nods. So I run to my bedroom and take it out of its secret place, in my favourite book, *The Faraway Tree*, right at the back of the bookcase.

I feel a little shy showing it to him. I've never shown it to anyone before. He looks at it and then at me and agrees we don't look alike.

My mother looks up at me from the picture. Her face is smiling, but it's one of the fakers. Her blue eyes are dull and without any mirth. Her mousy-blonde hair is tied back in a low ponytail. It's fine and straight, again the complete opposite of my afro hair.

'Maybe you look like your father,' Jim says.

'Ooh aah Paul McGrath,' I joke, but there's no merriment in my words and they fall flat between us.

'I asked Mrs Reilly for a photograph of him, but she got all weird and did that thing with her voice.' I say.

'All high, like she's being squeezed tight?' Jim asks and I nod. I knew he'd get it.

'She kept putting me off, but then when I pushed her, she told me that they didn't have a record of who he was,' I say.

'That sucks,' he tells me. 'I don't know who my father is either. My mam always starts to cry when I ask her about him. I've given up trying. Who needs a father anyhow? Losers.'

'Yeah. Losers,' I agree.

A tiny bit of me feels jealous of Jim, though. I know his mother is cracked, but at least she comes by every now and then. I think of mine and feel a pain in my heart.

'Does she ever call you?' he asks.

I shake my head no. 'I wrote to her a few times. I was real careful to make sure it was perfect, with no mistakes,' I say.

I was so proud of those letters.

Shame floods me now at how stupid I was.

'You have good writing. Better than mine,' Jim says. 'I bet they were great letters.'

He's not wrong about his writing. He mixes up his 'b's and 'd's all the time and his letters are way too big. I'm going to have to give him some lessons, because he'll get in trouble at school if not.

'I got Joan to put a picture of me in the last letter I sent, so she could see what I looked like now. I put on my best dress and stood in the garden by the rose bush for it. Joan had one of those Polaroid cameras,' I finish softly.

'What happened?' Jim asks, his voice so quiet I can barely hear him.

In our cocoon, made of white-and-blue cotton sheets, I suppose the sound of my silence is his answer.

He doesn't break my silence, doesn't question me any further, but reaches behind him to his stash of treats and hands me his Club bar. I know he's been saving this one till last; he loves to suck the thick chocolate off. So I push it back towards him. I can't take it. But he gives it to me again, insistent.

Neither of us say a word, we just sit there sucking our chocolate bars, lost in our own thoughts of absentee parents.

For weeks I would run to the postman, check through the piles of letters and when I saw a white envelope my heart would soar in hope. But it was never for me.

No reply. No card. No phone call. Nothing.

I look at Jim and hold up Dee-Dee. 'Until you came, all I had was Dee-Dee. She was my best friend.'

I take a deep breath. I want to tell him something, but I'm afraid that he might laugh. 'I'm glad that I have you now.'

He looks embarrassed and starts to push his Spider-Man truck up and down the walls made of sheets. But he doesn't laugh and I catch him peeking at me. I think he looks pleased with what I've said.

And even though he doesn't say it back, I know he thinks it too.

'Why did you leave their house, if it was so good there?' he asks when he turns back to me a few minutes later.

'I had no choice,' I admit. 'Joan and Daniel left Ireland.'

'Oh,' he says and his eyes are wide.

'I begged them both to take me with them. Daniel had gotten a job in the US, in some place called the Silicone Valley. They said that they couldn't take foster kids with them,' I say.

'Oh,' he repeats and his face is like one of those comic books, when it freezes into a shocked look at the end of a chapter.

I wonder what he'd say if I told him about how I pleaded with them the night before Mrs Reilly came to take me away. I feel a flush of shame overtake me again as I remember how much I begged and begged, but how it made no difference whatsoever. I still had to go.

'You could adopt me,' I whisper to them. 'Then you can bring me with you. I wouldn't be a foster kid any more. I'd be yours. And I'll be so good. I promise I'll be good.'

I hold my breath as they look at each other. Daniel looks uncomfortable and starts to fidget and Joan won't look me in the eye.

I don't wait for them to answer me, I just get up and walk out of the family room. I know the score. I ignore Joan's anguished cries that she wishes things were different.

'*Our hands are tied,*' *Daniel shouts at my retreating back.*

And even though I'm only eight years old, I know already that if they wanted me, if they really did, they could have made it happen.

Better not to tell Jim all that. And I don't want him to know about the day Mrs Reilly took me away from them either.

Joan cries and tells me that she will always care for me. But I don't answer her. I can see that my silence is hurting her. I know that she wants me to let her off the hook, to tell her I understand why I can't go with them.

But I don't want to make it easier for her. I hate her. I hate Daniel too and I hope that their plane crashes and they die.

Shame floods my body for thinking such a bad thing. And I know that it is my own fault that they don't want me.

Who would want me? My own mother didn't.

Mrs Reilly puts me in her car and takes me away. I can feel their eyes watching me as we drive off, but I keep looking forward.

Maybe they'll change their minds, Dee-Dee says. But we both know that's not true. So I move into a new temporary home. One where people keep trying to make me talk and unzip my lips.

But I am so tired. What good do words do anyhow? No one ever listens to me. They do what they want to do and send me away.

I turn my back to Jim and pick up my Simon game. I don't want him to see me cry.

'Why did you speak to me when you saw me on that first day?' Jim suddenly asks and his voice is gruff. I can't help it, I look back towards him.

Because you were the answer to my wish. Because I know that you were in pain and scared and I know what that feels like. Because … Just because.

'I dunno. Felt sorry for you, I suppose. Loser,' I say instead, joking to try to banish the tears.

He looks at me for a moment, locks his eyes on mine and even though he doesn't say anything, I know that he knows the real reason. And in that look, he is thanking me and I am thanking him too.

'You're alright for a girl,' he says.

He looks away and throws his Spider-Man car down to the ground.

'I feel sorry for you now, Belle Bailey, cos' I'm about to beat your record on that stupid Simon game of yours. Prepare to be destroyed.' He replies, picking it up and switching it on.

'In your dreams, Jim Looney,' I say.

5

Life itself is the most wonderful fairy tale of all.

Hans Christian Anderson

July 1990

It's one of those days where the heat is so strong, the air around me looks hazy. And even lifting my hand to move the pages in my book is too much effort.

'That story is for babies,' Jim says, flicking my Cinderella book closed as he passes me by.

'Get lost,' I reply and kick myself that I've not got a wittier retort. 'I'll have you know that Cinderella is a story for all ages.'

Strictly speaking, I know that I should have outgrown my Disney princess stage about five years ago, but no matter how old I get, I never tire of this story. My copy is battered and the corners of the book are curled from constant sticky fingers and thumbs working their way through them.

'You wouldn't catch me reading fairy tales,' Jim tells me. 'They are so lame.' He demonstrates said lameness by pretending to limp around the room.

I resist the urge to laugh. It only encourages him.

'You think you know everything, Jim Looney, but you're a mere ten,' I sigh and open my book again. He's such a pain sometimes. I should just go upstairs and hide from his childishness, but I'm too hot to climb the stairs.

'So does the princess always get the prince in these fairy tales of yours?' Jim asks, as I stick my nose back into Cinderella again.

I put my book down and give him my best withering look. I've been practising it in front of my mirror and think that it's pretty good. 'Of course they do. That's what always happens in fairy tales, you big eejit,' I reply.

'And you reckon that one day a prince is going to just rock up here to Drumcondra, on a white pony, and ask you to marry him too?' he says, as he balances his football on one foot.

'Don't be ridiculous.' I shake my head. Sometimes I just give up with him. 'We've had this conversation before, Jim. You know what's going to happen.'

He pretends to put a gun to his head to shoot himself. 'Not that again.'

'Haha, very funny.' I say. 'But you can't fight the inevitable.'

As he runs out the back door, I shout after him, 'I'm going to marry you one day, Jim Looney. You wait and see. I cannot wait for the day when you drop to one knee just like Prince Charming.'

Jim laughs, his usual response to my bold prediction. I'm sure many would be offended by his obvious mirth, but I'm not in the least bit worried by his reaction. First of all, he's a boy. Second of all, he's only ten. And okay,

I know I'm only two months older than he is, but it's a proven fact that boys don't mature as quickly as us girls.

Mind you, I have noticed something. I've been telling him he'll marry me for years now and even though he always laughs, he never says he won't either.

I think about going for a kick-about too, but it's just too hot. Tess has had to go to bed for a few hours. She said she was about to melt.

As it goes, I'm not too bad at football. Jim jokes that I'd give Paul McGrath a run for his money. With every 'OOH AAH Paul McGrath' that the whole of Ireland has chanted over the past couple of years, my life has gotten way easier.

The best defender Ireland has ever had, Jim reckons. All I know is that he has made it cool to be black. He's a legend in my books and one day I'll tell him so, if I ever get the chance to meet him.

'Your head is full of nonsense from all those fairy tales you read,' Tess says, as she walks into the kitchen. I jump at the sound of her voice. Despite her considerable size, she has always had this uncanny ability to sneak into rooms without making a sound.

'What, you mean there's no such thing as fairy god-mothers?' I say feigning mock horror.

'The only fairy you'll find around here is the one on top of the Christmas tree,' Tess says, laughing at her own joke.

'Fairy tales are magic. And magic exists. I've seen it. You just don't believe any more. It's not your fault, all adults stop believing, it's out of their control,' I say.

'Is that so?' Tess says.

'Yes. Fact,' I reply. 'But I'll not stop. No matter how old I get, I'll always believe.' I don't care what anyone says.

'Well, magic me up my fags, there's a good girl,' Tess says, laughing again. She's a regular comedienne, my foster mother. 'So one day my prince will come, what?'

She coughs up half her lung laughing again at her quip. I don't see what's so hilarious, I mean why can't there be true love in her future? Tess has always been quite vocal about her feelings on love. She doesn't believe in it, not one bit. Not the romantic kind, anyhow. In fact, in the two years I've lived here, I've never seen her go on a single date, now that I think of it.

'Love only exists in fairy tales and Disney movies. In the real world, here in North County Dublin, there's no such thing,' she laments.

I shouldn't take the bait, I don't know why I bother arguing with her, because she's proven to be unmovable in her opinions in the past.

As she plonks herself down into one of the kitchen chairs, her bum spills out on either side of it. I wonder if it will break, it seems to groan at the weight. She lights her cigarette, inhaling and releasing smoke with a satisfied smile. I fill the white kettle with water and stick it on. If she's having a smoke, she'll want tea.

Waving her cigarette in my direction, she tells me, 'There's no Prince Charming in my life, Belle. Love doesn't happen to the likes of me.'

'Why not?' I refuse to believe her. 'You know, Tess, Prince Charming could be just around the corner, waiting to bump into you.'

She snorts with laughter at this and her belly jiggles up and down, like a bowl of jelly. I giggle as I hand her a cup of strong tea and watch her as she stirs in three heaped teaspoons of sugar.

'That's too much,' I admonish. We've been learning about healthy eating in school and all that sugar isn't on the list of recommended foods in the pyramid.

She ignores me, by stirring the cup and then taking a big slurp. 'I've met a fair few princes in my time alright. I even married one. His name was Prince Liar Liar.' Her pale-green eyes fill and she dabs her tea towel over her face. I can't tell if it is tears or sweat that she is wiping away. She sweats a lot. Jim says it's because her body is weeping at the weight of heaving around what must be at least twenty-odd stone.

I'm a bit worried about her weight. And she smokes too much. I decide that I'm going to hide the biscuits. I push the fruit bowl towards her, pointedly. I want Tess to have her own Prince Charming. She's lovely and everyone should have their own special someone, like I have my Jim.

I just have to make her *believe*.

I pick up my book and flick to the last page. Cinderella is iridescent in a flowing white wedding dress, with flowers entwined through her golden hair. She looks up adoringly at her Prince, his head tilted towards hers, as if they are about to kiss.

Yuk. Something just occurred to me. Kissing. That could be a problem. I mean I want to marry Jim. Everyone knows that. But I don't want to kiss him. That would be gross.

I'll have the white wedding dress and the flowers and the castle to live in, alright, but I'm not ever, no way, kissing him. I better make sure he knows that, just in case he's under any illusions of my lips ever touching his.

I trace the words '*and they lived happily ever after*' written in fancy script on the last page. And bam, I realise something humongous.

'The happy ever after only happens on the last page.' I say to her, pointing to the words. 'You've just not got to your last page yet, Tess.'

Ha. I am triumphant and for a moment my words seem to make an impact. The look of disdain that normally lives on her face when talking about love is replaced with something that could be described as hopeful. But it doesn't last long, it's just a fleeting moment and disappears in a haze of cigarette smoke.

She rasps, 'Go away out of that' and snaps her tea towel at me. She pushes herself up from her chair, muttering to herself about silly girls as she walks out of the room.

I look out of the window at Jim, who is trying to dribble his football in and out of a row of flower pots he's lined up. It doesn't matter what Tess thinks, because as long as I believe, I can help make it all happen. And I've read enough books to know that me believing is the crucial part in this whole 'living happily ever after' malarkey. It all goes pear-shaped the moment you stop believing.

I'm not delusional. I do know that things are not picture-perfect for me. Like, for example, Jim and I didn't do so well in the whole parents' lottery. But I also know that it could be a whole lot worse.

It *has* been a lot worse. I rub the backs of my legs, as if doing so I can erase the stinging memories of my early childhood at home.

I'm not thinking about that now. I'm going to focus on here and now, because since I got to Tess's, life has been great. She's right at the top of my cool list, aside from her chain-smoking. I need to do something about that, I vow again. Hiding cigarettes doesn't work; she just gets another packet.

She keeps telling me that she has few comforts in life. How can I remove one of them? Especially when she's so good to us two.

A few months ago, Tess let us both pick new wallpaper for our bedrooms. Anything we wanted, she said. It was the first time in my whole life that I got to have a say about how to decorate my bedroom. We all went to Woodies and spent ages looking at all of the papers and paints. Jim, of course, has no imagination and has footballs all over his walls, his bed, his floor. It gives me a headache just sitting in that room.

I looked at every colour chart and pondered for ages. But jumbled up in my head were all the rooms I've ever slept in, a hodge podge of every colour in the spectrum. And then it came to me. I knew exactly how I wanted my room to look.

White. Every single part of it. Pure white.

Tess said I was mad, it would be a nightmare to keep clean. But I really wanted it to be that colour. So she made it happen. Even painting my wardrobe and pine bedside lockers white. She replaced the bookshelves with a new set, in white of course.

The bed linen is broiderie anglaise and so pretty. I love it so much in there. And even Tess has to agree that I'm really good at keeping it clean.

Actually, I think I'll go up there now to finish my book. I'm halfway through *The Lord of the Rings*. Dinner won't be for ages anyhow. I'm still stuffed from lunch. It was one of Tess's specials: deep-fried everything, with a side of fries.

Jim catches me watching him from the window. He starts to show off then, his skinny legs moving quickly as they weave the ball in and out. His wavy red hair flops over his forehead and he brushes it back before taking aim at the back fence again.

'He shoots, he scores, back of the net.' He shouts at his imaginary fans and then he turns to me. 'And the crowd goes wild …' He pulls his sweatshirt up over his head and runs around the garden.

'You big eejit.' I shout, laughing, and he takes a bow.

I know I'm lucky. Up until Tess and Jim came along, I'd never known proper love. But Jim's arrival seemed to have a knock-on effect all around me. When he came here, a ripple of fun, love and joy spread into all areas of my life. Sometimes I can't remember how bad things were before. And I don't want to. I've nearly managed to block out what it felt like back then. Nearly.

Every now and then I remember the fear, that feeling of being so scared all the time that I wanted to curl up into a ball and hide in a corner.

But there's something else that I remember even more than the fear.

The loneliness. What if she forgets all about me and leaves me here, locked up in my room? What if she never comes home?

I pick up a biscuit and nibble on it, looking at my best friend through the window. All I ever really wanted was someone to play with me. And being really greedy, I wanted that person to love me and me to love them too.

Jim Looney. My best friend.

I'll read later. Frodo and Samwise will have to wait.

Shouting to him as I run out the door, 'Get ready to cry, 'cos I'm going to take you down, all the way to Chinatown,' and I catch him off guard, grab the football from him and take aim at the back fence, our makeshift goalpost.

'That's how you do it.' I laugh and we both run towards the ball.

6

And that is how change happens. One gesture. One person. One moment at a time.

Libba Bray

December 1990

I can't listen to him for one more minute. He's driving me mad with his constant chatter about the big visit. You'd swear it was the Pope coming. I mean, I *know* it's a big deal. He's not seen his mam for a few weeks now, so of course he's excited. But come on. Enough already.

And it's not like we don't go through this every time she comes. Now that I think about it, she's been visiting more often recently. I think this could even be her third visit this month. It used to be only once a month at the most.

Don't get me wrong, she's alright – for someone who is as mad as a bag of cats, I suppose. And she loves Jim, so that makes her alright in my books. It's just you don't know what version of her she's going to arrive with, when she does call round. It could be the 'happy normal mammy' or the 'crazier than Michael Jackson and his pet monkey' version.

She's been okay for a while now, but last month when she brought the crazy with her, well, Jim was in bits for ages afterwards.

We were upstairs on the landing. There's this big window ledge, which we've put cushions on, so it's like a seat. We often hang out there and watch the world go by. Tess says we'll take root there one of these days.

Anyhow, there we were, waiting and watching for his mam to arrive. As it happens, we heard her high heels clipping the crazy pavement before we even noticed her arrival, because we were busy monitoring the slow trail of a spider up the wall.

So we look down and Jim is all excited, he's practically bouncing on the seat, but then his smile disappears. I knew without even looking that it must crazy mam time. I looked down and sure enough there she was doing this ridiculous zig-zag dance all the way up to the front door.

She was clutching a brown paper bag to her chest for dear life and her eyes darted to and fro around the driveway, as if she was expecting something awful to happen.

'What is she doing?' I asked, incredulous by the display below. I'd never seen anything quite so bizarre in my life before.

'She doesn't like cracked pavement slabs,' Jim replied. 'I haven't seen her do that for a while. I thought she'd gotten over it.'

His whole demeanour changed, gone was all his excitement and instead now his face looked worried and anxious.

My laughter at his mother's expense disappeared when I saw his face. He went downstairs, shoulders slumped and I followed on behind. She was as white as a ghost by the time she got to the front door and a line of sweat was over her forehead, matting her hair to it.

'Are you okay?' Tess asked kindly.

'I think I managed to avoid them all.' She answered. 'But they are everywhere. You need to get them fixed. It's dangerous. Anything could happen if you were to stumble on a crack.' She looked back at the driveway, as if she'd just managed to circumnavigate her way through a minefield.

'What happens if you stand on one of the cracked ones?' I asked. Tess kicked my ankle hard. 'Ow,' I yelped in pain. I thought it was a fair question. I was interested. I mean, it must be something bad if she went to so much trouble to avoid them.

'Stepping on a cracked pavement slab is unlucky. You could unleash some really bad luck forevermore into your life, with one false step,' she answered, starting at something on the wall behind my head.

The maddest thing of that whole episode was, that after all the effort of the bunny hop hop to the front door, when she got inside, she stayed all of five minutes, then hopped her way back down the drive again.

Told you, mad as a bag of cats. So as you can imagine, I've not got high hopes for this visit, I think crazy mam is due, we've not seen her for a few weeks.

And it's me who has to clean up the mess after she goes. When she left that time, Jim hid in his room for hours, wouldn't let me in. I wasn't going to say one smart word about her either. I knew that he was upset and didn't want to talk about it. I was upset too, upset for him. I wanted to go to him, comfort him, tell him how sorry I was.

'Leave the lad be. His mam isn't right yet,' Tess said, catching me as I was about to break into his room. She tapped her head three times. 'She suffers terrible with her nerves you know that. It's an awful affliction.' She shook her head sorrowfully and heaved her groaning body down the stairs again, with a purple snack in her hand, half-eaten.

I felt like crying for him that day. But I knew that would make him even sadder. So I bit down hard on my lip instead and sat outside Jim's door on the patterned hall carpet. I was there for so long waiting my bum went numb and I had pins and needles all the way up my two legs. But there was no way I was moving. I had to be there, so that when Jim did come out, he would see me and know that I loved him.

I couldn't make his mother's nerves any better, but I could make sure he knew he had a best friend. When he did come out, he looked down at me and said nothing. I didn't mind, though. I understood, more than anyone, that sometimes there are no words.

He was silent, sullen and I knew the reason why that was his heart was smashed into a hundred million pieces, again.

I didn't try to make him talk, I just fell into silent step with him, then we walked downstairs. I followed him outside and played football for ages with him and the garden was silent, bar the sound of our ragged breaths, as we ran and ran.

Then Tess shouted for us to come in for our tea. She had gone to a lot of trouble, makings all of Jim's favourites, to try and make him feel better. And by the time we were in the living room watching TV that night, he started to smile a little bit.

So here we go again, waiting to see which version of his mother turns up today. And to make matters worse, the big eejit has gotten it into his head that this time is the time that she's come to take him home. Something else we go through every single time. He always thinks the same thing, and each time he ends up disappointed.

Tess told me once that her grandmother suffered from her nerves too. She used to take to her bed for weeks when they were kids. I asked her if she ever got better and she just shook her head sadly. Maybe his mam can change. Maybe she can get better, unlike Tess's gran.

I just want him to be happy. And I know that if I'm thinking about the last disastrous visit, so is he, no matter how much he prattles on about how this is going to be different.

'How'd I look?' he asks, walking into the room. He's plastered down his hair to one side with half a bottle of gel, by the looks of it, and he looks pure ridiculous. He's also got on a grand-daddy shirt, in a blue stripe. It looks like a pyjama top. What is he thinking? His Irish jersey looks much better on him.

'You look stupid,' I tell him and as my words bounce off him, his face crumples.

Why did I say that? I feel awful. I want to take the words back, stuff them into my mouth again, but it's too late.

'Will I wash it out?' He asks, frantically rubbing his hair with the sleeve of his shirt and I feel like crying, the guilt is so strong.

Tess always says that jealousy is a shocking thing and she's right. Because I know that I'm being horrid all because I'm jealous. I've never ever got to feel the excitement of seeing my mam come to visit. Not that I'd necessarily want her to, I suppose. But even so.

Because despite the fact that Mrs Looney is off her head loopy-loo style, at least she comes to see Jim. At least she makes an effort to stay in touch and there's no denying she loves him. It's written all over her face.

I'm not being a very good friend and I know it.

'No, leave it alone, let me fix it. You don't really look stupid, I was just joking. You just used too much gel, that's all.' I run my hands through his glooped-up hair and restyle his wavy locks into a halfway decent style, using my fingers as combs. He looks like Jim again and I tell him, 'There, that's perfect. Your mam will love it, don't be worrying.'

'I just want it to go well,' Jim says for the one hundredth time, pulling at his shirt. He glances at the bouquet of flowers sitting on the hall table. He bought them out of his savings for her. I hope she knows how lucky she is, having him love her like he does.

'It will go well,' I assure him, even if I don't believe a word of it. She'll more than likely do another crazy dance all the way up the path, just to disappoint her son once more before turning around to go home.

I vow to myself that I'll be right by his side to pick up the pieces again. I already have two bars of his favourite Tiffin chocolate hidden in my top drawer upstairs, ready to console him.

After the last time, Tess has forbidden us from watching out for her upstairs. So instead she has us all sitting around the kitchen table, listening to Jim tapping his knee with his fingers.

Tess is on her third cigarette and it's freezing because she has the doors and windows all open to let the smoke out.

I've got to find a way to stop her smoking. Not just because she'll freeze us all out, but because that wheeze in her chest is getting louder all the time.

When the doorbell rings, we all jump and look at each other. Tess stubs out her cigarette and hides the ashtray under the sink. Jim fixes his shirt – again – and I take a deep breath.

I stand side by side to him when Tess opens the door. And we all hold our breath, waiting to see which Mrs Looney will walk through the door.

She looks nervous, but she's not out of breath. Maybe there was no crazy zig-zagging this time. Without looking at Jim, I can feel the relief seeping from his very core.

I look her up and down, taking in her bright-pink batwing jumper and her tight, white trousers. She's got on white high-heel shoes and I wish I had a pair like them. She's had her hair done and it looks glossy and swings onto her shoulders, like one of the models in a l'Oreal advert. Last time she was here, it was streaked with dark roots and she was wearing an awful blue and grey shell tracksuit.

She's practically unrecognisable.

This version is a new one. She didn't look like this the last visit.

It's great that she's smiling and when she pulls Jim into a big hug, I could burst with happiness for him.

Why is my stomach flipping about and why do I feel so uneasy?

'You've grown so much,' she says to Jim, her eyes look like they're about to pop out of her head. 'You're almost a man now, up to my shoulder already.'

'They're like weeds, the two of them,' Tess moans. 'I'm going to put a block on their heads one of these days. I can't keep clothes on them,' she quickly adds, 'Not that I mind, of course.'

'Of course,' his mam replies and they both look awkward.

'What's in the bag?' I ask, changing the subject. I wonder if it's the same bag that she had the last time she visited. She was clutching it like it was the crown jewels, but we never got to find out what it contained because she didn't stick around long enough.

Jim's mam smiles at me and thrusts the brown bag to Jim. 'It's for you both.'

We both smile in anticipation and peer into the bag when Jim opens it. Bars, in bright wrappers, purples, pinks, yellows all gleam up to us, accompanied by the most wonderful sweet smell of cocoa.

'I didn't know what your favourites are, so I bought a few of everything,' she tells us.

'Jim loves Tiffin.' I say, feeling superior. I know him better than you, I wanted to say. But I don't.

'Belle loves caramel bars,' Jim says.

'Oh, I don't think I bought any Tiffin.' She looks upset about that.

'It's okay. I love Star Bars too,' Jim says and pulls one out, ready to pull the wrapper off.

'I'll take them,' Tess says, swooping in and confiscating them. 'I am very careful with their diet. Just one bar each as a treat at the weekend. I'm all about their five a day. Healthy eating and all that.'

Jim and I snigger under our breath. Yeah, right. Five bars of chocolate a day, she means.

Tess does this all the time whenever the social workers come by. Pretends to be super-perfect or something. And the thing is, she is perfect. She doesn't need to pretend.

She tells his mam that she'll hand them out over the next few weeks, one bar a day, but Jim and I know that's rubbish.

'Let's leave Jim and his mam be,' Tess says, giving me a dirty look. She knows we're teasing her. She ushers me up the stairs to my bedroom. 'You go on into the living room, Mrs Looney. I'll send in some tea.'

'You'd swear she had servants, the way she's speaking,' I whisper to Jim. 'Good luck. She looks well, it's a good sign.' I squeeze his hand quickly before I run upstairs.

Did I mean that? I'm not sure. I know that I want Jim to be happy, but I'm scared of what his happiness might mean for me. It's all so complicated. His mam looks much better than the last time and that has to be a good thing, right?

Then there's that nasty voice in my head again.

When he asks her to take him home today, she might say yes, then what will you do?

I'll be on my own again.

I swallow back a lump of putrid, acidy sick that has burned its way up my throat. I don't want him to go. I feel ashamed again that I am being so selfish, putting my own needs ahead of his. He's my best friend. I should be on his side. End of. Jim has been talking about going home ever since that first day he arrived here. He loves her, crazy bits and all.

I quickly cross my fingers that she's well again and vow that I will be a better person if Jim gets his wish. I'll not say a word, I'll not cry. I'll just hug him and tell him I'm so happy. And I'll be okay, if he goes, because I have Tess.

I glance at Dee-Dee sitting on the end of my bed amongst an array of stuffed toys. I haven't played with her in a long time. She doesn't talk to me any more, but then again, I don't really talk to her. I pick her up and hug her, but I don't feel any comfort the way I used to.

Now that I've had a real best friend, I don't want a doll.

I perch my bum on our windowsill and flick my way through a battered 1983 Bunty annual. It's years out of date, but even so, I still like reading it. I envy Bunty's life and sometimes pretend that I'm her.

I'm living in a big house, blonde, pretty, rosy-cheeked and I'm living a normal, carefree life, with my mam, dad and little brother.

I forget about Jim and his mam for a while, as I get immersed into Bunty's latest escapade on a snowy mountain side.

I'm not sure I could pull off the cute ski gear she's donning, though. I'm so tall, my legs seem to be too long for everything. Tess goes mad every time I go up a size, she says that it's impossible to find a new pair of jeans for me that fit, so she has to get out her sewing kit to make some alterations.

A door slams and I look down. Jim's mam is leaving already. That flew by. She's got her arm around him as he walks her to the gate. She actually walks straight through the cracked pavement slabs. Another good sign.

I watch them hug for ages and feel weird watching them, like I'm snooping. But I can't take my eyes off them all the same. It's a lovely moment and I'm envious again. He's got one of his goofy smiles plastered over his face and that makes me happy at least.

Relief floods me as I realise that I'm happy to see him smile. Maybe I'm not such a bad person after all. I run downstairs two stairs at a time. I can't wait to hear all about it.

'Well, Jimbo, did she like your hair?' I ask.

And before he says anything back to me, I know. His face looks different. He looks happier than I've ever seen him in the past two years. I mean, we've laughed a lot. Once we snorted so much that I even peed my pants.

'She's taking you home,' I say.

He looks at me for the longest time. Then he nods. I make a tremendous effort to put a smile on my face, to make him believe that I'm happy for him. It must be working, I must be fooling him, because his goofy grin is back again.

'She's rented a two-bed flat in Ranelagh and the landlord has said that I can decorate my bedroom any colour I want.'

Green. He'll pick green, because that's his favourite colour.

I hear Tess sigh and the click of her lighter as she ignites another cigarette.

I'm losing him. Tess knows it. Jim just doesn't know it yet.

'How long do we have left?' I ask. I'm surprised that my voice sounds okay, considering the fact that I want to cry.

'You make it sound so dramatic, Belle,' Jim laughs at me. 'I'm just going to live somewhere else, that's all. Nothing else is going to change. We'll be best friends forever, you'll see.'

7

God puts rainbows in the clouds so that each of us — in the dreariest and most dreaded moments — can see a possibility of hope.

Maya Angelou

December 1990

I bolt upright, opening my eyes to the darkness around me. My heart is pounding and I try to scream, but no sound comes out. I need to alert everyone in the house to the danger.

But I can't open my mouth. It is as if glue has locked it together. I try to swing my legs over the side of the bed, but they won't work either. I've become paralysed.

Everyone will die and it will be all my fault, because I can't move or speak. Thick smoke stings my throat, restricting my airways. The heat claws at my skin, singeing it pink.

I watch my curtains alight with flames, dancing their way downward. They have their prey in sight: my books that are on the bookshelf to the left of the window.

I blink, once, twice and a third time. I tell myself, 'It's just a nightmare. It's not real.'

When I open my eyes again, the flames are gone, only darkness engulfs my bedroom. I've had a nightmare. The same one that has plagued me on and off for years. It's always the same, or a variation of such.

The house is on fire, me waking up in my bed, to feel the smoke and heat, but unable to warn anyone inside of the peril. Everyone perishes, burned alive, gone in an instant.

Ashes to ashes, dust to dust, if God won't have me, then the devil must.

I repeat the rhyme over and over and it helps calm me down. My breathing starts to regulate and my heart rate slows down to a more normal beat.

Right, time to try this again. I move my legs and swing them over the side of the bed. Good, they work again. Even though I know that it's been a nightmare, I'm still scared, afraid to let my feet touch the ground.

But the darkness scares me more than the fear of burning my feet, so I run across the carpet to the switch and flick it on. I can see again. The last of my nightmare disappears into the light that fills the room.

I get back into bed but know that trying to sleep is a futile task. So I lie down, eyes closed and listen to jumbled thoughts run around in my brain.

Try as I might, I can't stop thinking about things that I try hard not to think about. I'm back living with Dolores, my mother, and she keeps locking me in my bedroom. I can't stop remembering the fear of being locked up and the smell of smoke as it curled its way up to my bedroom, with me trapped in it …

'Get up, sleepy head,' a voice shouts.

I wake up to a series of painful prods from Jim. I must have eventually dozed off, closing my mind to my memories.

'Ow,' I exclaim, irritated and tired. 'What time is it?'

'It's nearly nine. Tess is going bananas down there. She wants us up and showered and looking our best before ten, because Mrs Reilly called and is coming over,' Jim informs me.

Mrs Looney didn't waste any time. She must have been in touch with social services already. I suppose arrangements have to be made for Jim's 'transition' home. I know the drill. Been there, done that, worn the t-shirt. Well, I haven't, but I've watched others before me go through it.

I put a smile onto my face. At some point before dawn and eventual sleep, I vowed to myself that I would be super-supportive, no matter how hard I find it. This is about Jim, not me.

'You might get home for Christmas,' I say, mustering up as much enthusiasm as I can.

This is Jim's home, though, right here with me. Not in some crummy flat in Ranelagh with his crazy mam.

Only she's not crazy any more, she's all glossy locks and high-heeled white stilettos.

And she's going to take Jim away, just before Christmas. I know it.

Last year we made a den in the sitting room and slept in it, side by side in sleeping bags. We were determined to catch Santa come down the chimney. But, of course, he remained elusive because we flaked out, missing the big man in red placing two filled pillow cases outside our makeshift home. This year we've plans to stay up all night to test the theory that Jim has, that Santa doesn't really exist. I don't agree and plan to prove that. As I keep telling him, of course he exists, because when I asked for a best friend, he gave me one.

'I couldn't sleep last night,' Jim tells me. He grabs my hands in his and looks at me with such intensity my stomach starts to flip. 'I've got a plan. Genius really. Get a load of this. I'm going to ring and ask mam to adopt you.'

'You can't do that,' I say. Can he?

'Why not? Why can't she take you with us too? Problem solved. Simple.' He grins, delighted with his plan.

'Do you think she would want me?' I can't breathe. A new life, with Jim. Adopted. A forever family.

'Of course she will. Sure, women always want a daughter. I bet she'd prefer a girl to a boy anyway. You can share my bedroom. I'll even let you pick the colours. But we're not having pink. Not a hope. Or purple,' Jim says.

'I don't know,' I say. But I do like green. We could have a green bedroom.

Jim grins at this. 'She really likes you. She told me that only yesterday,' Jim says.

I'm not so sure I believe that. His left eye always twitches when he's lying about something. I don't think I've been very nice to her, come to think about it.

Bad move there, Belle.

I mean, if I'd known that there was a chance that she might take me home with her too, I'd have been on my best behaviour every single time she visited, even on the crazy days.

I vow that the next time she comes I'll be so good that she'll forgive me for any of my earlier transgressions.

'I'm going to ring her now,' Jim tells me. 'I have her new phone number for the flat. You wait and see, Belle, it will be so much fun.' He pulls out a piece of paper from his jeans pocket, with her phone number scribbled on it in his large, loopy writing.

I feel excitement begin to bubble up inside me. 'Can you imagine the craic we'll have going to and from school on the bus every day?'

'The best,' and he laughs in response as he runs out of the room.

I better get ready. I know exactly what I'm going to wear. My good red jumper. It's the nicest thing I own. Tess says it makes my skin look like the colour of banoffi pie. And I'll tie my hair back off my face, like Tess always nags me to do. She says I look prettier that way.

I'll make her love me. You wait and see.

91

8

Things change. And friends leave. Life doesn't stop for anybody.

Stephen Chbosky

December 1990

If we're honest, we both knew it could never happen. Sure, Jim's mother had only just gotten her act together. She'd not said goodbye to the crazy for more than a few months. It was a big enough deal that they were going to let her take home her own son. There was no way she was going to adopt anyone, least of all me.

But we both had fun playing the sticking-our-fingers-in-our-ears-we're-not-listening-game for a bit. Until today, that is.

Even when Tess started to chain smoke in agitation at Jim's proposed adoption plan, we covered our ears as well as our eyes and ignored her.

Then the nearer it got to Mrs Reilly coming over, the quieter she got. She looked sad and not one bit like her usual upbeat self.

'She's always worrying about something or other,' Jim declared and I nodded furiously in agreement, even though I knew that wasn't true.

'She's happiest when she's worrying,' I declared.

He'd rang his mam as promised. The conversation ended much quicker than I thought it should have. That was the first sign that things were not going to Jim's plan. I shook the uneasy feeling off and decided that maybe it was a good thing. She probably said yes without hesitation, no need for a long deep and meaningful chat with Jim about it all.

'She'll come round to the idea. You'll see,' he told me, when he admitted that she seemed a bit startled by his suggestion.

I decided to ignore the fact that his smile was beginning to fade from his eyes once again.

She wasn't our only problem. We kind of guessed we might get resistance from Mrs Reilly, our social worker. She was the kind of woman who didn't inspire confidence at the best of times. In our experience she was consistently unenthusiastic about everything. She wore this same uninterested, blank look on her face. Tess couldn't stand her. She was fond of saying things like, 'Mrs Reilly, is a jobs' worth.' Or 'She's as much use as a chocolate teapot.'

For years now, I've had to go through the same routine with her checkups. She comes in, sits down in front of me and without even looking up, asks me a series of stupid questions. She is only interested in ticking boxes, that's all, I don't think she ever really listened to what I've replied.

Jim reckoned this could play to our advantage, though, in this instance. 'She'll probably sign off on the adoption, without even blinking. I mean, us both leaving at once, that's a win for her. She'll get a bonus or something for getting two of us out of the system in one go,' Jim declared.

I hadn't thought of it like that. Jim was the clever one in our particular double act. He always saw things that I'd miss. When Mrs Reilly arrived, we gave her the benefit of our most dazzling smiles. She looked instantly suspicious. I made a pot of tea and put the good biscuits out. Tess kept eyeing up the cupboard which was the current gaol for her Silk Cut Purple. She was failing miserably at cutting down too. I saw two empty cartons in the bin this morning.

Taking a deep breath, Jim laid out his plan to Mrs Reilly, concisely and firmly. 'So, you can see, it makes perfect sense for Belle to come live with mam and me.'

I was so proud of him.

Mrs Reilly didn't say anything for a few moments. She just looked at Jim in that same blank way she had down pat. But then she started to laugh, big bellowing guffaws. I looked at Jim and he shrugged his shoulders. We didn't know if her laugh was a good or a bad sign.

Wiping tears from her eyes, she said, 'You're not serious? Please tell me you're having me on.'

And in that second I knew we were done for. She wasn't even going to pretend to look into the possibility.

'We can't just go passing children willy nilly to random strangers.' She said, pointing a stubby finger at both of us.

'Why not?' I said. 'That's what you've always done to me.' I felt anger flush over me as I thought of all the houses I had been shipped between over the years.

'Don't be so cheeky,' Mrs Reilly flared up at me, her face flushed red. 'That tongue will cut you one of these days, it's so sharp.'

'Hey,' Tess jumped in, wagging her finger at her. 'Give the child a break. They're like Siamese twins these two. This is hard on them. On all of us,' Tess said, ending on a sob.

I looked at Tess in gratitude and inched closer to her.

'That's as may be, but Belle stays here. Jim, you get to go home. Enough of this nonsense now.' She then picked up a chocolate Hobnob and dunked it into her tea, as if she hadn't a care in the world.

I hated her more in that moment than I'd ever done before. As she sucked the chocolate off her digestive, I realised that she didn't care. Not one bit.

'I mean the very idea. A newly recovered manic depressive taking on not one, but two, children.' She shook her head and took another bite of her biscuit.

Things went from bad to worse after that.

'You'll start your new school in January.' Her face was back stuck in her brown manila folder again. So she missed the effect that those words had on us both.

The final nail in the coffin for the Siamese twins.

'But I don't want to change schools,' Jim said. 'I'll get the bus every day over here.'

Mrs Reilly snorted and looked at Tess, as if to say, are these two for real?

'That's just not doable,' she stated. 'I'm not a miracle worker.'

'Oh we know *that* much for sure,' Tess said. She looked really irritated now.

I couldn't look at Jim. I knew already how his face would look and I couldn't bear it.

Tess got up from the table and said to no one in particular, 'Sod it.'

Mrs Reilly's face was a picture when Tess took the packet of cigarettes out of the press, walked to the back door and lit one up. I think she knew better than to say a word, though, and take on Tess right then.

With every puff Tess took, Mrs Reilly mapped out Jim's future, far, far away from me. I could tell that she was getting irritated with Jim, that he wasn't more excited about it all.

'You're the one who wanted this, Jim. And now you're acting like I'm the bad guy here,' Mrs Reilly grumbled. 'If you'd rather stay …'

Jim's face went from sad, to angry and ended up worried at that threat. I panicked too at her words. What if our plans jeopardised Jim's chance to go home to his mam? I couldn't let that happen.

'You'd be wrecked going back and forth on the bus the whole time,' I said to him, mustering everything I could to stop my voice from wobbling.

'No I wouldn't,' he replied.

'You would. And when would you practise your football, if you were always on the bus,' I added.

That made him stop and think.

'It'll be okay. We'll still see each other. Lots and lots,' I said to him.

And even though he looked doubtful, he stopped arguing with Mrs Reilly and she left, with her brown manila folder, sniffing at the injustice of having to deal with the likes of us two.

Ever since then, I've put on a performance of a lifetime. I've told Jim that we'll phone each other every week. I'll write to him too. Of course he won't write back, because he's rubbish at that kind of stuff, but that doesn't matter.

Tess gave us a bus timetable this morning and together we marked out the times and routes for the weekends.

'We'll meet in the city centre on a Saturday. We can go feed the ducks in Stephen's Green. You love all that sappy stuff,' he says to me.

Tess sighs a lot. She's smoking a pack a day and I've given up nagging her to cut down. I don't have the energy for that right now.

'Best friends forever.' I keep telling Jim.

'You big sap,' he keeps answering. But I've got him smiling again, all the way to his eyes too.

Time has moved way too fast, as it always does, when you don't want it to. Now, finally, it's time for Jim to leave. His mam is here with Mrs Reilly and she's hugging Tess.

'I'll never be able to thank you enough,' she keeps repeating over and over to Tess.

They both start to cry and cling even tighter to each other.

'I don't know what they have to be sad about,' I say to Jim. He kicks his suitcase in response. I can tell he's mortified by their display of emotion. I stick my tongue out at him and make my eyes go cross-eyed and pretty soon he can't help himself and he starts to laugh again.

'I'll miss you around here,' Tess says. 'Come here and give me a hug, Jimbo.'

'Thanks, for, well, you know, like, thanks.' Jim, as always, when having to say anything remotely sappy, is gruff. But Tess knows that he only does that because he's really a big softie and is trying hard not to cry.

'It's time to say goodbye to Belle too,' Mrs Looney says.

I look at her and her eyes dart away from me quickly. I realise something. She has the exact same look on her face that Joan and Daniel had when they said goodbye to me four years ago.

Guilt. I'm so sick of seeing people look like that.

'You can come visit any time you like.' Her voice has gone all high and sing-song like. She's also wringing her hands like she's doing the laundry.

I can see Jim watching her, all worried that she'll turn back into crazy mam again and he'll not get to go home with her.

So I walk over to her and say, 'It's going to be okay Mrs Looney.'

She's Jim's mam and as much as I've tried to hate her these past few weeks, I can't. Because, at the end of the day, she's making him happy.

'Thank you, Belle,' she says and she gives me a hug.

I run to get a parcel I hid earlier in the hall closet and hand it to Jim. 'Sorry about the wrapping. It was either tin foil or the pink paper with bows on it I had for my birthday.'

'I don't have anything for you.' Jim looks distraught as he accepts my gift. 'But genius wrapping.' He pulls apart the silver tin foil, grinning.

'No way. This is your favourite,' he says, looking at my Simon computer game.

I shrug. 'If you ever plan on beating my record for highest score, you'll need this.'

'I can beat you anytime I like. I just let you win, 'cos, like, you're a girl,' he responds.

'In your dreams,' I say.

'Loser,' he replies and I laugh back, but it comes out more like a sob.

'Thank you, Belle,' he whispers, inching closer.

'Oh, for goodness sake, give the girl a hug,' Tess says, her tea towel wiping away her tears. We look awkwardly at each other for a second or two. We haven't done the whole hugging thing for ages now.

I step forward a couple of inches and throw my arms around him. 'It's me who should be thanking you,' I whisper.

'For what?' he asks.

'For being my best friend,' I say.

We pull apart and look at each other and I know that, like me, he's remembering it all. Playing Simon together, kicking the football, watching *Aliens*, the horror movie, behind our fingers, kicking our legs so hard so that we could out swing each other in the park, copying each other's homework, making faces behind Tess's back and laughing so hard that snot came out of our noses.

'Will you be okay?' Worry lines crease his face.

I want to be brave here and say, yeah, course, no biggie, but instead my mouth quivers dangerously.

'We'll see each other all the time,' he promises.

I don't answer and he asks me, 'You don't believe that? Don't go silent again, Belle. Don't you dare.'

'What if they move me again from here? You won't know where I am then.' There, I've said it. I've admitted my fear.

'I'll come find you. Wherever you are, I'll find you.' He promises me and I look into his blue eyes, nodding. I believe him. He'll find me.

We hear the click of Tess's lighter and the moment ends. Since the other week, Tess has given up all pretence to Mrs Reilly that she doesn't smoke in front of us and is puffing grey smoke into her lungs whilst dabbing a tattered tea towel to her damp face.

I run upstairs as he walks out of the door and sit on our window ledge, looking out. There's a crowd outside, neighbours, friends, who have come to wave him off.

He's popular around here. Everyone loves Jim. I can hear them all shouting their wishes to him and I bet he's scarlet from it all, but secretly chuffed inside. One of the neighbours has her arm around Tess, who seems to be sagging against her. She's crying a lot.

I better put the kettle on for her. She'll need tea.

But then a girl catches my eye. She's standing a bit back from the crowd, looking straight up at the window, her eyes locked on mine. I don't recognise her, she's not one of our friends. Maybe she's visiting one of the neighbours for Christmas. She's got short black hair, cut in a bob, with a fringe. I like her coat, it's bright red with big black buttons on it. I think I'd like a coat like that myself. With white stilettos like Jim's mam. And white skin-tight jeans.

Jim is about to get into the back of the car, to drive away, and I hold my breath, my hand waving to him.

Look up, please look up. Don't just go. Look up and see me here, waving at you. And of course he does. He looks up and smiles as he waves goodbye.

Then, as he if was never really here, he's gone.

PART TWO

PART TWO

9

If we wait until we're ready
We'll be waiting the rest of our lives.

Lemony Snicket

October 2005

'So, what you're saying to me is that there is no possibility, not even the slightest chance, that this Dolores, photographed here, is my mother?' I say. I look at the picture of the smiling woman, who is hoisting up a prop-sized cheque over her head in jubilation.

'No, afraid not, Belle,' Tess says. 'They have the same first name, that's it. Nice thought, though.'

'But you've not met my mother,' I persist.

It's been twenty-one years since I saw my mother. And while I remember moments in her company – mostly ones I wish I could forget too – her face has become grainy, like an out-of-focus picture. I hold up the paper beside the small Polaroid photo I possess. Shite, they are not even remotely alike. I squint my eyes, but I can't find even one feature that could make them the same person.

I never really thought that it was a possibility. I was ninety-nine percent joking. Tess knows that. Sometimes it's fun, though, to play make believe. I've developed a habit that whenever I hear the name Dolores, I look up and play the 'Are You My Mother?' game. So when I saw the article in the paper about a woman called Dolores winning gazillions of millions, sure, I couldn't help but daydream.

And you know what's the crazy part of all this? I don't think I even want to see her again.

I sometimes wonder if there are any happy moments that I shared with her hidden in my brain. That somehow or other I only remember the bad ones. But, try as I might, I can't come up with a single good one.

Memories of brown velvet sofas, brown curtains and a brown carpet, mixed up with my mother's back as she walks out of the house. Me sitting on my bed, cross-legged, staring at the door, hungry, waiting for her to return to feed me. Pulling a dining-room chair over to the kitchen press, climbing my little body up and looking at rows upon rows of tinned food, crying because I didn't know how to open them. Back on my bed again, but this time with a dry cereal bar, as the milk in the fridge was all lumpy.

Aside from those charming memories, all I have of my mother is this one photograph that Mrs Reilly gave me years ago. There was a time that I used to dream that my mother would come to her senses and wake up, realising she simply had to have me in her life. In that dream, she'd come rescue me, bringing me to live with her, in her beautiful home. The house would have a huge garden, with a swing on a big old oak tree. And my bedroom would be pink with a big double bed, with a white canopy over it and lots of pillows and cushions on it. There would probably be a pony in a stables adjacent to the house too. And life would be just perfect.

I can't fathom why I would even dream about such a thing. I should hate her for all she did to me, but I can't force myself to do that. Now that I'm an adult, I find myself trying to understand her, and what made her behave as she did.

Is she living a good life now? Without me in it? And despite the bad stuff, despite the fear and the loneliness of my early years, I wish her well. I want her to be happy.

One day, I'm not even sure when it was, I realised that I didn't want Dolores to rescue me. In fact, the opposite. Tess became my family. End of. The only mother I've ever known or wanted.

I smile at my foster mam, who will be seventy years old this year. I feel so protective of her. She's staring at me thoughtfully and wags one of her fingers in my direction.

'So let's just pretend for a second. If yer wan was your mother, what then?' Tess asks, looking at the new multi-millionaire on the paper.

'Well, for a start, I might find a way to forgive her for abandoning me, for a small share in her euro millions win!' I joke.

Tess cackles her trademark laugh. Even though she's not smoked for years, she's never lost her throaty voice.

'Pass me those chocolates,' she orders and then dives her head into the box, making a choice.

One of my finest hours was persuading her to give up smoking. That's well over fifteen years ago now. But I've never managed to get her to give up chocolates. Or her deep-fat fryer. At seventy, I suppose, maybe she's earned the right to eat a Turkish Delight or a bag of chips whenever she feels like it.

'You could still find her if you wanted to,' Tess throws into the conversation, nonchalantly, knowing full well she's just landed a grenade in front of me.

I look at her and sigh. 'I know. It's all I used to think about as a kid. I'd say to myself, when I turn eighteen I'll find her. Rock up to her front door and say hello, remember me?'

'Well, you're twenty-five now, all grown up and mistress of your own destiny. What's stopping you?' Tess asks.

'Ah, that's the million-dollar question. Well, to start with, if she wanted me, she would have been in touch long and ever ago, wouldn't she?' I say.

'True for you, but maybe she's scared to? Afraid of what you'll say to her, how you'll react,' Tess states.

'What could she possibly be afraid of? That I'll call her a selfish cow who abandoned me and never looked back, even once, to see how I was doing? I don't believe she even feels an iota of guilt for the years of abuse she threw at me. I was child, for goodness sake. How could she do that?' I say, and I'm surprised by how bitter I sound. I mean, I thought I was reconciled to all this, long and ever ago.

It takes Tess a few moments to answer me. 'I'm definitely not making excuses for her. But maybe she just couldn't be a mother. Maybe life just was too hard for her. It is for some people. Her behaviour is inexcusable, but I think it might help you, though, to talk to her. You might get some answers.'

'Maybe,' I say. 'But I'm not sure that I can be bothered.'

'Liar,' Tess remarks.

'Stop hogging the chocolates,' I tell her and grab the box to divert her attention.

'I think you should think about getting in touch, at least,' Tess says. 'It would be good for you. To get some, what does Oprah always say, you need to get some closure.'

'Get you,' I laugh. 'Listen, you're my family now, Tess. Whether you want it or not, you got stuck with me. That's enough for me. I don't need Dolores in my life, thank you very much.'

And that's at least partly true. But not the full story. Because sometimes, late at night, I find myself thinking about her and wondering where she is and what she's doing. Could she be thinking about me right this second, just as I am her?

Nah.

'For the record, I was never stuck with you, young lady. I wanted you, as well you know,' Tess snaps at me.

I know that's true. Over the years we've gotten closer than I reckon most mothers and daughters are.

She never took anyone else in after that boy Jim left. With it just being the two of us, well, we bonded, I suppose, as Oprah would say. She was so kind that Christmas, she knew I was missing him so much.

The turning point came after I overheard her talking to Mrs Reilly in the hall. It was shortly after Jim had left to go live with his mam. I'll never forget it.

'So this year you turn sixty, Tess. I know your plan has always been to retire from fostering once you hit that milestone year. So I wanted to reassure you that we've found a new placement for Belle. It's a house with another fifteen-year-old girl, so she'll have company there. And it's in the area too. She won't have to leave her school,' Mrs Reilly stated. 'I'm quite pleased with myself, if I'm honest. I worked hard to get the right place for her.'

I couldn't breathe. I never knew Tess was going to retire. I don't want to go. Not now. I can't start all over again. I collapsed onto the stairs and big fat tears started to splash onto my lap. I couldn't deal with this. I would run away. I was done relying on anyone else. Better off on my own.

But then, Tess spluttered in response, 'Over my dead body you'll take that girl from me.'

I couldn't believe my ears. She wanted me. Tess wanted ME.

'You want her to stay?' Mrs Reilly seemed incredulous.

Wagon. Was it that hard to believe that someone would want to keep me?

'That poor girl has had enough shoving and pushing from billy to jack in her life. She's going nowhere. This is her home, if she'll have me. I love that girl. She's like my own. And I can retire when she's eighteen,' Tess said. 'Not another word on the subject now.'

And I didn't care that Mrs Reilly was there, I didn't care that I'd been warned to stay in my room, I ran into Tess and buried myself into her warm, soft, squishy body. I'd never initiated a hug before and I know that I took her by surprise. But I wouldn't let go of her and then I felt her hands go around me too and she pulled me in tight.

'You want me,' I sobbed to her and my body heaved, assaulted by relief.

'Of course I do,' she said. 'You're my girl. My little butterfly. You always will be. As sure as if I had you myself.'

And that was when it all changed for me. I realised that I'd finally found a permanent home and with that knowledge came a shift in my outlook. I looked at Tess differently. I began to think of her as a mother as opposed to just somebody who made me egg and chips.

I know now that the day Daniel got that job, and he and Joan were shipped off to the US, was the luckiest day of my life. I don't even like to think about what might have happened if I'd stayed in that house with them. They were good people, nice, kind people, but they weren't my family. They didn't love me, not like Tess loves me.

I look up when Tess interrupts my reminiscing, 'If I was twenty years younger,' and I laugh as I watch her eyeing up McDreamy. Monday night is *Grey's Anatomy* night. It's one of our rituals, even though I don't live here any more. I always come here straight from work and we have dinner, then watch it together. Sometimes I don't know why I bother paying rent in my small bedsit because I'm here so much.

'I hope they get together tonight,' I say. 'I can't cope with all this on-off Meredith and Derek drama. They're meant to be.'

'You and your fairy tales.' Tess smiles. 'Always chasing happy-ever-afters.'

My hand hovers over the enter button on Google. I've typed in my mother's name, Dolores Freeman, and have been staring at the screen for ages, trying to get the courage to hit enter.

Ever since that conversation with Tess I've not been able to get her out of my head.

What if Tess is right and she's been waiting for me to make the first move all this time? She could be married, she might have children. I might have brothers and sisters, for goodness sake.

Before long my imagination has gotten out of control again and I've all sorts of notions in my head. But what I really need is the truth. Why didn't she want me? Why did she hate me so much?

Shit. I pressed enter before I have time to think myself into an even more melted head and watch as 673,000 hits come up on the page.

Okay, I think with a sigh, this might take a bit of time.

Dolores Freeman is a popular name. I start to go into each of the websites, one by one, and find women with the same name as my mother in all corners of the globe. There's a massage therapist in Hull, a retired nurse in Texas, an eighteen-year-old student in UCD and that's just in my first three hits. My eyes start to ache as I search and search, hitting enter and escape over and over again, into Facebook profiles, LinkedIn accounts.

I lament the fact that I don't know any private investigators. There was that guard I dated last year, but I shudder just remembering what it felt like every time he leaned in to kiss me. Nope, not even for access to his databases will I chance calling him.

Then I decide to engage my brain and I change the search to show images as opposed to text. Maybe I'll see her photograph, or at least narrow down the amount of times I have to check websites out.

You know the way, when you have a bright idea like that, but it never usually works out? Well, I thought that would be the case here. The pictures are easier to go through than all the text, but then suddenly, as I scroll down through two pages at speed, my hand freezes. Looking up at me is a picture of my mother.

My Dolores Freeman.

Older, granted. With more wrinkles and some grey in her brown hair, but most definitely her. I hover over the image for ages, just looking at her.

Do I want to do this? I feel like I'm standing on the edge of a cliff and by clicking on this image, I'm jumping.

Taking a deep breath, I decide to go for it before I have a chance to chicken out. The image is linked to a newspaper, the *Northside Chronicle,* and I hold my breath as it opens. I see that the article was written two years ago. I scroll through the text and read the caption written under the image.

As I read the words, my mouth drops open, in cartoon-like shock.

Dolores Freeman, 46, of Donnycarney, Co. Dublin, was found guilty of fraud on two counts and sentenced to five years.

I'm the daughter of a gaol bird. Wait till Tess hears this. That's that, then.

So why am I scribbling down the name of her solicitor – Aidan Turner?

10

Writing isn't letters on paper. It's Communication. It's Memory.

Issac Marion

July 2005

Dear Dolores,

Hello. I've been sitting here for hours, trying to work out how to start this letter. No matter how hard I try, everything I write seems so official and wrong and has ended up in the bin.

So maybe I should just get on with it. I'll start by saying, I'm Belle. As in, your daughter, Belle.

I hope it's okay that I'm writing to you. You see, I've thought of you often over the years and wondered how you are, where you are, are you happy? And it struck me that maybe you might sometimes wonder about me too. At least, that's what Tess reckons.

I'm not sure what you know or don't know about what happened to me after I was taken into care. Did Mrs Reilly keep you informed? In case she didn't, Tess is my foster mother. After a rocky start, between a few different homes, I went to live with her when I was eight. She's a wonderful lady. I love her. I'm extremely lucky to have her in my life.

A few weeks back, I learnt that you were in prison. I'm so sorry that life has turned out that way for you. I can't imagine what it must be like. Your solicitor has been very helpful. I called him and it was he who suggested that I write to you. He has kindly offered to get my letter to you.

Now that I'm writing this, I'm not sure what I should say. I'm twenty-five, still living in Dublin. I have a small flat, more of a bedsit, I suppose, but it's enough. And I'm near Tess's so I can call over anytime I like.

I teach English and History. Here's a photograph enclosed of my graduation from UCD a few years back. That was a happy day for me. Tess suggested you might like to see it.

I want you to know that despite how things started off for me, despite being in care, despite, well, I suppose, despite you, I'm happy. I have a good life. And please know that I don't want anything from you.

But I do have some questions that I'd like you to answer. I'd like to try and get some understanding as to why you treated me so cruelly. And I'd like to know who my father is. I deserve to know that much, at the very least.

I hope you write back.
Belle

11

Sooner or later we've all got to let go of our past.

Dan Brown

I realise I'm shaking, so I quickly sit on my hands, as they are in an uncooperative mood when I try to still them. I stare at the envelope in front of me. I'm afraid to touch it.

I would have said this morning that there's no way I would remember my mother's handwriting. Not over twenty years later, when the last time I saw it I would have been no more than five. But somehow I know I'd recognise that elegant script anywhere.

It's surprisingly quiet. Normally I hear the sound of traffic driving by the window, but today it's as if the world is partaking in a minute's silence for a little girl whose mother has finally gotten in touch.

I look up at the big white clock and watch the second hand slowly move. I reach for the letter and touch the white envelope. I wonder what her first words will be.

Did she sit for hours like I did, wondering what to say before she put pen to paper? Did she want her letter to be just perfect, worrying that she'd say the wrong thing? I took out so much, because I was afraid it sounded boastful. Or pointed, like I was having a go.

I wonder if there's a visitors' pass in here. Maybe she'll want me to come see her. Will I go?

Yes, of course I will.

The very thought of it causes my hands to shake even more. The only contact with prisons I've had before has been courtesy of *CSI New York*.

But this isn't Hollywood, it's Dublin and it's my life and before I can have another silly thought, I pick up the envelope and tear it open.

It's like one of those movies, when suddenly everything moves in slow motion.

As I unfold the single white sheet of paper enclosed, the silence in the room becomes deafening. I've never experienced a feeling like this before in my life and I've been in some pretty tense situations.

I realise that my mother's hand has touched this paper. This single sheet is the closest contact I've had with her in over twenty years. It's a sobering thought.

I wish Tess was here. I'm scared and not sure I'm brave enough to read.

It feels like I've waited my whole life for this moment. Oh feck, I can feel a lump the size of a lemon in my throat. I pinch myself hard, to try to steer the tears away in my age-old trick, and that nearly always works.

What do you really want? You say you want nothing. Well

118

that's a load of bollocks. Everyone always wants something. You're lying if you say otherwise.

And guess what, I've nothing to give you. I've no money. So you can jog on by if that's what you are after.

You wanted to know how I am. Well I'm peachy. How do you think I am? Stuck in this shit hole of a prison. How fucking stupid is that question? All that fancy education you got and you don't know shit.

You look like you've had a cosy life. You and your Tess. A teacher no less. It's funny that, as I used to be good at English. I could have been a teacher too if I'd wanted to. But I didn't get the chance to go to the University of Anything. Because I got pregnant with you.

And that fucking ruined my life.

As for your father, it could be Samuel L. Jackson for all I know.

When I first got pregnant, I thought Don Fields was the father. He'd a car, so he was handy to have around. He had a good job too and couldn't get enough of me. I told him the baby was his. It could have been. He was delighted with himself, started talking about names and prams. Bought a load of stuff for the nursery.

But then YOU had to ruin everything.

It was pretty fecking obvious you weren't his when you came out. His face when the midwife held you up. I actually laughed, it was comical. But everything went to shit after that. Don had his whole family out in the waiting room at the hospital, all dying to meet his new child.

When he looked at me like I was a piece of shit I knew it was game over. His bitch of a mother was calling me all kinds and Don broke off our engagement.

He might have been a boring old fart, but I could have had a good life with him. If it hadn't been for YOU.

So let me be very clear here. I've ignored your attempts to contact me in the past because YOU fucked up my life good and proper. End of.

Do you know what I wish for every day? The very same thing that my mother wished for and one day no doubt you will too. Because history has a funny way of repeating itself. I wish you had never been born.

I should have got rid of you when I could. Does that help you 'understand'? You were always crying and moaning, demanding attention. I had a pain in my arse listening to you. I was relieved when they took you off me.

I didn't want you then and I don't want you now. So piss off and leave me alone.

Dolores

I drop the letter to the ground and watch it as it descends slowly to the carpet, along with every ounce of hope I had in my heart.

I can't breathe. I feel hot and the room is closing in around me. I manage to make my legs work and push back my chair to stand up. But in my usual klutzy fashion, I knock it with my big feet and it falls with an almighty bang to the ground.

She never once referred to me by name.

YOU. It.

That's how she referred to me. Such small words, but so poisonous in their delivery. The hate and cruelty just bleeds from the ink.

I stand at the entrance to my flat and let the winter breeze wash over me. The cold stings my face and I welcome it.

I wanted answers. Well, I've got them now.

She's a monster. Vile, hurtful, nasty and vindictive. My mother, my flesh and blood. I feel shame flood me. My head tells me that I have nothing to feel guilty about, but that awful, sickening feeling of shame lingers.

YOU. I could hear her screaming that word at me through the page. YOU, YOU, YOU.

She could have just ignored me. Goodness knows she's had plenty of practice over the years.

I wish you had never been born.

My hands start to shake again. God dammit, why do I care so much?

I should never have written to her. I should have left that door firmly closed. What was I thinking? I know enough about my life now to know that I don't ever get the easy road. It's always hard for me.

I need to see Tess. I need to feel her warm arms around me, telling me that it will be okay.

I wish you had never been born.

To hell with my diet, I'm going to let Tess make me a fried tea. The works. Chips, onion rings and whatever else she wants to deep-fry. And I'm going to wash it down with wine. Lots of it. I'll stay at Tess's tonight and we can watch re-runs of *Grey's Anatomy* all evening. I'll spend the day in my old bed at home at Tess's. And I'll forget about that woman. I'll never think about her again.

I wish you had never been born.

I close my eyes and attempt to banish her voice for the millionth time.

As I turn the key in Tess's front door I can hear the low hum of voices in the kitchen. Who is it? The last thing I need right now is to be social to a nosy neighbour.

'Is that you, Belle?' Tess calls out when she hears the door open. 'Did you get my texts?'

I shake my head. 'I haven't checked my phone for the past hour or so. Something's happened?'

'You won't believe who has called to visit.' Tess's face is alight with excitement, then she stops when she sees mine. 'Oh pet, what's happened?'

'You first,' I say to her. 'Who is in there?'

She whispers loudly, eyes wide with excitement, 'It's only Jim Looney.'

12

Why do you go away? So that you can come back. So that you can see the place you came from with new eyes and extra colours. And the people there see you differently, too. Coming back to where you started is not the same as never leaving.

Terry Pratchett

Seeing him standing there, all grown up, after all this time, on top of hearing from my mother, is too much.

A high-pitched sound starts ringing in my ears and my vision starts to blur. Tess's kitchen begins to look and sound like an old TV with static hissing. My legs feel wobbly once more and the last thing I hear as they give way is Jim and Tess both calling my name. Then it all goes black.

'Sweet divine child you gave us a right fright.' Tess has a cold, wet facecloth on my forehead. Her answer to all ailments, that. She's sitting on the edge of my bed fretting about me.

I'm in bed? What the …

'How did I get up here?' I say.

'Jim carried you.' She tells me, like a proud mother hen. 'Can you believe it's him downstairs?'

So I didn't dream that. He really is here. 'He carried me? I must have broken his back.'

'He picked you up as if you were as light as a feather. I wouldn't have believed it, if I hadn't seen it with my own eyes,' she tells me.

Thanks, Tess. Way to make a girl feel good.

'Should I call a doctor?' she asks. 'You went down like a sack of spuds.'

'No. It's been a shit day, Tess, that's all. I had a letter from Dolores.'

'Oh, sweet divine, talk about blasts from your past all in one day, what with yer fella down there.' Her round face creases into a frown and she pulls me in for a hug. I stay like that for a few minutes and the warmth of her embrace does its job, as it always does. My head feels less cloudy and I begin to feel back to normal.

'What's he doing here?' I ask, peering out the door.

'Looking for you. He just arrived at the door, about an hour ago. Took me a moment to recognise him. He sounds and looks so different, doesn't he? I won't lie, I near had a heart attack when I realised it was him,' she says.

He looks the same to me. One glance in his direction and I didn't need anyone to tell me who it was.

'What did he say?' I demand. 'What does he want?'

'Just that. Asked if I had a forwarding address for you,' Tess says.

'Hello …' His deep voice echoes up from the hall below and we both jump when we hear it.

'We better go down. You can tell me about your mother

later on,' Tess says. 'It wasn't what you hoped for, I take it?'

'She's not my mother,' I reply. 'She's just Dolores. And there's very little to say, but yes, we'll talk later. Go on down and put the kettle on, I'll follow in a sec.'

I go into the bathroom and splash water over my face, the coldness stinging. Patting myself dry, I look in the mirror and assess the damage. Eyes a little bloodshot, but not too bad, all things considered. I'll have to do.

I look at the ledge at the foot of the upstairs hallway, the same one Jim and I sat on so many times in our childhood. So many memories shared with that man downstairs, right in this spot. But he's a stranger now. Just someone I used to know. Someone who promised that he'd never lose contact, but did just that.

I don't understand why he's back, I really don't. I suppose there's only one way to find out.

'Are you okay?' he asks, standing to attention when I walk into the kitchen. Tess has made the tea and hands me a cup.

I nod and feel a blush begin to creep up my neck, up to my cheeks. 'I'm not the fainting kind. I've never done that before in my life. Sorry.'

'Oh please don't apologise. It's totally my fault, for just arriving unannounced.' He looks genuinely sorry.

What's with his accent? He sounds American and nothing like the Dub that I used to know.

'It's been a rough day and I've not really eaten anything,' I offer in explanation and I bristle at the inference from him that he had the power to make me faint, just by appearing in front of me.

Tess seizes the opportunity to pick up a large box of chocolates. 'Jim bought these for me,' she tells me, delighted with herself. She has the cellophane off in under five seconds and opens the lid, passing them towards me. 'Here, you can have first pick, seeing as you're so hungry. Get your blood sugars up.'

Jim raises his eyes to me at that and we both smile in recognition. Tess never gives anyone first choice of her chocolates.

'You must have really gotten a shock when I fainted,' I say dryly to her and I contemplate taking the Turkish Delight just to wind her up.

'Any more cheek and I might change my mind,' she laughs. 'I'll make some tea for us in a bit. Will you stay for something to eat, Jim?'

He looks at me, as if waiting for permission. I shrug. It's no skin off my nose if he does or doesn't.

Liar, liar, pants on fire.

But I *am* curious as to why he sounds like Tom Cruise in *Far and Away*, failing miserably at an Irish accent.

If he throws in a 'begorra' I might have to hit him.

'We'll have the full works. A nice fry, with some chips. Proper ones. I always make my own, mind you,' Tess prattles on.

'You always did.' He smiles and looks towards the shiny new deep-fat fryer that sits on the counter top. 'That's a new addition, though,' he says.

'Belle got it for me. It's supposed to use less fat, or some such nonsense,' Tess says. 'But I can't get it to work.'

'What's with the accent?' I blurt out. I can't restrain my curiosity any longer.

'I've been living in Indiana for a long time. Mam married an American and we moved over there in '91,' Jim explains. 'I tried to hold onto my Dublin accent for as long as possible but sure, what can you do?'

I didn't see that one coming.

A hundred questions start fighting in my head to get out, but I stay silent. I feel a bit pissed off with him, to be honest. I'm not ready to play nice just because he's in Ireland on a holiday and wants to have a trip down memory lane. He picked the wrong day to call, because I'm all done with my past.

'How's your mother?' I settle on asking.

'She's really good. I've two little brothers and a sister. My step-father, Sam, he's a good guy. He adopted me,' he replies.

So it all worked out for Jim in the end. I'm happy for him. 'You got your happy-ever-after,' I whisper.

He looks up at me and replies, 'Almost. But not quite.' He pops a chocolate in his mouth.

I take another one myself and we both stare at each other.

'You still love the caramel, I see,' he says, pointing to the soft sugary goo that's spilling out of the chocolate case onto my fingertips.

Busted. And I can feel his eyes resting on my lips and I feel another blush creep up my chest. What the hell is wrong with me?

'Mam is the head of the PTA now, a soccer mom, just like those mothers we use to look at in the movies,' he says with a laugh.

If I close my eyes, I'm back out in Tess's garden playing football with Jim again and he has scored a goal. He's running around the garden, waving at the imaginary crowd, who are on their feet cheering. I try to reconcile that image with the man sitting in front of me.

I can't do it. He's no longer scrawny and lanky. He's very tall, over six feet at least, because I had to look up at him when I walked in. And he's broad. Strong, we already know, because he managed to carry all twelve and a half stone of me up the stairs to my bedroom.

I'm fecking scarlet just thinking about that.

But then I look at his hair and I realise that it's the same as it always was. Wavy and red, falling over one eye, just waiting to be brushed back.

And the eyes. I'd recognise them anywhere, unmistakably his. Okay, maybe he's not changed as much as I thought.

I realise that I've been staring and that I need to say something. 'I'm happy for your mother. Good to hear that things worked out for her. Have you any pictures of you all?'

He pulls out his wallet and takes out a family portrait. It was obviously taken at Christmas, and they are all wearing cheesy jumpers, in greens and reds, standing in front of a massive open fire, with garlands resplendent on top.

'Wow,' I say. 'It could be a Christmas card.'

'It was,' he replies, looking a bit embarrassed. 'It's the norm over there. We tend to go overboard at Christmas.'

'So does this one,' Tess says, pointing her finger at me. 'She already has my tree up in the living room. And her flat is like a little Christmas wonderland over there.'

The smell of sausages and rashers fills the kitchen as they sizzle in the pan. I get up and lay the table. I need to be busy. I can feel Jim's eyes following me around the kitchen and I'm disconcerted.

Without having to be told, I use the good cutlery and Delph tableware that Tess normally saves for Christmas. She nods approval when I take them out.

She feels at odds too, same as me, with our unexpected guest. I look at Jim and realise that we've lived very different lives. We don't know this Jim at all. But, there again, he doesn't know us either.

'Why are you in Ireland?' I ask.

'Just a vacation,' he answers. 'Gosh, that smell brings me right back to my time here, Tess. They don't do sausages like that back home.'

'Superquinns' finest. The only ones I'll allow in this house,' Tess tells him, waving her spatula in his direction.

'Smells delicious.' He compliments her and I'm pleased to see that he looks genuine in his praise.

'You're not married?' Jim asks me, looking down at my ring finger.

'Nope. Not married,' I reply. I feel a bit defensive, all old-maid like. But I'm hardly spinster territory yet. I'm only twenty-five. Some would say I'm still a baby.

I get the urge to start boasting that I've got loads of boyfriends. But before I get the chance to make a show of myself, Tess saves me by jumping in to big me up to him.

'She's way too fussy, that one,' Tess tells him, wagging a wooden spoon in my direction. 'She could have her pick of any man, look at her. Sure she's a gorgeous girl, but she nit-picks all the time.'

'I can well believe that. The having the pick of any man, I mean,' Jim says. 'You're beautiful, Belle.'

I look at him in surprise. Was that a bit flirty? I think it might have been. Tess nods, smiling, and then goes back to her pan, flipping the sausages over. She lowers her peeled and chopped potatoes into the fryer to a frenzied sizzle orchestra that's as familiar to me as hearing birds sing in the garden.

'Are you married, Jim?' I ask back. Fair is fair, he asked me. He doesn't wear a ring, but then again, a lot of men don't.

He shakes his head and winks at me, 'Haven't met a woman who could catch me yet.'

Yes. That was definitely flirty. I feel unnerved by it and that buzzing sound is back in my ears. He reaches over the table and places a hand on my arm, in concern, 'Are you okay?'

I want to say to him, no, I'm not okay. I thought you were part of my past and now you're here, looking all gorgeous, like Dr McFoxy, with your red wavy hair and I keep feeling dizzy.

But instead, I say, 'I'm good. Just hungry. Might have a slice of bread or something.' I pick up a slice of thick, crusty batch bread and spread Kerrygold butter on top thickly. He does the same and we sit companionably munching.

'Does my heart good, watching you two like that,' Tess says smiling. 'Just like the old days. I couldn't keep a sliced pan in the house with you both, you were always looking for bread and butter.'

'I think of those days a lot,' Jim says. 'You were very good to me, Tess.'

'Belle is a teacher, you know,' Tess tells him, but she's delighted with his compliment. 'She put herself through university, working on the tills in Superquinns at the same time.'

'That's awesome,' he says.

And this time he goes red when I giggle at him. 'It's just you saying "awesome". Get you, Jim Looney, all Americanised.'

'You were always teasing me when we were kids,' he says.

'Sorry,' I answer.

'No, I like it. You always made me laugh,' he replies.

Now it's my turn to blush.

'What do you teach?' Jim asks and he looks impressed when I tell him.

'What about you?' I ask. 'What do you do?'

'I'm a soccer coach. In a big high school in a place called Mishawaka,' he answers.

I say the name Mishawaka out loud and like how it sounds as it rolls over my tongue.

'That sounds almost like it's an Indian name,' I say.

'Yeah, I suppose it does. There's actually a huge Irish community over there. It's a cool place to live,' he replies.

'Awesome.' I tease and when he laughs he looks just like my Jim from years ago and a memory pops into my head so vivid it's as if it had just happened.

'This one.' I say, pointing to a number randomly in the telephone directory.

Jim dials it and we hold the phone up between us both. It's all I can do to stop the laughter from erupting as we hear it ringing. I stuff my hand in my mouth to suppress the sound and when the phone answers, Jim says, 'Is there any Walls there?'

The man at the end of the line says, 'There's no Walls here,' and in unison, we both screech down the line, 'Well what's holding the roof up so?'

As we howl with laughter, we drop the phone to the ground and stay laughing for hours over how funny we are. No double act out there is as funny as us.

Tess comes in to see what is going on and that makes us worse, tears and snot come out of my face, we're laughing so hard.

I look up at him and wonder does he remember? 'There's no Walls here,' I say and his face explodes into a smile.

'What's holding the roof up so?' he splutters out and we start to laugh again.

'Whenever I've told that story to friends, they don't get it,' he says.

'You had to be there …' I finish and we look at each other for the longest time.

'You both teach. Isn't that a coincidence?' Tess clatters a plate down in front of each of us, piled high with sausages, rashers, eggs, white and black pudding and chips. 'You always were two peas in a pod. I shouldn't be the least bit surprised that you both ended up doing the same thing.'

As the smell of Tess's fry wafts up to me, I realise that I've never felt so hungry in my life before. I spear a sausage with my fork and start munching, closing my eyes in delight as the salty pork hits my tongue.

'I've died and gone to heaven,' Jim tells a beaming Tess, mid-mouthful. 'We do a lot well back home, but we can't make a sausage.'

'Oh, it does my heart good, seeing you all grown up, back in my kitchen,' Tess says.

After we've eaten, we all sit back in our chairs, sated, mugs of tea in hand.

'Tess, you're not smoking,' Jim announces suddenly. 'I knew that something was different around here.'

'I wondered when you'd cop on that it doesn't smell like a smoke house around here any more,' I say.

'I'm off them nearly ten years now,' Tess beams. She's delighted with herself. 'Still miss them the odd time, like now, after a lovely fry.'

'I never thought you'd ever give them up,' he says in wonder. 'I'm so impressed. Well done you.'

Tess points to me and tells him, 'She nagged me nearly to an early grave. Sure I couldn't listen to her any more. I wasn't getting any enjoyment out of them, with her big eyes looking up at me, all accusing. Was easier to just stop.'

'I didn't think I'd ever see this day,' Jim says.

'Oh, I can be very persuasive when I want to be,' I reply.

'Something else I don't doubt.' He smiles at me and my stomach does this weird flop and I feel dizzy again. This time I can't blame hunger. Maybe I'm coming down with something.

We sit and chat for another hour and then Jim looks at his watch and jumps up. 'Time for me to go. I've stayed a lot longer than I thought I would. I don't want to overstay my welcome.'

I feel a familiar ache in my chest. Of course he's going. He was hardly going to sit here all night chatting to us. We walk him to the door and Tess gives him a hearty hug, telling him to come back again soon. He seems a bit taken aback by this. The hugs weren't plentiful back when he was here. But that was a different time. We're different people now.

'We're a family of huggers now,' I joke. 'In touch with our emotional sides.'

He seems to take this as an invitation and moves towards me but, and I don't know why I do it, I move a step back. Reflex, self-protection, I don't know what it is, but all the same, I move away from him and he sees that.

'Safe journey home,' I say and give him the benefit of one of my most special smiles, to try take the sting out of my rebuttal. I hold out my hand to shake his, feeling all formal and shy, to say goodbye once again.

He looks amused by this, but he takes my hand all the same and shakes it firmly. I sneak a look to see if his smile reaches his eyes these days. Damn the lighting in the hall, I can't tell.

'I'm not going home to Mishawaka, Belle. Not for a while, anyhow. I was hoping to see you again, as it happens. Would you come out for dinner with me?'

'Of course she will,' Tess says, giving me a shove forward, and I end up nose to nose with Jim Looney for the first time in over fifteen years.

There's that ringing sound again.

'Give him your number, Belle.' Tess prods me in the back again. I swear to God, I'm going to kill her. I turn around and give her the evils, but she's impervious to me.

I walk to the hall table and grab a post-it note, scribbling down my number on it and hand it to him.

'You've not given me an answer,' he says. 'Does this mean you'll come out with me?'

'You will,' Tess declares laughing. 'Sure, what else would you be doing tomorrow?'

'Tomorrow?' I squeak. This is all happening very fast.

'What's the point in waiting?' Tess says to the two of us. 'You've lots to catch up on. What could either of you be doing that's more important than that?'

'Quite right. That's settled so,' he replies and smiles. As he goes out the front door, he tips his hand to his forehead and salutes me. It's an odd mannerism, almost of another era. I feel something give in my heart. Honest to goodness I do. It's like a physical pain, as if something let's go.

Damn you, Jim Looney, what are you doing to me?

When he closes the door, I lean my back against it. 'I think I could be in trouble with him, Tess,' I say. 'I need to sit down. I'm feeling all a dither.'

'Ah sure. Listen here girl, you were in trouble with that fella the very first day you clapped eyes on him.'

13

Piglet: How do you spell love?
Pooh: You don't spell it, you feel it.

AA Milne

December 2005

'Do you remember us talking about this place?' Jim asks me. 'Back when we were kids?'

'I do. In our den made of sheets,' I reply.

'Tess was always going mad at us for robbing her good linen.'

'I can't believe you remember all that,' I say. 'To be honest I figured it was just a coincidence when we arrived here tonight.'

'No coincidence,' he says. 'And I keep telling you, I remember everything about back then. And if you remember, why wouldn't I?'

My stomach flips at this admission from him. It's so strange sitting here opposite him after all this time. I'd kind of gotten used to the idea that he was just a small part of my childhood. Okay, that's a lie. I'll admit he was a big part. A happy part. But one that had been closed down, never to be opened again.

'Do you remember telling me that one day you'd have your picture hanging in here?' Jim points to the dozens of photographs of Irish and international celebrities that line the walls of Trocadero's restaurant.

'I said a lot of things back then,' I reply, feeling a little stupid. 'I used to think I'd be a singer. Only one problem with that ambition, though. I can't sing.'

'You were always badgering me to sing a duet with you,' Jim says.

'I've had the time of my life …' we both say at the same time, laughing.

'Who sang that again?' Jim asks.

'Bill Medley and Jennifer Warnes,' I answer. 'I still play it on a semi-regular basis. Like an every other weekend, kind of thing.'

'I often think about that den we made. And Tess's face when she came home one day from Tesco to find her bed stripped of all its sheets,' Jim says.

Just hearing him say the word 'bed', and an image of us tangled together in my bed at home jumps into my head. For feck's sake. I need to get a grip.

'You were always looking at Tess's magazines, oohing and aahing over the celebrities. I was half expecting that I'd come to Dublin and find you married to a footballer or something.'

'Me, a footballer's wife?' I say and snort with laughter at the very thought. 'I'm far too low maintenance for that. But you did tell me you'd bring me here one day. And now you've kept that promise.'

He puts down his drink and stares at me. The intensity of this look makes me feel all breathless again. I can't cope, so I look away and take a gulp of my mojito. I can still feel his eyes on me, so I look down at the menu and do my best to suppress the tell-tale red flushes taking over my face.

'I keep telling you, I remember everything about those two years, Belle,' he says. 'It should have been the worst two years of my life, away from my mom. But instead it was the best.'

What is he trying to do to me?

'So does Trocadero's live up to your expectations?' I ask, looking around us, trying to bring the conversation to a less emotive level.

I've decided that my best tack here is to avoid eye contact with him. Because when I look at his eyes, things start to get all weird.

Jim looks around him. We're seated in one of the plush red-velvet booths near the back. We have portraits of Grace Kelly, Brenda Fricker and Stephen Fry watching over us, with knowing smiles hovering on their faces. They're looking at me right now, thinking to themselves, she so fancies the pants off him.

Shut up. I do not.

'In my memory, it seemed very glamorous here,' he says. 'And it doesn't disappoint, now that we're sitting here, in the flesh. I like it. Kind of mixes art deco with contemporary pieces. It's not too stuffy, either, despite the rich decor. Can't stand places that are so hoity toity I feel like I have to tighten my collar and put on a jacket,' Jim says.

I nod in agreement. He's right. 'The cocktails aren't too shabby either,' I say and he raises his glass to me.

As he does this, Tony Bennett starts to croon, *I'll be home for Christmas*, in his unmistakable rasp. We look at each other again, eyes locked. This time I can't look away. It's agonising, but beautiful, all at once.

I don't want to look away, but if I keep staring at him, I'm going to cry.

I mustn't cry.

'That's kind of eerily appropriate,' Jim says and his voice is all strangled. I realise he's emotional too. This here, us, sitting in this booth, means something to him. I'm not imagining this, whatever this is. It's not just me feeling it.

'But, this is not your home any more,' I say.

'Doesn't matter how far I've travelled, Dublin will always be home to me. And what's that saying? Home is where the heart is,' Jim says, his voice almost a whisper.

Then why did you leave?

'I used to go looking for you.' There, it's out. I've told him. So much for the grand plan of playing it cool. I've always been pants at that. I can't help it. I need to let him know how much he hurt me when he disappeared off the face of the earth. I know I've no right to be annoyed with the actions of a ten-year-old boy. No right to hold anything against him. But I am and I do. He swore he'd stay in touch, and he didn't.

He doesn't say a word in response. Just continues to stare at me with those big blue eyes.

'You said we'd never lose contact. I believed you,' I say.

He nods. One quick inclination of his head.

'And then I never heard from you. I was so worried. Tess said to me, 'Give him time. He'll be in touch,' I say.

Even though it was years ago, the memory feels as fresh today as if it were mere days that had passed.

'But days became weeks, which became months,' I continue, 'And you still didn't get in touch.'

I don't tell him that I used to sit on the window ledge on the upstairs landing. I'd look out onto the street, up and down, waiting for him to walk past, kicking his football, with a big grin on his face.

Tess used to come up the stairs and shake her head, telling me to let it go, tempting me back to the kitchen with biscuits and treats, to stop waiting.

'You know, even a year after you left, I'd get the bus out to Ranelagh on a Saturday. I'd just wander around a bit, go to the park, a coffee shop. I thought, I might just bump into you. How big could one suburb be?' Now that I've started, I can't seem to stop.

'Oh Belle,' Jim sighs.

I know I am painting myself as such a saddo here, but I don't care. I have carried this with me for a long time and I need to say it to him. If he can't take it, then so be it.

'I used to rehearse what I'd say to you when we'd bump into each other. I'd be cross you didn't get in touch, of course, but we'd laugh and then it would be okay,' I say. Damn it, a tear escapes and I swore to myself I'd not cry.

He leans in across the table and wipes the tear away with his thumb. He looks down at the droplet and we sit in silence for a moment, staring at that tear drop on his thumb.

'I'm so sorry I did that to you,' he says. 'Can I explain? Will you give me the chance to try to do that?'

'Yes.' As if I can say no to him.

'At first, when I moved back in with mom, everything was different. But in a good way. She was so happy to have me there. I was on a high. Every day she had different itineraries planned out for us. We went to the pictures, to museums, on walking tours of Dublin. She played football with me in the park and we even went swimming. It was non-stop.'

He shrugs, looking embarrassed.

'You didn't have time to think about me. I get that Jim. That's allowed,' I tell him.

'But then, a few days before Christmas I asked mam could I call round to see you. I missed you. I really did. I couldn't wait to see you to tell you all about what we'd been doing. But it was the strangest thing. As soon as I mentioned the visit, she got all weird. Her face grew taut and she started popping pills, saying she'd a headache. It didn't take a genius to work out that she wasn't happy about my suggestion. So I dropped the subject, afraid to upset her. I figured I'd leave it for a few weeks,' Jim says.

Our waiter ambles over and seems to sense that a deep and meaningful is happening, so starts to back away.

'Two more of these,' Jim says, pointing to our mojitos, catching the waiter's eye before he goes.

'After Christmas I brought the subject up again and the same thing happened. I got the message loud and clear,

141

that she didn't want me to see you or Tess any more,' Jim continues.

Ah. So that was it.

'We spoke about it last week. I told her I was coming home to Ireland and that I was going to look for you,' Jim says.

'Did she remember me?' I ask.

'Oh yes, of course she did. She admitted that she had a considerable amount of guilt about playing a hand in us losing touch,' Jim says.

'I think I understand why she felt like that. Tess and I were all wrapped up as part of a bad memory for her,' I say and he looks surprised at my words.

'Yes. That's pretty much what she said.'

I take a deep breath and say to him, 'You did the right thing by cutting ties with us. Your mam had been through a rough time. She had to do what was right for both you and her. Give yourselves the best chance.'

He shrugs. 'I didn't think it would be forever, though, Belle. Just for a while, a few months, till she got used to having me again. I just couldn't risk her getting sick again, disappearing on me,' Jim admits.

I look down in surprise, feeling his thumb stroking the top of my hand. Somehow or other we're now holding hands across the table. I'm not sure when it happened. I don't recall moving my hand towards him. I don't pull it away, though. It feels natural, like it's exactly where it's supposed to be.

'So how did the trip to Mishawaka happen?' I ask.

'It wasn't long after Christmas that mam came home and said she'd met this guy. He was an old boyfriend, but he'd been living in Indiana for years. I'd never seen her like that before, all happy and girly, laughing all the time. She introduced us and I really liked him,' Jim says.

'Next thing I know, they are getting married and we are moving to the US, to live with Sam,' he tells me. 'It happened quickly.'

'Wow,' I say. It must have been such an exciting time for him. I can picture him boarding the flight, excited, thrilled. He'd have been beside himself. A memory of Jim and I running around the garden, as kids, in a cardboard box we'd fashioned into an aeroplane jumps into my head.

'Blast off,' I say and he laughs.

'Okay, I'd forgotten that. We played with that aeroplane for ages,' Jim says.

We sit in companionable silence for a few moments, just looking at each other, holding hands. I realise that I could stay like this forever.

'Were you happy?' I ask.

'Yes I was. I am. It's a good life over there. School was good. I was a minor celebrity over there for a while, the new Irish kid. Kept getting invited to people's houses. They loved hearing my accent,' he says. 'And I got to play soccer. I taught those yanks a trick or two.'

'Natch,' I say.

'Natch,' he laughs, 'We used to say that all the time.'

'We did,' I reply.

'I left home after university and now live in a condo, not too far from mom and dad. It's cool,' Jim says.

Then why are you here? I think. If it's that cool, why come back?

'I want you to know that I've thought of you often. I know that must be hard to believe, when I didn't get in touch. But it's the truth,' he says.

I can see that he's not lying. Every word he's spoken has been so earnest. And I've no desire to milk the situation. I need to let him off the hook.

'I won't lie, I was upset at the time, but we were kids. You were only ten years old. It was a long time ago and things are different now. I'm glad you're here and have explained, though, because it does help,' I say.

'Am I forgiven?' he asks.

'There's nothing to forgive, Jim,' I say. 'Don't worry about it one more second.'

'And what about you, Belle? Were you happy?' he asks.

Now there's a loaded question. I take another sip of my cocktail and ponder it. 'Yes. In the end, I was. I am.'

He looks at me, waiting for elaboration that I find hard to give. It's difficult to sum up fifteen years. I'm not sure where to start.

'After you left, I got it into my head that Tess was going to send me away. Mrs Reilly was over and I overheard them talking in the hall about Tess retiring. I thought I was on the move again. Shipped out to another house. Thankfully I was wrong,' I say.

'Mrs Reilly. The old bag. God, I couldn't stand her,' he says. 'Do you ever see her?'

'Nah, never. She's long gone,' I say.

'But you never left Tess's?' he says. 'She didn't retire?'

'She told me that I'd have a home with her forever. And she was true to her word. When I turned eighteen and started college, she let me stay with her. Rent free.' I say.

'She's a good woman,' he replies.

'The best. I'd be lost without her,' I say. 'She's been more of a mother to me than mine ever has been or is likely to be. And I'd not have gotten through university without her support.'

'Did your mam ever come to visit?' he asks with such tenderness that I feel teary again. 'Are you in touch?'

I shake my head. 'You know what, I don't want to talk about Dolores. Do you mind? I'll tell you about her, but for now I don't want her intruding on tonight.'

'Enough said. Let's change the subject. Hey, do you still have that gimpy doll? What was her name?' he asks.

'Dee-Dee and less of the gimpy. Yes of course,' I say. 'She's in a shoe box in my wardrobe.'

'Please say you don't still talk to her,' he teases me. 'You were forever having conversations with her back then.'

'I get more sense from her than most, I'll have you know. But for the main, she remains silent these days,' I say.

I look up at him and decide to go for broke, 'Jim, can I ask you something?'

'Sure,' he says.

'What made you come to see me now? It seems very sudden,' I ask. I suppose he could have been planning it for ages.

145

'It was the weirdest thing. I just kept thinking of you. Of us. Of the fun we used to have together. I won't lie, I'd not given you much thought for years. But then a few months back, I was dating this woman. A nice lady,' he says.

I feel a stab of jealousy assault me and I'm unprepared for the depth of how much it stings. But then I smirk at his use of the word 'nice'. That's never a good thing to be called when dating someone.

'She was talking about her childhood one evening when we were out for dinner. She spoke about her friends, what they used to do together. That kind of thing. And of course she asked me who my childhood best friend was. I thought of all the lads I pal around with back home, friends from school, university and the neighbourhood. But the only name that came out of my lips was yours, Belle,' Jim says.

'Oh.' I'm not sure what else to say.

'And ever since then, you have been on my mind. I'd go by a park and see a girl with black curly hair and perfect caramel skin and think of you. I'd hear someone laughing and I'd think of all the times you laughed with me, at one of my bad jokes,' he says.

He said my skin was perfect. Perfect no less. I think I sighed out loud, I couldn't help it.

'In the end I thought, to hell with it, I'm going to go find you. So here I am.' He holds up his hands and then leans in close, 'Is it okay that I'm here?'

'Yes,' I reply. I wish I had a witty retort to throw back at him, like I used to. But I've nothing more than that one word. I have an urge to climb over the table, knock the beautiful glasses and silverware to the ground and start kissing him. I glance at the picture of Grace Kelly to my left and I'm sure she's egging me on to do that. But Brenda Fricker is tutting her disapproval. She's not down with the whole making-a-show-of-yourself-in-a-posh-restaurant kind of thing.

Damn it, Brenda. You win.

'You should have let me go halves,' I say. I dread to think how much that bill was, the number of cocktails we ended up drinking.

'I don't know what kind of men you've dated before me, and I'm not sure I want to know about them,' he says. 'But in my world, if I take a lady out on a date, I pay.'

I feel like I could swoon at these words. First of all, he's called this a date and second of all, he insinuated that he might be jealous of previous boyfriends. I feel a warm glow move from my toes up to my ears.

We walk towards the taxi rank, side by side, shoulders almost touching.

'It's cold,' I shiver, as a cold blast of air whips against my cheeks. He stops and touches my arm to stop me too, then takes his scarf off and wraps it around my neck. It's so long he has to wrap it around me several times. It's the most sensual thing I've ever experienced.

'Belle,' he whispers.

I can't speak. I can't move. I am frozen in this perfect moment.

He moves an inch closer towards me. I can feel his breath, warm, on my lips. And they tingle in anticipation.

'May I?' he whispers so softly, it feels like a caress against my cheek.

I must have answered him with my eyes, because he leans in close. Then, his lips touch mine and I know for sure, what I've always known.

I love Jim Looney.

14

When I saw you, I fell in love
And you smiled, because you knew.

William Shakespeare

Christmas Eve, 2005

'When you were ten, you predicted that I'd be on my knees one day begging you to marry me,' Jim says. 'Well I guess you were right. Because here I am, begging you, Belle.'

Oh boy.

'I can't live another day without you,' he continues.

Nor I you Jim, I think. You are my everything, once more.

'I need to know that this time, it's forever. I need to know that nobody is ever going to keep us apart again. I need to know that we never need to say one more goodbye,' he says.

A lifetime of hellos, with no more goodbyes, I think. I cannot think of anything I want more than that.

'I have loved you for so long. I loved you when I didn't even understand what love was,' Jim says.

I feel like I've been waiting my whole life for this moment

and now that it's here, I don't want to miss a beat, a look, a moment of it.

Then he takes a breath, a long and steadying one and says, 'Belle, will you do me the honour of marrying me?'

I hear the crowd hold their breath as they wait for my answer.

'Yes,' I scream, 'Yes. Yes. Yes.'

As the crowd cheers, surrounding us as we embrace on the Ha'penny Bridge, he stands up and lifts me up off my feet, into his arms.

I lean down to him, nose to nose, to seal the deal with a kiss but he says, 'Wait,' and places me gently back on firm ground.

He peels off my glove from my left hand and ties the red ribbon from the silver bell around my ring finger. It's the silliest ring I've ever seen, but it's also the most perfect.

I hold it up into the air to show the crowd around us and they all cheer when it tinkles as I wave my hand around.

And then he kisses me.

15

Nothing makes us so lonely, as our secrets.

Paul Tournier

June 2007

'Belle, wake up, Belle.'

I lash out, my arms connect and hit Jim.

'Wake up. It's just a nightmare, come on, wake up.'

I look around me and the flames and smoke disappear from the room as my nightmare dissipates.

Jim pulls me into his arms and holds me, rocking back and forth, until I stop shaking and my heart rate slows back down.

'Same dream?' Jim asks.

I nod.

I haven't had one in a long time. But this is the third night in a row. It doesn't take a rocket scientist to work out why.

Dolores is getting out of prison in a few weeks.

Not that she was in touch with me or anything, or likely to be. There's only been the one letter. Her solicitor sent me an email, more out of courtesy than anything else, I think, letting me know. I emailed him back and thanked him for his consideration, but asked him not to contact me about her again.

On the surface I've been very brave and hard-nosed about it all. I tell myself that I don't care. That her words or actions can't hurt me. But I suppose when you are asleep, you are at the mercy of your subconscious.

'Want to talk about it?' Jim asks.

I shake my head. What's there to say?

'Ever since you heard from the solicitor, you've been all jittery. I'm not sure that it's healthy that you still have her letter,' he states.

I look at him, ready to accuse him of breaching my trust. Was he snooping in my handbag?

But he's way ahead of me. 'I saw you reading it yesterday, then putting it back in your bag.'

Oh.

'Bin it. You've got to stop torturing yourself. It's been two years,' he urges. 'I mean it, throw it away.'

'It's not that simple,' I sigh. How can I make my husband understand when I don't understand it myself?

'She can't hurt you any more,' Jim whispers into my hair, as he pulls me in again towards him. 'I'm here now. I won't let her hurt you again.'

I relax back into him and close my eyes. 'She used to leave me on my own.' There's no one I trust more than my husband. It's time to tell him everything.

He doesn't move away from me, doesn't make a sound, but he pulls me in tighter. I can feel his heart hammering away in his chest, in competition with my own.

'Back then, it was just my normal. I knew she was going out as soon as she put on her makeup. She wore this bright-red lipstick. I still get shivers when I see someone wearing a similar colour,' I say. 'When I was very small, I didn't even know she was gone half the time because I was asleep.'

'Fucking unreal,' Jim says, his body tensing in anger. 'How could a mother do that?'

But it was real. My real at least.

'Then when I was four, at least I think I was four, I woke up in the middle of the night. I was scared so I went looking for her.'

Now I realise how stupid that was. She wasn't the maternal type who would have wiped away my tears with kisses. 'I couldn't find her. I panicked, thinking something had happened to her, so I rang the guards.' I say.

'That was very clever of four-year-old you to do that,' Jim answers. 'And brave.'

'I didn't feel very brave, just scared. They came to our flat and a social worker took me. The next morning, mam came and got me. She was all smiles for the guards as she swore it would never happen again, a one-off. Even back then, I could tell when she was pretending. Her smile didn't reach her eyes,' I say.

Jim rubbed my hand gently with his thumb and, save for the sound of his heart beating, he was silent.

'When we got home, she was so angry. I remember cowering in the corner of the kitchen with her screaming at me. I swore I'd never call them again. And then she laughed and said, "too right you won't".'

'Was that the end of it?' Jim asks gently. I look at him and shake my head slowly.

'This story is not one of the happy-ever-afters, Jim,' I say. I realise that this is the first time I've ever talked about this. I've hinted about it with both Tess and Jim, but the detail, the scary, horrific, vile details, I've never spoken about. I save those for my dreams. But it feels good to share it with Jim. I need him to know what it was like for me. To understand.

'She started to lock me in my bedroom when she went out. So I couldn't call for help if I woke up or get her in any more trouble with the social workers,' I say.

'She's some piece of work ...' I can feel Jim's anger pouring from him.

I take a deep breath.

'Then one night, I woke up as I could smell smoke in the flat. There was a fire in the kitchen, but I was locked in my bedroom and I couldn't get out. Dolores wasn't there.' I'm surprised at how flat and emotionless my voice sounds. I should be sobbing here, at the relief of sharing my past, no? I feel strangely cold.

Jim pulls the duvet up over me as I shiver and I'm glad he doesn't say anything, just waits for me to continue.

'The smoke stung my eyes. And my lungs hurt, it hurt to breathe. My nostrils felt like they were bleeding. I didn't know what to do.' I tremble at the memory.

'I walked over to the window and started to bang on it. I was up high, in a flat, on the third floor and the windows were those old sash ones. I didn't have the strength to open them. So I kept banging on the window and crying, hoping someone would see me. But the street was empty. Nobody was watching,' I say.

'Oh, Belle.' Jim says and I pull away from him and look into his eyes.

'I think I passed out, but next thing I know I'm in an ambulance and on my way to hospital. I was terrified. The sound of the sirens, the flashing lights.' The trembling won't stop now, as I catapult back into that time.

'She should be strung up for what she did to you,' Jim says.

Yep.

'I've always wanted to know if she felt bad about that night. I get that she doesn't love me. I even get that she thinks I ruined her life. But I could have died! Does she have any guilt at all about that? Does she care?'

I move in closer to my husband, who continues to cradle me in his arms.

'I don't think she's capable of guilt or love. From everything you've told me, she's an evil, cruel woman. End of,' Jim says.

What if I turn out like her? What if I have children and I have her twisty, cruel genes? What if history repeats itself for the third time, as she predicted?

'What happened after that?' Jim asks.

'The social workers took me away from her. I was placed in foster care for the first time.'

'Thank God for that. Foster care, bad and all as it was at times, was safer for you than with that nut job,' he says.

I can't seem to stop shaking, I feel bitterly cold, right down to my bones.

'I'm going to make you a cup of tea,' Jim says, wiping his eyes to hide the evidence of tears. He kisses my forehead softly. 'Back in a moment.'

We sit, side by side in our bed, drinking the warm brew. Sometimes in silence and sometimes in conversation. The floodgates have opened and I find myself remembering moments of my childhood that I thought I'd long forgotten. We eventually fall asleep, somewhere in the early hours, Jim cradling me in his arms, keeping me safe.

And there were no more nightmares.

We decide to go out for breakfast to the local café in Artane, where we now live. We're both ravenous, the way you often are after some big emotional episode.

As I munch my scone, Jim tucks into a hearty full Irish whilst reading *The Irish Independent*.

I love mornings like these, where we don't have work and we get to just *be* together.

I thought that we couldn't be any closer than we are, but last night's confession has made us even stronger. Why hadn't I told him before? Of course he would understand. Of course he would be there for me. I thought that it wasn't possible to love him any more than I did, the day we got married. But I realise that's not true because our love is stronger now than it ever was.

'We could do this,' he says suddenly, pointing to an article in his paper.

The trials and triumphs of one foster family in Dublin,

'We could,' I reply, laughing at him.

'I mean, when you think about it, we've been there, done that, worn the t-shirt,' he continues.

'Do many foster children ever do that? Go on to foster themselves?' I ponder.

'Will we give it a go?' He says, catching me off guard.

I start to laugh some more, thinking he was joking. But then, he puts down the paper and turns to me, all serious.

'Imagine if we could just make one child smile. A child who's in the system and scared. Just like we were. Wouldn't it be worth it just for that? To make that one small difference.'

He's serious, I think. Feck. I've never considered it before. Could we? Should we? I find myself feeling exhilarated at the thought.

And before I know it, I am running around the table, to his side and saying, 'You had me at the word "smile".'

PART THREE

16

A child born to another woman calls me mom. The depth of the tragedy and the magnitude of the privilege are not lost on me.

Jody Landers

January 2013

'It's uncanny,' Jim whispers to me. 'Tell me you see it.'

We're in the kitchen, making a snack for Lauren, our new foster child. She arrived an hour ago, and like many children that have been to our house over the past five years, she's scared, lost and vulnerable.

Lorcan, our social worker, has just left. We don't know how long Lauren will be with us, but this one could be a long-term placement. There's no father or grandparents in the picture and her mother is not fit to take care of her, with no sign of that changing for the foreseeable. She's had some sort of breakdown, it appears.

'Well?' Jim persists.

Of course I noticed it. The second I opened the front door it hit me immediately.

161

'Yes. I saw it, Jim,' I reply, smiling at him.

'Gave me quite a turn, I have to admit,' Jim continues. 'I mean, it was like going back in time to when we were kids. She's your double.'

He looks at me and says, 'I know it does your head in when people go up to you and say that they know someone the image of you. And more likely than not, it's just because they're black too. You do know I'm not doing that.'

'Relax. Racial generalisation may be alive and kicking in Ireland but I know that you are not guilty of it. Listen, if I'd a euro for every time an eejit came up to me and said, "oh I saw this woman on the train, the spitting image of you, she had afro hair too." Well, I'd be rich,' I say.

But it's more than her colouring, her facial features are so like mine were at that age too. It's uncanny. We have the same skin-colour tone, the same hair, our lips, eyes, all mirror images of each other.

'She could be your daughter,' Jim says and then quickly reddens, looks stricken with the statement. 'I'm sorry. That was insensitive of me.'

He's only saying what I'm thinking, though. Yet it still hurts to hear it out loud.

It's like life is playing a cruel joke on me. The first foster child we have had in our house since … well since then, and what does the universe serve up? A mini-me.

'Are you okay?' Jim asks. 'You've gone awfully quiet again. I hate it when you do that.'

'Old habits die hard,' I say, but I smile to reassure him. I know how much he worries and I don't like that.

He knows me well, my husband. Whenever I feel threatened, I go quiet.

'This isn't about me, Jim, it's about that little girl in there. She's frightened, she's vulnerable and she needs us.' I pick up the tray, with milk and cookies on it, and bring it inside to the family room.

Lauren is sitting on the edge of the sofa, her body tense with fear and my heart contracts, in recognition.

What secrets are you hiding, little one? What traumas have you experienced in your short life?

I know that a neighbour called social services and when they arrived at her house, they found Lauren, dirty, hungry and very distressed. She had been living on cornflakes, dry, as there was no milk in the house.

One of the reasons Jim and I wanted to foster was that we felt we could really empathise with the kids, because we'd been through similar situations ourselves.

But this one just feels so close to my own, I'm thrown by it. I ate dry Weetabix and nothing else for two days once, on one of the occasions my mother disappeared.

Lauren's mother, it appears, has given up on life, on herself and, horrifically, on her daughter. That's the bit I always struggle to understand.

I stifle a sigh and try not to judge. But sometimes, in moments like these, I feel a rage and fury bubble beneath the surface and I feel like ranting and raging at the world and its cruelty to children.

'Is that your favourite toy?' I ask. Lauren is clasping a teddy in her hand. It's brown, with a Babygro on it, that was once pink, many moons ago. The teddy is limp, the stuffing inside now flattened from years of hugs and cuddles.

'It's my Rosie,' Lauren answers.

'She's lovely. I bet she's your best friend,' I say and Lauren nods, a smile threatening to appear, as she thinks about her special toy.

'I used to have a best friend like that, when I was a little girl. Her name was Dee-Dee,' I say. 'I brought her everywhere with me.'

'Do you still have her?' Lauren asks.

'Yes. But I keep her in a special box now, to keep her safe.'

'Can I see her?' She asks and for a moment I want to say no, because Dee-Dee represents a time in my life that I prefer to keep boxed up.

But somehow or other, I need to get Lauren to trust me, to realise that I'm an ally. Maybe Dee-Dee can help do that for me.

'Come with me,' I say to her and offer my hand out. She looks at it for a moment and then her little hand reaches out to mine and she lets me lead her to my bedroom. As I feel her little fingers in mine, I think, right in this moment, I'm falling for this little girl.

I reach into my wardrobe and pull out a box. It's just an old shoe box, nothing fancy, but it has a few things in there that are too special to throw away. I've tied the lid on tight with a green ribbon that has a thin layer of dust sprayed onto it now. I open the ribbon and lift the lid from the box. On top lies a white school shirt, signed by my classmates, on my last day of school. My school report is there too, with mixed reviews from my teachers throughout the years. Some photographs, of foster carers and children who came and went from my life over the years.

'Is that you?' Lauren asks, as she spies a photograph of me, taken when I was no more than four or five.

I hate that picture. The sadness in my face, well, it slaps me hard. It's difficult to look at it and not be transported back to that time.

'You look like me,' Lauren says.

'Yes, I do,' I reply.

And even though I can't see it, somewhere at the bottom of this box is a picture of my mother, and her letter. I don't carry it in my handbag any more, but it's still here, burning a hole through the cardboard with the hatred it contains in its words. I'm not feeling that masochistic today. I leave that be.

Instead, I pick up Dee-Dee and hold her tight, in an embrace as old as time.

Hello old friend. It's been a while.

Dee-Dee's silent, though. She stopped talking to me many years ago. But even so, just holding her in my hands evokes so many emotions, of secret conversations held, that saved my life, I think.

How many tears have stained the fabric of her dress, I wonder.

Taking a deep breath, I show her to Lauren. 'Rosie, meet Dee-Dee. Dee-Dee, this is Lauren's friend Rosie.'

I take one of Dee-Dee's hands and pretend to shake her hand with Rosie's soft teddy paw.

Lauren giggles, 'She's pretty. I like her dress.'

'Yes, she is. I used to think she was the most beautiful doll in the world,' I say.

'Who gave her to you?' Lauren asks.

What do I tell her? With some of the children who have been in our care, I've shared some of my experiences as a foster child. It helped. It was appropriate. For others, the short-term placements really, I suppose, it never came up.

My instinct, my gut, tells me that Lauren is going to play a big part in our lives. I feel it deep inside of me.

That connection I felt, the moment she placed her hand in mine, has only gotten stronger, the longer she sits by my side.

'When I was a little girl, I was in foster care too,' I say. 'And one of the ladies who took care of me for a few years, well she gave me Dee-Dee.'

Lauren's eyes are round with shock at this piece of news.

'I used to talk to Dee-Dee all the time,' I say.

'I talk to Rosie,' Lauren replies. 'She talks to me too.'

'Well, of course she does. She's special because she's your best friend,' I say. 'But, you know what, if you ever want to talk to someone else, I'm here too. I'm a pretty good listener.'

'My mummy used to be a good listener,' Lauren says. 'But now she doesn't listen to me at all.'

I resist the urge to jump in and ask any questions or rush with platitudes or sympathy. Gently does it with this one.

She looks down at Rosie sadly. I wonder what the teddy has just whispered to her.

I pull her into me and give her a hug. I don't hold her too tightly, I don't want to frighten her, but I'm relieved that she doesn't pull away. So we sit, with her and Rosie in my arms for a moment or two.

'Will we go have those biscuits now? See if Rosie wants one?' I ask, when I feel her pull back.

She nods and smiles for the first time since she walked into our house.

Tess's influence in our fostering is strong. Biscuits and milk are the treats of choice for all newcomers to our house.

As we walk out the bedroom door, Jim is there hovering, watching and waiting, worrying.

'She's smiling,' he says.

I whisper to him as we walk by, 'We're not going to stop till we make her smile like that every day, do you hear me?'

'Yes,' he replies and kisses my head.

Lauren has just finished her second bowl of Weetabix.

'That's four in total. There's a record in this house of six in one sitting, held by Bobby,' Jim tells her.

'Who's Bobby?' she asks, mid-mouthful.

'You'll meet him soon enough. He was our very first foster child and he stayed with us until he was 18,' I say.

'But he never really left. Half his wardrobe is still in the spare room,' Jim says. 'I swear that guy has more clothes than David Beckham.'

'And later today, you get to meet Nana Tess,' I say. 'She was my foster mother. I lived with her for a very long time. She cannot wait to meet you.'

'What's the plan for today?' Jim asks. 'Sun is shining, even though it's January and it's the weekend.'

'How about the park so? And don't forget it's your turn at youth club tonight,' I remind him. 'But before we do anything, I reckon this little monkey needs a bath.'

I pick up Rosie and say to Lauren, 'How about, while I give you a bath, Jim gives Rosie one too?'

'And then, when that's done, it's time for the tree. I think you'll like that,' Jim says.

Lauren looks puzzled and we smile at her.

'Every child who comes into our house gets their name added to our tree,' I tell her.

I point out the kitchen window, into the back garden, where an old oak tree stands resplendent in the pale morning sunshine.

Jim holds up a small wooden plaque that he spent last night etching her name onto.

'That says Lauren,' she says, in awe. 'I can read my name.'

'Yes, you can. Well done,' Jim replies. 'And after you and Rosie here are washed, we'll go out to the garden and hang this to the tree with all the other names. We've got quite a few nailed to it now.'

'Wow,' Lauren says, clearly delighted with the idea.

I smile at my clever husband who came up with this scheme. And he beams back at me.

That evening, Tess hands me a glass of wine, 'She go down okay?'

'She's a sweet kid,' I say. 'I read her a bedtime story and then we sang a song together. She loves Taylor Swift, apparently. There'll be no lullabies for her.'

'Ah the sweetheart,' Tess says. 'Remember, I'm here to help out any time you need me.'

'Oh she was all about Nana Tess earlier. You're a big hit already,' I tell her.

'I've the easy bit, just come in and play with her, give her a few treats,' she says. 'You and Jim are the ones doing all the hard graft.'

It doesn't feel like work, though. After we made the decision to foster and completed all our training courses and checks, we had our first placement – Bobby. And it's been non-stop ever since. I don't think we've had more than the odd week where there's been nobody in this house.

I said to Jim the other day that we had it all wrong back then. When we first started it was upside down in our heads. We naively thought it was all about the children, what we could give to them. Ha. It's us who have been changed. It's our lives that are so much better since these small people came into it.

Five years of crazy, noisy, fun, scary, lump-in-the-throat fostering. And I'd not change a single day of it.

Tess always says that every day is a school day when it comes to fostering, and she's so right.

'Do you remember Erin?' I say to her.

'Oh God yes. Spiky little thing wasn't she?' Tess answers.

'She grunted at us for days and for an eight-year-old she had a pretty hefty left hook. I'd the bruises to prove it,' I say. 'She was difficult to love.'

I didn't bond with her immediately like I had the other three before her. And the guilt of that was crippling. When I confessed this to Jim, I was consumed with shame. It seemed awful that I was struggling to like her, never mind love her.

He admitted that he was struggling with the same issue. We thought, shit, we better call social services.

But before I hit dial to Lorcan's phone, I had one of those 'aha' moments. I was like Erin when I was a kid. Spiky and uncommunicative.

So I put down the phone and waited. I had all the time in the world and I had my breakthrough a few days later. Erin was struggling with her homework and I was trying to help. It wasn't going well. I was stumped. She exhaled this long, agonising sigh of frustration. And I felt so protective of her and wanted nothing more than to take that sigh away.

I thought to myself, feck you and your spiky boundaries, Erin, I'm coming in.

I pulled her in close to me for a hug and didn't let go, even when she gave me a few thumps to push me away. Then, after what felt like an eternity, but in fact was more likely a moment, she kind of fell into my hug. She let go.

And in that moment, so did I.

I let go of all the anger I felt to foster parents who hadn't bonded with me. I realised that it didn't mean that they were bad or nasty people. I had just made it difficult for them to get to know me, never mind love me. Yes, I had my reasons for being so quiet, but it must have been hard for them too.

I look at Tess and marvel, once again, at this woman who never gave up on me.

'I often wonder what would have happened to me, had you sent me packing after Jim left,' I say to Tess. 'No one would have blamed you. You'd done more than your fair share.'

'You would have been just fine, no matter where you ended up, because you're a fighter. You're strong and fearless. But I was never letting you go. I had a feeling about you the moment I met you,' Tess says.

'That's how I feel about Lauren,' I admit. 'Just like that.'

'I know that it's okay if we don't feel immediate, warm, squishy feelings about every child we foster. In fact it's probably healthier if we don't. But there's something about her ...'

'Be careful, Belle,' Tess says. 'You don't know how long she's staying yet.'

I take a sip of my wine and decide to ignore that. Life is full of uncertainties. Who knows anything for sure?

And who is to say that Lauren won't stay here with us, like Bobby did. He's such a big part of our family now. Lauren could be the same.

'Penny for them?' Tess asks.

I fudge what I was thinking. I don't think Tess would approve of my running away with myself. She's right, we don't how long Lauren will be with us.

'Sorry, I was miles away. Just thinking about all the children we've had come in and out of the house these past few years.'

'Any regrets?' Tess asks. She looks worried.

'None at all. It's Jim and me who have gotten the most out of fostering, not the children. We're the lucky ones,' I say, quick to reassure her. And that's so true.

'But, it's okay to admit that sometimes it's a challenge,' Tess says. 'I know that more than most would.'

'A few times, I've felt like throwing it all in, but Jim and I are in this for the long haul. When we decided to start fostering, we knew it was a lifelong commitment,' I say.

Tess nods in approval. 'That's what it was like for me too. Once I had that first child, that was it. Oh lord, look at the time. Come on, put on *Grey's Anatomy*. It's about to start.'

17

The trouble is, you think you have time.

Buddha

December 2015

'What time is Bobby calling over?' Jim shouts from the den.

'In about an hour or so. You know Bobby, though, he's his own man, always has been, he could arrive any time,' I reply.

I've always admired that about him. He beats to his own drum, even when it drove me to distraction as his foster mum, he still held firm to that.

I remember the first time we allowed him to walk home from school alone. Jim and I were beside ourselves, worried that we were doing the right thing. When is the right time to give your teenage foster son a bit of independence? Especially when it's one like Bobby, who spent his waking days like a coiled spring, ready to fly off any second.

In the end, unable to decide ourselves, we rang our social worker, Lorcan, to get his approval, before we gave Bobby the green light.

'Despite the ridiculous amount of time we spent in a classroom learning how to be foster parents, this topic was never covered,' I joked to him.

'Foster parents always panic more.' I could hear the smile in his voice. 'Relax.'

'The word is chillax,' I replied, quoting Bobby. Jim and I were getting down with a whole new language with him in our lives.

'Get you, with the lingo,' Lorcan laughed. 'But, you'll never hear me use that word. Ever. As for your young ward, well, Bobby's fifteen not five. So, of course let him walk home alone. You can't make a show of him in front of his pals, by babying him. He won't thank you for that,' Lorcan told us.

So we let our new addition to the family loose in North County Dublin the next day. We then paid for that by going through two fraught hours while we waited for the bold laddo to come home. He walked in the door eventually, without a care in the world. And the only thing on his mind was his stomach, as he was 'bleeding starving.'

He shrugged when Jim exploded with worry, couldn't see what the big deal was at all.

'How could you put us both through that? We've been out of our minds here,' Jim complained.

'Relax your kacks. You'll give yourself a heart attack,' He quipped back and I giggled when Jim turned a funny shade of red. 'I was just having a kick-about with the lads, Jimbo.'

Looking back on it now, we were lucky we managed to all come out the other side of that placement. Bobby stayed with us for twenty-two months in the end. Somewhere in that time, amid the drama, he became a permanent fixture in our hearts. And a regular visitor to our house too now, even though he's been gone a few years.

'My turn. Me want a go,' Lauren shouts, as she clatters her way into the kitchen. She's wearing a pair of my high heels and is dragging a small red step behind her. 'There,' she declares as she places it in front of the kitchen counter, beside me.

'Okay, Little Miss Impatient,' I smile, lifting her up onto the step. 'You can put these vegetables into this bowl right here.'

She grins as I lean down to kiss her forehead. As I dice carrots and onions, she makes a pile of them and then transfers them one by one into my bowl. She sticks her tongue out, deep in concentration as she moves them. I never get tired of looking at her.

'Ah, here's my two girls, slaving away at the cooker. That's what I like to see,' Jim jokes as he comes in.

'I'm helping Belle,' Lauren says.

'I can see that. What would we do without you?' He leans down and kisses her head before swiping a piece of carrot.

'It's ages since Bobby's been over. I can't wait to catch up with him,' I say.

'I get to relive my precarious youth by listening to his exploits,' Jim says.

'You've never done a precarious thing in your life,' I joke.

'Ah, you'd be surprised my love. You're making his favourite, I see?' Jim asks.

'Of course. I think half the attraction when he comes to visit is food,' I say.

'Please say that's dessert I can smell too,' Jim says.

And I nod towards the oven, where a pie is baking.

'I'll have to get Bobby to call around more often. shepherd's pie and then apple pie for afters too.'

'Quit your moaning. You don't do too bad for yourself, Jim Looney.' I point towards his stomach, which only has the slightest paunch.

'I've no complaints, Mrs Looney. I know I do very well, thank you very much,' he answers and blows a kiss in my direction.

'No regrets?' I ask.

'No regrets, just love,' Jim replies, as he always does when I pose that question.

After his whirlwind proposal we waited a whole six months before getting married. 'It will never last,' was muttered both in front of us and behind our backs. But here we are, nearly ten years on, still living life with no regrets.

Well, that's not quite true. But I block the thought from taking root and ruining our family dinner.

'Is he still dating that girl, what was her name? Rachel or was it Tricia? I can't keep up with him any more,' Jim says.

'Tricia was the latest one, but that's over too, I think. He and Rachel haven't been together since Easter. At least according to Facebook, that's the current situation,' I reply.

Thank God for Facebook status updates. It's the only way I can keep track of him and his girlfriends.

'He's some lad. Do you remember that first night he arrived here? He was on his phone chatting up some girl at the time and he was what? All of fifteen?' Jim smiles. He looks proud of him, though. Typical man. 'He's a good-looking lad. No wonder he has the pick of them. Hey, what's that frown for?'

I hadn't even realised I was frowning. I quickly smile and say, 'Ah, I just worry about him. He never seems to stick with anyone for more than five minutes. I know he's only young yet, but I wish he wasn't quite so fickle.'

'You just want to wear a fancy hat. When he meets the right girl he'll settle down and he's loads of time for that yet,' Jim says.

'Jeepers, speaking about the time, I better go get Tess, before she's on the phone giving me hell. See you in a bit,' he says as he walks out the door.

'Can I watch my programmes now?' Lauren asks. She's bored of helping now.

'Sure thing. But just until Tess and Bobby get here, Lauren. TV stays off when they visit, that's the deal?' I remind her.

'Pinky promise.' She says, offering me her little finger. Deal sealed with a shake, she skips off happily to the den. I assemble the layers of meat and gravy, vegetables and mashed potatoes into my big casserole dish, then pop it into the oven.

Time to change into a different top, freshen up a bit. But I don't get far, because Lauren comes running in with my phone.

'It's ringing,' she shouts.

'Thanks, honey. Oh, it's Lorcan.' I answer, before it switches to voicemail. 'Hey you.'

'Hi, Belle. You okay to talk for a second?' he asks.

'Sure, you sound fierce serious, is all okay?' I can feel the hairs on the back of my neck rise. I wonder if he has an emergency placement for us. We had one only last week, a child whose parents were in a car crash and had nowhere to stay. Relatives were on their way back from Australia to take over, but until then we had to step in. I must check how they are all doing.

'All is fine, but I do need to have a chat with you about Lauren. Can I call around later?' he asks.

'Yeah, Bobby is coming for dinner, he'd like to say hi, I'm sure,' I tell him. 'Plenty in the pot if you fancy joining us for dinner too? It's pie night.'

'Pie night, oh I think I could have my arm twisted for that. Having a bitch of a day so I've not had a bite to eat. I'll call over on the way home from the office, about five, that okay?' he says.

'Perfect. By the way, should I worry? About your chat?' I ask.

'We'll talk when I get there. But when have I ever given you something to worry about?' he replies.

Liar, liar pants on fire, Lorcan. I can always tell when he has bad news to impart.

'It's Tess.' Lauren's little voice singsongs throughout the house. 'Belle, Tess is here. Come quick. And Bobby is parking his car too, look. Everyone's here.'

Okay, no time to change. I'll have to do as I am. I squirt some deodorant on, then pull my thick hair back into a low ponytail.

'You've lost more weight,' I remark when I hug Tess. 'You okay? Been eating alright?'

'Eating all around me, as normal. But I'm doing keep fit in the community centre twice a week,' Tess boasts. 'Best fun I've ever had. We sit on these chairs and do the keep fit from there. The instructor is quite hunky. He has a look of that Dr McDreamy.'

I giggle just picturing Tess in a tracksuit kicking her legs about. I never thought I'd ever see that day. 'Good for you, Tess. It suits you.'

As Jim pours some sparkling water into glasses, I tell him, 'Lorcan is stopping by on his way home from the office.'

'Another temporary placement?' Jim wonders.

'Maybe.' I'm not so sure, though. I whisper, careful to avoid Lauren overhearing me talk about her mother, 'Wonder, is it Alicia again?'

'You think she's done another disappearing act?' Jim asks.

I shrug. She's been good the past few months, I'll give her that. Alicia hasn't missed any of her meetings with her daughter. We don't have time to chat about it any more, because Bobby walks in.

'Alrigh, houz it goin?' I swear, his Dublin accent gets stronger by the day and I spin around to give him a hug.

'Let me get a look at you,' I say and look him up and down. He's wearing his customary Adidas tracksuit and runners, but it's his face I search. I can always judge how much partying he's doing by the circles under his eyes.

And today he looks wrecked. 'You're tired. How much sleep have you had lately?'

'I'm grand. Not a bother on me. Come here to me, darlin'', he grabs Lauren up into his arms. 'I've got a present for you.'

'I missed you,' she announces, her two arms wrapped around his neck. I love watching them together. They are so close, I don't think they could be any more so if they were indeed siblings.

'And me you. You're getting big. Belle is feeding you well,' he says. 'Speaking of which, I'm starving.'

'Some things never change,' Jim laughs. 'Come on, let's go into the kitchen and you can fill us all in on what's going on in the madcap world of Bobby.'

'This and that. You know yourself,' he drawls. Bobby is one of life's duckers and divers. He'd not got the best start in life. Both his parents are heroin addicts. We did the best we could to show him an alternative way to live his life, during his two years with us. My biggest fear was that he'd follow in their footsteps, but he swears that he'd rather chop his arm off than ever touch drugs. Cigarettes and beer, well that's another thing.

But as Tess says, you'd never be done worrying about kids. Comes with the territory.

I make a pot of tea and we all sit down around the kitchen table to catch up. Lauren is on the floor playing with a *Frozen* jigsaw, her present from Bobby. He's gone from hero status now to god with that particular gift.

'How's all the family?' I ask, bracing myself for the update. Let's just say it's usually colourful.

'Haven't seen Ma and Da for ages. Don't want to either. They're still on the quare stuff. Paul is back inside. Banged up for dealing. Again. Fecking loser,' he spits out.

'I'm sorry Bobby,' I say and I am. Paul is Bobby's older brother and he did the best job he could for years while their parents were off their heads on heroin. He was father and mother to Bobby, doing all he could to keep him safe. But it was inevitable that he'd get mixed up with the wrong crowd. When he was sent to jail for firearm offences and sent to a young offenders institute, social services had no choice but to put Bobby in care. I'll be forever grateful that it was our house he came to.

Bobby got four honours and two passes in his leaving certificate in the end. Thanks to the long hours Jim patiently gave him, helping him study and play catch up on all the work he'd missed.

To think there was a time we thought he'd never even finish third year, never mind do his final exams. He's come such a long way.

Some of the stories he shared with us shocked us to our cores. And I'll be honest, I'm not easily shocked. I've seen it all.

A few short weeks before he was placed with us, he'd had a gun pointed to his head. Imagine that? A child having to process that fear, that brush with death? Well, I feel my blood run cold at the thought.

But that wasn't even the worse of it. He then went on to watch both his parents overdose. Found them both on the floor of the flat. Only for Bobby getting help as he did, they'd both be dead.

I look at Bobby and I'm so proud of him. A lesser person would have cracked under the weight of the knocks life had thrown at him, but Bobby isn't one of them. He's a survivor.

'Paul swore he was staying away from all that when he got out last year. I thought he was going to do it too. For Lulu's sake. He's lucky to have her, she's a dote,' Bobby continued.

'What age is she now?' Tess asks. Lulu is Paul's daughter.

'Three,' Bobby tells her. 'God love her. She doesn't know what's going on, where her daddy has gone.'

We all sit in silence for a few moments. I look around at my family and realise that we have all felt what that is like, in some shape or form.

It's all getting a bit sombre, so I decide to lighten things up.

'Who's ready for Secret Santa?' I ask and my answer is in their whoops and hollers of 'Bring it on.'

Every year we do this. We each pick a name out of a jar, and for the month of December, we are that person's Secret Santa. Twenty euros budget for the gift. It's more about the fun of guessing who you have, than what you get.

I've had all sorts over the years. I always seem to get one of the kids as my Secret Santa so the gifts have been eclectic, to say the least. My personal favourite so far was a salad spinner. One of those plastic Tupperware ones that you put lettuce leaves in, to spin the water off. A Bobby special.

I go and get my jar, which I've already filled with all of our names, folded up, ready for each of us to choose.

I come in singing, as I do every year, my own version of *Let it Snow*, knowing full well that they'll all be joining in within seconds.

'Oh the weather outside is frightful,
But this gift is sure delightful,
I'll leave it and quickly go,
Because who I am you cannot know.'

'Me first,' Lauren demands jumping up and down, so I hold the jar down low for her.

I then pass it around to each person and there's lots of sly looks as we each try to work out who has who.

I take out the last name and have a peek.

Jim.

Aw, I've got Jim. I've never had him before. This is going to be fun. An idea jumps into my head immediately. What if I could get him a Simon game, like the one we had back when we were kids? Wonder would they have a 1988 version on eBay maybe? Someone clearing out their attic. That would be cool.

'I know exactly what I'm going to get mine already,' Tess says.

'Anyone want to swap with me? I've no bleeding idea what to get,' Bobby says.

'Language,' I say.

'Soz,' he smiles apologetically.

'No swaps allowed. Is there, Belle?' Lauren says with glee.

'That's right, no swaps. And don't forget to include the gift this time, is all I'm saying,' I tease.

Everyone starts to roar with laughter at this and Bobby replies, 'It was an easy mistake. Yez are all hilarious.'

'Buy … yourself … a gift,' Jim says, tears coming out of his eyes, as he clutches his side.

'Tess's face ...' I add.

'Well, I must say, I was a bit put out,' Tess says. 'Imagine opening a card and that's what you're told. Buy yourself a gift. Charming.'

'It was supposed to have a voucher in it. To buy the gift with,' Bobby shouts above the din of us all laughing. 'You know that.'

'I want a present. Not just a card, Bobby,' Lauren says, fearful that the same fate awaits her this year.

'Oh me darlin', if I had you, you'd be getting a massive present,' he replies.

Mollified she continues with her jigsaw.

'Give us a biscuit or something, Belle, when you're finished slagging me off, my stomach thinks my throat is cut,' Bobby says.

'Me want a biscuit too,' Lauren's singsong voice pipes in, never one to miss an opportunity.

'After all my exercise this morning, I think I deserve a slice of that,' Tess says, looking at my apple pie cooling by the window.

'What are you all like? When Lorcan gets here, I'll be serving dinner, so no biscuit, no pie, no nothing till then,' I say.

'She's fierce bossy,' Bobby says to Lauren, who nods solemnly.

'She never lets me eat biscuits,' Lauren declares, also feeling hard done by.

'She was the same when I lived here,' Bobby replies. 'It's a wonder I didn't fade away.'

'As a child she was impossible,' Tess chips in. 'I wasn't allowed to enjoy even the odd chip with her in the house.'

I get ready to throw my best retort their way, but the doorbell goes. 'Saved by the bell,' I tell them all, wagging my finger at them.

'That smells unreal,' Lorcan states when he walks in, loosening his tie as he goes. 'Hello one and all. Salutations.'

'Howaya,' Bobby says.

'Hello young man,' Lorcan nods to him. 'Good to see you. Keeping out of trouble I hope.'

'But of course,' Bobby winks. 'By the way, if you need a new fridge freezer, I can hook you up with one. Mates rates.'

'Bobby,' I chastise him. He loves to bait Lorcan when he comes over, looking for a reaction.

Lauren is hiding behind Jim. I don't think she'll ever trust Lorcan. She'll always associate him as the man who took her from her mam.

'Hi, Lauren. How are you?' He says to her, trying to coax her away from Jim. But she buries her head somewhere in his armpit.

'When will they learn that I don't bite? Not children at least,' Lorcan winks as he accepts a drink.

'Hey, share don't scare. And I keep telling you, don't take it to heart with Lauren. Jim and I still get shivers when we think about our old social worker, Mrs Reilly. She was alright, as they go, but we couldn't stand her back then,' I admit. 'Actually, scrap that. She was an old bat. Nothing like you.'

'Ah, I'm one of the good guys. But there's always the odd one who gives us a bad name.' He says, holding his hand up. But then his face clouds a little. 'I need to talk to you and Jim about Lauren, when you have a sec.'

I catch Jim's eye and nod towards our sunroom. 'Let's get this out of the way before dinner.' I close the door behind us, leaving the others chatting.

'How has Lauren been these past few months, with her mother back in her life?' Lorcan asks.

'It's been difficult and quite an adjustment for her, after all, Alicia is a stranger to her in many ways,' I say. I'm irritated already at the mention of Alicia and feel my body stiffen.

Ever since Alicia has come back into Lauren's life, our lives, it's confused everything for me. Take her last visit, for example. Lauren spent hours making a card for her mother, colouring in the picture with such care. She asked me to help her write it. Which of course I was happy to do, but every loving word she wrote, cut me, just a little. And when Alicia walked in the door and Lauren ran into her arms, the look of joy mirrored on both mother and daughter's faces, well that cut me a lot.

I don't think it's possible not to be affected.

Jim shoots me a worried look. He jumps in and tells Lorcan, 'It's going well, as far as we are concerned. Lauren looks forward to seeing Alicia now. She doesn't seem as distressed as she was at first.'

Even though Jim isn't saying anything I don't know to be true, every word he's spoken feels like a betrayal to us and our family unit here.

She's not your daughter, though, a little voice whispers. I know. I know. I KNOW.

'Listen, we all know that Alicia has been suffering from mental illness for years. It's been a rough road for her, but she's turned things around. We've had a full assessment done by a psychologist. We're happy with her progress,' Lorcan continues.

I bite back an unkind retort, bully for her, then feel bad, because the ironic thing about all of this, is that I *do* like Alicia. Part of me has even been rooting for her to recover and get her act together. She's a nice woman and I can see how much she wants to get better and that's more than a lot of the parents I've come across since we started fostering.

More than Dolores ever did.

The first time Alicia called to visit Lauren, she took me by surprise. I had this image in my head which was completely wrong. I'd imagined that any woman who could hand over her child would look bedraggled, unkempt and, I suppose, hard-looking. There'd be no love, only madness in her eyes. I told myself that I'd not like her, I'd remain aloof. I'd be professional, of course, but I'd keep my distance.

She was pretty much the opposite of what I'd imagined her to look like. Bang went my theory on what a stereotypical vision of someone who had her baby taken into care looked like.

Nope, there wasn't a bedraggled hair on her head. In fact, Jim said she looked like an advert for Gap or Next when she arrived here the first time to see Lauren. She had even brought with her a pretty tin, full of homemade cookies, doing a good impression of *Desperate Housewives'* Bree Van de Kamp.

And she's always been friendly and eager to please whenever she visits too. And respectful to both Jim and me. She can't thank us enough for all we do for Lauren.

So you see, that's why it's confusing for me. I don't want to lose Lauren. She's happy with us. She loves us. But the thing is, I didn't bargain on liking Alicia.

It has crossed my mind once or twice that it's all an act. I like to think that I'm wise to be a little cynical, because I've seen a lot of crazy stuff go on, both as a foster child and as a foster parent. But you would have to be blind not to see that she wants to have her daughter home again and is willing to do just about anything to that end.

As if reading my mind, Jim compliments Alicia, 'She's been on time for every single visit. She is always extremely thoughtful and understanding of how confusing it must be for Lauren. And considerate of us too.'

Even though I'd just been thinking the same thing, Jim annoys me, once again, by saying it out loud.

This is all going to end badly. I know it is.

Lorcan and Jim both turn to look at me, with their big concerned heads on them that make me want to throw something at them.

I know what Lorcan is going to say before he even opens his mouth.

'The plan with Alicia and Lauren has always been about reunification.'

What an awful bloody word. I've always hated it. Sounds painful and, actually, that's what it is. Painful.

'We feel it's time for Lauren to go home to her mother. We'd like you to talk to Lauren about this in the next few days,' he adds.

I can feel two pairs of eyes boring into me now.

Well, they can both go to hell, I don't want to look at them. I know that Jim's eyes will share sadness at the thought of Lauren no longer being in our lives. But he'll be more philosophical about it too. And that pisses me off. I want him to shout and scream and fight for Lauren to stay.

Exactly what I intend on doing.

'How do you feel about this?' Lorcan asks us both. 'Do you agree that it's time?'

No it's not time. It will never be time.

I remember the last visit. Alicia and I were chatting over coffee and Lauren was running backwards and forwards between us both. And I couldn't take my eyes off Lauren's face when she was in her mother's arms.

Every time Lauren looks at me, I can see only love in her eyes. She adores me. I know she does, as I do her. But I saw another truth on that day. She loves her mother too.

So is it time? Yes, dammit to hell, I think it is.

Sometimes I hate that voice in my head.

When Alicia left last week, Lauren stood at the door for an age, refusing to come inside to play or watch TV. She missed her mother and she had only just gone.

She missed her mother.

Yes, okay, maybe it is time.

But I can't say that out loud. I can't do anything to facilitate the removal of a little girl that I love with all my heart.

Fuck reunification. Fuck social services.

'You always knew she would have to go home one day,' Lorcan says again. 'Belle. What do you think?'

And fuck you, Lorcan Colter. That's what I think. You can forget about pie now. Go get a bag of chips for yourself on the way home.

But I don't say any of that, of course. I rarely curse, but right now there are no other words to convey how I feel.

'When Jim and I decided to foster, we swore that we would only do it if we could love ALL the children like they were our own,' I say to him. I'm surprised at how strong my voice sounds, because in my head I feel like I'm choking. My airways feel restricted, as if the breath won't come out.

He nods like one of those puppies whose heads go up and down in the back window of a car.

'We love Lauren like she is our own daughter,' I continue.

'That's obvious to us all,' Lorcan says. 'You have been amazing, both of you have and Lauren is such a confident, happy child as a result of that.'

But I don't care how many compliments he fires at me, I'm furious with him. I'm furious with Jim. I'm furious with every goddamn one of them.

'You social workers,' I say, waving a finger at him. 'You can't have it every way. You can't expect us to love these children like our own on the one hand and then do a Halleluiah dance when you come in talking about reunification.'

I dare him to interrupt me. He stays quiet.

'So while this is a good thing for Alicia, forgive me if I cannot share more enthusiasm about Lauren leaving us, right now.' I stand up, shaken. 'I better check on dinner.'

'Belle …' Lorcan says, rising to follow me.

'Leave her,' Jim says. 'Give her time to get her head around this.'

I turn back to Lorcan and say, 'You'd be wise to heed my husband's advice. Leave me be for now.'

I'm not sure how I manage to get through dinner. But somehow or other, I dish up shepherd's pie onto the plates and pass them around and we sit down together, Walton's style, to eat it. I can feel Jim's eyes on me, worrying about me as he always does. I know I should check to see how he feels, because this is hard on him too. But I don't want to. I don't want to know if he's happy or sad about the news. I only have space in my head right now for me.

Thank goodness for Bobby, because he keeps everyone entertained with his latest romantic breakup story.

Lorcan, meanwhile, keeps trying to catch my eye, so I give him what I hope is a withering look. It must have been effective, because he shoves some more pie in his mouth and looks away.

'You're quiet,' Tess remarks, as I load the dishwasher after dinner, 'And that worries me. Because whenever you stop talking, I know that's when you are most upset. What's going on?'

'They're taking Lauren from me,' I whisper.

Tess leans in close, her face knowing. 'I was afraid of this. I knew you'd take it bad when it happened. Ah I'm heart sorry, I really am.'

I wipe my hands on the tea towel and walk out to the garden. I need to get away from the chatter and banter.

'You're hurting right now,' Tess says, following me into the garden.

'You reckon?' I say. She makes a face, so I continue, 'Can I not have even five minutes to feel upset about the fact that the child I think of as my own is leaving me?'

'Of course you can.' Tess is reasonable and understanding. 'I felt like this when Jim left. I cried for weeks over him, I missed him so much.'

I'm surprised by this admission. I never knew she'd been that upset. She hid that well from me and I guess I know why now. She didn't want me to see that, she did that for me.

'What I always told myself when one of my kids went back home, was that my sadness was only matched by their happiness,' she says.

I find it hard to make a smart retort to that. 'Stop being so wise, Tess. It's hard to argue with that.'

'So many times, people have said to me, I NEVER could be a foster parent; I would just get too attached,' Tess says.

I nod. It's true, it's something I've heard dozens of times too.

'But it's inevitable that after a long-term placement, you can't avoid the heartache of raising a child and then having them leave your home,' Tess says. 'It sucks to high heaven, but it's life and that's the way it is.'

I sulk silently to Tess's pearls of wisdom.

'Do you think Lauren is going to be okay with Alicia?' Tess continues.

'Probably,' I admit. 'Alicia seems to have her act together. She loves her, there's no doubt about that. But Tess, I can't forget the state that Lauren was in when she came here. Alicia is great now. She's all Bree Van de Kamp, with her home-baked cookies, but I still remember a little girl who ate stale cornflakes and nothing else for weeks because her mother couldn't get out of bed to shop or cook.'

'I hear you,' Tess says. 'But you'll have to trust Lorcan and the system. Trust that they will keep an eye on Alicia.'

I know she's right. But I'm uneasy. I want to do what's best for Lauren, but I'm terrified for her safety if it all goes pear-shaped.

'The positive impact you have made on Lauren and Alicia, well that's incredible. You and Jim have both helped Alicia get her act together. I've seen you with her too. You've helped her learn how to be a parent again, by allowing her into your home, to watch and learn from you both,' Tess says.

I nod. I know Tess has a point here and Lorcan has told us several times that Alicia's progress has been greatly enabled by her knowing her child was so loved and well taken care of. She could focus on herself and not worry about her daughter, get her act together.

'Putting those two back together again, well that's pretty incredible and it completely outweighs any heartache you may be experiencing right now. You have to remember that,' Tess says.

I know that every word she says is right. But what my head and heart feel and know are different.

'You have to let her go home,' Tess says. 'That's the deal with fostering. I told you both that when you came to me to ask advice on starting down this route.'

'I don't have to do anything,' I mumble. I feel like stamping my size eights at the injustice of it all.

I turn to Tess and decide to fill her in on what I was thinking over dinner. I wonder what she'll make of this.

'Do you know what I was thinking? I was wondering how far we could get if Jim and I ran away with her. We could go to the States, you know. He's got citizenship. Start again over there,' I say.

'Oh, sweet divine, will you listen to yourself, Belle. That's not how this works. You're not a stroppy kid any more. You're an adult. You have to say goodbye when the time comes and be ready to say hello to the next child,' Tess says. 'That's just the way it has to be.'

Easier said than done.

18

Life is magic, the way nature works seems to be quite magical.

Jonas Salk

December 2015

I look at the clock – again. It's only five minutes since the last time I checked. For goodness sake, where is he? I told Jim it was an emergency. What is keeping him so long?

It's only been an hour since Bobby called and dropped his bombshell, but it feels so much longer. I need to hear what Jim makes of it all. I'm up the walls here. I look at the clock again and decide to call him if he's not back in the next five minutes.

At bloody last. I can hear our front door opening. It has to be him.

'What's wrong?' Jim rushes in, sweating and red, out of breath.

Oh shit. I probably made it sound like someone was dead. Looks like he ran all the way over here from school too.

'Bobby called. He bumped into Alicia in the pub last night. She was on a date,' I blurt out.

'That's allowed surely?' Jim asks, leaning over to try to ease what looks like a stitch in his side. 'Since when is dating banned?'

Okay when I say it like that, it sounds pretty lame. But he doesn't know everything yet.

We walk into the kitchen and I pour him a glass of water.

'Here, drink this before you collapse. And actually, no, it's not allowed. At least not when the guy in question is an ex-con, with a rap sheet as long as your arm,' I say.

I am triumphant in imparting this important news. This changes everything. Now I have justification for not wanting Lauren to leave us. It's her safety that is at risk.

'Okay. You've got my attention. Go on,' he says, once he's downed his pint of water in one go.

'Well, Bobby said that this guy is seriously dodgy. He's dangerous too. Seriously off the wall, off your head territory. Bobby said he's known for being a "little shit". He has been done for GBH loads of times too. We have to call Lorcan, warn him about this,' I say, waving my mobile in front of Jim's face.

'Hold on a second, Belle. Does Bobby know for sure that the two of them are definitely dating? For how long? Is it serious?' Jim asks. 'We need facts before we can go charging in like bulls in a china shop.'

'I don't know the ins and outs of Alicia's love life,' I sniff. 'But I do know one thing. I'll not have Lauren exposed to that type of individual. I'll not have her at risk. We have a duty of care here.' I've worked myself up into a right tizzy now.

I'm furious at the thought of Lauren even being in the company of someone who is violent. Our sweet, kind, sensitive child. She deserves more. I have to protect her. This isn't about me, it's about her.

'Okay, I'll ring Lorcan. Not you, Belle.' He grabs the phone from my hand. 'You're too emotional,' Jim says.

'You say that like it's a bad thing. Of course I'm fecking emotional.' But I can feel my anger already dissipating.

Jim dials Lorcan's number and swats me away, laughing, as I hover in close to him, to listen to the conversation. He fills Lorcan in on Bobby's observations, calmly.

'So you can appreciate our concerns. We have to advocate the best interests of our foster child,' Jim says.

I nod in approval at this statement. 'Tell him we're *very* concerned,' I whisper loudly.

'You heard that? Yeah, she's in a bit of a state over it. Yeah, I know,' Jim laughs.

'What did he say?' I ask. Somehow or other, I think whatever it was, it was at my expense. Jim holds me away from the phone with one arm and finishes up his conversation. 'You'll look into it? Great.'

'He's going to tell Alicia she can't have Lauren back? Do you think he will? Maybe she can stay with us?' I splutter out in a rush.

'Don't,' Jim says. He's not laughing any more, he looks deadly serious.

'Don't what?' I reply feigning innocence, although I know what he is forbidding.

'Don't start thinking that this can change anything. We have no idea what's going on with Alicia. We have to trust that she will act on the best interests of her daughter,' Jim says. 'That she will know the difference between a good or bad guy.'

'But Bobby said …' Jim cuts me off before I can finish.

'Bobby nothing. He doesn't know Alicia does he? Lorcan will look into it,' Jim says.

'For all we know she could have all sorts parading in and out of her house,' I say.

'She never seemed that type to me,' Jim replies mildly.

Me neither. But do we really know her? I don't think so. Look at how many people Dolores fooled for years.

'If Lauren stays with us, we can give her a future. She can go to college. She can be anything she wants to be.' I start to pace the floor, I fill the kettle then put it down again. I don't want tea. Maybe coffee. No, I don't want that either. I just want to know that Lauren is going to stay here with us, damn it. Where I can keep her safe. I can't let her mother let her down or hurt her ever again. I just can't.

Jim looks at me with concern. 'If Lauren stays with us, we'll make sure she gets a third-level education, but she can still have that if she goes home to Alicia,' Jim adds gently.

Sometimes I could throttle my husband. Why does he have to be so bloody even-minded all the time?

'As much as I enjoy having you shout at me, I have to get back to work now.' Jim says. 'You going to be alright?'

'Sorry,' I mumble, feeling contrite. None of this is his fault, I know that. I walk over and give him an apologetic kiss.

'I know this is hard on you. Remember that it's hard on both of us, though,' Jim says.

'Yep,' I mumble against his shirt.

'Listen, I've got to split. I've a meeting with one of the kids in half an hour about his CAO application for college.' Jim is now a careers guidance teacher in the local technical college. Kids love him; he has a good way about him. 'Try to stay calm, Belle.'

You know when someone tells you stay calm. That. I can feel my temper beginning to rise once again.

He then decides to spin his Russian roulette gun one more time, right in my direction. He's a brave man, my husband. 'Maybe this is a good thing, if you think about it.'

I look at him and cannot believe what he's saying. 'Good? Are you for real? How can any of this ... this mess, be good?'

'Maybe, think about it for a second, well maybe losing Lauren has shown us both that it's time for us to have our own baby. I don't mean we should stop fostering. But who says that we can't do both?' he says.

Not this again. I hold my hand up, to stop him saying any more. I'm so upset I can't speak. He knows how it is for me to think about babies. Just the word brings me back and the memory is so painful, I wince.

The cold gel makes me squirm, even though I knew it was coming. I hold my breath as the midwife starts moving the ultrasound over my tummy. It's silent in the room, save for Jim's breathing. I realise I'm holding my own breath and I exhale quickly, afraid that I could be hurting the baby by doing that.

Duh dum, duh dum. Duh dum duh dum.

'Can you hear that?' The midwife asks, smiling at us both.

I nod, unable to articulate that, yes, I can hear that beautiful sound.

'That's our baby's heartbeat?' Jim asks, his hand squeezing mine so tightly it hurts.

'Well it's not mine,' the midwife jokes and points to the screen. 'This is his head, his arms, his legs. He's a lively one by the looks of it. I would say you are about ten weeks along, judging by this scan.'

We watch in awe as our child bounces around the screen, doing somersaults in my tummy. I think, he's putting on a show just for us.

I have never felt love like it before.

'Belle.' Jim's voice brings me back to the present, to our kitchen. 'You can't keep blocking this conversation. I have feelings too, I need … I need to be heard.'

Then more gently when he looks at me and sees my face, 'We'll talk later, okay?'

Before I have a chance to respond, he's gone.

I look at the clock and see that I've another hour before it's time to pick up Lauren from school. I need to get out of here. If I sit here I'll start to cry and I'm afraid if I do that I won't be able to stop. So I wrap up warm, because it's cold outside but dry. Lauren has been hoping for snow and, looking at the sky, it wouldn't surprise me if it comes.

I tear off at high speed, but when my feet start to slide on the icy footpath I slow down to a safer gait. I know where I want to go. To the park. It's so cold, it's unlikely that there will be many in there and I need the solitude.

'Afternoon, Belle.' I nearly walk into Mrs O'Leary and her dog Missy, I'm so lost in my own thoughts.

'Sorry,' I shout, 'Can't stop …'

I feel a bit guilty. I know she's lonely and loves a good natter with us if we bump into her. I'm just not in the mood for company.

My feeling about the park is right. It's empty but for a dog that is sniffing around for some scraps to eat. I feel sorry for it and search my parka coat for something to give him.

'Sorry, mutt. You're out of luck,' I say and he moves away disgusted.

I head for the swings and wipe the seat with a tissue. Realising that it's a lost cause as the tissue disintegrates to mush, I decide to chance the cold, icy seat. My bum will warm it up soon enough.

I walk backwards as far as the swing allows and run forwards as quick as my legs will go, to lift off. Then I kick my legs out in front of me and back down again. With each swing, I move higher and higher and I welcome the cold air as it stings my nose and cheeks. Closing my eyes, I allow myself to just enjoy the sensation of moving up and down, over and over again.

How many times have I done this over the years? Trying to swing away my sorrows, I guess you'd call it. Whatever it is, I seem to find myself back here a lot both with and without the kids.

The dog barks and I open my eyes reluctantly to see why. A group of boys is coming in with skateboards. I'd

201

say, by the looks of them, they're eighteen or nineteen. Not boys any more, they are on the brink of being men. They are all dressed in their trademark uniform of hoodies and tracksuit bottoms. I half expect to see Bobby amongst them. It seems like only yesterday when he was part of a skateboard gang, in this park.

I feel a quick surge of pride at the part that Jim and I played in getting this place built. It was my idea, one of my rare good ones. It was shortly after Bobby came to stay with us and I couldn't believe that there was nowhere for the kids to go, at the weekends and after school. The nearest park was a good ten-minute drive and the youth club wasn't up to much, due to lack of interest from both kids and parents. So I called door to door, campaigning and gathering support from the locals. And then I formed a committee and both Jim and I spent a year, tirelessly fund-raising, looking for grants from the council, asking youth groups and the local schools to help out.

It was worth all the hard work, because now we have a vibrant youth club in the community hall. And this fantastic park. Bobby loved them both and we've had many of our teens use them while they stayed with us.

Jim sometimes jokes that I only got the park built for my own pleasure. As I swing higher and higher, I realise that there's a grain of truth in that.

Lauren loves it here too. She adores picnics. We often pack a light lunch and come here on Saturdays, easily spending an afternoon playing in the park or walking around the beautiful grounds.

And we've certainly gotten good use out of it with the many kids we've fostered. Playing outside is not just about letting off steam. Something magic happens to kids when they are let loose in a park. It's somewhere where they can just be kids again. I don't think I could put a number on the amount of times I've watched a child forget about some of their pain and sorrow, while they played in this very spot.

And that has to be a good thing. Because there are some sick people in this world. What's that joke? You need a licence for a dog or TV but kids? Anyone can have one of those.

Thing is, I don't think that Alicia is one of the bad ones. My gut tells me that she's got this. But I'm nervous. What if she blows this second chance? And deep down, I can't help but worry. What if she's another Dolores? I vowed that I would make Lauren smile every day. I cannot allow her to face anymore disappointment or hurt. She's finally in a happy, good place.

It must be time to pick up Lauren, I realise, and start the walk to her school. I ache in the knowledge that my days are numbered doing this simple pleasure. I'm going to miss it so much. Her little hand in mine, skipping along beside me, trying to keep up with my longer gait. And I learn so much on these walks. She never stops talking, telling me all about her day. And with every chatty comment she makes, I think, we're doing something right here. She's happy.

I feel my phone vibrate and pull it out of my jeans pocket. It's Jim.

'Hey you, I'm just on my way to get Lauren,' I say.

'Lorcan rang. Listen, he's been in touch with Alicia and she's not dating that guy,' Jim says.

'She would say that,' I say, sighing.

She's not a liar, though.

'Apparently she went on one date, but that was as far as it got. She worked out for herself that he wasn't for her. Lorcan was a bit pissed off, to be honest. He reminded me that Alicia is allowed to date whomever she wants. He lectured me about boundaries,' Jim says.

'He did what?' I'm pissed off now and can feel my red mist descending. 'How dare he?'

'We've got to remember that it's not our place to be judge and jury. We're here to help and support,' Jim continues.

He sounds so reasonable, I want to scream once again. My calm that I managed to get back, somewhere on my fifth or sixth swing, is gone once more. 'I can't talk about this now, Jim. Lauren is coming out. But believe me, this discussion is far from over.'

19

Our hearts grow tender with childhood memories and love of kindred, and we are better throughout the year for having, in spirit, become a child again at Christmas-time.

Laura Ingalls Wilder

'Oh Fristmas tree, Oh Fristmas tree.
Thy leaves are so unchanging
Oh Fristmas tree, Oh Fristmas tree,
Thy leaves are so unchanging'

I giggle as Lauren sings her little heart out. She always muddles up her Fs and Cs, it's so damn cute. Nat King Cole's silky voice fills our living room and I can't help but smile. We have boxes from the attic strewn on the sofas, on the floor, on the table. I stand back to admire my tree, in all its glory. It's a nine-foot California Douglas Fir tree, shipped over by Jim's parents to us a few years back.

When we went on our honeymoon to Indiana, Jim's mother remembered me admiring the US trees. They are always so much bigger than ours and I was practically salivating looking at them all.

It's without doubt the best Christmas present we've ever received.

Even though it takes me a whole afternoon to just put it together and in its stand, it's worth it. I love putting it up, truth be told. It just looks so resplendent and grand even now, when it's naked without any decorations to adorn it.

The anticipation of dressing the tree is so delicious. I love this, the whole build-up to Christmas, making it special for the whole family.

Tess and Bobby will be here, as always, and as it will be Lauren's last Christmas with us, we need to make it special.

In a few weeks, we'll all head up to the Dublin mountains to pick our real tree out. Jim used to think I was crazy insisting on two trees, but now he's as bad as me. Wouldn't be the same if we didn't have both types. The Nordman Fir tree goes into our hall, so that as soon as we arrive home and walk inside our front door, the smell of pine greets us. I've learnt, though, that it's better to only put up a real tree a few weeks before Christmas, rather than at the beginning of December, if we are to have any chance of it lasting till the New Year.

I don't think I could choose which I prefer more. The real or the artificial. Both so beautiful in their own ways.

But for now, it's all about this artificial beauty. As far as I'm concerned, once this is up and decorated in our family room, then it's official, I'm gonna call it and say it's Christmas.

I hear people complaining all the time that the festive season begins way too early every year. I suppose I'm one of the annoying ones. Because I start to hum 'Jingle Bells' in November and cannot wait to see the Christmas adverts hit our TV screens. I wonder what the John Lewis advert will be like this year. I'm still not over those two penguins.

Jim, thank goodness, is as bad as me when it comes to this holiday. He moans that it's a case of, if you can't beat them, join them. And I let him get away with that, even though I know it's nonsense. He's as big a Christmas nut as I am. In fact, I can hear him up in the attic, right this minute, singing along off key to Nat.

He's on a search for a missing box. Our angel for the top of the tree has gone walkabout. Weird, because I distinctly remember putting her away with the rest of the ornaments. But she's not here and for the life of me, I can't work out where she has disappeared to.

'I swear there's been gremlins in the attic messing with everything,' Jim grumbles when he walks back in a few moments later. 'I'm admitting defeat. I can't find her. I've looked everywhere.'

I hand him a glass of mulled wine. I don't really like the taste of it myself, but love the smell it gives in the house. And ever since Tess gave us a bottle the first year we got married, we've made it a tradition to drink some while we decorate the house. I look in despair at my tangled web of fairy lights.

'Why is it that no matter how careful I am at putting these babies away every year, I still end up with this mess when I take them down from the attic,' I grumble.

So much for the hanger trick, I think. Last January, I'd spent ages winding the lights around a hanger, imitating something I saw on Pinterest. I thought to myself it was a genius idea at the time. Ha. Now I just have a hanger to contend with in my muddle of wire and lights. I swear, next year I'm just going to buy new lights.

'Let me. Let me try.' Lauren demands, grabbing the lights from my hand and mixing them up all over again.

To hell with it. I give her the ball of lights and figure they will keep her occupied for a bit while I sort out the rest of my decorations. I've got quite a collection now, accumulated over the years. I pass Jim my fireplace mantel garland. It's green with bright-red berries scattered through it. It also has white fairy lights entwined around it, which by some miracle have stayed untangled in the box.

'Don't forget to hang our stockings too,' Lauren reminds him.

I hope her stocking will be here on Christmas Eve. Does Alicia even celebrate Christmas? I shoot a worried glance at Lauren and hope that the little traditions she's grown to love here don't get lost when she's with her mam. She'll have her own way of doing things, I know that. I just hope she makes it magical for Lauren. I catch Jim looking over at me. He looks worried and, I suppose, who can blame him? I've been up and down, mood-wise, these past few days. I just can't stop worrying about Lauren.

I cannot let my anxieties about Lauren ruin today, though. I want her to have this memory, unscarred by my demons. So I give Jim what I hope is a reassuring smile. He smiles back, looking relieved.

'Look at me, I'm going to be as tall as the tree any day now,' Lauren says, standing on tip toe.

'I hope you don't grow to be nine feet tall or we'll be in trouble,' Jim says, laughing.

'The first tree I ever had was about your height,' I say to her.

I had a tiny apartment, studio, really, that I used to rent, back in my single days. The miserable tree we had there was about three foot tall. But I suppose it went perfectly with the tiny space I was living in. There is no comparison at all to the tall, green, resplendent specimen before us now.

Tess couldn't understand why I wasted my time putting up a tree in the flat, when I'd spend most of the Christmas holidays with her anyhow. But I've always liked to have my own decorations.

'Tell me about your tree,' Lauren demands. 'I don't remember it.'

I laugh and tell Lauren that she'd never seen it, because that was back before she was born. 'It was small and meagre, and even the two dozen cheap and nasty baubles that came included with it couldn't disguise that fact.'

'I can vouch for that,' Jim says. 'I didn't know whether to laugh or put it out of its misery when I saw it the first time.'

'You didn't even see it at its worst. By then, I'd replaced most of the original baubles with new ones.' I walk over to the box of decorations and rifle through it, finding what I'm looking for pretty quickly.

'And see this one here?' I hold up a small silver bell on a red-velvet ribbon. 'Well, this is probably the most special one we have. Jim bought me this the day he proposed.'

'Show me.' Lauren's greedy little hands snatch it. 'It's so pretty.' She starts running around the boxes, ringing it. Then the song changes on the CD and Doris Day's voice fills the house.

> *Silver bells silver bells*
> *It's Christmas time in the city*
> *Ring-a-ling hear them ring*
> *Soon it will be Christmas Day*

'You couldn't plan that,' Jim remarks, shaking his head.

'I know. Lauren, why don't you hang the bell right here?' I pick her up in my arms and she hangs the silver bell on a branch halfway up the tree. It's always the first of my ornaments to go up and the one that my eyes always look out for when I walk into the room.

'A lifetime of memories in these baubles,' I say.

'No regrets?' Jim asks, walking over towards me.

I turn around and quickly put my arms around him. 'No regrets. Just love.'

The sound of rustling behind me spins me round to see Lauren nose-deep in my boxes, picking up decorations and admiring them, one after the other, then flinging them behind her with abandon, as only a child can.

'Some of these are breakable,' I remind her, catching a glass slipper that almost hit the ground.

'It's a good job it's a nine-foot tree, the amount of decorations you've now collected,' Jim states, shaking his head. I suppose we do have a lot, but some will have to be held back for the Normand Fir when we get that.

We each start to place the decorations on branches with care. Lauren is working on the lower ones, I'm in the middle and Jim works up high. It's a good system, one we've used for years now. We all sing and hum along to the Christmas CD as we work, stopping every now and then to remind each other of a memory a particular bauble stirs.

Jim nudges me in my side and holds up the Do Not Disturb sign that we pinched from our honeymoon suite. It's circular and in red velvet, so quite decadent, and it makes a fine decoration now.

'Speaking about memories, I've a few good ones triggered by this sign,' Jim says, winking at me and I giggle.

'Play your cards right and I might make a few more with you later on,' I reply playfully.

It's amazing really, but after only ten minutes or so, our tree is already looking gorgeous. It's an eclectic collection, and I'm sure many would say it can't compete with perfectly themed trees that are decked out in golds, or purples or reds and whites. But this suits us, suits our family. There's something about the mix of my Disney ornaments rubbing shoulders with more elegant gold-and-black decorations, which I bought in my fancy phase, that just works.

I sigh as I take it in and can't help but think that our tree is the most beautiful in the world. End of.

Jim brings over the box that contains all of our personalised decorations. You know the ones, where you can have your names added to various themes. It started with us getting a figure of a couple on their wedding day, with our names written underneath with the date of our wedding. That was a gift from Jim's parents. I loved the idea of it and then when Bobby came into our lives, I had to get one for him. Since then, we've gotten into the habit of getting one for every child that is with us for Christmas.

When he comes to our tiny glass angel, with a gold halo above its golden hair, he pauses. It sits in the palm of his hand, tiny, as it's no more than the size of his little finger. I watch the emotions flash across his face. I know what he's thinking about and my heart contracts in mutual pain too. I walk to his side and he looks at me, pain and longing all over his face.

This decoration was bought to remember our angel baby. He places it gently beside all of the named decorations, with the names of our foster children written on them. Just beside the 'Jim & Belle' one.

An angel baby that I never got to hold in my arms, a baby I never got to kiss. But a baby that I loved from the moment I found out that I was pregnant, to the moment that she was no more. Like a thief, stealthily creeping into our house in the dead of the night, a miscarriage stole both our baby and our hearts.

Jim kisses the top of my head and we stand silently for a moment, until Lauren demands our attention.

'Put this up. I made it,' she squeals and I pull myself back to her.

Jim holds my hand as we both stop to admire her handmade cardboard Rudolph reindeer.

'Let's put that in pride of place, right at the front,' I say to her.

'Beside your bell?' she begs.

'Yes, beside our bell,' I answer. Looking at her as she flits around the room, so full of excitement and bursting with happiness, well, it's infectious.

'It's beautiful,' Jim says, when the last decoration goes up.

'This tree is a memoir of my life, you know. Each ornament holds a precious memory,' I say.

'It's beautiful and I'll never be sorry that I got to share this life with you,' Jim says.

I'm the lucky one, though, and I need to remember that. I kiss him quickly and do my best to ignore Lauren, who is pulling on my jumper.

'But we still haven't found our angel for the top of the tree yet,' Lauren moans, insistent that we give her our attention.

'I'll keep looking. It has to be up there somewhere,' Jim says. 'Angels don't just disappear into thin air.'

'Let's turn the lights on first,' I say. 'Lauren, you get to do the honours. Push this switch, right here.'

Jim puts his arm around me and I lean into him, as I've done hundreds of times over the years, placing my head in the crook of his neck. I love this man so much, my partner in crime, my best friend. And I feel bad that I've been so difficult with him these past few weeks.

'Maybe this time next year, we'll have a little crib over there,' he whispers in my ear.

He's said that to me before. Those very same words. Does he realise that? Oh God, the joy, the absolute magical joy the first time he said them.

I hold up a handful of pregnancy tests to Jim. All with two beautiful lines, confirmation of what I already know. I'm pregnant.

'It's a … you mean, you're … it means we're having a baby?' Jim stutters.

'Yes,' I smile, delighted with myself.

'It will be a girl, I just know it and she'll look just like you,' Jim says.

'You don't know that,' I say laughing, but secretly I'd love a little girl who looked like me. I've never had anyone look like me before.

'You're crying,' I say, as I see tears splashing onto the pregnancy tests in my hand.

'So are you.' He wipes my tears away with his thumb, then kisses me. I start to laugh against his lips and he joins in and we dance around the Christmas tree, hysterical with joy.

'This time next year, there'll be a crib over in that corner too,' Jim declares.

I sigh and wish that life wasn't so cruel. Because there was no crib. No baby. Just a hole into my core, so deep that I want to crawl inside it and die.

20

The story of life is quicker than the blink of an eye, the story of love is hello, goodbye.

Jimi Hendrix

December 2015

How do you explain to a six-year-old that their home is going to disappear? There are no words that can cushion that shock.

I know this to be true, because I've been that child, worn that t-shirt. I've had foster breakups so many times I could write a book on them. Everything from, 'It's not you or anything you've done,' to 'It's for the best, we're thinking of you really,' to my personal favourite, 'I'm jealous really. Starting a new life, wow, it's so exciting.'

I suppose one good thing is that I know what NOT to say. Problem is, even the lovely, caring, kind foster parents who said goodbye to me, well, they couldn't find words that made it any easier.

So here's a truth I know. Breakups are messy. No matter what age or the circumstance.

It's weird being on the other side of the equation, though. I'm the adult, I'm the one saying the goodbyes.

I've had some practice already, with children who were only with us a short while. Children, who despite their short spells with us, I loved, grieved and still miss today.

Most days one or other of them will pop into my head and I'll wonder how they're doing.

So with all that practice, why is Lauren so hard, and why does it feel so different from every other time? That's the million-dollar question, I suppose.

Because it's Lauren, that's why.

Because I've allowed myself to dream of keeping her. Forever.

Because, even though she isn't, she's *my* daughter.

Because, whenever someone says to me that she's the image of me, I burst with pride and never correct them.

Because, when she walked into our lives I think she might have saved me.

My eyes rest on our bookshelf, which is heaving with books. We've got such an eclectic collection there, everything from Harlan Coben to Claudia Carroll and Dr Seuss. And sandwiched amongst all of those is a special book. The book of us. Jim brought it home one evening shortly after we had been given our foster license, his eyes alight with excitement and promise of the future we were about to start.

'*We shall have a page for each child that we have in our home. No matter how short or long their stay, they get a spot.*'

He's such a softie, really, my man. The first page opens and there we are, Jim and I on our wedding day.

Jim Looney, the big ride. *My husband*. Love so fierce explodes in my heart that I want to reach inside the photograph and pull him towards me.

As I flick through the pages of the book of us, so many memories come back, of moments both treasured and loved. Snaps of babies I held and sang lullabies to. And then children I nursed through nightmares and sleepless nights, bugs and colds and flus. And the amount of tears I cuddled away, well, I think they could fill a lake.

I smile as I touch a photo of Bobby's cheeky face, grinning up at the camera. I always knew you were a keeper, I think, smiling back at him. There's Imelda, our truculent teen, who tested us to our limits. No smiles from her, no matter how we'd pleaded. I'd swear she was giving us the finger when we took this pic. And I'm glad that she was herself for the shot. No fake smile just for the camera. Nobody should have to do that. Ah, there's my little spiky Erin, sitting close to me. By the time she left, she had become my shadow. I still hear from her the odd time. I love that. Oh jeepers, there's the Murphy boys, all three of them. Now they were a challenge. Look at them smiling despite being covered head to toe in red chicken pox.

'That was a red-letter week,' Jim says, startling me.

'How long have you been there?' I ask, once my heartbeat goes back to normal. I feel a bit self-conscious that he was watching me.

'Only a few minutes. You know what? I often thought that if we'd had the Murphy boys as our first foster kids, we'd never have gotten beyond them. We didn't sleep for the full week, did we?' he says.

'They didn't have a square inch of their bodies that wasn't covered with spots. God help them.' I feel itchy just thinking of it.

The funniest thing was, they were only with us for a few weeks, to give their parents a break because they were going through a rough time. And Murphy's Law – ha! – they were sick for the whole time they were here. We had so many plans to spoil them, give them treats. But instead they got cold baths and Sudocrem.

When I get to the end of the photographs, I stare at the blank page that awaits its next snap. Lauren. She'll be next. Soon her face will be just another photograph memory in this book.

'I'm not sure I have the strength to let her go,' I say.

Jim crouches down beside me and rests his chin on my shoulder. 'Me neither.'

Isn't it funny how you just connect with some people more than others? It was like that with Lauren. As soon as she walked in our door, shyly behind Lorcan, I felt like I knew her already. When she took my hand that first day, she took my heart too.

And back then, when she came, I was broke. She fixed me. And I suppose I fixed her too. But no matter how hard I try to avoid it, I know that she needs her mother now. And that pain, that truth, is unbearable.

'I'm going to miss her. I love her just as much as you do, Belle. You're not going through this on your own,' Jim says.

I look up at my husband and don't doubt how hard it is for him one bit. But I'm not sure he gets how much more complicated this is for me right now.

'A number keeps going around and around my head, Jim,' I say. I've got to try help him understand how I feel.

He looks at me, eyebrows raised. 'Go on.'

'106,' I say.

'106 what?' Jim says, half a smile playing on his lips. I think he reckons we're about to play a game or something.

'Hard to believe it, but it's been 106 times that I've said goodbye to people in my life. Lauren will be the 107th,' I say.

The weight of that number lies on my shoulders. It's a lot of people. I feel weary from it all. Tess often used to moan about being bone-tired, at the end of the day, when we were kids. Well, I get that now, because every bone in my body aches. I'm bone-tired too, and I feel like I've not slept for such a long time.

'I didn't know you kept count.' He looks shocked. 'Jesus, Belle, that's a lot of goodbyes.'

He might be even more surprised if he knew that not only do I know the total number, I can break it down into different categories. Want to know how many foster parents? Or maybe you'd like to know the number of foster brothers and sisters I played happy families with? Now I get to add my own foster children to the list.

And let's not forget my mother and father, although to be fair to them, I never had to say goodbye, because they never bothered to even say hello.

So this is really just one more goodbye. I should just suck it up and get on with it. But it's the hardest one. I blink. Then I pinch myself. Stop.

'I'm worried about you,' Jim says. I look at him and see concern making lines on his face. I hate that I'm doing that.

'Are you not sick of this? The never-ending drama that is our life?' I say.

'It's not all bad is it?' He looks almost wounded at my words.

'It's not all good,' I reply, even though I know that this statement will hurt him.

'That's not fair. We have a good life here. We've got a house over our heads, we've made a difference in so many children's lives and let's not forget that we have each other,' Jim says.

'I wish you could get into my head. So you can get where I'm coming from. I love our life. I love you. But right now, it feels like it's been a never-ending saga,' I say. 'I could give any soap opera a run for its money. You couldn't make it up.'

'No one can argue that you've had it harder than most, Belle,' Jim says. 'But there's more to this. What's really going on with you?'

'I'm scared. I can't stop worrying about what happens if Alicia falls apart again. Remember Lauren when she arrived here. She had been living on nothing but cornflakes and a stale loaf of bread for God knows how long. I know what that feels like. I can't bear the thought that Lauren will ever have to go back to that. I don't know whether I want to cry or scream at that memory.'

'I get angry when I remember that too. But there's no guarantees in life. We both know that. We have to believe, though, that Alicia has got this. Plus she's got support now, she didn't have that before,' Jim replies.

'She's happy with us,' I say.

'Yes. But she can be happy with her mother too. It's what she wants,' Jim says. 'Listen, Lauren is a bright kid, she'll pick up on the fact that we are upset if we are not careful. That's not fair on her.'

I can't disagree with that.

'If I thought for one second that it wasn't the right thing for her to go home with Alicia, I'd fight all the way to the courts to keep her. But Alicia is ready. We know that. And so is Lauren. We've done a good thing here, Belle. We're sending home a lovely, happy, joyful kid to her mam, who is waiting with open arms for her,' Jim says.

I nod, as he speaks. 'Jim Looney, you're always able to talk me down off a ledge when I need it. I need to remember that part – we have done a good thing here. I'm also going to try to stop putting the ghosts of my past on Lauren's shoulders.'

'I'll always be here to talk you down. Same as you do for me. But remember, you're not on your own. Yes, you still have goodbyes to say, but you're doing them with me. And guess what? You'll never have to say goodbye to me. I promise you.' Jim takes my face in his hands and locks eyes with me.

I throw my arms around his neck and squeeze him tight.

'We will get through this, together, do you hear? What do we always say? When life gives you lemons, slice them, then toss them into a large gin and tonic,' Jim jokes.

'Let's go talk to Lauren,' I say, grabbing his hand. 'Together. Then I might need you to fix me one of those G&T's.'

We find her in the playroom, cross-legged, doing a jigsaw puzzle. Her tongue is sticking out in concentration, as it always does, as she tries to find a home for one of the pieces.

'Wow, that's a really good job,' Jim says, admiring her work so far.

'I'm very good at jigsaws,' Lauren boasts, in total seriousness and we both laugh.

'Can you leave that for a few minutes? We need a chat,' Jim says.

She jumps up and runs over to him, giving him a hug. 'Eskimo kiss.' It's her new favourite thing to do, nose-to-nose kisses with each of us. I feel my heart contract as I watch two of the people I love most in the world rub noses.

'I'm hungry,' Lauren states and forms her perfect mouth into a pout. 'Can I have a Frube?'

'No Frube, but I'll go get you a snack,' I say, moving towards the door.

'Afterwards,' Jim says, touching my arm lightly. 'We'll get you some milk and maybe even a cookie, but after our chat.'

'I like Oreos,' she informs us, her little head tilted on one side.

'I'll bear that in mind,' I say, smiling and feeling like a fraud.

I wonder if this is how all those foster parents felt when they told me I had to leave too?

This is different, though. Lauren is going to her mother, I never did that. She's done moving. This will hopefully be her last one. I look at Jim and realise that all this time, when I thought Lauren was like me, it's him she's like.

'It's been fun spending so much time with your mam, hasn't it?' I say to her, forcing myself to smile.

'She gives me Oreos too,' Lauren says. 'And she's really good at colouring in. She never goes over the lines like I do.'

'That's pretty cool,' I agree.

'How would you like to spend more time with her?' Jim asks. 'Maybe go for some sleepovers in her house?'

Her face breaks into a smile that makes my heart break in two and there's no need to guess what her answer is.

'Yes please.' She's jumping up and down, beside herself with the excitement. 'Can I go now?'

'Not today.' Jim smiles, even though his eyes look suspiciously glassy. 'How about this weekend? And if you like it, your mam would really love it if you can stay there forever. Wouldn't that be great? To live with your mam.'

'But I live here, silly.' Lauren looks at Jim, then me and laughs. 'I can't live there and here too.'

'No, you can't.' I say. I pull her into my lap and smell her unique smell and wonder where I will find the words to help her understand.

She looks from me to Jim and back again to me once more. 'I won't live here?'

'No darling, you won't. But that's a good thing. Just think how much fun you will have every day with your mam if you lived with her every single day,' Jim tells her, holding her hands between his.

'But I'm going with you to choose our tree for the hall. And I've been making a special decoration for it. It's a star,' Lauren says. 'You promised I could do that. A promise is a promise.'

'Yes, I did and you still can. We'll still do all of that but, when you get ho ...' I stop myself. This won't be her home soon, I need to start remembering that. 'When you get back here. And I bet you will be helping your mam do her decorations too. Imagine that, you'll get to do lots of Christmas tree decorating.' I can see that this idea is appealing to her and doing its intended job of halting any tears.

'Can I bring my teddy on the sleepover with me?' she asks.

'Yes of course you can. You can bring anything you want from your bedroom. Except the bed. That wouldn't fit in your suitcase,' I joke and she giggles.

'Can you come too?' She looks up at me and my body weeps with sadness.

'No honey, I can't. But Jim and I will always be here if you need us. Our door will always be open,' I whisper into her hair.

This seems to satisfy her and she sighs in contentment as she snuggles in close.

'Right, that's settled so. Only one thing left to do. Race you to the kitchen for cookies.' Jim shouts as he's halfway out the door, with Lauren chasing him, squealing in delight.

That's that then.

21

Sometimes the hardest part isn't letting go but rather learning to start over.

Nicole Sobon

Lauren left a few moments ago to spend the weekend with her mother, a trial run before she goes to live there again.

'Can we talk?' Jim asks

'I'll make us a coffee,' I tell him, putting on the kettle.

'It's harder than I thought it would be,' Jim admits. 'When we did our training, when we waited and waited for our first placement, I really thought I had it all sussed, knew what I was getting myself in for. But nothing prepares you for this, does it?'

He gets it. Relief floods my body. Thank goodness he gets it.

While my head knows that Lorcan is right, Lauren should be back with her mother, my heart screams another truth. I can be as logical as the next person when pontificating about the importance of keeping a family together, but my heart isn't ruled by logic. My heart cannot be a cheerleader for this betrayal, for this hurt.

I've been thinking about something for weeks now. I never thought I'd ever consider it, but it's in my head and won't leave. I need to tell Jim. And cheered on by his own admission a moment ago, I feel less anxious about admitting how I feel.

'I don't think I can do this any more.' There, I've said it. 'It's too painful.'

Okay, maybe he doesn't get it, because his face is a cartoon picture of shock at my admission.

'You want a break for a bit, you mean?' he asks. 'We can tell Lorcan that. Give us a few weeks at the very least to get our heads sorted.'

'I don't know.' I shrug. I want to be honest with him. I can't lie. 'I'm just so tired. We've not stopped since we did our training. First it was getting the house ready. All the visits from social workers, us jumping through hoops to make this a safe environment.'

'I hated that part too,' Jim says. 'Sometimes I wish that we were our own bosses and no one had the right to tell us where to put our bleach.'

'We chose this life, though,' I sigh.

'We did. And I love it. I thought you did too.' I can see Jim is hurt. I don't think we've ever really been on a different page. What did Tess always say about us? Two peas in a pod.

Honesty sometimes isn't the best policy, it seems, judging by the look Jim is throwing at me. I need to make him understand where I'm coming from.

'What happens next, do you think? Lorcan calls us and he has another placement. We snuggle, kiss, parent them. I can't do that without loving too. It's not in my DNA,' I say.

'Thank God for your DNA,' Jim says. 'Your capacity to love is what made me love you.'

History has a funny way of repeating itself.

Dolores's words continue to taunt me. What if that's in my DNA too? I feel like I'm losing my mind, words jumbled up inside of me, driving me to distraction.

'Do you not get tired of the lack of control, Jim? We have absolutely no say in the future of these children. Decisions are made about them and we have to just accept it.' The injustice of it all seems unbearable.

'You really thought that Lauren was ours, didn't you?' Jim says.

'Yes,' I admit and he sighs long and deep. A deep furrow has appeared in his forehead. Was that there yesterday? He walks over, closer to me.

'I'd like a forever child too you know,' Jim says. 'Maybe it's time for us to try again. It's been nearly three years now. What do you think?'

I can hardly fathom that it's been three years. To me it feels like yesterday.

'Don't go all quiet on me again, Belle. I hate it when you do that,' Jim pleads. 'We need to discuss this.'

What do you want me to say, Jim? That I think about our baby every single day. That it's a load of bollocks that time eases all pain, because three years later, I still hurt every bit as much as I did when our baby died inside of me. I couldn't even do that one simple job. Keep my baby alive.

'I need to understand what's going on in your head. Are you saying that you don't want to foster any more and you don't want to try for another baby either?' There's that edge to his voice that has been growing more and more these past few weeks.

'I don't know. I'm so sorry,' I answer and my words float up into the air, landing with a thud right in between us.

22

At one time, most of my friends could hear the bell. But as years passed, it fell silent for all of them. Even Sarah found, one Christmas, that she could no longer hear its sweet sound. Though I have grown old, the bell still rings for me. As it does for all who truly believe.

The Polar Express

You could cut the air with a knife, it's so tense. I can feel Jim's disappointment in me, seeping into every nook and cranny, sucking the joy out of Christmas. I feel like I'm letting him down. But I am powerless to change that.

I know he is biding his time to corner me, so we can have our big 'talk'. The thing is, I don't need him to sit me down or say a word for me to know exactly what he wants me to agree to.

The big, fat, grey elephant that has been sitting in the middle of our room for years is now standing up on his two rear legs and screaming for attention.

I'm so pissed off, though, I might just grab my Morphy Richards electric knife and cut up that cute bastard elephant into a million little pieces.

'Stop it,' I say to Jim and he looks up at me in surprise.

'What?' He asks, feigning innocence. He knows what, though.

'I can't be doing with all this, Jim. I know you have stuff you want to say. I can feel the unspoken words just aching to spill out of you. But today is not the day for that. This is Lauren's last weekend with us. Let's not ruin that memory for her,' I say.

'You're right,' he agrees immediately.

'So we're agreed, we park the subject for now? That means no more remarks about cribs or such,' I say to him.

'Understood,' Jim replies. We sit in silence for a few moments listening to Lauren chattering away to her 'baby', which today is a brown stuffed monkey.

'Will we watch a Christmas movie or something? We can let Lauren choose it?' Jim asks. 'Take our minds off things.'

'I'd like that.' And it does sound perfect.

Lauren agrees and after a lengthy debate on which movie to choose, she finally opts for *The Polar Express*. It's been a favourite of ours in this house, for a long time.

'How about I make some hot chocolate, before we stick it on?' Jim asks.

'With marshmallows?' Lauren is bouncing in her seat beside me, at this question.

'I'll take it that's a yes. I was thinking of doing a Jim special. Marshmallows, whipped cream and chocolate sprinkles on top,' Jim says.

'Throw in a Wispa bar and I'll love you forever,' I say.

'Done.'

'All aboard.' Tom Hanks' voice bellows out a few minutes later, and we sink back into the soft cushions on our big sofa, side by side, slurping our hot drinks.

When the train barrels onto the young boy's quiet street, in a veil of steam, we all gasp out loud. It's startling and exciting. No matter how many times I see it, I feel that same magic tickle my senses.

'She's got a nightdress like mine,' Lauren says, pointing to one of the little girls on board the train and looking down at her own one.

'That she does,' I say.

As we sip our hot chocolate, our eyes take in the wonderful sounds and colours on the screen before us. I wish it could be like this all the time.

The closer the train gets to the North Pole, the greater the excitement grows in our family room. Lauren bounces between Jim and I, and insists on giving us an ongoing narrative to the events that are unfolding on the screen.

When the train thunders through the wilderness, with rollercoaster abandon, she snuggles in close to me as this bit always scares her. I need to tell Alicia that. Lauren might seem fearless, but there are times when she freaks out.

She doesn't like ladders or heights. Yet, she'll jump into a pool without a care. She doesn't like spiders, but she thinks mice are cute. I think I'll make a list for Alicia.

For now, I'll put that to one side and concentrate on this moment. My family, together, watching a Christmas movie. When the reindeer enter the courtyard at the North Pole, prancing and pacing with silver bells ringing from their harnesses, all three of us hold our breaths in awe.

'It's the most magical sound in the whole world,' Lauren sighs. And I can't disagree.

She runs over to our Christmas tree and searches for our silver bell. When she sees it she reaches up to take it down. Even on tippy toes, though, she's too small, so Jim goes over and gives her a lift up. Her face full of bliss, she rings the bell as her little hand clasps it and in that moment, with perfect cinematic timing, Santa walks out into the courtyard to the elves and children.

'Why can't he hear the bells?' she asks, pointing to the little boy on the screen, bewildered that he cannot hear what everyone else can.

'He doesn't believe,' I say to her. 'You only hear the bells ringing if you believe in magic and in Santa Claus.'

'I believe,' she gushes, her eyes shiny. 'Do you believe, Belle?'

'Yes, I believe,' I say.

Liar, liar, pants on fire.

I used to believe, but then I realised that magic only exits in fairy tales. I wish I could go back and bottle some of that belief I had when I was ten years old.

Before the end of the last credits, Lauren's eyes have grown heavy with sleep and she sags against my shoulder. Jim picks her up into his arms and carries her to bed. The sight of my husband with a child in his arms makes me ache.

Jim is an amazing father. If ever a man was born to be a father it's him. But what if I can't give him that?

'I'm not sure you do believe any more,' Jim says to me, when he comes back to the living room. It's dark now with only the flames of the open fire dancing light onto the floorboards in front of us.

I shrug. I look to the door and yawn. I think I'll go to bed, before he pushes this further. He promised earlier he would drop the subject, but he's got a determined look on his face.

'You used to believe in magic,' he says. 'One of the things I loved most about you as a kid was your unwavering belief that happy-ever-afters do happen.'

That feels like a lifetime away to me.

'You made a believer of me back then too,' Jim says.

'I reckon that Tess was closer to the mark back then. She always said that there was no such thing as fairy tales,' I reply.

'Nope, I don't agree. I'm positive that we have a happy-ever-after coming. I can almost touch it, it's that close,' Jim says. 'We just have to be brave enough to go chase it.'

'Maybe this is our happy-ever-after already. We got married. We've fostered. Can that be enough for you, for us?' I say.

'It's everything. And if this is as good as it gets, that's fine with me. It's more than most get,' Jim says. 'But I think that there's another ending meant for us. I think that we are going to have a baby of our own.'

We are just so far apart on this subject, it's not even funny. Has Jim not even considered the risks?

'What did that hobo say on top of the train?' I ask Jim. 'In the movie, *The Polar Express*.'

'I can't remember,' he says, looking confused by the change in the subject.

'Seeing is believing. That's what he said to the little boy. Seeing is believing. Well, when I think about us having a baby, all I *see* is that day in the hospital. And that's kind of sucked any magical belief right out of me,' I say.

'It doesn't have to be like that again,' Jim says.

'I'm not strong enough to take that risk. I can't put myself through that again. I wouldn't survive it,' I say.

'I never took you for a coward,' he says.

He doesn't understand. I sigh. 'I'm tired. I'm going to bed.'

Jim gets up and starts to pace around the room and throws a look at me that is both wounded and full of accusation.

'That's right, go to bed. Run away from a real conversation,' Jim explodes.

'I am tired,' I say. Now I'm the one throwing wounded looks.

'Well before you go, let me respond to your accusation,' Jim says.

I don't know what he's talking about for a minute. What have I accused him of?

'So I don't understand, do I?' he demands.

Oh, that accusation.

'Yeah, you're right, what would I know about any of this? I was only the father.' He pauses for breath, then continues. It's as if an avalanche is rolling down a mountain side at breakneck speed, and his words tumble out between us.

'Every time someone said to us, "It wasn't meant to be" or "It was for the best", do you know what I was thinking?' His voice rises with every word.

I shake my head in response, my body tense with fear, with horror.

Jim continues, 'I was thinking "you asshole" or sometimes even "shut the fuck up", that's what I was thinking.

But of course I never said that. I smiled and thanked all the well-wishers for their kind words.'

It occurs to me that both of us don't always say what we are thinking on this painful subject. I feel shame, that maybe I've been so wrapped up in my own grief, I've not asked Jim about his. When did I get so self-centred?

'I was so focused on your pain, I'd bite back my anger at the world,' Jim says.

I move to touch his arm, my heart aches for my husband. He looks broken. But he's moving too fast for me, continuing to pace around the room.

'I used to get nightmares, you know. You're not the only one. Not as much any more, but that first year, they were a regular enough occurrence,' he says.

'You never said,' I say and I'm ashamed that I never knew. Should I have noticed? Yes, I bloody well should have.

'I didn't want to burden you, Belle. You had enough going on, dealing with your own grief. But now, looking back from this particular vantage point of hindsight, maybe I was wrong. Maybe I should have been more vocal, so you would understand now, that I KNOW what it's like to be scared. Truth be told, I'm shit scared, but I still think it's worth the risk to at least try. I believe that we can do this,' Jim says.

Finally he stops pacing and he sits down on the couch.

We sit in silence for a long time, both locked in our own world of pain.

'Do you ever think about what it would be like if our baby had lived?' I ask.

Jim nods. 'All the time. I sometimes think that in a parallel universe, we've got a three-year-old now. She will be starting playschool in September. She's wilful like her mother, and kind and funny and beautiful too. Just like her mother,' he says.

'What did we call her in this other universe?' I whisper.

'Rose,' he says. 'After my grandmother.'

'I like that name,' I say. 'I thought I was the only one to do that. Think about the milestones, I mean,' I say in surprise.

I inch my bum closer to him on the couch. I touch his hair on his forehead and stroke it, pushing it back in a gesture that is as old as we are.

'We are good at this,' Jim says.

'At what?' I ask.

'Parenting. Just think about it. We've worked our way through every single possible age and stage of a child, from new-born to stroppy teen and all in between. We have this sussed.' He chances a wink as she says this last bit.

'We're not too shabby, I suppose.' I agree, nudging his shoulder with my own. 'Except for that time we lost Erin in Tesco.'

'That child was like a ninja. We should have chipped her, she was forever running off. But, losing children aside, we have a lot we can offer a child. You have to admit that,' he says.

I nod.

'I just want to try one more time. If it doesn't happen, then at least we'll know we tried,' Jim says. 'Will you think about it?'

'I think about little else these days,' I say.

His face changes and the young, cheeky Jim I'm used to disappears. He looks older and weary. I've done that. I've made him frown and fret and now he has aged. Right in front of my eyes.

'Please Belle,' he begs.

I want to say to him, come on, right now, let's do it. But I can't. I'm stuck in this goddamn no man's land called fear.

Fear of what might happen if I don't get pregnant. Fear of what could happen if I do get pregnant and if I lose a baby again. Fear that I'm my mother's daughter and that I'd be the third generation to wish their child had never been born.

I wish I could just brush it aside. I wish I could banish the thoughts that I know are irrational. But I'm paralysed with fear and they have taken root and are growing like weeds in my head.

I walk over to him and hold him close, wishing that things could be different. 'I'm so sorry I wasn't there for you, when you needed me.'

'You were. Every day, being with you, loving you, being loved by you, well that's what got me through it,' Jim replies.

'I love you, Jim. Always know that.'

23

There are no goodbyes for us. Where ever you are, you will always be in my heart.

Mahatma Gandhi.

I stand at the foot of our driveway. My smile feels manic, I wonder, does it look that way to everyone else? I am waving so hard, my shoulder aches in protest, but I welcome the pain. I can feel Jim's breath on the back of my neck and hear his chest heaving as he breathes in deep and long.

This day that has been thundering towards us at break-neck speed is now here. I'm not ready for it, not one little bit.

My sadness is only matched by her happiness.

That's what Tess said before. This thought, I cling to like a life raft, with both my hands. It anchors me. It allows me to smile and wave, even though my heart has a deep chasm running through it.

Lauren twists in her car seat to get a better vantage of Jim and me. She waves back and is smiling. I've been checking all morning and there's no doubt, it reaches all the way to her eyes. That makes me happy. That is all that matters.

'It's the hardest part. Saying goodbye,' Jim says.

'For us, but not for Lauren. She's saying hello to a new life. There's a difference.' I close my eyes and a number flashes in my mind, making me dizzy.

107.

I'm done.

24

Giving up is the only sure way to fail.

Gena Showalter

December 2015

'I can't do this any more, Belle. You've not said a word for days since Lauren left. I miss her too,' Jim says.

'I'm sorry,' I mumble and wonder how the hell he puts up with me. I wouldn't if I was him.

'You don't have to apologise. I'm not looking for that. I'll even go as far as to say that I get it. I understand. But please remember that I'm still here and you are cutting me out. I miss you. I miss us,' Jim says. 'I think we need some time off. Some fun.'

I look at him and wish I could find words to make things alright. He doesn't deserve this.

'We could go get our tree for the hall? We haven't done that yet and it feels bare out there,' he suggests. 'Then we could go out tonight. For a drink or something to eat?' My husband is trying so hard, the least I can do is try to look enthusiastic.

'That sounds wonderful,' I say and when he smiles, I vow to find a way to get out of this funk I feel myself in. I've put off doing the real tree, only because Lauren is gone.

I'm worrying a lot of people right now and it's not on. Tess was over last night. The troops have been called in to rally around me. I heard them both whispering in the hall. They need to work on their technique, because I could hear every word uttered.

Maybe Jim is right, I do need to forget about everything for a while, have some fun.

'Give me five minutes to freshen up, then let's go get that tree,' I say.

'Dress up warm. It's freezing out there,' Jim says.

When I come back down a few minutes later, I find him in the hall and he's wearing his Dr Who scarf again. Jim Looney, the big ride.

'You wore that the first time you ever kissed me,' I say.

'Why do you think I've kept it all these years?' He asks. 'I'm hoping, that maybe, before the end of today, I'll be getting another snog, courtesy of the magic of this beauty.'

I run over and kiss him lightly on the lips and we both giggle like teenagers as we jump into his car, sticking our wellies in the boot. It gets mucky on the trails on the farm. I switch on Christmas FM, my favourite channel, dedicated to carols and festive songs. It's the perfect accompaniment to our journey. We both can't help but sing along and I realise that it's impossible to stay in a bad mood when belting out *I Wish It Could Be Christmas Every Day*. I glance at Jim and he's grinning away too.

It's busy at the farm, at least another dozen or so cars are queuing to go in the gates. I can feel a bubble of excitement begin to form. I love this annual tradition.

'So are we going to go pre-cut, or do I bring my hacksaw?' Jim asks.

'Do you really need an answer for that?' I ask, raising my eyebrows, pulling the hacksaw from the boot.

He laughs and says, 'Come on my little lumberjack, let's go get our tree.'

We start to patrol the rows of trees, one after the other, touching and feeling them as we walk by. Having done this very same thing for years, we both know what we are looking for. We want a green, full, lush tree. Around the six-foot mark, although we can go a little higher if we need to.

'Isn't there something about the smell, the look of these beauties that is just so … traditional?'

'Hmm … Hey, what about this one?' Jim shouts from the middle of a cluster of trees. 'Traditional enough for you?'

'Nice but not quite right. It's too pointy. Let's keep looking.'

'Ah, here, look at this. Now this is what I'm talking about,' Jim says, standing in front of a huge tree.

'That's mahoosive. Won't fit in the hall,' I say, pulling out my tape measure from my coat pocket. I quickly measure it and confirm that it's close to seven feet. 'Remember our first year choosing a tree?'

'It was like the chainsaw massacre by the time we'd finished trimming that beast,' Jim jokes. 'I thought we'd never fit it in. Fair enough, onwards we go.'

'Look Jim,' I say, pointing with excitement to a tree to the left of us. 'It's perfect.' I run over and sniff it. Jim lifts the branches and taps on the silver bark of the trunk in a knowing manner. I *know* he hasn't a breeze why he does this, but he saw someone else do it the first year we were tree-hunting.

As I measure the tree, which is bang on the head six feet tall, Jim declares, 'We have a winner here.'

He gets on the ground and starts to cut it down. 'Go on, say it, I know you want to,' I tease him.

Like a kid, he looks up at me and says, 'What did one lumberjack say to the other?'

'I don't know, what did he say?' I answer, giggling, even though I know the answer.

'I don't know either. Why don't you axe the tree?' He explodes into laughter at his lame joke.

'Every year …' I laugh.

'I'm nothing but consistent. And every year you laugh,' he replies and then, again as he always does when the tree falls, 'Timber.'

Delighted with ourselves, we head back to pay for our tree and bring it home.

'Hungry?' he asks.

I realise that, for the first time in days, I'm ravenous. 'Like I've never been before.'

'Me too. Let's stop on the way home and then we can have a drink when we get home,' he says.

We find a pub within a few minutes, a bit off the main road. It's small and has a large open fire in the centre of it. It's also full, with lots of people like ourselves looking for a late lunch.

We sit in silence for a few minutes, just enjoying the atmosphere. It's noisy, but not overly so that it interferes with us chatting.

'This was a good idea,' I say to Jim when our food comes out. Being in a new environment, away from home and our usual surroundings, is good for us. 'I wish we didn't have to go home,' I sigh looking around me.

Jim jumps up. 'Back in a second.'

Ten minutes later, he's back with a pint in one hand and a gin and tonic in the other.

'Drinking this early?' I say, feigning mock outrage.

'Ah it's five o'clock somewhere,' he jokes.

What is my husband up to?

'You said you didn't want to leave here. Well, I can't make that happen, but we can play hooky for a night anyhow. They do B&B here. I've booked us a room. We're having a few well-earned drinks,' he says.

'You genius,' I declare and lean forward to kiss him firmly on the lips.

'I do try,' he smiles back. 'Seriously, we work hard. Let's just have some fun for the afternoon and evening.'

25

The mind replays what the heart can't delete.

Unknown.

'Look at you rocking your bump.' Our midwife Shelly says, smiling at my long-sleeved t-shirt. It has an arrow pointing down towards my ever-growing belly.

I never thought I'd be the type of pregnant woman who wore slogan t-shirts. But I can't get enough of them. My favourite is a thought bubble saying, 'I'm related to these people, I'm not coming out.'

'Jim got it for me.' I smile at my husband, who has a big goofy smile on his face. Today we find out whether we are having a boy or girl. It's our big scan, twenty weeks, so we're halfway through our pregnancy.

'Feeling well?' Shelly asks as she lifts my top and squeezes the cold gel over my belly again.

'Wonderful,' I reply. 'If you put aside the heartburn, constant dashing to the loo and being liable to fall asleep at the drop of a hat.'

'Spare a thought for me, Shelly. I'm the one who has to keep doing mad dashes to the all-night garage, because herself

245

has a longing on her for trifle. Or Fanta orange. And last night, she decided at quarter to twelve, midnight mind you, that she simply had to have mashed potato,' Jim complains.

But he's smiling and I know he loves pandering to my every whim. I feel cherished and loved and special.

Shelly laughs along and then gets to work running the ultrasound over my tummy. We stop laughing and are silent, anxious to see our little baby again. Jim clasps my hand and we both hold our breaths. The expectation of hearing that glorious duh dum duh dum of the heartbeat once again is intense.

Why is it so quiet, though? It feels different to the last time. I look at Jim, but he's smiling. I feel every nerve in my body stretch in worry.

Shelly reaches up and turns the machine off and on again, like a troublesome TV.

'Modern technology,' Jim quips. But his voice sounds strange. Strangled. The smile is still on his face, but it's not in his eyes any more.

It's too quiet. I have an urge to run out of the room, blue goop all over my tummy and keep running till I fall down.

The silence in the room grows louder. Shelly keeps searching my tummy, pushing the wand in firm swipes. Now there's only the sound of static from the machine.

'I'm just going to get the doctor to double-check something for me,' she says.

'Is there something wrong?' Jim asks.

'I'll be right back,' she replies, and avoids eye contact as she leaves the room.

I look down at the blue gloopy gel smeared all over my tummy. It doesn't feel cold any more. We sit in silence, neither of us able to voice our fears. I look back up to the screen again and reach my hand to touch the baby that is still on the screen.

You're just sleeping, my little baba. Just having a little rest, and you're not in the mood to perform for your parents. That's okay. But it's time to wake up now, little one. You're giving mummy and daddy quite the fright here.

I bolt upright, my body sheathed in sweat.

'Nightmare. Just a nightmare,' I say to Jim, who's looking at me, concern all over his face.

'Same one, about the fire?' he asks.

'No. Not this time,' I answer and wipe away a tear that has escaped.

I stand up to go to the bathroom and stub my toe on the side of the bedside locker.

'Son of a ...' I yelp in pain.

'What time is it anyhow?' Jim asks, reaching for the phone. 'Ten a.m. Wow, we better get a move on, think check out is ten-thirty. God my head hurts, think I may have overdone it on the pints.'

'Good night, though,' I say to him, leaning in to give him a little peck. 'I needed it. Thank you.'

Twenty minutes later, we're in the car and on our way. 'Once we get home, I'll light the fire, make you a big dirty fry and we can put on one of them box sets we've been meaning to tackle,' Jim says.

'I love the sound of that. We should do it more often. Just us two, have some fun,' I say.

'Me too,' Jim replies. 'We don't know what's around the corner for us …'

He looks so longingly at me. I try to stifle a sigh. I don't want to discuss this, I don't want a row, I don't want to lose the happy feeling we have right now.

But Jim is on another page and wants to talk, it appears. 'For God's sake, Belle. Just say something,' he says and I feel like something is unravelling in my head.

I keep my voice low and calm, even though I don't feel that way. 'Do we have to do this right now?' I ask.

'We're just talking, where's the harm in that?' Jim says.

'No harm. Except I have told you over and over that I can't do this any more, but you keep ignoring me and pick, pick, picking at me. Have another baby. Foster another child. Stop crying over Lauren. Pick, pick, pick,' I say.

'That's not fair.' Jim holds up his hand as if to fend off the nasty words that are coming from my mouth. And I know that I'm being unfair in many ways. But none of this situation is fair as far as I'm concerned.

Maybe if he feels a fraction of how I feel, he'll get the fact that I just want to leave this subject alone.

'Have you any idea how sick I am of listening to your voice, go on and on at me? I was the one who felt the life inside of me die. I felt that. Not you,' I say.

When I see his face crumple in pain, I know I've gone too far.

'I had to watch you go through that hell, completely helpless. Don't you dare say I didn't feel that,' he shouts back, taking his eyes off the road. 'I've told you what it's like for me. Don't you ever listen to a word I say?'

'If you felt it like I did, you wouldn't ask me to go through it again,' I scream.

'I hate this, Belle. Fighting over something that should be a good thing. A baby, for fuck's sake,' Jim says.

'We had a baby. But she died. She didn't wake up, Jim. I had one job to keep her safe and I couldn't even do that. Maybe I'm not so different from Dolores after all,' I say. I don't feel like fighting any more.

'Don't say that. You are nothing like *her*. It was nobody's fault. Just one of those things,' Jim says.

How many times have I heard that? Yet why can't I seem to believe it? I can't shift the feeling of shame and guilt that somehow or other, all of this is my fault.

'You can't keep doing this to yourself,' Jim says. The fight is gone from him too. I see only love in his eyes and concern.

'I don't know how to stop,' I say. It feels a bit like our Christmas tree falling. Unstoppable once it begins to topple. I know that I have been unreasonable and cruel to Jim. He has been patient when time after time I've said to him, not now.

'So you won't even consider trying again?' He sounds weary now too.

'I don't think I can,' I say and watch something close down in my husband's face.

'I give up,' Jim says and puts his foot down to accelerate.

I switch on the car radio, to fill the deafening silence that engulfs us. Jim refuses to look at me, staring at the twisting country road in front of us. I start to reach for his arm, to tell him I'm sorry, but I stop.

Frank Sinatra starts to croon in the background – *I'll Be Home for Christmas*. I choke back a sob, remembering so many other times I've heard this song with Jim, evoking only happiness and joy, not the sadness that fills the car now.

You can count on me … As Frank sings this line, Jim turns to look at me with such disappointment embedded into every inch of his face, I flinch.

I've never felt more alone in my life and that's saying something.

But then, the car starts to spin. I scream Jim's name. I hear him curse as he grapples the steering wheel. We bounce across the road and hit the edge of the ditch and for a moment I think Jim has regained control, turning onto the road again.

Tires screech on the wet gravel and I have never been so scared in my life.

'Jim …' I scream as we spin a full 360 and hurtle towards the ditch, headlong into a large tree.

This cannot be how it ends for us. We have so much more to do …

26

You are my person. You will always be my person.
Christina, Grey's Anatomy

Where am I? I look around, trying to get my bearings.

Car … crash. We've crashed the car. Jim … But I can't speak, I can't find my voice.

I push down the airbag and turn to my right, holding my breath. Let Jim be okay. Let him be okay. His face is covered in blood, his eyes are closed and a tree is lying awkwardly between us, part of it on his shoulder.

What the? A tree? And then I realise. It's our Christmas tree. The nose of it is through the front window of our car and splintered glass is everywhere. I look down at my hands and see cuts and red blood dripping and it's that sight that sends sound to my windpipe.

'Jim …' I sob. 'Jim.'

I scrabble to take my seat belt off and lean towards him, pushing the tree back into the rear of our car. The car is filled with smoke and smells like gunpowder. I have to get us out of here, now.

My eyes sting and my head hurts. I think I've banged

it on the window. But I know I don't have the luxury of even thinking about my own injuries. I have to get help for Jim. He's so silent, but I can hear his breathing. I can hear him … that means he's alive.

I try to get my bearings, but it's difficult in the smoke. I peer through the window and see green leaves and the trunk of a tree. The front of our car seems to have disappeared, crunched up like an accordion.

I'm afraid to touch Jim, but every part of me wants to climb on top of him, kiss him, hold him, make him wake up. But I feel numb and more scared than I've ever been in my life.

'I can't lose you, Jim,' I sob. Damn it to hell, Belle, don't you fall apart now. You have to get help. You've got to get Jim out of here.

Don't let this be number 108. Please God, please don't let it be that.

I can't open the doors, they're jammed shut, buckled from the impact. I climb into the back of the car, over the blasted Christmas tree and try the right back door. It moves open an inch, but no more. So I inch my way over to the left back door, but that won't budge at all.

Where's my phone? I'll call for help. I try to think where I had it last. Probably on the dashboard. We both tend to leave our phones there. I climb back into the front of the car, careful not to jar Jim. He looks pale, worse than before and I'm not sure if I'm imagining it or not, but there seems to be more blood. I pull off my sweatshirt and use it to mop up the blood as gently as I can. Then

I crawl onto the floor the car and with my hands start searching for the phone. I can't believe my luck when, within seconds, my hand rests on it.

But that luck is dashed quickly when I realise we have no signal here. We're on a small country road in the middle of the Wicklow mountains. Rural, with little cell coverage. I climb back to the rear of the car and lie on my back and with all my might start to kick the right door.

I kick and kick and kick with all my might and it opens a little further each time. 'Jim, hold on, I'm getting us out of here.' I wipe sweat, tears and snot from my face and push my legs hard against the door with all my might.

'Hello, are you okay?' I hear a voice shout.

'Help. Help us please.' I scream back to the man's voice.

Then I see him, through the window and he pulls the door as I continue to push with my legs. And between us we get it open.

'Call an ambulance.' I beg. 'My husband is hurt.'

'I've already done that. It's on its way, love. I saw the accident happen, I was behind you. I rang for help straight away,' the man says. He holds his hand towards me, 'Come on, let me get you out of the car at least.'

'I'm not leaving Jim,' I say, and I must have sounded firm, because he doesn't argue with me, just takes his phone out to check where the ambulance is.

Within a few minutes, I hear the siren in the distance. There's a lot more blood on Jim's head and no matter how many times I wipe it away, more appears. By the time the paramedics appear at the door, I am hysterical. I try to hold it together, but I cannot stop the tears. My body is shaking and trembling.

A lady, who tells me her name is Jacinta, leads me gently from the car and assures me that her colleagues will take good care of Jim. But I don't believe her. A blanket is placed around my shoulders and she examines me, declaring that I'm very lucky to have escaped with a few scratches and bruises.

I'm not sure how long it is, but I'm pretty sure it's not more than five minutes, and Jim is taken out of the car, carefully put on a stretcher, camed towards the ambulance.

'Belle, let's get you inside,' Jacinta's voice says, with kindness. I move into a seat in the ambulance and allow my eyes to once more lock with Jim's. And then as the sirens start again, he opens his eyes. 'Belle,' he croaks and I sob as I clasp his hand between mine.

'He's had a bad head injury. Let him rest,' Jacinta tells me.

I nod but I lean down close to him and whisper, 'I'm so sorry, my darling.'

He opens his eyes a fraction, but the effort seems too much for him. I lean in again, 'Don't worry about a thing. You just need to rest up, Jim Looney, do you hear? For once do as I ask, okay? We'll have the rest of our lives to talk, okay?'

He squeezes my hand and I feel elated. If he can do that, it must be a good sign. I turn to Jacinta.

'Will he be okay?' I ask. 'He's all I've got …'

'Let's just get him to hospital as quickly as we can and we'll let the doctors sort him out. Right now, he's stable. But he's lost a lot of blood,' she says.

The sirens continue to blare and the lights flash through the back window. The last time I was in an ambulance, I was four years old. Taken from my home, from my mother who didn't love me enough to stay home, from a fire that almost killed me.

This cannot be how it all ends. Alone, losing the person I love most in this world.

I look down at Jim and whisper to him. 'No regrets?'

But he doesn't answer me.

'You need to go home, Mrs Looney, get some sleep.' The nurse tells me and I shake my head no.

'It's late. At least go home and get changed, have a shower. We'll call you if anything changes. You've been here for twenty-four hours now,' she continues.

I look down at my clothes, blood-stained and dirty. A hot shower sounds good. Both Tess and Bobby have been here, but I sent them home late last night. The nurses were kind enough to let me sleep here, but not surprisingly rest eluded me. Every sound in the hospital is exemplified in here. Jim has woken once or twice, but only for a moment. Yet, each time, I know that he's looked for me.

'Please, Mrs Looney. Just go for a few hours,' she repeats again. What was her name? That's right, Annette Hoyne. She's a nice woman.

I stand up and my body aches like I've been hit by a … I smile as I realise what I was thinking. Like I've been hit by a tree head-on. I have pains in places I never thought it was possible. My shoulders and neck, in particular, feel tender and I can only move in slow motion. 'Okay, I'll go home for a little bit. But you better call me if Jim awakes.'

I grab a taxi and as it's early. We're home in ten minutes. It feels weird walking in our front door. The Christmas wreath usually makes me smile, but now it seems all wrong. It's too cheery and full of Christmas joy and that's inappropriate when Jim is in hospital.

I go upstairs and strip off my clothes, leaving them in a puddle at my feet. I'm not even going to wash them, they're going in the bin. I'll never be able to wear them again without thinking about our crash.

The hot water scalds my body but I welcome it, turning it on full power, so that it pummels my aching bones. The nurse was right. I needed this. I stay in the shower and try to close my mind off to anything but how the water feels on my body.

Once I'm dressed in jeans and a t-shirt, I stand in our bedroom but seeing Jim's book, turned on its face, half-read, makes my knees buckle. What if he never gets to finish it? I sink to the floor and allow myself to cry. As the sobs rack my body, I give in to them and with every tear I plead with whatever gods are listening, to let Jim finish that book, finish his life with me.

'Don't take him away from me … please … I need him,' I sob out loud. The need to touch him, to be with him is all-consuming and I know I have to get back to the hospital immediately. Wiping the tears from my face, I walk over to our wardrobe to hunt down a sweatshirt. I'll wear one of Jim's. And I know the very one. A grey hoodie that he wore a lot the year we met. He doesn't wear it often now, so where did he put it? I pull a chair over to our built-in wardrobes and reach up on the highest shelf, fumbling with the piles of unworn old jumpers and sweatshirts that I've been meaning to give to charity for years. Ah, there it is. I spy it at the back. Reaching in, my hand touches a box.

My shoe box of memories.

I know I should ignore it. I know that, right now, I have no business opening it up and revisiting the ghosts that it contains. But it's as if my hand has a mind of its own. I can't control it. I reach in, holding my breath, and see my mother's letter. My eyes scan the words, as they've done hundreds of times. And when I get to the final paragraph, my heart splinters into a million pieces, as it always does.

You fucked up my life good and proper. End of. And look where I am today? This is all on you.

I wish you had never been born.

This is all my fault. If we hadn't been arguing, if I had just stopped being so wrapped up in myself for one minute he would never have been distracted.

Maybe Dolores is right. It would it be better for everyone if I was never born. I know he would never say it, even think it, I know he loves me, but would his life be different without me in it?

Folding the letter up, I stuff it into the back pocket of my jeans and walk downstairs, Dolores' words bouncing around in my head. I stand in our living room and look around at our decorations. And in the same way as when

I walked in our front door, they seem so wrong. They mock me with their bright, festive colours of celebration.

What on earth have I got to celebrate this year? I'm here, on my own, no child, no Lauren and I can't bear to even contemplate it, but what if there's no Jim … I feel anger sweep through my body. Adrenalin hides my aches and pains and so I welcome the red mist and allow it to completely take over.

Like a woman possessed, I start running around the sitting room, grabbing decorations and throwing them into a pile in the middle of the floor.

'Christmas is cancelled,' I scream and run at the tree and, with all my might, push it until it topples over and lands in a heap.

Baubles and decorations fall and the silver bell silently rolls towards my feet.

27

One day your life will flash before your eyes. Make sure it's worth watching.

Unknown

Mater Hospital, Dublin

'I'm so sorry, Jim.' I brush back his wavy hair from his forehead and apologise once again. He must be sick of me saying it. I'm careful to not hit the tubes that are coming from his nose and mouth. A large bloody gash has been stitched together with white tape under his eye. A dark bruise is already tainting his pale skin. His arm has been strapped to his body and, if that wasn't enough, he has several broken ribs to contend with too.

The room is quiet, but I can hear footsteps, chatter, trollies rolling outside in the corridor. Jim sleeps through all of this. The nurse says the drugs have taken good effect, knocking him unconscious.

I did this.

'If I could switch places,' I say. And I mean it. I would die for him. I wonder, does he know that?

Annette, the nurse, comes in and checks his stats. She takes his pulse and scribbles down the details on his chart. Then deftly changes the saline bag on the drip for a new one.

'He'll be out cold for some time,' she says to me. 'You get on home.'

I shake my head and think about the massacre of our Christmas decorations from my last trip home. Probably safer if I stay put.

'Is there anyone I can call for you?' she asks and I smile my thanks.

I look at my phone and think about calling his parents in the US. I've been putting it off, but now it's the middle of the night over there. They'll be fast sleep. Better wait until the morning. Tess and Bobby have been in already and worry was etched on both their faces. Maybe I'll call Tess and ask her to come in again. The company would be nice and she could be here in minutes.

Before I have a chance to consider any more phone calls, the machines start to beep. The room swells in indignation at the intrusion. And then Jim starts to react to whatever is causing the beeps. He thrashes on the bed. I scream for help and start searching for the help button.

I run to the door to scream for help again, but before I reach it, the door opens. Two nurses run in.

'Move aside.' One of them pushes me away and I call his name, over and over, Jim, Jim, I'm here.

'Wait outside.' The nurse says to me, 'Let us do our job, Mrs Looney.'

This can't be happening. I can't lose my husband. I won't survive it.

I feel like a pressure cooker about to explode. I look at the door and back to Jim, who is being held down as they inject something into him.

You fucked up my life good and proper. End of. And look where I am today? This is all on you.

I wish you had never been born.

Stop it. I can't do this any more. Stop. Please make it stop.

I start to run, down the white sterile corridor, away from the pain. I run away from the noise of the machines and I run away from my husband.

'Hey watch it!' A man shouts as I knock into his shoulder.

'I'm sorry.' I cry as I pass, but I don't stop. I keep running, faster and faster. I don't pause even when I reach the front entrance, just fly out of the sliding doors, onto the street.

A blast of cold, icy air hits my face, but it's not going to stop me either. I continue my mad dash, without any thought to where or what I am running to. I just need to escape. I navigate the front steps by jumping over them, two by two and then I'm on the street. I pass the ambulances, the cars, the red-brick houses and the many people who are going about their business, wondering who the mad woman is running for dear life.

If I keep running, if I don't stop, then Jim will be okay. A madness has overtaken me and every time my feet pound on the footpath, I pray that Jim doesn't die. Let him live.

It should be me in there, not him. He doesn't deserve this.

You're losing it, a voice pops up into my head. Maybe.

I look up and see that I'm on O'Connell Street. The avenue of trees that line the street are alight with Christmas fairy lights. I pass by groups of people, dressed in bright, ridiculous jumpers with reindeers and Santa Clauses emblazoned across their chests.

'What's the big hurry, love?' A taxi driver asks as I run past. 'Want a lift?'

I dodge in and out of Christmas shoppers, arms laden down with bags of presents and run till my lungs sting with the exertion.

I run until I can run no more, until the pain of my bruises hurt so bad that my body feels like it's on fire. But this is what I want. The pain is a blessed relief from the pain of guilt that floods my being.

I wish you had never been born.

I look up, wondering where I've ended up now that I am spent. Of course I'm at the foot of the Ha'penny Bridge, right back to the beginning of Jim and me. The Looneys. The lights that adorn the pretty bridge bounce light onto the river below. Panting from exhaustion, I walk onto the bridge and lean over the side, looking down into the black abyss.

I should have gotten rid of you when I could. My life would have been so much better if you had never been in it.

I've spent years trying to forget those damning cruel words from Dolores. Maybe, though, it's me who has gotten it all wrong. What if Dolores is right?

If I'd never have been born, Jim would be in America, living a good life with his mam and dad. His own family.

He could have the forever child he so desperately wants. He wouldn't be lying in a hospital room fighting for his life.

I wish you had never been born.

Cold wind whips my hair into a fever around my face. It stings my eyes and tears of cold, of pain, of loss blur my vision. I look upwards to the grey-marbled sky.

Time stands still and it's just me and that angry sky. I look down towards the brown waters of the Liffey below me. I just need to climb over and let go.

The colours in the water change, they no longer look murky, but ice blue. I feel myself move towards the edge, raising my legs to climb the railings. The calm water whispers to me. They whisper that it's time. It's time to just let go.

I close my eyes to everything and feel calmer than I've felt in my whole life.

'It's really cold up here.' A voice shatters that momentary peace and I look away from the water, back down to the bridge, startled. A young girl, no more than eleven or twelve, is looking up at me, smiling. I ignore her and contemplate my next move.

I wish you had never been born.

I look back towards the river.

'I'm cold. Are you?' The child continues, persistent. I turn around and look at her. She does look cold.

'Where are your parents?' I say, looking up and down the bridge. But there are no likely candidates.

She shivers again, and her face looks a little blue. Oh for goodness sake. I heave myself back from the railing and jump, but to the bridge below me.

'Here.' I say, as I pull my scarf off and wrap it around her neck.

'That might help,' I say. 'Come on, where are your parents?'

The bridge is still empty bar us. I look to my right and left and can see nobody searching for a missing child. It's late for a young girl to be out and about on her own. Something doesn't seem right.

'I like it here,' she answers me. 'It's one of the prettiest bridges in Dublin, I think. I come here to listen to the music a lot. Can you hear it?'

And as if by magic, like she's conjured it up, I can hear carol singers' voices drift up towards us. They are coming from Dame Street by the sounds of it. And they are giving a rousing rendition of *Good King Wenceslas*.

'I like that song, but it's not my favourite. I love *O Holy Night* the most,' she tells me.

'That's my favourite too.' I say, looking at her a little closer. What is it about this girl that reminds me so much of someone? Is she from around Artane? Does she go to school with Lauren, I wonder. I've definitely seen her before.

'How old are you?' I ask her.

'How old do I look?' she replies.

I've dealt with enough children in my care, to know when someone is dodging my questions. But still she just smiles at me, like a little, irritating Mona Lisa.

'At a guess, eleven,' I say. But going on thirty, I think.

'Oh I'm much older than that,' she replies, beaming at me now.

'Do your parents know where you are?' I say, the niggly feeling that I've seen her before takes root now.

'I don't have any parents,' she answers. And for a moment, her smile vanishes and a sadness surrounds her whole body.

'Everyone has parents,' I reply, gently.

'You know that's not true,' she says and the bloody smile is back again. It's like she's in on a joke, that's so obvious, I should get it too.

'Okay, I'll buy that. But who looks after you? Foster parents, family?' I ask

'I have lots of people taking excellent care of me,' she smiles.

She does look well looked-after, there's no doubt about that. Her coat is immaculate, her hair shiny and cut into a blunt bob, rosy cheeks, that are not malnourished in the slightest.

'Why were you running so fast earlier?' she asks. 'Were you running away?'

'Yes, I think I was,' I reply. Now we're reaching some common ground. Maybe she's a runaway too.

'And why were you up on the railings?' she continues to probe. 'It's not safe up there.'

I flush at the question and feel shame that I almost jumped into the cold water below, in a moment of pure helplessness and desolation.

'What's your name?' I ask her, deciding to ignore her question. I can't answer it when I don't know how to answer it myself.

'Nora,' she replies, smiling, like she's not got a care in the world.

'That's pretty. You don't hear that name very often any more,' I say.

'It was very popular when I was born,' she answers.

'Do you have a second name?' I ask.

'Nope. A long time ago, yes, but I don't use it any more. Nora works just fine for me.'

I realise the person who would know what to do in this situation is Jim. I need to get back to him. I've done some stupid things in my time, but running from the man I love takes the biscuit.

The sound of the machines' beeping jumps back into my already full head and I shudder as I think about what is facing me back at the hospital.

I need to get back there immediately, but I can't leave this young girl on her own. I might not be able to take responsibility for her right now but I know someone who can and will. Lorcan. He'll know what to do with a runaway. If I can get him to meet me at the hospital, I can hand the problem of this slightly annoying young girl called Nora over to him.

'Listen, Nora. I've got to get back to my husband. He's been in an accident and is in hospital,' I say. I don't want to worry her, but she seems unfazed by my news.

'I've got a friend, his name is Lorcan and he works with lots of boys and girls, just like you. I know he can help us find whoever takes care of you,' I say.

I wish she'd stop staring at me like I'm an imbecile. I hit redial to pull up the recent calls I've made. That's weird.

It's blank. I know for a fact I've called Tess several times today. I hit the contacts list, to search for Lorcan there, but it's like a ghost town. Not one single name is entered in what used to be a packed list.

'Anything wrong?' Nora asks.

'No,' I say. But I start to get an uneasy feeling. Is this some sort of scam? Jim's mother was going on about smartphone fraud the other week. I wished I'd listened more to her now. Is someone watching me now, someone who has taken all my information from my phone?

I shiver at the thought of it.

Doesn't matter, sure I know Lorcan's number off by heart. I've used it often enough.

It occurs to me that my phone going blank and the girl in front of me could be all tied up together. But then I feel a bit stupid, allowing silly conspiracy theories in my brain.

What's his number? Think, think. I enter the eight digits and hope I've remembered correctly. Thank goodness Lorcan's clipped voice answers after a couple of rings.

'Good evening. Lorcan Colter speaking.'

'Oh thank goodness it's you. It's Belle. I need your help,' I say.

'Belle? Belle who?' he answers.

'Belle Looney. From Artane. How many Belles do you know?' I ask, wondering if he's been drinking. I suppose it is the season to be merry, he could be on his Christmas night out.

'Are you sure you have the right number? I don't know a Belle Looney.'

'Is this Lorcan Colter? As in social worker Lorcan?' I ask, feeling sweat begin to break out under my arms, despite the icy cold.

'Yes. It is. How can I help?' His voice now sounds more suspicious than anything else.

'It's Belle here. As in Jim Looney's wife.' Still no response to that. Okay, now I'm worried.

'We're foster parents. You have placed dozens of children with us over the past five years,' I say.

'Not with me you haven't,' he answers. 'Is this some kind of joke?'

What the hell is going on?

'Lorcan. I don't know why you don't remember me, but I am a foster parent from Artane. And my husband Jim has been in an accident.' I speak slowly, hoping that he'll suddenly remember us. 'I need your help.'

'Were you injured too?' he asks.

'No.' Give me strength. 'I'm fine. Jim is in hospital. But there's a little girl here, about ten or eleven, called Nora. She's lost. And I can't leave her on her own. She says that she has no parents. I need to get back to Jim, I can't deal with this right now. So can you come to take her?' I say.

'Where are you?' He tells me, I can hear him reaching for a notebook and pen.

'I'm at the Ha'penny Bridge, but I'm heading to the Mater Hospital now. I can bring her with me, if you can meet me there,' I say.

He agrees and I turn to Nora, who is now singing *Silent Night*, along with the carollers up on Dame Street.

'He doesn't know who you are, does he?' she states.

'Eavesdropping on conversations is rude,' I say, but every hair on my arms rises in alarm.

She ignores this mild reprimand and tells me, 'He couldn't know who you are, because you don't exist any more.'

Okay, no doubt about it, there is something weird going on. I look around me, wondering if this is some kind of MTV Punk'd programme.

'*You* don't exist Belle. Lorcan has never met you,' she says again.

'Don't be so silly,' I say. 'Stop this game, whatever it is.'

'Do you really wish you had never been born?' She asks me and looks so sad. I never said that out loud. How the hell does she know that I was thinking that?

'How do you know that?' I ask her. 'Who are you?'

'I'm Nora,' she replies, smiling at me. 'I told you. And you got your wish, Belle.'

'How do you know my name?' I shout. I look around me again, wondering when whoever is behind this whole thing is going to show their face. Am I in danger? Should I just run?

'I like that name,' she continues. 'You know that every time a bell rings an angel gets its wings?'

'I've heard that before alright,' I mutter. 'Once again, how do you know my name?'

'I know everything about you, Belle. I've been watching you for a long time,' Nora says. 'Your whole life, in fact.'

'Don't be so ridiculous,' I say. 'You're a kid and I'm thirty-five.'

She shrugs.

This is a scam of some sort, I realise. I have no idea what she's scamming, but I reckon it's money. If you want to solve a mystery you always follow the money. I read that somewhere.

'What do you want?' I say to her. 'Just spit it out. I don't have time for this. My husband needs me.'

'Yes you do.' Nora says and smiles again, like she's privy to some big secret that I'm not. 'You have all the time in the world, Belle.'

'What do you mean by that?' I say to her. I look around again, waiting for someone to come and mug me. But I don't even have my bag with me. I'll be slim pickings.

'I don't know what your game is, Nora. But I'm not playing any more,' I say.

'I don't have a game, honestly.' She grabs my arm. 'I'm not here to steal anything from you. Or skim or scam or whatever else you think.'

Had I said that out loud? I'm out of my depth here, I don't know if I'm having some kind of breakdown that is making me imagine things, but I'm beginning to get worried.

She's only a kid, a cute one at that, but she's freaking me the hell out.

I start walking back towards the Mater hospital and she follows behind me.

'Where are we going?' she asks.

'To the hospital. Lorcan is going to meet us there and then you are going to go with him. And I'm going to sit with my husband and beg him to wake up and come home with me,' I say.

'There's no point going back there.' Nora says. 'Jim's not in the hospital any more.'

Have I fallen and cracked my head? Am I dreaming? I pinch myself hard. Time to wake up.

'You're not dreaming,' Nora says, reading my mind once again. 'And you really should stop all that pinching. It's an awful habit you have.'

'How do you do that? Is it some kind of an app or something that lets you read minds?' I demand.

I realise that sounds like a whole lot of crazy, but it's all I've got.

She thinks this is funny and starts to laugh.

I glower at her.

'Only, you weren't joking,' she says. 'You wished that you had never been born, right?' she says.

I nod. 'I didn't mean it.' I say, feeling foolish. Why am I even talking to her?

'Well, that's funny. Because you've been thinking it a lot lately,' she says. 'We've been getting a lot of oh woe is me, life is horrendous, poor Belle, with the awful life.'

'Stop it. I do not think anything of the sort,' I say.

'Well, I wish you'd make your mind up, because I've granted your wish. I thought you'd be happier, to be honest. Here you go, you've never been born.' Nora smiles at me, like she's just given me the winning numbers for the lotto.

'Hey.' Someone moans, when I stop dead in my tracks and they walk into my back. I move to one side. Did I hear her correctly? I need to get this child help, she's not just annoying, she's delusional too.

'Listen, Nora, or whatever your name is. I've not got time for this. But I will get you help. Why don't you just stay quiet, till we get to the hospital?' I say.

'Whatever you want,' she says.

I start to run again, this time towards the hospital. I'm aware of Nora jogging along beside me, so I push myself to run even faster. The strangest thing is that I don't hurt any more. My ribs and bruises feel fine and when I glance at my hands, all the cuts and scratches are gone.

I need to get to Jim and away from the crazy. I run through the front doors and don't stop until I get to Jim's ward.

'Can I help you?' A nurse asks me when I rush by the nurses' station.

'Sorry,' I pant. 'I just need to see my husband. He's in room 108.'

Room 108. Why didn't I notice that bloody number before now? I slow down and suddenly don't feel in such a rush to open the door to his room. I'm terrified.

My hand feels like it's no longer connected to me and I watch it push the door open in front of it. My eyes move to the centre of the room, to the bed. But it's empty.

I run back to the nurses' station. My head is screaming, no, no, no. This is not happening.

'Jim Looney. What room is he in?' I say to Annette, the nurse who I have spent the past few days with.

She looks puzzled. Oh no. She looks down to her chart and back up to me, 'No one of that name here. Sorry.'

This is the very same nurse who told me to go home not an hour ago.

'You don't remember me? My husband, Jim, was here. In room 108,' I say.

She looks at me, not a flicker of recognition on her face. 'Sorry. But I see so many people come and go, I can't remember everyone. Are you sure it was me who treated your husband?'

'Yes. It was you. Earlier today,' I say. Come on, lady, you can't have forgotten.

'Maybe you're on the wrong ward?' she says, giving me a way out.

I turn to Nora and she shrugs as she says, 'I told you.'

28

Have I gone mad? I'm afraid so. You're entirely bonkers. But I'll tell you a secret. All the best people are.

Alice in Wonderland

I need answers and child or no child, Nora needs to tell me what the hell is going on. I search the corridor for somewhere we can talk. It's busy, though, staff, patients, all bustling about the corridors. Then I spy a waiting room and open the door, pushing Nora into it ahead of me.

'Right, Nora. Picture a rope. It's thin, frayed and worn. It could snap at any second,' I say.

'Oh goody. I love games. Yes, I can see it,' she says.

'Well, I've been swinging on that rope for years now. Trying to claw my way to the top of it. Some days I get close to the top, others, like this past month, I'm slipping fast towards the end. But you know what? I'm done. I am now at the end of my rope,' I say.

Nora's smile vanishes and she looks at me with sympathy.

'You have to help me here. No more games. What is going on? Where's my husband?'

'I told you already …' she replies, but I grab her arm and interrupt.

'I mean it, tell me where Jim is.'

'I believe he's in a pub in Artane, right this minute.' Nora beams at me.

'He's in a pub?' This comes out in a shriek. My husband, who last time I saw was hooked up to machines, is now in a pub having a rare old time.

'Yes. I believe so,' she says.

Think, Belle. None of this makes sense. I'm going to just rule out her madcap story about wishes granted. I run my hand over my head, searching for a bump. Did I hit my head harder than I thought in the accident? Maybe that's it. Delayed reaction.

'Let's just cut to the chase here. What do you want?' I demand.

'Nothing,' Nora smiles again and I want to scream.

'Everyone wants something,' I say, my hand resting on my mother's letter in the pocket of my jeans. That's what she said and she's right. 'I want my husband. How about that for a start?' I say.

'I can see that you're struggling right now. And, to be fair, it is a lot to take in. So how about I take you to him?' Nora says.

At last! Now we're getting somewhere. 'Yes, take me to him immediately.'

I just hope that he's not in any danger. If I can get him back to hospital straight away, it could be okay.

'You have to remember something. He doesn't know

who you are, Belle. You don't exist. So therefore you never married him,' Nora warns.

Oh, for goodness sake, she never gives it a rest this one. 'So you are sticking with your story then, about granting my wish?' I say.

'It's not a story. It's a fact,' she answers, shaking her head in disapproval at me.

Then a thought strikes me. I'm here taking the word of an obviously delusional child. Why am I even humouring her story? If he's not in hospital, maybe they've just sent him home.

That nurse is more than likely overworked and can't remember her own name, never mind every patient that comes in. Sure Jim is a strong man. He's never sick. I think the last time he had a cold was about ten years ago. He's made a rapid recovery from the crash, the hospital would need his bed. Plus he'll know how worried I am.

When I think about it logically, there's only one place where he is right now. Sitting at home in our kitchen wondering where the hell I am.

I dial his number, trembling with anticipation. Voicemail.

'Jimbo here. Leave a message.' Is that Jim's voice? His American twang has gone and all that is there is a strong Dublin accent.

I start to tumble down the rabbit hole at breakneck speed.

'Jim, ring me please. It's Belle here. I'm worried about you. Are you okay? I love you …' I hang up and will the phone to ring.

I can't just sit here, though. Adrenalin is pumping through my body as my anxiety levels grow. I've got to get out of here. I can't just sit in this hospital waiting room, I need to sort out whatever mess we've landed ourselves in.

I need to find my husband and then I want to go home.

As I walk towards the main entrance, Lorcan walks in through the sliding doors. In all the panic, I'd forgotten he was on his way. I've never felt so relieved to see anyone ever. He looks around and looks straight through me. I wave, but his eyes have moved on from me already.

'Lorcan,' I shout. Then louder again, 'Over here.'

As his eyes reach mine, I run towards him. 'Are you the lady who called me about the child?' he asks.

'I'm Belle, you eejit,' I say and fling myself at him for a hug. I've never needed one more than I do now. But his arms don't move around me, and he takes a step backwards. A panicked look has crept over his usually reserved face.

Oh no. This is so bad. 'You don't recognise me?' I whisper.

'I'm sorry, no I don't. Should I?' he answers. 'Listen, I came as fast as I could. You said there's a child here who needs my help. Where is she?'

I turn around to point to Nora, but she's gone.

'Her name is Nora. I found her on the Ha'penny Bridge earlier. She's about eleven, I'd say, no more than that. Annoying and delusional. She says that she's got no parents, but is well looked-after. I don't know, it doesn't feel right. I'm worried for her, that she's in danger.' I start to look around the hospital corridors but there's no sign of her. 'She was here a second ago.'

Five minutes later, we still haven't found her.

'She's definitely lost?' Lorcan asks. 'Is there any chance she's gone back to her parents? Maybe they found her here while we were talking and they've left.'

'She said she had no parents,' I say. But I suppose she could have done that. Should I mention to him about the whole 'I no longer exist' scam?

'Do you think she's a foster kid? Is that why you rang me?' he asks.

'Something is off about her. She kept saying to me that she'd granted me a wish,' I say.

'What wish?' he asks.

'She said that she'd arranged it so that I'd never been born,' I say.

He looks at me like I've sprouted a second head. 'That does sound worrying.'

Wait till you hear the rest of it, Lorcan. In for a penny, in for a pound and all that.

'Funny thing is, I do know you. And you know me. You had dinner at my house only the other week. You often call in for a bite on the way home from the office. We're friends,' I say.

'Belle. That's your name, right?' He asks. His face looks concerned. Kind.

I nod.

'I've never met you before in my life. I'm getting on a little and get the odd bit forgetful. Like this morning, I couldn't find my car keys. But I would never forget a friend.' He is insistent. 'I don't know you.'

He thinks I'm mad. Of course he does. Sure, I think I'm mad now too.

'I've got to find my husband,' I say. 'He was in an accident and now he's not here any more.' I can feel big fat tears begin to splash onto my cheeks.

Lorcan's face changes to sympathy. 'Don't cry. I've never been good with tears,' he says.

'I know,' I reply. 'Your mother was a crier. She was always sobbing. If you see someone boohooing now it makes you think of her and you freak out.'

His face changes to suspicion in an instant. 'How do you know that?'

'You told me, years ago, over a bottle of wine and a game of gin rummy with me and my husband,' I say.

'I don't know what's going on here,' Lorcan says. 'But I don't like it.'

'Neither do I,' I reply. I move towards the entrance. 'I've got to go find my husband. If you see a young girl in a red coat, dark hair, that's Nora. Help her.'

'I tell you what, I've a few calls to make. I'll do them here, in the lobby. That way if she comes back, I'm here to help her,' he answers. 'But, maybe you should get some help too. You sound a bit … off.'

So polite. Off. Yes, off my rocker.

I leave and jump in a taxi, giving the driver my address in Artane. I'm going to head home and hope that Jim is sitting at our kitchen table, drinking coffee and eating a chicken sandwich. Just as the car is about to leave, the door opens and Nora jumps in. 'Don't forget about me.'

'Where the hell have you been?' I demand. 'My friend Lorcan came to get you. He's still inside waiting for you.'

'I saw him. He's a nice man, I've always liked him. Much nicer than that Mrs Reilly. She was a cold fish, wasn't she? But I can't go with him. My job is to stay with you,' Nora says.

I can't find any words to respond. I keep thinking that I'll stop being shocked, but every five minutes I'm faced with another statement from Nora that sends me spiralling in circles.

We drive in silence for a few minutes, as the taxi navigates the evening traffic. We're moving at a snail's pace and every traffic light seems to be against us, turning red, just as we get close. I feel nauseous, my stomach is flipping around like a tumble drier on high speed. I'm cold and my hands feel like ice.

'I'll see if I can speed things up,' Nora says, then leans forward and looks out the driver's window. The strangest thing happens, the lights change from red to green in an instant. The stagnant traffic starts to inch forward, then gathers speed. We continue all the way home without another single stop. Every light turns green just as we approach it.

'I've never had a run like that before in my life,' the driver says. 'That's the darndest thing. Not a single red light all the way home. Might do the lotto later, wha'?'

'It sure is the darndest thing' I say and look at Nora, who ignores us and looks out the window deep in thought.

I grab some money from my pocket and pay the driver, then walk up to the front door of our house. Where did I put my keys? I dig deep into each of my pockets and find them. Fumbling with anticipation and hope, I can't get the key to turn in the lock. I start again, taking a deep breath. No, the stupid key won't even go in a quarter of the way. I might as well be pushing a square peg into a round hole.

Oh thank goodness, the outdoor light comes on. It's Jim. He's coming. The sound of the lock turning from the inside is the sweetest sound I've heard in the longest time.

Jim, I knew you were home.

'Can I help you?' a young woman asks, looking wary and more than a little harassed. She has a baby on her hip, who is wailing up a storm.

I look back and Nora is standing by the gate. She seems unsurprised to see them here and has a look on her face that has a distinct twang of 'I told you so'.

'Can I help you?' harassed mother asks again, as she rocks the baby against her hip, shushing its tears.

'Is Jim here?' I whisper.

What if she tells me that she's his wife and that screaming baby is his? The very thought sends shudders through my already trembling body.

'James, you mean?' she asks. 'Yeah, he's inside.'

Oh no. This can't be true.

'Is he okay?' I ask. 'Can I see him?'

'He's fine and dandy. He's not the one up every night doing feeds. Lazy bastard. One second and I'll get him. Who will I say it is?' she asks.

'Belle. It's Belle,' I say and watch her close my front door shut.

Except it's not my front door. It's red and I painted ours a bright yellow last summer.

When the door opens and the woman appears with a man, half asleep, who is not my husband, I don't know how to feel.

'Yeah?' the man says.

'You're not Jim,' I answer.

'Never said I was,' he replies.

'I'm sorry. Wrong guy.' I say and he turns without a word, scratching his arse as he walks back down our hall.

She makes a face, looks me up and down and says, 'Are you one of the mums from the mother and toddler group? I've baby brain, not getting much sleep these nights.'

'No, I'm not. I used to live here, that's all. And I'm looking for someone, I thought that he might have been here. Can I ask, how long have you lived in this house?' I ask.

'Two years or so,' she replies. She looks wary again, a look that seems to be passing over everyone's face I see at the moment.

I take a step backwards and mumble an apology for bothering her. First Lorcan, now this.

'Come on,' Nora says. She takes my hand and leads me towards the shopping centre down the road. If I close my eyes I can pretend that it's Lauren, swinging on my hand, skipping beside me.

I allow myself to be led by this strange young girl down the street. We pass rows and rows of houses, of neighbours, friends, who don't know who I am any more.

My neighbour, Mrs O'Leary, walks by, her pet dog Missy barking at us both as they pass us. She looks straight through me. I have never walked by without her stopping me for a long chat before.

When we come to our community centre, I have to blink twice to make sure my eyes are not playing tricks. It's boarded up. That cannot be right. I was here only last Friday supervising Youth Club. I stop and walk to the padlocked door and give it a futile shake.

'Where is everyone? The youth club should be in full swing by now,' I say.

'There's no youth club. The knock-on effect of you not being in this little part of the world is huge. You and Jim weren't here to set one up,' Nora says. 'It's an awful pity because the children have nowhere to go now in the evenings.'

I look up and see lots of kids sitting on the walls outside the shopping centre, just hanging around. This was exactly why we wanted a youth club, to prevent this.

We walk into a small café, one that I've had tea and scones and full Irish breakfasts in dozens of times. We take a seat near the back and Nora orders two hot chocolates for us.

'May we have marshmallows and cream please?' she asks.

The waitress gives her a friendly smile and compliments me, 'What a well-mannered girl you have.'

I feel like I'm having an out-of-body experience.

Nora pulls out a notebook from her pocket and starts to scribble in it. I watch the world go by and try not to think. I'm scared. I'm in trouble. And I don't know how to make it right.

Nora spoons a large dollop of sugar into both steaming mugs when they arrive. She puts a straw in each one and then pushes one of the mugs towards me. I have the strangest sensation that she is the adult and I am the child.

I place my hands around the white mug and allow the heat of the drink to warm me.

The sugary chocolate tastes better than I remembered and quietens my tummy. I begin to thaw.

'I always feel better after a hot drink,' Nora tells me.

I'm not in the mood for banal chit chat. 'Let's have a quick recap. You heard me wish that I'd never been born earlier this evening. So you granted said wish and now here I am, without a husband, a home or a single person who knows me,' I say.

'Yes.' She smiles like she's just given me the winning lottery ticket.

I decide to just park that for a moment. 'Who are you?' I say.

'I'm Nora,' she says.

'Nobody likes a smart arse. I know you're Nora. Where are you from?'

'A better question would be, what am I?' she replies.

'Go on, then. What are you?' I decide to humour her.

'You'll love this. I'm an angel,' she replies.

That's it. All pretence that this is a normal situation is gone. 'I don't believe in angels,' I say.

'You don't believe in a lot of things any more. That's the problem,' Nora says.

'*Do you believe, Belle?*' *Lauren's little face asks me, as she rings the silver bell.*

'*I don't think you do believe any more.*' *Jim says.*

'Where are your wings?' I say.

'Not all angels have wings. Depends which division you

work in. Plus, you have to earn your wings. They don't hand them out willy nilly, you know,' she replies.

Am I having this conversation? It appears I am, because I continue to ask, 'What division are you in, then?'

'I'm what you would call your garden stock guardian angel variety. I've been watching over you, ever since you were born,' Nora says.

The feeling that I've seen her before strengthens. Her face, her smile, it's not the first time I've seen it. I can't remember where, but I'm sure.

She nods at me. 'Déjà vu some call it. Memories, I prefer.'

'Can we have some music on?' Nora asks the waitress.

'Sure thing.' She flicks a switch on the radio and *O Holy Night* fills the room, sung by Mariah Carey. And I get it. I remember.

'You were that girl on the Ha'penny Bridge. The night that Jim proposed. You were singing this song.' I say, but I have no idea how that can be.

'The voice of an angel, you said. I have to admit, I giggled a lot when you said that,' she says.

I remember a little girl in a red coat, staring up at me, as I sit on the window ledge in Tess's house.

'You were there too, the day that Jim left,' I say.

'One of my worst moments, that was. And you've had some pretty horrible ones to witness, in fairness. I hated seeing you so upset. And there was nothing I could do. Jim had to go home. That was his destiny at the time,' she says.

All of the hopefulness and loneliness that I felt for a lot of my early childhood is back in full force.

'I did work hard to get him back again to Ireland, so that you two could meet again,' Nora says. 'I spent ages whispering your name in his ear.'

I feel mollified by that. Maybe she's on my side. 'Please tell me that Jim is alive. He's not hurt?' I ask.

'I promise you, Jim is as alive as you are right now and quite well. Although not as happy as he could be. He's a bit of a loner,' Nora says.

That doesn't sound like Jim. He is always the life and soul of every occasion. People just gravitate towards him, always have done.

'He never met *you*, was never married, never in that car crash. Remember that. So he's a different Jim than the one you have known,' she answers.

But he's alive. Something good has come from my wish. My husband is not hooked up to machines, fighting for his life. He is alive and well. That's all that matters.

'I want to go see him,' I say.

'You can go anywhere you like,' she tells me. 'You are the master of your own destiny.'

'I've not got much money on me,' I say.

'Don't worry, I've got lots of money. I told you, I'm well taken care of and now, I'm taking care of you.' She holds up a wad of notes and winks at me.

Holy shit, there must be hundreds there. 'Put that away,' I chastise her.

'Always the mother,' she murmurs. 'That's one of the things that's most special about you, Belle. You are a born mother. Okay, let's drink up and go to your Jim.'

29

Don't worry when you are not recognised, but strive to be worthy of recognition.

Abraham Lincoln

As we arrive at the doors of the pub, I check the time. It's seven o'clock now. Damn it

'You can't come in here,' I say to Nora. 'No children are allowed after seven.'

'Technically, that's incorrect. I'll be 293 years old next May, so you'll find that I can go anywhere I like,' she responds, smiling.

The fact that I just take this nugget on board, without questioning, worries me.

'That's as maybe, Nora, but I'm not sure the owners of the pub will take your word for that. You look like a kid and kids aren't allowed in pubs after seven o'clock,' I say, 'So we have a problem.'

She walks over to a bench under the window outside the pub. Trails of cigarette butts litter the ground and nicotine smoke lingers in the cold night. She sits down. 'Go on. Go find Jim. I'll wait here. Although I'm sorry to miss seeing you two meet. Should be a fun moment,' she says.

'I can't leave you on your own,' I say. It's not safe for a child, even if they are really an angel and hundreds of years old. Plus, I don't feel in such a rush to go inside any more. Lorcan's blank look when I waved at him taunts me. I can't bear the thought of Jim doing the same.

'Shoo … go on … I can take care of myself,' she says. 'But just to keep you happy, I'll take off for a bit.' She laughs and then disappears in front of my eyes.

'Nora?' I shout. This is beyond crazy.

'Pretty cool, eh?' She says to me, appearing once again on the bench. 'Your face is such a hoot. It never gets old seeing people's faces when I do this.' She nods in my direction.

'Excuse me if I seem a bit perturbed by the disappearance and reappearance of a fecking guardian angel!' I say.

She's done this before, I realise. I don't know whether that's comforting or not. How many more people are wandering around Dublin right this minute, with their lives in chaos thanks to a meddling angel?

Be careful what you wish for. Those words never felt so true as they do right now. A gang of young lads come out of the pub, half cut, lighting up their cigarettes. They are noisy and, angel or not, it's no place for a little girl to be. 'Disappear again. I'm going in to find Jim,' I hiss to her.

And with that, she's gone.

I've been in this pub many times with Jim for a drink and in this version of my non-life, not much is different. The walls are full of dusty souvenirs from flea markets.

A row of signed jerseys from the Dublin football team is pinned to the wall. A low hum of chat and laughter fills the busy bar. Gangs of after-work colleagues, in for a quick drink to re-energise after a hard day at work, are gathered around tall round bar tables. Two capped pensioners, sitting beside each other at the bar, nurse a pint of Guinness, silently ignoring each other. A gang of girls, who look too young to wear the impossible high heels that they totter on, giggle as they stand by the juke box.

But amongst this mayhem there is no sign of my husband.

I scan tables full of giggling women, drinking wine and vodkas, and couples who gaze at each over a bottle of lager. A solitary woman, in her fifties, sits with a glass of wine. Sadness surrounds her and I wonder what her story is. I glance over in the direction of the pool table. A long shot, as Jim has never been much of a pool player. But there is quite a crowd and he could be there, I suppose, watching a game. I squeeze my way through a large group of people, all with glasses and pints in hand, laughing and joking. My eyes dart from left to right. But he's nowhere to be seen.

Part of me feels relief. I'm surprised by this. Maybe it's better that I don't find him. Because if Jim reacts to me like Lorcan did, I'm not sure I can bear it. But then I think of my man, my love, *my* person. This is Jim I'm talking about. There's only ever been him. There is no world where he will not know me.

I glance at the gents and wonder if I should chance going inside. He could be in there right now. I imagine his face if I barge in, as he's mid-flow. But then the door swings open and a large elderly man comes out, pulling up his zipper and I shudder. No, I draw the line at going in there.

Nora was adamant that he's here and so far she's been right about everything else. I realise that somewhere between Lorcan and the harassed mother in my home, I've accepted her angel story. So I'll trust that she's right about Jim too and decide to grab a seat at the bar. Maybe if I stop looking, he'll find me.

Actually, now that I think about it, the thought of a gin and tonic sings to me. I've never needed a drink more than I do right now. Jim always said slice up those lemons and make a G&T. Maybe he's right. I find a spot near the two old capped codgers and try to catch the eye of the barman. He's at the tills, with his back to me, ringing in an order.

His shoulders hunch forward and he stands with his feet one foot apart. I know that stand. I know it as well as if I were looking in the mirror at myself.

It can't be.

The barman with his back to me has a shaved head. But the build is the same, from the broad shoulders and strong arms to the slim hips. My eyes rest on his bum and there's no doubt.

He may no longer be rocking a headful of foxy red hair and it makes no sense that he would be working behind a bar, but when the barman turns, so does my stomach. It's Jim. Without a doubt. But just a different version of him.

'Howya darlin', he drawls. It's that same Dublin accent from the voicemail earlier. Where has his American twang gone?

'Jim?' I say.

'The one and only,' he replies, smile wide. I search his face for recognition, but none comes.

'It's Belle.' I look at him, stare into his eyes and will him to know me. To recognise the love we have for each other. This matters, Jim, this matters. Don't let me down.

He leans in over the bar and I move closer to him, hope rising, like flames from the ashes.

'Was it you who left that weird message for me?' he says.

I nod and the flame goes out. He looks me up and down and shakes his head. He hasn't got a barney who I am.

'You don't recognise me,' I say. What now? Do I become the crazy lady? Or just skulk away, pretending I'm okay with the fact that my husband has forgotten me.

'Sorry darlin'. Were we, I mean, did we?' He whistles and winks at the same time, in a manner that I don't think I've ever seen my Jim do. It feels like I'm in one of those stupid farces. I expect to hear a horn blaze and the live audience to start clapping.

Yes we did, Jim. Many times.

But I don't answer him.

As I start to run through my options, my face must betray me. His face softens, in sympathy and perhaps regret. 'Was I wasted? I don't want to be a prick here, but I don't remember you. Ah here darlin', don't cry. I'm sorry.'

'You weren't wasted,' I answer.

His face tells me that he doesn't believe that. 'I must have been, because you're the kind of girl I'd remember.'

I flush under his scrutiny and wish I was wearing something nicer. How messed up is that?

'What are you drinking? Don't tell me, let me guess. You're a gin and tonic kind of girl, I'd wager,' he states.

'Yes!' He remembers my drink, I'm elated. That has to mean something.

'You've a great smile,' he says. 'You should do it more often.'

'Are you married?' I dive right in and ask my husband.

'Oh, you don't mess about do you?' He laughs and my heart skips a beat. The laugh, that's all Jim. My Jim. The lovely, carefree one that loves me.

He places my drink in front of me and answers, 'I'm not married. Never will be either.'

'That's a definite statement to make,' I say.

'Because it's the truth. Settling down is not for me,' he answers. 'It's a mug's game.'

No it's not. And for the record, you love marriage, every bit of it. You tell me all the time that asking me to be your wife was the best decision you've ever made. But I'm so relieved that Jim isn't with anyone else.

'Are you happy?' I ask him.

'Delirious,' he says. 'You're full of questions, aren't you?'

He moves along the bar, clearing glasses and pulling pints, but his eyes keep darting back to me. 'I can't work you out. You don't seem crazy. But you're not making a lot of sense either,' he remarks, coming back.

The not being crazy remains to be seen. He continues, 'I'm good with faces. I'm sure I would have remembered meeting you.'

I lean in again and look into his blue eyes, searching for my husband. We have looked at each other, nose to nose, hundreds of times and I am so close, I could just kiss him.

'You're trouble. With a capital T. I've worked that much out,' he says, stepping backwards before I get the chance to make a fool of myself.

'I've been called worse,' I say. The gin tastes wonderful. Maybe I should just sit here, with my husband who isn't my husband, and get drunk.

'What do you want?' he asks.

'Truthfully?' I ask.

He nods.

'I want you to remember me,' I say.

He sighs and wipes down the bar for the second time since we started to talk. 'Listen, Belle. You seem like a nice girl. And I feel shit that I don't remember you. But I don't.'

I don't know what to do. I wished for this. I wished for a life where I had never existed. But I never believed for one second that this would mean that my husband would forget me.

'We knew each other when we were kids,' I say.

He looks surprised. 'You from around here?'

'We were in the same foster home together,' I say.

His face changes. The smile disappears and he looks suspicious once more.

'You were at Tess's?' he asks. 'Because if so, I don't remember you.'

I nod. 'We used to hang out together. A lot. In the park and we had a den. We made it out of sheets. We would play that game Simon, the memory game, for hours,' I say.

He shakes his head. 'I don't think much about back then. My childhood wasn't the kind that makes you want to revisit it.'

'I'm sorry about that,' I say.

'I still think you've got the wrong guy. Because you stand out. You're not the kind of girl that a bloke would forget. And when I was at Tess's, there were a few kids who came and went, but none that looked like you.'

'Maybe,' I say. I try another tack. 'The Jim I knew went to live in America with his mum. She married a guy called Sam. Is that you?'

'What the?' he says, shock flashes across his face, then he looks angry. 'Listen, you've got the wrong guy. I never lived in America. My mam never married anyone. She's at home, out in Ranelagh, doing shifts in Tesco. I told you, wrong guy.'

He walks away and serves a round of drinks to two giggling girls. Despite my best efforts to catch his eye, he ignores me. He's doing a good job of being the congenial bar man and flirts with the two girls. They look at him through long, black false eyelashes and whisper in each other's ears, as they look him up and down. I just want to go home, climb into bed and sleep this crazy day away.

There's one big problem with that. I don't have a home to go to.

I look at Jim again. There was something about his face when I mentioned the name Sam earlier. My instinct is that I need to push that a little further, see what that was. Once he's finished serving the girls, he wanders back to me and leans his long frame onto the bar.

'There was a Sam,' I say to him, 'In your life.'

'Maybe. But there are a lot of Sams in this world,' he replies. 'Not exactly an uncommon name.'

'Tell me about the one you knew,' I say. 'Humour me.'

He sighs and starts slicing a lemon methodically into thin wedges. 'When I was a kid, my mam dated a guy for a short while called Sam.'

'And?' I say.

'I didn't like him. Mind you, I didn't like much about anyone back then. They didn't last. She finished with him,' he says.

I feel so sad hearing this. Because they are such a great couple, so in love with each other, even all these years later. 'How's your mam now?' I ask.

'Bat-shit crazy, Belle, that's how she is. She's so doped up on Xanax half the time she doesn't know her own name, never mind mine,' he answers.

I grab his hand and squeeze it. I want to climb over the bar and pull him into my arms and hold him until all the sadness in his face disappears. 'I'm so sorry, Jim.' It's not meant to be like this.

He looks at me, really looks at me. I feel dizzy. I recognise the sensation. It's the same way I felt that day he walked into Tess's home, when he came to find me.

'Oi, Jimbo. Stop flirting and come serve us.' A voice shouts and Jim shouts back, 'One minute.' But his eyes never leave mine. 'Jaysus, I'm dying of the thirst,' the voice persists.

'Trouble written all over your face.' His finger touches my cheek for just a moment. 'I knew that's what you were, from the moment you walked into this bar,' he says.

He felt something just now, I know he did. As he serves the impatient customer with the big gob, he glances back at me, over and over again. I can sit here all night, Jim Looney. I spent years waiting for you, I can easily wait a few more hours. If I wait for him to finish work, maybe we can go somewhere to talk and I'll make him listen. I'll tell him everything, the whole Nora shebang.

'I can't figure you out,' he declares. 'But right now, I've a bar to run.'

'I can wait until you finish, then maybe we can talk?' I ask.

He gives this some thought, then replies, 'No can do darlin', I've a date later on.' He nods towards the taller of the giggling girls from earlier.

A little part of me dies at the thought of my man even breathing the same air as one of those girls, let alone sharing it.

'I hope you find your Jim,' he shouts over his shoulder and then turns his back, dismissing me.

'I hope so too,' I whisper. I wait to see if he will turn around. That would be a big fat no, then. I walk out of the noisy pub and feel a hand slip into mine. I look down and Nora is beside me, pulling me away.

'He didn't know who I was,' I say. 'He was different. The same but different all at once. How can that be?'

'His life was different because you weren't in it,' Nora says. 'He was a mixed-up kid when he went to live with Tess. And he didn't have the friendship of a young girl called Belle, who made him smile and laugh. He got mixed up in the wrong crowd.'

I can remember that first day Jim arrived at Tess's. He was like a feral animal, waiting to lunge at anyone who looked at him crossways.

'Without your friendship, he focused on a lot of stuff he shouldn't. And then when he went home, he gave his mother a hard time. Poor Sam didn't stand a chance. As soon as Jim met him, he did everything in his power to split them up,' Nora says.

My head reels and my heart aches for this mess.

Nora looks up to me and her eyes are pools of water. 'You want to see Tess?' she asks. Of course, she can read minds. She's a fecking angel.

'Yes. I do,' I say.

So I follow this 292-year-old in the body of an eleven-year-old, who holds her hand out to the passing traffic. And, of course, a taxi appears within seconds.

30

Certain things, they should stay the way they are. You ought to be able to stick them in one of those big glass cases and just leave them alone.

J.D. Salinger

As we drive past the park Jim and I raised money for, Nora asks the taxi driver to slow down. 'Isn't it such a pity, to see it like this?'

Graffiti stains the walls that surround the park lands. A broken bottle is at the entrance and I can see litter blowing across the gravel cement pathway.

'It's very different in my world,' I sigh.

'Help, help!' a voice cries.

'Did you hear that?' I ask, as I take my seat belt off. 'One second …' I jump out and run to the entrance of the park and Mrs O'Leary is fighting off two kids with her walking stick. Her dog, Missy, is barking up a storm, trying to bite their ankles as they pull her handbag from her.

'Hey!' I scream and run towards them. The bigger of the two hooded kids screams, 'Leg it!' and runs away. The younger of the two trips and falls, just as I get to them, so I grab the back of his hoodie.

'Hey, you little shit …' I hold on tight to him, as he kicks and flails to get away. 'Mrs O'Leary, are you okay?'

'Oh dear, what a palaver. I was just walking my Missy when they jumped out. Hooligans,' she says.

'Sit down for a moment, let me deal with this first,' I say to her. I turn the kid around and pull his hoodie down.

It's not a boy. I assumed it was a boy, because of the jeans and the hoodie.

'Lauren. What on earth?' I cry out in surprise.

Her face registers shock as I say her name. 'How do you know my name?'

'I know you and I'm so disappointed. Why on earth would you do this to Mrs O'Leary?' I say.

'Big deal,' she says, attitude seeping out of her.

I'll give her big fecking deal.

'Who was that with you?' I demand.

'None of your business,' she shouts.

'Where's Alicia?' I ask.

At the mention of her mother's name she stops trying to squirm her way away from me.

'Are you with Alicia or with a foster carer?' I ask.

'Get lost, loser,' Lauren shouts and I cannot recognise this wild child with the sweet, innocent girl I know.

'I'm going nowhere. Not till I get some answers, Lauren. Do I need to call Lorcan, your social worker?' I ask.

That got her attention. 'Don't do that,' she says. 'He'll take me away again if he hears I'm in trouble.'

'Right. I'll not call him if you sit down on this bench with me and tell me what's going on. If you run, I'll call him, do you hear?' I say firmly.

She must believe me, because she sits down on the far side of the bench Mrs O'Leary is perched on, enjoying the banter between us all.

'You need to be firm with the likes of her,' she says to me.

'Duly noted,' I reply. 'Are you hurt?'

'Oh not a bit of it. I've fought off bigger and bolder than the likes of this one and her friend,' she adds. 'Right, I'll carry on home. I think I need a cup of tea.'

'Take care,' I say to her and then sit down beside Lauren.

'Where are you living right now, Lauren?' I ask.

'I'm with my mum. With Alicia. She's a flat in Beaumont,' she answers.

I nod. Okay, that's good. 'I bet Alicia won't be happy to hear about all of this.'

She shrugs and doesn't reply.

'You said that Lorcan would take you away again?' I say. 'Has this happened before? You getting into trouble?'

She shrugs again. Oh boy, this is going to take a while.

'Come on. I'm taking you home.' I grab her by her arm and we walk back out to the road, where the taxi is parked up waiting for us.

'Hello, Lauren.' Nora smiles brightly at her. 'Nice to see you again.'

Lauren gives her the benefit of her biggest scowl.

'We're taking Lauren to her mother's house. I assume you know where that is?' I ask.

'Oh goody,' Nora says and gives the driver his instructions.

Five minutes later, we're outside a block of flats, which are behind a green grocer's. 'These look nice,' I say. 'Go on, lead the way.'

I follow Lauren as she slowly makes her way home. When we get to the third flat on the right, she stops and rings the doorbell. It takes a few minutes for Alicia to come to the door but, when she does, she's one unhappy mother.

'Where the hell have you been?' she screams and grabs Lauren's hand, shaking the girl. Then when she spies me, she asks, 'What's she done this time?'

'Tried to steal an old lady's handbag in the park,' I reply.

Alicia narrows her eyes. 'I'm ashamed, I really am. How could you, Lauren?'

'What do you care?' Lauren demands.

'Don't speak to your mother like that,' I admonish. 'Remember your manners, young lady.'

Alicia and Lauren both turn to look at me then, like I've two heads.

'Thank you for bringing her home. I'll have words with her, I can assure you,' Alicia says.

'May I come in?' I ask.

'Are you a social worker?' Alicia eyes me up suspiciously.

'No. Not at all. I am a foster parent, though. I know how hard it can be. Maybe I can help,' I say.

She slams the door shut firmly in my face.

That would be a no.

I don't know what to do. Should I stay and see if they let me in or go as I've no rightful place to talk to them here?

301

'Such a mess those two,' Nora sighs from behind.

'It seems that way,' I say. 'I never even got to give her a hug.'

'I find that it can be tricky hugging someone when they are trying to bite and kick you,' Nora states.

'What's going on with them?' I ask.

'Well, Lauren has been in quite a few foster homes these past couple of years. Problem is, she didn't make a connection with anyone like she did with you and Jim. So she was moved around a bit, each time she got angrier. And Alicia, knowing her daughter was unhappy, found it hard to concentrate on her own recovery, so took her home too early. It was a disaster waiting to happen. Things have been spiralling out of control for quite some time now, it's going to end in tears,' Nora says.

'But Alicia is doing so well. She's so together now,' I say.

'Yes, because of the impact you and Jim made on her. She saw the kind of parents you were with her daughter. You made her want to be a better parent,' Nora says.

I'm floored by this.

'She's a good woman. But she has internal demons that she finds hard to keep at bay sometimes. Only, Lauren is now fuelled by this anger and hatred, it's affecting everything,' Nora continues.

All my worries and fears about Lauren being in danger with Alicia have been realised right here. I am powerless to help, because in this world I no longer exist.

'You see how far-reaching the impact of your life is on others?' Nora asks. 'Now, come on, we need to get moving. I know you want to see Tess.'

302

Our taxi is still waiting and, as soon as I sit down tiredness overtakes me. I close my eyes as the taxi rolls on its way to Drumcondra. I know that before I get there, Tess won't know who I am. I've accepted this mad world that I find myself in at the moment. But I also know another truth.

Tess is one of the kindest women I've ever met in my life, with the biggest of hearts. I'm pretty sure I can get her to invite me in and listen to me at the very least.

I picture the scene. We are sitting down to watch *Grey's Anatomy* together. We have gallons of hot, sweet tea and the prerequisite Milk Tray chocolates. Once we've had our fill of Dr McDreamy, I'll creep upstairs to my old bedroom. She's kept it the same all these years. And when I close my eyes, Tess will tuck the duvet around me. Tomorrow, I'll work out what to do with this crazy, mixed-up world. Tess might even have a suggestion on how I can get back.

Click your heels three times, Dorothy.

I imagine Tess in a Glinda the Good Witch fairy dress and giggle.

Nora sighs and that exhalation shoves the giggles back down my throat. All thoughts of Dr McDreamy and chocolate dissipate. I open my eyes to look around and realise that we're nowhere near Tess's house.

'Where are we?' I whisper, but I don't want to know the answer. The hairs on my arms stand up in fear.

'Almost there,' the taxi driver answers, mouth noisily chewing gum.

'This isn't the way to Drumcondra,' I say. I should never have left this to Nora. She's given the driver the wrong address.

Only Nora doesn't make mistakes. I've worked that out already too.

The driver ignores me. He continues driving in the opposite direction from where we need to go. All the while chewing that bloody gum.

'Tess isn't in Drumcondra any more,' Nora says. She keeps looking out of the window, avoiding eye contact.

Do I want to know where Tess is? Actually, yes I do. Maybe she's living it up with a husband and dozens of kids in this world. Maybe she's got a great life going on. There's no need for me to assume the worse.

'You loved it there, didn't you?' Nora says. 'You were happy at Tess's.'

'Yes,' I say. 'There was a lot of laughter in that house. There still is.'

My memory floods with an image of Tess. All twenty-odd stone of her, dressed in a shell tracksuit. She's wearing a baseball cap twisted to the side.

It was the day after Jim had left with his mother. I was miserable and nothing she had done could lift me from my depression. Tess had tried everything she could to make me smile, but I was resolute in my determination to be miserable.

Then, in she walks to my bedroom. All squeezed tight into that silly outfit, trying to look serious.

'You look ridiculous,' I say in horror when she walks in. Please don't say this is a new look for her.

She looks at me, winks and then does this weird stance with her two hands in the air.

'What are you doing?' I ask. The trackie bottoms look like they are about to burst at the seams any second. She grabs a cassette player from the hall and presses the play button. Then, with my mouth wide open in shock, she bursts into song.

'Now, this is a story all about how
My life got flipped-turned upside down
And I'd like to take a minute
Just sit right there
I'll tell you how I became the prince of a town called Bel Air ...'

As she sings the whole theme song to *The Fresh Prince of Bel Air*, start to finish, word-perfect, the more I laugh.

And the more I laugh, the more she throws herself into her surprise performance. My sides start to groan and ache as I double over in glee and mirth at her antics.

My Tess. My hero.

'You know why she did that, don't you?' Nora says.

'I know,' I say. She wanted to make me laugh. And boy, oh boy did she succeed. 'It was a lucky day, the day I found Tess.'

'I thought that day would never come,' Nora says. 'I always knew that she would be your forever home, that you would get your happy-ever-after. But it was so hard watching you in pain before then.'

I ache now to see Tess. I want to tell her how much I love her. Does she know how much she changed my life? I think I've told her that, but I need to say it again. I want to laugh with her, our belly laughs that usually end up with me groaning in pain.

I want to forget about everything except for her big arms around me, pulling me in close for another soft, warm embrace.

'She knew all that,' Nora says, reaching over and gently clasping my hand.

The taxi driver indicates to the left and I feel the blood drain from my face.

'You said knew,' I say in horror. 'No!' I whisper as the driver slows the car to a stop. Nora looks at me with such sadness that I know it is true, no matter how much I beg it not to be.

'Keep going,' I say to the driver. 'I'm not going in there.' Don't make me go in there. I can't bear it. But Nora hands the driver his fare and gets out. I find myself opening the door, even though I don't want to, and looking up at the entrance to Glasnevin Cemetery. I follow Nora, who takes me down a long gravel path. We pass graves, centuries old and full of history, before we come to the newer ones. My mind frantically goes through options of who might be in here. Anyone but Tess.

Finally, she stops and I close my eyes tight, refusing to look at the gravestone.

'Open your eyes,' Nora says with gentleness.

I take a deep breath.

Focusing on the grey marble stone in disbelief, I read aloud the engraving in front of me.

In loving memory of
Teresa (Tess) McNulty

Every Time a Bell Rings

11th February 1945–24th December 2005
Reunited with her parents, Eileen and Joseph
A smile for all
A heart of gold
One of the best this world could hold
Never selfish
Always kind
A beautiful memory left behind
Good night, God bless, sleep tight.

I am standing in front of Tess. My mother. My heart. And she's gone.

She died ten years ago. Oh Tess. I'm so sorry. I hope you died with love by your side. I hope you were not in pain. I hope that you are at peace now. I hope you know you were loved.

I wipe the tears from my face and turn to Nora. My jaw clenches and every muscle in my body tightens. I've had as much as I can take from this little angel.

'This isn't funny any more.' I shake my head sadly. 'She's dead and that's too far. You've gone too far.'

To be fair, Nora doesn't look like she's enjoying herself any more than me. In fact, the opposite. She's crying.

'Change it. She doesn't need to pay for my mistake. Just because I made a stupid wish never to be born, don't take it out on Tess,' I say.

'You still don't get it,' Nora says and sighs with regret. 'You didn't cause Tess to die. She did it all by herself. She never stopped smoking.'

She continues, 'The reason Tess is still living in your old world is because of you. Here, in this world where you were never born, she didn't have anyone to nag at her to give up. She didn't have anyone to try for.'

'Cancer?' I ask. 'She died from cancer?'

It had always been my fear for her. The reason why I never stopped begging her to throw away her cigarettes and eat better.

Nora nods.

I picture her, in hospital, with her ragged body full of tubes. A pain knifes my side, a physical stabbing ache.

'I'm so sorry, Tess,' I whisper to the cold, unmoving stone.

'Without you in her life, she didn't have a reason to take better care of herself,' Nora says. 'It was such a waste, because she had so much more to offer the world.'

'Was she alone when she died?' I ask, but I'm not sure I want to know the answer to that. I can't bear the thought of her being on her own.

'I was with her. I stayed right to the last moment. She died in a hospice in Clontarf,' Nora says. 'It was peaceful in the end.'

I sink to the cold ground, my legs buckling under the weight of guilt. I could have prevented this.

I don't want to be part of a world where Tess isn't part of it. I don't want to be here, do you hear me?

'I'm done. Turn things back to the way they were,' I demand. 'Make this stop.'

'It's not as simple as that Belle,' she answers. 'I'm so sorry, I wish I could do that, but it's not up to me, how this plays out.'

'Well, let me speak to whoever is in charge,' I say.

'Why, you're in charge,' Nora says. 'You wanted this. You got it.'

'I didn't want *this*,' I shout. 'Don't you dare suggest I wanted this.'

'Come on, let's go for a drive,' she states, with a shrug, and walks away ignoring me.

I run my hand over the gold engraved words on the gravestone, my fingers lingering on her name.

Tess McNulty. Goodbye Tess from your little butterfly. I'm so sorry. I'm going to do everything I can to make this better.

I navigate my way through the gravestones and follow Nora. Once again, I feel like the roles have reversed. I'm the child and she's the adult. Everything is upside down in this world, nothing makes sense.

Nora holds her hand up as we exit the black wrought-iron gates. And once again, as before, a taxi miraculously appears and pulls up beside us.

'Neat trick,' I say, wondering what else she can do.

'I've got loads more, even better than this one,' she boasts.

It's going to get annoying, Nora reading my mind the whole time.

'I know,' she says.

'So where next? I'm not sure I can take any more shocks,' I say.

The tiredness of earlier nips at my eyes again. 'You don't happen to have a nice hotel ready for us, by any chance?'

'Not a hotel,' she replies. 'But I do want to bring you somewhere. It might take your mind off yourself and your own troubles for a while.'

We sit in silence for twenty minutes or so, listening to Michael Bublé croon Christmas carols on the radio. I do my best to not think about anything. I try to close my mind to all thoughts of Jim, Tess and Lauren. Not just because those thoughts are painful, but also because Nora's ability to read my mind feels invasive. For a long time as a child my thoughts were the only thing that were mine. And now, that's no longer the case.

I find myself nodding off as the car bumps along and wake when I feel white fairy lights shining their light into the taxi. We have arrived on O'Connell Street again. Was it only a few hours ago that I ran down this street, distraught, frightened, away from Jim? And now, I would give every-thing to be able to run back to him again. I can't fathom that so much has changed in such a short space of time.

I look at my watch and see that it's nine o'clock. The late-night shoppers have gone home but the street is not empty. In their place are evening revellers out for the night. Girls totter up the street in impossible heels and miniskirts. Men, wearing festive jumpers, with Rudolf ears, move from pub to pub, laughter ringing through the night. They all look so carefree and happy. I envy them. I wonder what would happen if I just ran from the taxi, into one of the pubs and join in.

I could make new friends. I could allow gin and tonic to help me forget that I'm in a world where Belle Looney does not exist.

The taxi stops and Nora pays the driver, whispering something to him that makes him laugh. I pick up my pace to catch up with her, as she runs off down the street. Where on earth are we off to now?

She disappears down a lane and once again I feel protective of her. Has she no concept of danger? She might have all the answers, but she's still a child. I shout her name as I run but she's no longer in sight.

Damn it, Nora, where are you?

I turn a corner and walk bang into a queue ahead of me. There seems to be about two dozen people in it. They seem to be nearly all male, by the looks of it. What are they queuing for? There's a building on the right-hand side. It must be that.

I skip the queue, walk to the top and see a sign over the open double doors.

Soup Kitchen.

Oh. I didn't even know that this was down here. All these years living in Dublin and I had no idea that this was here.

'Over here, Belle,' a voice says and I look up in surprise. A man in his forties is standing at the door and beckons me forward.

'Howya. Nora's gone in already. She said you were following on. Thatta way,' he says, thumbing the room behind him.

What have you gotten me into now, Nora?

I walk into a large community centre, with long tables lined up in the middle. Benches are on either side and I watch as people begin to shuffle down to sit. They have trays laden with food in their hands and place them on the tables in front of them.

Frank Sinatra is belting out *It's Beginning To Look A Lot Like Christmas*, and in this room, it certainly is.

Tinsel, in reds, purples, whites and greens, is draped across the ceiling, from one beam to the next. A Christmas tree stands in the centre of the room. It's alight with multi-coloured lights, covered in more tinsel and red and gold baubles.

I can see people of all ages in the room, including quite a few kids that look no more than fifteen or sixteen.

That's hard to see. Are they homeless too?

My heart contracts and I feel a lump the size of an orange in my throat. I mean, I know what it's like to not have a family. But I've never not had a home. I always had somewhere to sleep.

I head up to the top of the room and look around for Nora.

'You must be Belle,' a woman's voice shouts over to me. I nod hello to a young girl who is currently handing out sandwiches and soup behind a long table.

'You're working with me this evening. I'm Sophie.' She says.

She nods towards an apron and some plastic gloves. Right so. No comfy bed but some work.

'What do I do?' I ask, as I tie the apron around my waist.

'First night?' she asks. 'You've not done this before?'

I reply. 'I've kind of been thrown in the deep end here by Nora.'

'Listen, if you pour the soup, that would be a great help. I'll do the sambos and teas or coffees. It's ham or tuna tonight, by the way. Oh and the soup is vegetable. It almost always is,' she smiles. 'Safer that way. Keeps the vegetarians happy.'

I soon find my rhythm as I ladle spoonfuls of the aromatic soup into plastic cups. I then place a lid on their tops before handing over to the waiting masses.

The soup is carrot, orange in colour, with what looks like fresh parsley scattered through it. It smells delicious. Beside me is a large platter piled high with buttered brown soda bread. Everyone is encouraged to help themselves to this. Most don't need to be asked twice, they are quick to grab a handful.

At the end of the table is a tin filled high with custard creams beside a box full of bananas and apples. Most stop and stuff their pockets as well as their trays with bread, biscuits and fruit. They move quickly, with urgency, and I suspect for many, hunger is a strong motivator.

I watch Sophie in awe as she chats to everyone when they get to the top of the queue. She knows many by name. Some respond, others just snatch the food and run, ignoring all conversation. But no matter the response, at all times, she smiles at them and only speaks kind words. It encourages me to do the same.

An hour passes by in a blink as we continue serving each person.

'Thanks, Belle. You've been great.' Sophie says, as the last person takes their seat.

'No problem. I'm glad to help,' I say. And it was true. I've enjoyed myself. Nora was right. It has been a blessed relief to just do something and not think for an hour or so.

I look around at the packed hall. With plastic plates and cutlery, most are eating their evening meal in silence. There seem to be two noisy tables at the back, where friends have congregated. They must know each other because they are chatting in that familiar way that only friends can do.

As I watch their faces taking pleasure in each other and the food that is in front of them, I realise that there is much I could learn from them all. I've forgotten how to enjoy the simple things in life. I need to start focusing on good stuff, because that's aplenty. My family, my friends, my community. I have a lot to be grateful for.

'You're coming along with me and Stu on the soup run. We're on route two. It's a nice dry night at least. But cold,' she says.

'Where is Nora?' I ask. I've not seen her once since we arrived at the kitchen.

'Oh she's gone out on another soup run an hour ago. She says she'll see you later,' Sophie says. 'Right, we better go. Stu has the van loaded up already, bless him. He's no patience, though. You know what men can be like.'

31

No act of kindness, no matter how small, is ever wasted.

Aesop

I settle myself in between Sophie and Stu in his van and we head off, into the dark night.

'You said this was route two. How many routes are there then?' I ask.

'Five in Dublin city centre. And we do the run 365 nights a year,' Sophie answers.

'Rain, hail or sunshine, we're out and about,' Stu says.

'Even Christmas Day?' I reply. I'm surprised by this.

'I think that's the most important day to do it,' Stu replies. He's driving up Dame Street towards Christchurch.

'There's over 5,000 people sleeping rough in Dublin on any one night,' Sophie tells me. 'Scary isn't it?'

I didn't realise it was that many. I can't imagine what it must be like for them, in particular on a cold night like it is now.

'For a lot of them, when we arrive, it's gonna be the first thing they'll have eaten today,' Stu says. 'Some might be asleep, so we just leave the food and drink by their side.'

'What do we have for them?' I ask.

'Sandwiches, soup, tea, coffee. We've got plastic ponchos if they need one, to keep dry and clean, some treats for the more sweet-toothed of our clientele,' Stu tells me. 'Although with Sophie here, they might not get a look in.'

'Hey!' she laughs in response. But then takes out a Mars bar from her jacket pocket, waving it in the air. 'Helps me work, rest and play.'

'And do you both do this every night?' I look at them in wonder.

'Oh lordy no. There's a hundred or so part-time volunteers. We have a rota,' Sophie answers. 'But I'm here every week, at least one night.'

'It's show time,' Stu says and pulls over to a loading bay just before Christchurch Cathedral. He nods over to his right. There are a couple of sleeping bags huddled together.

Armed with canteens of tea, coffee and soup, and bags of food, we walk over to them.

'Something to eat, lads?' Stu asks and three heads emerge from the huddle in front of us. They are of indeterminable age, but somewhere north of forty, I'd guess. Weather-beaten faces, chapped and red from the cold, smile as we pass out the hot drinks and sandwiches.

There's lots of light-hearted banter between us all and I'm grateful that I'm part of it.

We continue up towards the cathedral in search of more who are sleeping rough and spot another candidate.

A man sits on a large piece of cardboard, with his head buried between his knees.

'Would you like some food, a drink?' I ask.

He doesn't look up, keeps his head down low.

'We'll leave you something here pal, alright,' Stu says, dropping to his knees and leaving a pack of sandwiches and some fruit on the ground. I pour some soup into a cup and place that beside the food.

He never looks up once, just keeps his head down and we move on. But when I look back, he's blowing on the cup of soup and taking a sip.

We continue our search and I lose count of how many we feed. One guy asks me for clean socks and I begin to apologise to him, that I don't have any. But then Stu digs deep into the pockets of his coat and pulls a pair out.

'I've always a couple of pairs with me,' he says. 'Here you go, pal, Penny's finest.'

I make a promise to myself that I'll go to Penny's and buy dozens of pairs of woolly, thick socks and never leave home without a pair or two in my bag, so that I can give them to the homeless, if they ever need them.

Home. I realise with a start, that right now, I'm homeless too. I have nowhere to go and have more in common with these people than they may realise.

As we walk back to the van, I spy a bundle in the corner of a shop front. He wasn't there an hour ago.

He is shivering, despite the many layers of clothes that he is wearing. That's how cold it is. A hoody tracksuit top, with a body warmer over that, and navy baggy bottoms, that only accentuate how thin he is. His hands are clasped together, as if in prayer.

'Would you like some food?' I ask.

He looks up and I know why I'm here. Of course there's a reason why Nora arranged for me to be on this particular soup run.

Sitting on a cardboard box in front of me is my boy.

'Bobby.'

Dull eyes look up to me in suspicion and fear. He starts to grab his things, ready to take flight.

'Bobby, please don't be afraid. I don't want to hurt you,' I say.

I pull out sandwiches and snacks and place them on the box beside him. Then I pour a cup of soup and give it to him.

'You look perished. This will warm you up.'

He takes the cup, but his eyes still dart around him, fearful and scared.

'I've got this,' I say to Sophie and Stu and they tell me to take my time, heading back to the van.

'Things pretty rough right now?' I ask.

He shrugs.

'Have you been sleeping on the streets for long?'

'Couple of years,' he replies and it takes all of my will-power not to sit down and scoop him into my arms right here and now. He takes a sip of his soup and closes his eyes as the warmth hits him.

'Do you see your family at all?' I ask.

'I got no family. I've got nobody,' he says.

'What about Paul?' I ask.

He shoots a look at me, 'How do you know Paul?'

'I don't really. But I know you and I know he's your brother,' I reply.

'Well, he ain't my brother any more. He put a bullet to his brain two years ago,' he says. 'He's in the ground now, with the worms.'

Oh Bobby, no, my poor boy.

'Maybe he had the right idea,' he says, his voice flat.

I reach over and place my hand over his. He starts to pull away, but I keep my hand there and he stills.

'I'm going to help you,' I say. 'You're not alone. You have somebody.'

He looks at me and says, 'I don't know you, lady.'

'Maybe. But I know you Bobby. And I love you,' I say.

He pulls his hand away this time and starts to shove the sandwich and fruit into a plastic bag.

'You're fucking crazy.'

'Could be,' I reply. 'But I do know you.'

As he stands, so do I and I turn to him and I blurt out, 'The munchkins in *The Wizard of Oz* scare the bejaysus out of you.'

He stops in his tracks and turns to me, his face a picture of shock. 'How do you know that?'

'I know a lot more. You don't like toast, you hate tuna and anything fishy, which is why I've given you a ham sandwich. You love that song *I Would Walk Five Hundred Miles*, and can do a mean Scottish accent. In fact, you are a brilliant mimic and can turn your hand to most accents,' I say.

He has now given up all pretence of walking away and is a rapt audience as I recant his many idiosyncrasies.

'You have a scar over your left knee. You were messing with Paul's knife and cut yourself when you were eight. You should have had stitches, but you were too scared to get help, so you just patched it up yourself as best you could,' I continue.

'How do you know all this?' he says.

'That's a long story, Bobby. But can you just believe me when I tell you I know you and I care about you,' I say.

He looks at me and slowly nods.

'Will you come with me?' I say and he nods again.

'We need to find Bobby somewhere to stay tonight,' I say to Stu and Sophie.

They don't ask any questions and I'm grateful for this. 'I'll ring around, see where there's a bed free,' Stu says.

A few minutes later he confirms that he's found a spot in one of the shelters for Bobby.

'Let's get you sorted,' I say to Bobby and we both jump in the back of the van.

A few minutes later, we arrive at the hostel.

'Will you do me a favour?' I ask.

'Maybe,' he replies.

I write down Jim's name and the pub.

'Go find Jim tomorrow. Tell him that I sent you. He's going to help you,' I say.

'Will you be there?' He says.

'I'll try. But if I don't see you tomorrow, I'll find you,' I promise him.

'What are you?' He says, placing his hand on my arm. 'Some kind of angel?'

I start to laugh at this, of all the things to say to me. 'No, not an angel. But I am your friend. I meant it when I said you aren't alone. Will you do as I ask and find Jim tomorrow?'

'Yeah,' he says. But then he looks down at the paper, and back up to me again and says, 'Thanks. I will do.'

'You want a lift anywhere?' Stu shouts to me as I walk away from the hostel. I'm so grateful for the offer, because I know exactly where I need to go right now.

'Will you bring me to Artane, Stu?' I ask.

'Sure thing Belle,' he says. 'Hop in.'

I need to see my husband.

32

Happy is the man who finds a true friend, and far happier is he who finds that true friend in his wife.

Franz Schubert

The last of the stragglers are leaving the pub when I get there. I look around and see only an empty room full of the stale smell of beer and spirits. Jim is behind the bar, stacking glasses and shouts as he hears the door, 'We're closed.'

'Hello again,' I say.

'Oh here's trouble again. I thought I told you to scram,' he says. But he's not frowning. He's smiling. He's happy to see me, I know he is.

'I thought you had a date,' I say.

'Maybe I changed my mind,' he replies. 'Lock that door behind you and I'll get you a drink. I need one myself. Been a long night.'

I walk back to the double doors and close them tight, reaching up to the black iron locks, sliding them closed. Jim has placed a gin and tonic on the bar counter and walks around to join me. He hops up onto the bar stool and takes a sip of his lager.

'Well, what have you been up to tonight?' he says.

'I've been volunteering at a soup kitchen,' I say.

'Yeah right,' he says, then realises I'm not joking. 'Oh, good for you. I didn't have you pegged as the Florence Nightingale-type.'

'It was fun,' I say. 'My first time doing it, but it won't be my last. I learnt a lot.'

'Good for you,' he says.

We sit and sip our drinks. 'Can I put some music on?' I ask him, pointing to the CD player.

'Knock yourself out,' he says. 'There's a Christmas compilation CD in it. Tis' the season and all that.'

I lean over the bar and press play on the CD and Noddy Holder's voice shouts out, 'It's Christmas!'

'It sure the hell is. Tonight I had three Christmas work parties in. The gang from Artane shopping centre were lethal. Never seen a group put away shots like they did,' he laughs.

'What's your favourite Christmas song?' he asks. 'Actually, don't tell me. Bet you're a *Last Christmas* kind of gal.'

'Busted!' I say. 'Love that song, that video. But it's not my favourite.'

'Okay, let's see. You like the crooners. A bit of Michael Bublé maybe?' he asks.

'I'm more old school than that,' I reply.

'Oh, Frank Sinatra or Tony Bennett?' he asks. 'Ah Tony it is, your face gave it away.'

'*I'll Be Home for Christmas* is one of my favourites and special to me, but it's not my number one,' I tell him.

323

He leans over the counter and picks up the CD case. 'Here we go, track twenty-one.' He pushes the buttons till Tony's voice fills the room.

'So go on, spill, why is it so special to you?' he asks.

'Oh, the usual story. My first date with the man I love, well, this song was playing in the background. It's special.' I shrug.

'You still love that guy,' he says. 'Look, you're blushing.'

'Yes, I love him,' I respond. 'With all my heart.'

'Don't let him know you were leaving love messages on my phone so.' He laughs. 'I'm not sure I'd like that if it were me.'

I smile and wonder what he would say if I told him that he was on that first date with me.

'I think I can guess your favourite song,' I say to him

'Go on, give it your best shot. But I'm pretty confident you'll not get it,' he says.

'Well, you tell everyone that your favourite song is *Rockin' Around the Christmas Tree*,' I say and smile when I see his face.

'But, really, you're an old softie and your true favourite is *All I Want for Christmas Is You*.' Haha, I'm right, his face is a picture as he realises I've nailed him.

'I can't work you out. I really can't,' Jim says. 'There's something about you that I just can't put my finger on.'

Should I just go for broke and tell him?

'Do you want to hear a story?' I say.

'Go on.' He takes another drink.

'In another life, we were best friends. We met at Tess's and I suppose you could say that we saved each other.' I look at him to gauge his reaction. So far so good.

'Tess was a nice woman,' he says.

'Yes. She was more of a mother to me than my own ever was or could be.' I take a deep breath. 'I visited her grave tonight. She died ten years ago.'

Jim shakes his head, 'I'm sorry to hear that. She was good to me and I was a little shit when I lived with her. In and out of trouble all the time.'

'In my world, you were never in trouble,' I say.

'That doesn't sound like me. I got suspended for fighting from school more times than I had hot dinners,' he says.

I can't fathom a Jim like that. 'You fought for me once or twice,' I say to him. 'When kids were picking on me. But you were never suspended.'

'So we were besties as kids? Always living with Tess?' he asks.

'No. Not both of us. I stayed with Tess, but when we were ten, your mother came to get you. She met a guy called Sam. He's a good man. They fell in love and got married. Jim, he adopted you. And you loved and respected him. You called him dad.'

I can't read Jim's face any more. 'They had two children, your mam and dad. You have a brother and a sister who adore you. You all moved to Indiana in the States. You were happy,' I say.

'That's some imagination you have on you,' Jim declares.

'Maybe.' I take another drink.

'So how does it all end up? Am I still in the US, in this other world of yours?' he asks.

'Nope. You came back to me. When we were twenty-five, you came home to Ireland and found me. You know when we were kids, I'd always joke that one day you'd beg me to marry you,' I say. 'And three weeks after our first date, on Christmas Eve, you dropped to one knee on Ha'penny Bridge and proposed.'

'And what did you say?' Jim asks.

'Yes. Of course. There was never any doubt in my mind. We got married and we live up the road, in a doer-upper house. We never seem to find the time to do the doing up, though. Maybe that's because we foster kids. Your idea, as it happens,' I tell him.

Something flashes on his face. 'You've thought about fostering before, haven't you? Wondered how you could help kids like you?'

He stands up and walks around the bar, to re-fill our glasses. 'How do you do that?'

'I know you, Jim. That's how,' I say.

'What could I give a foster kid? Barman, living in a flat, yeah, that would really make some kids life,' he says.

'You've made a difference in a lot of kids' lives. You are a good man. You ever think about teaching? Because you are a teacher in my world. You used to be a soccer coach in America, but when we got married and settled down here, you started to do career guidance in the local school instead,' I say.

'This Jim of yours sounds like a real stand-out guy,' he jokes. 'I think I prefer his life than I do mine.'

'Oh, he's pretty cool. You'd like him a lot. Most do,' I say.

'So, tell me this then, Belle, you with the crazy imagination. If your world is so good, what the hell are you doing here in mine?' he asks.

'I messed up,' I say.

'How?' He looks attentively at me.

I decide to cut to the chase. No point being evasive or holding back. 'We lost a baby and I've been a little bit broken ever since,' I admit. And in another gesture as old as we are, Jim leans over and with his thumb, caresses away the tears that start to fall.

'I'm so sorry,' he says. 'You would have a beautiful baby.'

I smile. He said that to me over and over when I was pregnant.

'Go on, tell me more about how you messed up,' he asks.

'We fought. Doesn't matter why, but we fought, while we were on our way home from the Wicklow mountains. You sped up, you were pissed off with me and then the car skidded and we crashed,' I say.

'Am I alive?' he asks. His face has turned a funny shade of white.

'I don't know,' I say, once more going for the hard truth. 'I panicked at the hospital, your machines were going mental, beeping and the nurses were all around. I can't explain why I did it, but I ran out of the hospital and didn't stop till my sides hurt.'

'I sometimes feel like doing that. Running,' Jim says.

'You do?' I'm so grateful to him that he didn't judge me. I should never have left his side.

I look him straight in the eye and hit him with the punch line. 'Get ready for the best part. I wished I'd never been born, an angel called Nora appeared and told me she'd granted my wish. So here I am, in this world where nobody knows who I am.'

It feels so good to say it out loud to him. His face, however, isn't one that shows he believes a word.

'You really believe this story, don't you?' he says.

I nod and he says, 'I don't know whether to give you a hug or call the guys in white coats.'

I giggle and hope he opts for the former.

'I think I could well be crazy. I mean this world doesn't make sense to me. Everything is upside down and different.' But then I look at him, really look at him. But maybe not as much as I thought at first.

'At first I didn't recognise you, I thought you were so different to my Jim. But now …' I drift off, not knowing how to complete the sentence.

'Now what?' Jim whispers.

'Now I recognise you,' I say.

We both sit for a moment, listening to the music, drinking our drinks and say nothing further. I have no idea what's going through his mind, but at least he's not throwing me out the door of his pub.

'Tell me about our life,' he eventually says.

'We're happy. We're in love, proper love-story stuff too.' When he laughs at this, I say, 'No, seriously, we are. We are both teachers, but I just do relief work now, as I focus on the foster kids more. We have a nice house,' I say. 'We both volunteer at the community centre, at the youth club. We've fostered lots of kids, some on temporary placements, some long-term.'

'That's pretty cool,' Jim says.

'You'd say awesome in my world. Yankee doodle dandy,' I tease.

'I don't think I've ever used the word "awesome" in my life. Deadly … Maybe.' He says.

'Tess is alive too. That's been one of the hardest things to take here, her death. Our house is always full and loud,' I say.

Lauren's face flashes into my head. Happy and laughing, not sullen and angry like earlier.

'We like Italian food, walks on Donabate Beach and *The Walking Dead*. We're saving like mad to go on holiday, you want to bring me to Yosemite Park and go camping. I want to go to a spa. We might do both,' I say.

'Sounds pretty "awesome".' He jokes and I giggle and reach up to touch his face.

It is. More than any words could describe.

'So how do you get back there?' he asks, sitting in front of me again. 'That's the question.'

I shrug. 'I don't know how and I'm not sure I want to. Because in that world, I don't know if you are alive or not. And if you are dead, then I can't be there. I can't live in a world without you, Jim.'

Our eyes lock and we stare at each other, for a moment, for a lifetime. I feel something pass between us, he feels it too, I can see it in his eyes.

I whisper, 'You have no idea how much I love you. And I know you don't know me in your world. I know that I sound like the craziest woman you've ever met.'

He nods.

'I know you don't love me. But if I stay here, in this upside-down world, at least I can come back here every night and breath the same air as you. I might very well develop a drinking habit, but at least I can see you every day,' I whisper.

Adrenalin floods my body and my senses are heightened in the silence. Jim stares at me for the longest time. Then, he leans in and kisses me. Softly at first, but soon with urgency and I am lost in a tangle of emotion, as his hands search my face, my hair, my body.

33

We are all here on earth to help others; what on earth the others are here for I don't know.

W.H. Auden

Before I open my eyes, the bittersweet smell of stale beer and cider assaults me. Hundreds of drops of alcohol spilt onto the table tops and red grungy carpet have left their mark. I hear a truck trundle by, on the road outside and a car door slams shut. I'm lying, spoon to spoon with Jim and can feel his breath, warm on my neck. Jim made a makeshift bed out of blankets and towels robbed from the back kitchen.

'Morning,' his voice says. He's awake. My stomach turns over, just hearing his voice.

I flip over and smile at him. 'Morning.'

'That was something else last night,' he says. 'Unexpected, at the very least.'

Yes it was. Something we've done hundreds of times before, yet it felt like our first time last night.

'I need to go,' I say.

A look, regret, I think, crosses his face. We both sit up

and he says, 'Not before you have a cup of tea. Some toast. At least let me make you breakfast.'

So, with hot buttered toast and a cup of tea, we sit at the bar again, facing each other, shyly, but both wearing the same tentative smiles.

'I have a favour to ask,' I say.

'Shoot,' he replies.

'There's a man, a young man, called Bobby. He needs your help,' I say.

'Okay.' He replies. 'I'm listening.'

'In our other life, he was our foster son. He's a great kid. And we both love him and him us. He's like both of us, really. He's lost. He's paying the price for the sins of his parents,' I say. 'But despite all of that, he's a good man. And you could be good friends here. You'd like him.'

'What do you want me to do?' he asks.

'Give him a job, here in the bar. Give him a sofa to sleep on in your flat, till he can get his own place. Give him a reason to live,' I say.

'That's a pretty big ask, Belle. I don't know him,' he says.

'Yes you do. Remember what you said last night, that you have thought before about helping others. You just didn't know how. Well, I'm telling you how you can make a difference right now, right this minute,' I say.

He pours another cup of tea and, mug in hand, walks around the bar, mulling over my words.

'You've messed with my head, Belle. Since you walked into this bar yesterday, everything feels different,' he says.

I feel bad for him, I really do. I can't imagine what it must be like for him, trying to compute the last twenty-four hours.

'I feel like I know you,' he whispers.

Because we're meant to be, that's why. No matter what mixed-up world we are in. You're my person and I'm yours.

'And even though your whole "other world" story is the maddest thing I've ever heard, I want to believe that it's true,' he says.

I stay silent and watch my husband as he grapples with how he feels and what he knows.

'You know what I keep thinking?' he asks.

I shake my head.

'Even if you are madder than a bag of cats, that I don't care. I want to see you again,' Jim says.

My heart sings. It really does and little pieces of it that splintered over the past twenty-four hours start to meld back together again.

'I want to see you again too, but right now, I have to sort out this mess I'm in,' I say. 'I have to get back into the city and find Nora.'

'This Bobby bloke, how will I find him?' he says.

'You'll help him then?' I ask. I am floored by his generosity.

'I'll give him a trial here. That's all I'm promising. But I do need some help for Christmas anyhow, it's getting busy,' he says.

'And a place to sleep?' I ask. 'He's homeless and needs somewhere to stay too.'

'I'll throw in board too. But he better not fleece me. If I wake up and my DVD collection is gone, I'll come look for you!' he says.

I run over to him and throw my arms around his neck. His tea spills everywhere, but he doesn't complain when my lips find his.

'What are you doing to me Miss Trouble?' he says. 'You better come find me again. I don't want to say goodbye.'

'I promise,' I say. 'I have to be cheeky now. Can I have some money too? For a bus ride into the city.'

'Where you going?' He asks, not hesitating for a second before reaching into the till for a fifty-euro note.

'I'll get this back to you,' I say.

He waves aside my promise. 'You never answered me, where you going?' he says.

'To the Ha'penny Bridge, to see a friend,' I say.

'Nora. The angel,' he replies.

I nod. I just pray she's there.

'Will you be back?' he asks

'I don't know, Jim. But I'm going to do everything I can to find my way back to you, in this world or in our own. I promise you,' I say.

The roads are busy with early-morning commuters, making their way to their desks. I'm grateful for some time to sit and think about the previous night, before I find Nora. What if she's done a disappearing act? Panic runs over me. Yes, I've found Jim but I don't want to stay in this world. I want our old life back.

Once I get into the city, I start to make my way to the bridge. As that's where Nora found me. It's cold and I fasten my borrowed parka coat up tight. I wonder if Bobby is awake yet too. Will he call Jim, like he promised he would? I hope I've done enough to make a difference there.

The clouds are low and grey. They appear to be hanging lower than normal, as if they could drop any second and land with a crash on the ground in front of me. Tess would say that the sky is full of snow. That's what I'm seeing now. I remember, as a kid, watching the sky in the thick of winter, hoping for a snow day. Because then our school would close and Jim and I could stay at home and play.

The bridge is empty and my heart sinks. Maybe Nora is having a lie-in, I think wryly. I walk to the centre and stand close to the white railing, holding on tight to them and looking down to the river below. So much has changed since the last time I stood here.

'I can remember when this bridge opened,' Nora's voice says from behind me and near gives me a cardiac arrest. 'Back in 1816. It's gone through so many changes since then, but I like it now. It's pretty, don't you think?'

'For goodness sake. My heart,' I say. But I'm so happy to see her, I grab her and hug her close to me.

'You thought I wasn't going to come, didn't you?' she says.

'Put it this way, I never thought I'd say this, but I'm glad to see you,' I say.

'I keep telling you, you've got to start believing again, Belle,' Nora says.

I'm trying. I really am.

'As quick as the council get rid of these, more appear.' Nora says, pointing to the dozens of padlocks that are fastened to the white railings.

'I like them. They're so romantic, a public symbol of lasting love, locked together,' I say. I read the names of couples inscribed in marker on some of the padlocks. John & Fiona. Shelley & Anthony. Evelyn & Seamus. Mike & Tina. Fiona & Michael. Carmel & Roger. Adrienne & George. Ann & Nigel.

'Some people throw the keys of the padlocks into the River Liffey. As a gesture of everlasting love,' Nora adds.

'Everlasting love. I like the sound of that,' I say.

'You and Jim are everlasting,' Nora remarks.

'That's what I want to talk to you about. I need to get home. To my home, to my Jim,' I say. 'I'm begging you, Nora.'

'It's not as simple as clicking your heels three times,' Nora replies. 'I can't control what happens. And you're not done here yet.'

What else have you got in store for me, Nora? I'm not sure I can do any more surprises. 'Will Bobby be okay?' I ask her.

'I think he has a chance. You've done a good thing there,' Nora says. 'I didn't see that one coming, that plan you hatched. I like getting surprised.'

'Jim and Bobby have always had a strong bond. They like each other, enjoy each other's company. I'm hoping that this is still the case,' I say.

'It's up to them now,' Nora says. 'I'm curious as to who you would like to see today, though?'

Nobody.

Liar, liar.

Nora raises her eyebrows and smiles knowingly. Damn her and her mind-reading. 'Come with me,' she says and once again I follow.

34

From Childhoods Hour, I have not been, as others were.
I have not seen, as others saw.

Edgar Allan Poe

'So, Dolores. What do you reckon she's up to here, then?'
Nora remarks.

I don't want to think about her, thank you very much.
But of course we all know that's not true.

'I mean you made that wish, you wished you had never
been born, because she put that little seed into your head
with that nasty letter of hers, all those years ago,' Nora
continues.

'So she's not dead then?' I ask. And when Nora shakes
her head, I feel relief seep into my bones. Maybe I do
care.

Why does it matter? I mean, I don't have a relationship
with the woman. She's shown me quite clearly for over
three decades that she has no feelings for me whatsoever.

But it does matter. I need to know how she is. How was
life for her, without me in it?

'Is she happy?' I ask. 'Without me in her life?'

'You'll see,' she remarks in that know-it-all manner that a child has no business having.

'You keep forgetting. I'm not a child. I'm 292 years old,' Nora remarks.

Damn this whole mind-reading malarkey.

We're heading out of the city, towards the south side. It's funny, but I don't come out this way that often. The other side of the Liffey, but I rarely have reason to visit over here. We pass through Ballsbridge and twenty minutes later I am back to where it all started for me. I'm back in Dun Laoghaire, driving down the street where I spent four years of my childhood.

Nora reaches over and clasps my hand, squeezing it tight.

I brush away tears as they splash their way onto my cheeks.

'I shouldn't be this upset, just being back in this area. It's ridiculous,' I say.

'No it's not. I know it's often said that time heals all wounds. But I'm not so sure that's true. You just learn to live with some of them and patch them up as best you can. And that's okay. It's okay to be remember the bad times, because it helps us recognise the good ones,' Nora says.

Our car pulls up outside a brownstone terraced house.

'This is Dolores's house,' Nora says.

'She's in there,' I say, looking up the driveway. 'I don't want to see her.' I can feel my heart beating loudly in my chest.

'I didn't say that,' Nora says. 'It's her house, though. Come on, follow my lead. You need to see this.'

Nora is skipping up to the front door before I even have my seat belt off. I clamber out of the car and run after her. She rings the doorbell and smiles when the door opens.

'Hello?' A man, in his late fifties, I'd say, stands looking at us enquiringly.

'Hello,' Nora says, with her trademark big smile. 'You're Don?'

He's Don, the boyfriend that Dolores told me about all those years ago. The one that wouldn't marry her when I came out, all black, ready to mess up her world.

Oh, I get it. She married him after all and now they live here. I'm not sure how to react to this.

Don can't help it, Nora's megawatt smile does its trick. He smiles back and the wary look disappears from his face. Nora has that effect on people, they react well to her.

'My mum and I are cousins of Dolores. But it's years since we've been in touch. As we were in the area, we thought we'd come to visit,' Nora says. And I find myself shaking his hand, smiling at him too.

I used to imagine what he looked like, this man that almost married my mother. I'd sometimes play a game when I was younger. What if I'd not been born dark-skinned? Would he have married mam and would we all be living the dream together? One big happy family. I look up at the pretty house and wonder, is this the life I could have had?

His eyes don't leave Nora's and an expression that I can't read takes over his face. 'You'd better come in then.'

A bright-purple hall leads us into a big open-plan kitchen and family room, painted in yellow and orange. He likes colour, that's for sure. And to look at the guy, you'd think he was more of a beige kind of decor man. He's dressed in a jumper and chino slacks. Conservative. A Christmas tree is in the corner of the room, a wonderful mix of handmade decorations and tinsel adorning it. Years of children's arts-and-craft projects from school right there on every branch. A large white star sits atop this tree.

'I'm more of an angel girl myself,' Nora says with a cheeky grin, pointing to the star.

To the left of the tree is a gallery of photographs on the wall. I scan them quickly and see there are three children at various stages of their lives, from gummy, smiling babies, to adulthood. Black and white canvases stand alongside colourful prints, filling every inch of the wall.

'Your children?' I ask.

'Yes. I'm going to have to start a new wall soon,' he says and we all laugh. 'That's my eldest, Siobhan.' He points to a picture of a pretty woman with auburn hair, with a baby nestled in her arms. 'And my grandson, Alfie.'

'A gorgeous picture,' I say and he nods in agreement. A doting grandfather if ever I saw one.

'And these two are the terrible twins, Adelle and Ciaran.' He points to them both in cap and gown at their graduation. 'They're off touring the world for a year. Last Skype call they were on a beach in Bali.'

'Lucky them,' I say. 'You must be so proud, Don, they are lovely children.'

He starts to fiddle with his Nespresso coffee machine as he answers, 'Nobody luckier than me. Good kids, each and every one of them.'

'And their mam, Dolores?' I say pointing to the pictures. I am pretty sure this is true, because Ciaran is the image of her and I can see a lot of her in Siobhan too.

'Yes.' His face changes, the smile has gone and a hardness has crept into his countenance.

I note that there is not a single photograph of Dolores anywhere. And somehow or other, I reckon that she's not Susie Homemaker in this world either.

'Where is she?' I ask gently.

'She left when the twins were babies. Siobhan was only a toddler,' he replies.

Oh.

'Not the mothering kind, she told me. And I'm afraid I was a bit of a let-down for her,' Don says.

'I'm sorry,' I say and I genuinely am. I wish that in this life, Dolores had been different.

'We should never have married. She didn't love me. I'm not sure what she wants in life, but it sure as hell wasn't me,' he says.

'Do you know where she is?' I ask.

'She's been in and out of prison. For fraud. Social welfare fraud. She was claiming child benefits for the kids, even though she wasn't here.' Now he looks angry and who can blame him?

'Are you okay?' he asks and I realise that he's talking to me. 'You look a bit pale there.'

I'm not okay. Not one bit. I've spent the best part of my life blaming myself for my mother's pitiful life. For being born.

You ruined everything.

'Here, sit down,' Don urges.

I take a seat and place my head in my lap.

I could have had a good life if it hadn't been for you.

Oh Dolores, you were never going to have a good life. I didn't screw your life up. You are far too good at doing that all by yourself.

All those years, I pictured a world for Dolores where she didn't get pregnant. A world where she had married Don and lived happily somewhere in the suburbs.

I take a sip of the cold water that Don has produced and wait for the blood to stop rushing around my head.

'Were you close to Dolores?' Don asks. 'I'm sorry, if this is all a shock.'

'We weren't close. But we did know each other. I was just curious as to how her life turned out,' I say. 'I really am sorry that she didn't do more for …' My voice trails off as I look at the pictures of the family.

'We've done okay.' Don says. 'And the kids are good. Most of the time.'

I stand up. I need to get out of here. I feel like an imposter snooping.

'Thank you, but we'll be on our way. Happy Christmas, Don,' I say and we shake hands. Nora gives him a hug and I watch his face change once again, back into happy, carefree Don, without the shadow of Dolores.

'Where are you spending Christmas?' Don asks us. 'With family?'

'I'm not sure yet.' I realise I've no answer for him. I imagine a Christmas without Jim and Tess, Bobby and Lauren.

'Come on, let's go,' Nora says and she heads towards to the hall door. We walk away from the house down the tree-lined street in silence. 'I know something that will cheer you up.'

There's a park on our right and Nora runs over to the playground. We each grab a swing and start to kick our legs back and forth, as we swing higher and higher.

As the cold air whooshes through my hair and stings my face, I begin to feel calmer. I open my eyes and see Nora is now gently swinging beside me, so I slow down and match her rhythm. 'I can't believe she did that. To those beautiful children. She had it all.' I am incredulous.

'Her path in life was set from the get-go,' Nora replies.

I could have had a good life if it hadn't been for you.

The pain from that letter feels as sharp today as it was back then.

'All this time I thought I was the reason her life was in such a mess,' I say.

'I know. And it couldn't be further from the truth. The only reason Dolores had the life she had is because she's spent a lifetime working hard to make a mess of things,' Nora says.

I feel tired. I feel so bloody tired that I want to curl up into a ball and sleep for an eternity.

'So who does she blame here in this world, for her misfortune? If I never existed?' I ask.

'Her parents, Don, the children, her friends, the universe. It's always someone else's fault with Dolores,' Nora says.

All this time, I held onto guilt and blamed myself it was my fault that her life was such a disappointment.

'Listen to me, Belle. Listen hard. Dolores is the master of her own destiny. We all are. None of this has ever been your fault.' Nora says.

How many wasted hours have I spent worrying about my mother?

'Everything happens for a reason,' Nora continues. 'Dolores had a life. A good life. Yes, things have happened to her that have been difficult. Her own mother was a hard woman.'

History repeating itself, as she told me.

'But you know, better than anyone else, that you can't always control life's circumstances. What you can control is how you react to them.'

I think of all the years I allowed her voice in my head, criticising me, blaming me, pointing her finger at me.

'It's time to mute her voice,' Nora says.

'Zip it, lock, put it in your pocket,' I say, repeating a phrase that Lauren often uses.

'You do know that you're not your mother,' Nora says, leaning over and touching my arm. 'You are your own person. A good person.'

I've never said out loud how much I fear that I'm like my mother. That some of her genetic badness will come out in me at some point. And to hear that thought denied is a gift.

I am not my mother.

She's just a person who shares some DNA with me. But I am not her and she is not me.

I know that so many factors have shaped me into who I am today. And a big part of that, one that I have never really come to terms with, is my early days with Dolores and how she treated me.

Why wasn't I good enough? Why didn't she love me enough? Why did it matter, one little bit, the colour of my skin? Why didn't she hold me close, skin to skin, mother to daughter and just love me?

'She was supposed to love me,' I say.

Nora nods, her eyes glistening in sympathy.

'When I found out that I was pregnant, this primal, all-consuming love overcame me. When I saw our baby on the scan for the first time, it became my everything. That's the bit I can't understand. Why didn't she feel that too? She was supposed to love me unconditionally.' Loss pierces my soul.

'She'd forgotten how to love,' Nora replies.

I look up at the sky as I can feel the build-up of long-held-back tears.

'There are always consequences for everything we do. Do you truly believe that Dolores has no regrets? She hasn't come out of this unscathed. She's a damaged woman,' Nora says. 'And at the end of the day, she's all alone.'

We gently sway back and forth. A young couple pushing a pram walks by, their eyes never leaving the sleeping bundle wrapped up in blankets before them.

Nora twists her seat around so that she is facing me. 'What about you? Do you have any regrets?'

Yes. But I'm not talking about that now.

'How long will you go on blaming yourself?' Nora asks.

I said I'm not talking about that, Nora.

'It was nobody's fault that your baby died.' Nora is persistent.

Stop it, I don't want to talk about it.

'You have to. There can be no more hiding, Belle.' Nora strokes my hand gently in hers.

I close my eyes and remember.

I'm tired. And fat. With a bladder the size of a pea, it seems. That's three times in the past hour I've run to the loo.

But I've never felt more beautiful. All my life I've tried to find clothes that hide my tummy, my bum, my thighs. But now, as my bump grows, my confidence in my body does too.

I stand up and walk to my long-mirrored armoire. I turn to check out my silhouette. Yesterday someone asked me how long did I have to go and spluttered in disbelief when I said twenty weeks. I know that I look at least six months pregnant already. Am I bothered? No! I love that. I want my bump to get bigger and bigger and when my belly button pops, I'll rejoice.

Yes I'm fat, tired with a pea-sized bladder, but that's not all I am. I'm deliriously happy.

I think it's time for a song.

My baby book says that from about twenty-three weeks little junior here can hear sounds. A daily soundtrack of my heartbeat and voice, and sounds from the outside world, are so important to the baby.

I got so annoyed with Jim yesterday. He was shouting at the TV. Liverpool were not doing their thing, playing badly. Well, the poor baby got an awful fright, the shouts coming from him. So I've banned all shouting. Told Jim to take his football hooliganism to a different house. I don't care how bad the match is going.

The book also recommends singing to your bump. It's a way to form a bond with it, an attachment before the baby arrives. And the theory is that when the baby comes into the world it will already know your voice.

Well, I don't think I need any help with the bonding part, as I've totally fallen in love with my little baba already. But just in case, I talk and sing constantly and make Jim do the same too. He was all self-conscious at first. But now he has me demented, bending down and whispering to the baby about all sorts, all day long. Usually he bangs on about sports. I told him the other day that the poor child will probably come out, and instead of crying will say, 'Up the Dubs!'

For my lullaby sessions, I have a catalogue of songs that I like to mix up for the baby. Jim teases me about the cheese factor, but I don't care. I feel all fromage frais-like these days. I sing Brahms Lullaby, Toora Loora, Hush Little Baby *and to mix it up a little,* Shake It Off *by Taylor Swift. But my absolute favourite is* Hushabye Mountain.

How would you like that, little baby? Yes, that will do nicely, I think.

A gentle breeze from Hushabye Mountain
Softly blows o'er Lullaby Bay
It Fills the sails of boats that are waiting
Waiting to sail your worries away

I look up and Jim is watching me.

'You are going to be the most wonderful mother,' he says. 'That's a lucky baby in there.'

I hope so. I have so many hopes and dreams for this little one.
Now where were we, little one?

So close your eyes on Hushabye Mountain
Wave good … bye to cares of the day
And watch your boat from Hushabye Mountain
Sail far away from Lullaby Bay.

My back starts to ache. A dull, low ache.

'I might go to bed myself,' I tell Jim.

Then I feel it happening. A tear. Something giving way inside of me.

I feel the baby inside of me pull away.

My dreams that night return to childhood nightmares of flame-filled rooms and abandonment. Loss.

But as night turns to day, my fears seem silly and I have persuaded myself that I am worrying over nothing.

Cold gel on my tummy. A monitor beside me with a baby on the screen. A white hospital room filled with silence and the laboured breaths of worry.

No heartbeat.

The doctor is called and he tells us, gently, sorrowfully, but firmly, our baby's heart has stopped beating.

I know exactly when it happened. I felt the tear.

It was my fault. It was all my fault.

'It was my fault.'

Nora moves from her swing and comes closer to me. This 292-year-old child pulls me towards her and holds me close.

'It was not your fault,' Nora says.

'I felt it. I felt the moment that it happened. I didn't imagine that it could be losing her, though,' I say.

'Whether you were lying in bed or cooking dinner, it was going to happen. You did nothing wrong,' Nora continues.

'Then why do I feel so guilty?' I whisper.

'You need to blame someone and yourself is as good as anyone,' Nora says.

So wise for one so old.

'If loving a baby and wanting a baby could prevent a miscarriage then you would have a three-year-old right now,' Nora says.

'I loved her so much,' I say.

My body racks with grief. I cry for the baby that I sang to. I cry for the baby that I had so many hopes and dreams for. I cry for the ache that just won't go away inside of me ever since she died.

'Let it go,' Nora says. 'This burden you took upon yourself to carry, it's not yours to do so.'

I've held onto so much for so long, I'm not sure who I am without it all inside of me.

'You know, you have always been one of the most compassionate people I know,' Nora continues. 'It's time that you showed yourself some compassion.'

Easier said than done.

'Try,' Nora says. 'Say it out loud and maybe then you'll believe it.'

'It wasn't my fault,' I whisper.

'No it wasn't,' Nora is emphatic. 'No more than it was Jim's.'

'My baby died but it wasn't my fault,' I say and as the words are said out loud, walls of guilt that have surrounded me for years come tumbling down. I am no longer a prisoner.

My baby died and it was nobody's fault.

I can't control how my mother feels about me. I am not to blame for her life.

But I can control how I feel about myself. I am not a bad person.

And I can control how I love.

I want to love life, I want to love Jim. And I want children in my life. Foster or our own. I want children.

I'm starting to believe again. Fairy tales do exist. I swore when I was a kid that I'd go to my grave, old and wrinkly believing in happy-ever-afters. Well, that's exactly what I'm going to do.

Dusk has crept up on me and the park is now bathed in half light, half darkness.

'There you go,' Nora says, 'I knew you'd get it!'

I kick back my legs, joyfully, and start to swing. As I look up into the darkening sky, twinkling stars appear above me. And for the first time in a long time, I feel at peace.

35

Our greatest weakness lies in giving up. The most certain way to succeed is always to try just one more time.

Thomas A. Edison

'Where are we going?' I ask.

'You'll see,' she says and I feel hope. 'Am I going home?'

She starts to hum *O Holy Night* and I begin to get excited. 'Oh look, it's a jumble sale. Let's take a peek before we grab a taxi.'

I follow Nora into the small community centre and wander around looking at piles of household trinkets and books that are on sale.

'I think you might like to look at the stall over there. Lots of toys on it,' Nora says, winking at me.

And before I even get close, I see it. Simon, the memory game. It's the original one, just like ours. I run over and pick it up. I swear this could be the same one.

'How much?' I ask the lady.

'Oh, let me see, how about a euro?' She smiles at me.

I reach inside my pocket and pull out a ten-euro note. 'Here. Take this. It's a bargain at that price.' I hold it in close to me and know it's the perfect Secret Santa Christmas gift for Jim.

'Oh, how generous of you. For that price, I'll even give you one of these lovely gift bags to put it in.'

'Perfect.' I take the bag and turn to Nora, who is looking pretty pleased with herself right now.

'I know, I'm a legend,' she says.

'That you are my friend. That you are,' I reply.

We're in a taxi a few moments later and I feel lighter than I've done for years. This is all going to work out. We're all going to be just fine. I cannot wait to see Jim to tell him so. As we pass by one of Dublin's many famous bridges, O'Connell Bridge, I notice a crowd beginning to gather. What's going on over there?

'Stop!' I shout to the driver, as I suddenly realise what is going on.

'Where are you going?' Nora shouts as I jump out of the car.

'That's Bobby over there,' I say, pointing towards the crowd. I push my way through the rubberneckers gathered on the bridge and hope that I am wrong. But balancing on the top of narrow railings on O'Connell Bridge is my Bobby. What on earth is going on?

'Let me through,' I plead with the un-cooperating crowd. 'I know this man.'

They move apart at this and I can feel their fear and excitement as a real-life drama takes a new twist in front of them. I stand a few feet away from the young man who doesn't know me, but he is my son all the same.

'Bobby,' I whisper, afraid that if I shout I'll cause him to topple over into the water.

He turns to glance my way and looks at me without recognition for a moment.

'He just walked up and climbed the safety railing, just like that,' a woman stage whispers behind me. 'I tried to talk him down, but he's having none of it.'

I inch my way forward and pray for the right words to get through to him.

'Bobby,' I say again, gently. 'Do you remember me? We met last night. On the soup run.'

His eyes show recognition and he nods. 'Go away lady.'

'I can't do that Bobby,' I say. 'I can't leave you.'

He looks towards the grey, murky water and I realise he's about to jump, just like I had planned to only a few days previously. Nora stopped me and now I have to stop him. But I have no idea what to say, no idea what to do.

'You're my son, Bobby!' I scream, over the gasps of horror all around me. He wobbles as his hand grasps the railing behind him.

'I have a mother and it sure as hell ain't you.' Sadness fills his every word. He looks back to the water again.

'Did you call that number I gave you?' I ask gently.

'No, what's the point?' He says, defeat permeating from his every fibre.

'There's every point,' I say to him. 'You can't give up.'

'Yes I can,' he says.

'Jim, my friend, he has a job for you,' I say. 'I spoke to him last night. He has a flat and he says you can stay with him too and he will give you a job in his bar,' I say.

'Why are you doing this? Why are you helping me?' he asks.

'Because I care. Because in the world where I come from, I threw away it all away. I had a boy just like you in my life. I loved him like a son.' Now I feel my own tears whip towards his. I'm close to him now. I have inched over slowly as we talked. I hold my hand up to him.

'Please Bobby,' I say. 'Take my hand.' He refuses it and looks to the water again, tears streaming silently down his face.

'What do you think is going to happen when you jump?' I demand.

He looks down to the now-choppy water and back to me again. 'I get to disappear.'

Oh Bobby, when did life get so bad that you just wanted to do that? As I feel the cold air on my face and look down to the swirling, dark waters. I can hardly fathom that I ever felt like he does right now.

'It's going to be cold. It's going to hurt like hell when you hit that water. And you might not die,' I say to him.

He shrugs and as he moves a foot away from the railing, I try to reason with him one more time, try one more time to save this boy.

'I wished I had never been born too,' I calmly tell him. 'But it didn't work and now I've lost everything.'

He moves his foot back to the railing. 'What happened?'

'I felt like you, at my lowest. Something snapped and I could not continue. So I wished I'd never been born. I got my wish. And now I'm living in some kind of no man's land, hell,' I say.

'I'm on my own already. It's not the same,' Bobby says.

'Yes it is,' I tell him. 'I have nobody now. But if you want me, I can be here for you. I'll be your friend. I'll help you through this. And you can help me too.'

He looks at me, tears whipping off his face into the wind. The woman behind me whispers that the coastguard has been called and is on its way below.

'I can't do one more Christmas on my own. I'm done with that.' He looks broken and I just want to fix him back together again.

'I understand,' I say and I do. Because I am on my own too. I have lost everyone that is special to me. He turns away from me and I know that no matter what I say, he is lost to me.

Or maybe not. I climb up on the railings, ignoring the protests of people around me.

'You jump. I jump,' I say to him. I hold my hand out to his and grasp the railing behind me for dear life.

'No you won't,' he sobs, but there's doubt on his face.

'I will. You have to realise that everything you do creates ripples throughout your life. In ways that you cannot even comprehend. Every single life has value, Bobby. Yours too. And you have the potential to impact others in such a positive and meaningful way,' I say.

He doesn't move. But his hand is back holding the railings. I feel hope that my words are reaching him.

'I didn't believe this until recently. I had no idea that so much that we do every day affects others. In a positive way. You matter Bobby very much,' I say.

'I don't feel like I matter,' he says.

'Just allow yourself to think something, for one minute,' I say. 'Imagine that some of the best days of your life haven't happened yet. If you jump, you'll never find out what they are.'

He lifts his hand and I reach mine out towards his. 'Take it,' I say to him. 'Take my hand. I've got you and I won't let go.'

He leans over and his fingertips touch mine. They are cold, like ice. I loop my fingers around his and squeeze. 'I've got you,' I say, smiling in relief. He smiles and inches towards me and I can hear cheers from the crowd.

Then his right foot slips on the icy rail and he lunges forward. I lean forward to grab him, shouting his name. He clambers for me, grabs my leg and then I feel myself falling with him. The sound of silence is deafening. I hear nothing until I hit the icy water and then it goes black.

36

If light is in your heart,
You will find your way home.

Rumi

Christmas Eve, 2015

I open my eyes as a bright light beams down on me. It's happened. I'm dead. Do I become an angel, like Nora? That wouldn't be so bad, I suppose. But then the crushing realisation hits me. If I'm dead, I never get to feel Jim's arms around me, ever again.

Jim, I'm so sorry. I've messed up really badly. I never meant to leave you. Jim, my darling, I'm so sorry.

'Give her something to calm down,' a voice says and then it goes black again. My body aches. I feel like I've been hit by a truck. I open my eyes, slowly, and see those same bright lights again.

Why am I so sore, if I'm dead? That doesn't make sense. My right side, from my face right down to my legs, feel bruised and battered. Nora. Where are you? Don't leave me now.

'I'm right here,' Nora says and turn to my right and she's

sitting beside me, smiling that goddam beautiful smile.

'Am I dead?' I whisper and when she shakes her head in denial, tears pour down my face. I've never been so relieved in my life.

'Is Bobby okay?' I ask and can't bear to wait for the answer. Please let him be okay.

'Bobby is fine,' Nora smiles some more. 'Don't worry. He's in a room down the corridor, but is unharmed, physically at least.'

'I had his hand …' I say. 'But it just slipped away and then he was falling and so was I …' It's too much and I start to shake. I'm wearing a thin, short-sleeved hospital gown and feel so cold.

'Your clothes were a little wet when you were brought in. Jumping into the Liffey will do that for you,' Nora smiles as she pulls the blanket over me and tucks me in. Once again, I have this weird topsy-turvy sensation that she is the adult and I am the child.

'You saved his life,' Nora said. 'You were so brave and I've never been so proud of you.'

'It was instinct. He's my child. Of course I'd give up my life for him,' I say.

'You were on your way home too. You knew that. You knew that I was bringing you back. And yet you gave that up, to stay here and save Bobby. There is no limit to a mother's love, it seems. To love someone more than yourself …' She sighs with contentment.

So I've lost my chance. I don't regret it one bit, staying behind for Bobby. But I'm so sad. Maybe I can still find a way to make this right. If I can find a way back home again, to a world where Bobby doesn't feel despair. To a world where Jim and I are together, as one, as we should be. To a world where Tess is watching *Grey's Anatomy* munching chocolate but always with two arms open to catch me when I fall. To a world where … where I might dare to dream of having my own children …. Because I am a mother.

I turn to Nora, to tell her all this, but she just places her finger to her lips. 'Sshhh …' she says. 'I knew you'd work it all out in the end.' Her smile is gone and now tears pour down her porcelain cheeks.

'I've left it too late, though? Haven't I?'

She walks over to me and embraces me. This wise angel.

'It takes someone really brave to be a mother, Belle. And there is no one braver or stronger than you. You've spent your life fighting battles. To be loved, to be wanted, to be accepted. But you don't need to fight any more. You just need to start living life in all its glorious wonder,' Nora says.

I close my eyes and hold her tight and wish with all my might that I can go home. I want to do that. I want to live. Oh please let me have a second chance.

'I thought you'd never wake up,' a voice says, cheerily. 'You were exhausted.'

I look up as a nurse walks into the room. My arms are empty and Nora has gone.

'How are you feeling?' she smiles brightly.

'Okay.' I say and reach up and touch my cheek where I hit the water. The swelling has disappeared. My arm …

I'm wearing my clothes again. And they are bone dry. Does this mean …?

'What happened?' I ask.

'You don't remember?' the nurse replies. 'Well, you fainted. Right outside Jim's room. I think the shock of everything just got too much for you.'

I hold my breath until it stings. She said Jim. It must mean I'm back. But what am I facing? 'Is he … is he alive?' There, I've asked it.

The nurse walks over to me and gives me a look of sympathy. 'Oh, you poor poppet.'

He's dead. I'm back but he's dead. I'm too late. I never got to say goodbye.

'What are you crying about?' the nurse continues. 'He's doing just fine. You can go see him if you like. He's asking for you.'

'He's alive?' I say.

'Yes, of course he is. He's suffered a severe trauma, but he's stable now. Stop fretting, he's going to be just fine,' she replies.

'What day is it?' I ask.

'Christmas Eve,' she smiles. 'And it's snowing outside. I think we're going to get a white Christmas after all.'

I swing my legs out of the bed and stand up. The nurse is right by my side to steady me, but I don't need her help. I feel light, healthy, sure-footed. I've never felt better, in fact. I smile my thanks to the nurse and run towards Jim.

His eyes are closed and he is so still. I stand at the door and just look at him. My heart is beating so fast, surely he must hear it over there. My legs do not cooperate at first. They feel like jelly and I wobble my way towards his bed. I reach over and touch his hair. His beautiful, wavy, foxy hair that is falling over his eyes once again. In a gesture as old as we are, I brush it back from his face and he opens his eyes and smiles at me.

'No regrets, only love,' he finally whispers to me.

Sometime later, I awake to feel Jim's hand gently stroking my hair where I rested my head on the side of his bed. 'Hey you,' he says.

'I have so much I need to tell you,' I say, awake at once.

'Me too,' he replies. 'I know you're scared and that's why you lashed out, but we have to ...'

I hold my finger up to his lips. 'Can I go first?'

He nods.

'I'm not scared any more, Jim,' I say.

He looks at me, doubtful, but I think he must see something in my face. He nods at me to continue.

'Something happened to me, something quite beautiful,' I say to him and then falter. Damn it. How do I explain this?

'Me crashing the car?' Jim jokes.

'No, that was the worst moment of my life. Seeing you unconscious, with blood trickling down your face, I thought I'd lost you. And then, for a while, I did.' I say.

'Takes more than a bang on my thick head to get rid of me,' he says with a smile. 'I'm made of strong stuff.'

'I happen to love that thick head of yours,' I say and then, touching his hair again, 'But never cut your hair. Promise me that.'

'Listen, the only reason I keep it is that it seems to invite you to touch it constantly. And I never get tired of that,' he says with a smile. 'But I can't guarantee that I won't go bald one day. Will you still love me then?'

I think of the other Jim, with his shaved head. But still beautiful, hair or no, in every way.

'Yep, I can safely say, that even with no hair you'll still be hot.' I lean in to kiss him, to prove my point.

'So, what's this beautiful thing that happened?' Jim asks.

'It's hard to explain, a long story and one day I'll tell you it all. But for now, let's just say that a friend helped me understand how wonderful life really is,' I say.

'Sounds like a wise friend,' Jim replies. 'I happen to think that every day.'

'I've spent the best part of my life feeling guilty about being me,' I admit. 'Guilty that I somehow caused my mother to not want me and I ruined her life.'

Anger flashes over Jim's face. But before he can say anything, I tell him, 'Listen to me. That's gone. I understand now that I'm not my mother's keeper. I am not responsible for her life. Only my own.'

'You really believe that now?' Jim asks.

'Yes I do,' I say. 'And there's more.'

'Do I need to brace myself?' he asks, looking a bit bemused by my words.

'I love fostering. And I don't ever want to stop. I want to keep helping children, whether it's for a few days or years like we had with Bobby and Lauren. My heart can take it whichever way the cards fall. Because I know that what we do makes a difference,' I say.

'That's such a relief to hear you say that. I love fostering, I would hate to give it up, but I would, you know, in a heartbeat for you. It's killed me these past few weeks, watching you in so much pain,' he says.

'I know that and I can't thank you enough. I miss Lauren, as I know you do. But I know now that I was mourning much more than the loss of her. It was a lot about our baby too,' I say.

Jim's eyes fill with tears and he nods, 'I know.'

I take another deep breath and say, 'I no longer blame myself for the miscarriage.'

'The doctors told you it wasn't your fault,' Jim jumps in.

I smile at him and say, 'I know, darling. But I didn't believe them until recently. We lost our baby and while I'll never completely recover from that, I know it's time to move on.'

He sits up, winces and grabs my hands. 'Do you mean …?'

'I want to have babies. Lots of them,' I say.

Jim's beautiful smile lights up my heart and I smile back. Then he starts to laugh and I do too and we cannot stop, as mirth and joy overtake us.

'Everything okay here?' Annette, the nurse, pops her head in to check on us.

'We're going to make babies,' Jim says, laughing. 'Lots of them.'

'Not right this minute, I hope,' Annette laughs. 'Matron might not approve.'

'But I've good news for you both, though. Do one more night here and tomorrow, by lunchtime, you can go home,' she says.

'Out for Christmas day,' he answers.

'Yep. Happy Christmas you two,' she smiles.

37

No one is born to be a failure. No one is poor who has friends.
Frank Capra

'So everyone knows that dinner is cancelled?' Jim asks, as I wheel him out the ward in a wheelchair, towards the hospital entrance.

'Yep. I rang Tess and Bobby last night. Told them that we were going to postpone our celebrations this year. I think we might have them all over for New Year's Day instead. You should be back to full health by then,' I say. 'If you listen to what the doc says and rest up, that is.'

'Sir, yes sir!' he jokes. 'Listen, all I want to do is snuggle up in front of a fire with my gal and watch TV. I've had enough adventure this past couple of days, thank you very much.'

That I can empathise with. I keep expecting Nora to jump out from behind a plant pot and scream, 'surprise, guess who's back?' But ever since I woke up in hospital the other day, she's been silent.

I never thought I'd say it, but I miss her.

'We can have an alternative Christmas day this year,' I say.

We've certainly never had one like this before. I'm normally so organised.

'Look at the time,' I say to Jim, checking out my watch. 'I'd be knee-deep in stuffing and bread sauce by now.'

I can feel my stomach grumble at the thought of it. Maybe, tomorrow I'll make a roast for us, the full works. I wonder if the local Spar will be open, so I can pop in and grab some milk and bread for today.

Also right now, more than lamenting our no-turkey Christmas, I'm a bit worried about how cold and unwelcoming our home is going to be. We have one of those houses that takes ages to heat up. With this cold spell we've had, it must be like a big freezer right now. And that's not even mentioning the Great Christmas Decoration Massacre of a few days ago.

'When we get in, you go jump into bed straightaway,' I say.

'Hey, you'll have to go easy on me, I'm not sure I'm up to much,' Jim winks at me.

'Haha, funny guy. Jump into bed, because it's going to be the warmest place to be, I reckon. I'll light the fire in the sitting room and get the heating on. Then we can have that snuggle in front of the fire you've been wishing for.' I give him a kiss and hope that it's not too long till he's back to full health.

I should have gone home yesterday really, to sort the house out. At the very least, I could have done something about the Christmas tree. But I just couldn't bear to leave Jim. I keep thinking that if I let him out of my sight, I'll end up in another weird parallel universe without him.

I couldn't believe it when Annette, Jim's nurse, said I could sleep on the chair in his room. She muttered something about being a sucker for a good Christmas love story and when she found me curled up beside him on his bed, she didn't even raise an eyebrow, just smiled at us.

I need to get her some chocolates. And flowers too.

'So as you're not knee deep in stuffing, what's on the menu for today? Melted tuna cheese toasties?' Jim asks.

'I think I can rustle up something a little better than that,' I say. 'I've a freezer full of food. We won't starve.' My mind starts to run through options. Parma chicken with pesto sauce, perhaps. Or maybe I could do my Madeira chicken dish with creamy parsnip mash. Jim always loves that.

'Did Bobby and Tess mind?' Jim asks. 'Having their plans changed at the last minute, I mean.'

They always come to us for Christmas Day. I felt awful telling them about the way things had panned out. But they were only worried about Jim.

'I have a feeling that they might pop around this evening to say hello,' I say. 'I think Bobby is going to Tess's house for lunch anyhow. They were only worried about you and wanted to help in any way they could.'

'I know that. By the way, I know you are keeping something from me. You've always been a crap liar,' Jim says.

I decide to ignore him and say instead, 'Tess wanted us to go to her for dinner today. She was quite annoyed with me when I said no.'

'We can call there now if you want to?' Jim says. 'I know I said I wanted to just get home, but what do you want?'

'It feels like such a long time since we've been home, Jim,' I say. 'I need to go there, be in our house together. So that's where we're going.'

He looks at me, as if he's going to say something, then stops in his tracks as we get to the entrance of the hospital. 'Look at that.'

It's snowing and soft white flakes are making a blanket on the ground. It powders the branches of trees, which sag under the weight.

'Oh,' I laugh as a snowflake lands on the tip of my nose.

'How often do we associate snow with Christmas? And it never happens, does it?' Jim says.

'A winter wonderful,' I sigh. 'It's so gorgeous. Oh Jim, it's beautiful.'

'It's getting heavy too, it's sticking. Let's get home before we end up stuck here for the night,' Jim remarks.

Annette has thoughtfully ordered us a taxi and we find him waiting within minutes, just outside the loading area.

'Happy Christmas,' the taxi drivers says. 'Nice day for it, wha'?'

'Sure is,' I say.

'It's all very good right now, everyone all buzzed with their white Christmas shite, but wait till it turns to grey sludge tomorrow. The traffic will go to a standstill. Everyone will be moaning then, wha'?' He continues, full of the festive cheer, I note.

Jim throws his eyes up to the heavens and smiles.

'Ah, we can worry about that tomorrow or whenever. For now, I'm just going to enjoy how beautiful it is,' I reply,

369

giving him the benefit of my best smile. Not even a grumpy taxi driver is going to ruin my mood right now.

I've been putting off reminding Jim about the state of the house. But as we are now en route, it's time to 'fess up. 'Jim, I need to tell you something,' I say.

'Oh lordy,' he says.

'After the accident, I kind of lost it a bit more,' I admit.

'Okay.' Jim looks amused. 'That's not like you, losing it, I mean.'

I let him off that remark. Probably because it's true. 'This wasn't my run-of-the-mill freak-out, this was big-time losing it,' I say.

'What did you do?' He asks, beginning to look a little alarmed now. 'Have we a house at all to go home to?'

'Well, I pretty much wrecked our Christmas decorations,' I say. There, I've said it.

'Define wrecked,' Jim says. There's a hint of a smile hovering around his lips right now. I hope he keeps smiling when he sees my mess.

'Well, I may have, kind of, knocked the Christmas tree over. Then pulled all the lights down. And let's just say that in the brawl between me and the Christmas wreath on the door, I won.' I feel so bad picturing our beautiful wreath in smithereens in the hall.

'So the tree, the wreath, anything else?' Jim asks.

'A couple of snowmen didn't make it either,' I say.

'Did it help? Smashing it all up?' Jim asks.

'Enormously,' I say, feeling sheepish, as I remember how good it felt to hear the snowmen crash against the wall.

Jim starts to laugh and I'm so relieved, I join in too.

'So you don't mind that it looks a bit like a festive war zone at home,' I say.

'I don't care one iota what the house looks like. All I care about is that I'm with you,' he says and kisses my hand. 'And sure, at least it will save us having to take them all down after Christmas.'

'Thanks for not being annoyed,' I say. But I'm annoyed with myself. And now, after everything that we've been through, I can't even really work out why I did all of that.

'I wish I could have chosen something else to take my temper out on, though. Other than our lovely decorations,' I say.

'Yep, you didn't really think that one through. I mean, you could have done some serious damage to that awful pot Tess gave us last year,' Jim says.

'Or that picture your mother sent us, the one with that creepy girl looking out the window. I swear it's haunted. Those eyes follow you wherever you walk,' I say.

'Tell you what, let's dump those anyhow. We'll call it an aftershock!' Jim jokes.

'Deal,' I say.

'Hey, we're passing the Ha'penny Bridge,' Jim says. 'Look how pretty it looks.'

The driver stops and says to us, 'Just a minute mind.'

'I asked him to detour here on the way home,' I say to Jim. 'We missed our usual Christmas Eve tradition, but I thought we could cut straight to the finale today, even if it's a day late.'

'What a wonderful idea,' Jim says, and holding hands we slowly walk up to the centre of the bridge.

We look at each other and with no words know that each of us is remembering that moment right here, when Jim proposed.

I lean into my husband and kiss him tenderly.

Jim Looney, the big ride.

Ignoring the beep from the taxi driver, I pull my mother's letter from the back pocket of my jeans.

'I've been holding on to this for too long. It's time to let it go,' I say.

I open up the letter and watch the page dance its way amongst the snowflakes to the water below.

This time the water stays silent as it eats up Dolores' words.

There. That's better.

'Come on, let's go home,' Jim says.

A few moments later, our taxi turns into our road. It looks so different under the white powder of snow. Trees glisten with white, silvery snow and cars are laden down with snow blanketed on their bonnets. Kids in scarves and hats are building snowmen in their driveways, their laughs and giggles echoing down the road.

'Hey, look, the lights are on,' Jim says, pointing to our house.

I look and yes, they are on. That's odd.

'I must have left them on the other night,' I say to him. 'I was in a bit of a state.'

'That must have been awful for you. It's one of my worst nightmares, ever hearing that you've been hurt,' Jim says.

'It wasn't the most fun thing I've ever experienced,' I say.

Jim pays the taxi driver and we shout Happy Christmas to a couple of kids on the other side of the road, who've made a whole family of snowmen.

'Cute,' I say to them and they smile, sticking carrots in all of the frozen faces.

I hold onto Jim's arm as we tip-toe through the snow up to our front door. I'm not taking any chances at him taking a slip and banging his head again. Just the thought of that makes me shiver.

'I thought the wreath got it?' Jim says. 'Look at that.'

I look up and pinned to the front door is a large green wreath, with red berries laced through it. White snow powders the leaves and my stomach starts to flip.

What on earth is going on? I destroyed our wreath.

The door opens and standing grinning in front of us are Tess and Bobby.

'Welcome home,' Tess says ushering us in. My mind flashes back to a time, decades ago, where she ushered me into her hall. That time I was scared, but now, seeing her, this woman I love so much, I am undone.

'Oh Tess,' I say and throw myself into her warm, soft embrace. 'I missed you so much.'

'There, there,' she says, as I bury myself in her arms. 'Hush, Belle. You're okay. You're home now.' She pulls back and wipes the tears from my face with her hands.

I look over and Bobby is in Jim's arms, hugging him unashamedly.

'Bobby,' I sob and pull him into my arms too. 'Are you okay?'

'Er, yeah, I'm not the one who was in a crash,' he says, but he still hugs me back tight all the same.

'If you are ever in trouble, you come to me and Jim, straight away. You hear me?' I say to him.

Jim gives me a funny look and says, 'It's been a worrying time for Belle, you'll have to excuse her being so emotional.'

'Come inside, out of the cold,' Tess says and we close the door behind us.

'What's that smell?' Jim asks and his stomach grumbles loudly.

'Dinner, of course,' Tess says. 'Surely you didn't think we'd let you guys come home to a cold house. What do you take us for?'

We walk into the kitchen and the most wonderful aroma hits me. I cannot believe my eyes as I see saucepans bubbling away on the stove.

'We've got some home-made roasted sweet-potato soup for starters. Courtesy of the Kavanagh's next door,' Tess says.

'When I called over yesterday to put the heat on, your neighbour Catherine asked me what was going on,' Bobby says. 'When I told her about Jim's crash, she was so worried. And then this morning, when I got here, she was over with the soup. Made it especially for you both.'

I feel tears sting my eyes at their generosity. Mind you, I'm not surprised. They are amazing neighbours.

'And that's not all,' Tess says. 'You've got some home-made shortbread biscuits, dropped in by Mrs O'Leary this morning. She said she'd heard about Jim outside mass.'

'I called Lauren's mam too,' Bobby says. 'I wanted to arrange to drop over some presents for Lauren. Anyhow when I told her about the crash, she was really upset. And when I got there with the presents, she had made a trifle for you. Looks pretty good too.'

'All I had to do was sort the dinner. And you'll both be thrilled to know that I didn't use the deep-fat fryer once.' Tess winks at us both.

'We've turkey, with two stuffings,' Tess says. 'Pork stuffing for Jim, and chestnut for you. And ham with a maple glaze on top.'

'It's good. I've already robbed a bit for a sambo,' Bobby says. 'Bleeding starvin' I was.' And he ducks as Tess tries to swipe him with her tea towel.

'Parsnip and potato mash, roast carrots and butternut squash and peas. Oh and some Brussels sprouts, but Bobby went all Jamie Oliver on me and put bacon and walnuts in with them.' Tess shakes her head ruefully. 'He was watching some programme on the telly and got ideas.'

'I've filled your fridge for you too,' Bobby says. 'You don't need to leave the house for a week. I promise you won't go hungry.'

I walk over to the fridge and open it in disbelief. It's heaving at the seams, filled with patés, cheeses, cream, salads, prosecco and a huge trifle.

'Jeepers,' I say and then start to cry again. 'I can't thank you both enough.'

'Would you go away out of that?' Tess says. 'Sure we're your family, what else would we do?'

'Er, I thought that you'd been bleeding burgled when I got here, by the way,' Bobby says. 'Some mess you had there in the sitting room and in the hall.'

'Long story,' I say sheepishly.

'I did my best,' Bobby says and pulls me by my hand into our living room. But I can see he's trying not to smile. What is he up to?

'Close your eyes,' he tells us both and we do so obediently.

'Right, open them,' he says and when we do, we are dazzled.

The curtains are closed and the lights are off, save for the dozens of twinkling fairy lights bouncing around the room. Standing in the corner is our Christmas tree: tall and resplendent, filled to capacity with our baubles and decorations.

'Oh my,' I say and reach over to clasp Bobby's hand.

'There were a few broken balls, but I glued them back together. It's all there. I tried to make it like you always do, Belle,' he says.

'You made it better,' I tell him and hug him close.

'But I couldn't find your angel anywhere,' he says.

'Don't worry, it was already missing. I need to get a new one,' I say.

An open fire roars, the flames licking the hearth and the sound of crackling fills the room.

'Cheers mate,' Jim says gruffly and ruffles Bobby's hair.

'Sit, sit,' Tess says to him. 'Don't you be doing too much.'

'I'll get some drinks,' Bobby says.

'Dinner will be in about thirty minutes,' Tess says. 'Can you wait that long, or do you want a chocolate to keep you going?' She holds up a large box of Milk Tray, hopefully.

We both giggle. Some things never change.

'Let's leave them till tonight, we can watch the Christmas specials with choccies and Prosecco,' I say to her and she is practically giddy at the thought. Bobby comes in and hands us a glass each and pops open the cork on a bottle of bubbly. He quickly fills each of our glasses.

'Impressive,' Jim says to him, as he does so without spilling a drop.

'I hope you don't mind that we came over?' Tess asks. 'It's just, well, we couldn't stay away.'

'We wouldn't want it any other way,' I say and I mean every word.

'Who's that?' Tess grumbles as the phone rings. 'Stay where you are, you two. I'll get it.'

She walks back a few minutes later, holding the phone out. 'It's Lorcan.'

I take it, thinking of the last time I spoke to him. 'Hello.'

'Hey, Belle, hear Jimbo has been in the wars,' he says. 'Is he okay?'

'He will be. Just needs a little TLC for a few days and he'll be back to fighting fit,' I say.

'You okay? Last time we spoke, you weren't best pleased with me,' he says.

'I'm good. I know that Lauren is where she should be,' I say. Doesn't stop me missing her, though. 'Just promise me that you will keep a close eye on them both and any sign of problems with Alicia, you bring her straight back here to us.'

'You have my word. Listen, I was trying to get you both yesterday, but obviously you weren't picking up,' he says. 'I have a family who need help. Mother is going into hospital middle of January for a hysterectomy. Dad died a few years back. The grandparents are too old to step in and no other relatives around. Four kids. All teenagers, ranging from thirteen to seventeen. Three girls, one boy.'

'Sounds like hormonal hell,' I say.

'Yeah, that's about it,' Lorcan says. 'But I need to find temporary foster parents for them, for four weeks. You up for it? Or do you think it will be too soon after Jim's crash?'

Am I up for it? Only a few days ago, I swore to myself I'd never foster a child again. But I look at Bobby, our first foster child, and know that there is only one answer I can give.

'Of course I'm up for it. Bring it on, Lorcan,' I say. 'Merry Christmas, old friend. Stop by sometime for a drink.'

'Merry Christmas to you too and I might just do that tomorrow or the next day.' He hangs up and I turn to Jim, who is looking at me expectantly.

'Four teenagers coming our way mid-January. You better get better quick. And Bobby, you'll have to put the bunk beds up,' I say to him.

'So you're still fostering?' Tess asks, a smile dancing on her lips. 'I thought you were done with all that.'

'Don't be so ridiculous,' I say. 'That's what we are. Foster parents.'

'Hey, I nearly forgot, some kid called round here earlier with a present for you, Belle. I'm not sure who she was,' Tess says. 'Sweet little thing. She wouldn't come in. Just left you these two parcels.'

Tess walks over to the tree and pulls them out from the pile under it, one wrapped in green-and-white-striped paper, with a large red bow tied around its centre. The other is a Santa gift bag. It can't be?

I look inside the bag and, yes, it's the gift for Jim. 'This one's for you. Happy Christmas from your Secret Santa.'

He opens up the bag and when he sees the game inside, his laughter bellows out through the house. 'Oh you are so going down to china town, Belle Bailey!'

'Not that game again,' Tess says laughing. 'Sweet divine, that brings me back.'

'Good present?' I ask and he kisses me his thanks. I think I did good.

'What's the other one?' Bobby asks.

'I'm not sure, but it's wrapped very pretty,' I say. 'This is my first present this year.'

'There's more under the tree,' Bobby says. 'From me and Tess and Lauren too.'

'I don't have yours wrapped yet,' Jim says and I shush him with a kiss.

'Did you open your own presents yet? They were somewhere under the mess of the tree,' I say to Bobby and Tess.

'No of course not,' Tess says. 'They're still under the tree, waiting till you guys got home. We can open them after dinner.'

I carefully untie the bow and open the parcel. Inside is an angel, about fifteen inches high. She's dressed in a long white gown, with wings covered in white feathers. But she's not like the angels that I've normally seen in shops, with blonde hair and blue eyes.

'She looks like you,' Jim says and I nod in amazement. Same hair, same caramel skin. She's a lot like Dee-Dee, I realise.

'I've never seen an angel like that,' Tess says.

'Who's it from?' Jim says and I reach inside the box, looking for a card or note. I find a tiny card folded in two and read it out loud.

I heard that you were missing an angel on your tree, Belle. Merry Christmas and always remember, it's a wonderful life you have, my friend. Don't waste a second of it.

Love always, Nora x

'Thank you, Nora,' I whisper through trembling lips, and I walk over to the tree to place her on top.

'Need some help?' Jim asks and he takes the angel from me and places her gently on the top branch. And as he does so, my silver bell rings out through the living room.

Every time a bell rings, an angel gets its wings. Atta girl Nora, atta girl.

'Now Christmas is just perfect,' I say and turn to rest my head in the nook of Jim's neck. 'Merry Christmas, my darling.'

38

Look, Daddy. Teacher says, every time a bell rings an angel gets his wings.

Zuzu, It's A Wonderful Life

Nora

I've been an angel 292 years, roaming Dublin, taking care of my many charges. I've had some pretty amazing moments. I can still remember the sound of the first baby boy born into the Rotunda Hospital in 1757. I was by his side right up till his death fifty-five years later.

I saw the electric lights get switched on in Dublin in 1881 for the first time and laughed in glee alongside the hundreds of amazed men, women and children who watched in awe.

When Patrick Pearse stood in the GPO in 1916 and announced a new Irish Republic, I cheered, so proud of the man he had become from the boy he once was. And I wept when lives were lost over and over in the days that followed.

So many babies born, my charges, and I've stayed dutifully by their side, until they breathed their last breaths. Some gone far too early, others, like Mary McEvoy, who hung in until her 101st birthday to finally sigh her last breath.

My only job throughout all of this was to watch and whisper words of encouragement when they needed it, and smile in pride when I see them living their best lives.

107,212 days of watching and whispering and loving. And today is my last day.

It's time for another angel to step into my shoes.

It's my time.

Epilogue

Because when you stop and look around,
This life is pretty amazing.

Dr Seuss

'Oh sweet divine, I'm dizzy,' Tess moans, lowering herself onto a park bench. 'That little man has my heart broken. I've no sooner spun him on the roundabout and he wants another go.'

I giggle at Tess's face, which is redder than normal and marvel at her energy.

'Come on, Nana Tess, one more time, pleeeaase,' George shouts. Our foster son is eight and has been with us for over a year now. He's bright, happy and wild and there's a chance he might be with us forever. But I've learned to take one day at a time. No more planning too far ahead. For now, we're a family and that is okay with me.

'Bobby, Bobby, push me higher!' A little voice squeals with excitement and my heart constricts with love.

'She's no fear that one,' Tess says, smiling at the little girl, who is not even three yet. She has that effect on people. I've noticed that most can't help but smile in her company.

I jump up from the park bench and sit on the empty swing beside her.

'Come on, Jim, I need a push,' I say to him.

'I'd hoped she'd outgrow this,' he moans to Tess, but he's smiling as he walks towards me.

'You wouldn't want me any other way,' I say and shiver in excitement when he pulls me back and pushes me forward with all his strength.

'Higher, higher!' I squeal.

'Look at me, mammy.' I look to my right at my daughter, who is fearless and kind, loud and quiet, stubborn and generous, loving and, best of all, all ours.

'I see you, darling,' I say, watching in awe at the little girl who calls me mammy. 'You are almost touching the heavens.'

Nora, our daughter, was born in September, exactly nine months after that fateful Christmas. Our very own angel, and we are in constant awe that we created someone so perfect in every way.

'She looks more like you every day,' Jim says and I know it shouldn't matter who she looks like, but I'm so glad it's me. My little mini me.

'Let me down,' I say to Jim and his strong arms pull me to a standstill. I jump off the swing and say to Tess and Bobby, 'Back in five. I'm gonna steal my husband for a quick walk around the park.'

He loops his arm over me and we walk shoulder to shoulder to the path, around the park, the sounds of George and Nora echoing behind us.

'Happy?' he asks even though he doesn't need to.

'More than I ever thought possible,' I say and look down to my tummy.

I have a secret. A delicious secret that I have been waiting to share, at just the right moment.

'What are our plans this Christmas?' I ask.

'You asking that already?' he laughs. 'We've not even gotten through the summer yet!'

'Oh you know me. I like to prepare early,' I say. 'Besides this year, we'll have our hands full.'

'Why?' he asks.

I stop and take his hand, placing it on my tummy. He looks down to where his hand rests and back up to my face again.

'A baby?' he asks.

I nod. 'A little brother or sister for George and Nora, due on Christmas Eve, by my calculations.'

'Another baby.' He spins me around and around in his arms. 'Belle, I love you, you clever, clever woman. No regrets?'

He's right of course. I am terribly clever. 'No regrets, just love.'

Acknowledgements

Dear Reader,

You know, it's been a long-held ambition of mine to write a Christmas book, so can you imagine my excitement when my editor suggested that I do one this year? Yep, I was over the moon. The story of Belle Bailey and Jim Looney is inspired by one of my all-time favourite movies, *It's A Wonderful Life*. Have you seen the 1946 Frank Capra classic? If not, then check it out. It's … well, it's wonderful! It never fails to reduce me to happy, joyful tears by its conclusion. My Christmas wish is that you love *Every Time a Bell Rings* even a fraction as much as I do the movie that inspired it.

I have many thanks to give and I can think of no better place to start than with you all! Thank you, oh fabulous reader, for continuing to support me and my books, for cheering me on, whether we meet in person, on Facebook or Twitter, or on my website. I love chatting to you all and every word I write, I do with you in mind. Know that every word of encouragement and review you give me, is cherished.

Special thanks must go to Charlotte Ledger, my incredible editor and friend, who not only suggested I write this book, but also came up with the beautiful title. I'm so grateful for her endless enthusiasm, passion and keen editing eye. I know how lucky I am to have her by my side, supporting me.

There are so many people to thank at HarperCollins both in Ireland and UK, who work tirelessly behind the scenes to get a book onto the bookshelves, real or virtual. I am very lucky that I get to work with Kimberley Young, Tony Purdue, Mary Byrne, Ann-Marie Dolan, Cait Davies, Katie Sadler, Jaime Frost, Rebecca Glibbery, Dawn Cooper, Lucy Vanderbilt and so many more.

Thank you to my agent, Tracy Brennan, for all your hard work on my behalf and for encouraging me at all times.

One of the themes in *Every Time a Bell Rings* is that of foster care. During my research I spoke to my friend, foster parent Margaret Madden. Her help was invaluable and I'll be forever grateful. I am in awe of the selfless love and devotion that all foster parents, including Margaret and her husband Declan, offer children every day.

Congratulations to Annette Hoyne, who won a competition to have a character named after her. I believe that nurses are walking angels. I hope you like that I've named a lovely nurse after you.

Writing can be solitary for many, but not for me, because I have a gang of talented writerly friends, who, whether they know it or not, have kept me from turning into a crazy lady on many an occasion. When I mutter about deadlines, edits and bestseller charts, they always listen, advise and understand and are happy to share G&T's and cake with me. They're good like that. In no particular order, thank you, my talented friends – Lynn Marie Hulsman, Claudia Carroll, Alexandra Brown, Maria Nolan, Louise Hall, Paul O'Brien, Hazel Gaynor, Margaret Madden, Tanya Farrell, Catherine Evans, Sharon Thompson and Fionnuala Kearney. You may not realise it, but at some point over the past year you've kept me sane!

I have to give a shout out to Elaine Crowley and all the gang at Midday. Whenever I join you on the panel, I laugh so much that my sides hurt. To the team behind Focal – Wexford Literary Festival, you have been a huge support to me, right from the start. I'm forever grateful that we stumbled across each other. To the IWI'ers, the group I mentor, thank you and remember to always keep dreaming and writing!

To my family and friends who support and love me, I thank you. My parents Tina and Mike O'Grady, siblings Fiona and Michael Gainfort, John and Fiona O'Grady, Shelley and Anthony Mernagh, my mother-in-law Evelyn Harrington and siblings-in-law Adrienne Harrington and George White, Evelyn and Seamus Moher and Leah Harrington, my nieces and nephews Sheryl, Amy, Louis, Paddy and Matilda, my aunt and uncle Ann and Nigel Payne. So many friends, thanks for all the laughs – Maria Murtagh, Liz McNulty, Siobhan Kirby, Davnet Murphy, Fiona Murray, Rosaleen Philpott and all the lovely mammies I've met since Amelia and Nate came into my world – too many to mention by name. I would like to say a special thanks to three friends who forever go the extra mile for me, I can never thank them enough – Sarah Kearney, Catherine Kavanagh and last, but certainly *never* least, Ann Murphy (my person).

Thank you to my mother, Tina O'Grady, who kindly loaned her recipe for Christmas Pudding to Nana Tess, one of the characters in the book, and to you all too, because it's here in the book for you to enjoy as well. I hope you love it as much as my family and I have done, for many, many years.

Finally, I'd like to thank all my H's – Roger, Amelia, Nate and Eva, to whom this book is dedicated. Thank you for the huggies, songs, laughter and love that we share every day. I couldn't do this without you all, wouldn't want to. We'll make this Christmas one to never forget, I promise.

There's nothing more for me to say, but pour yourself a glass of something nice, open the chocolates and enjoy *Every Time a Bell Rings*. Much love to each and every one of you and have yourselves a merry little Christmas …

Carmel
xxx

Tess's Christmas Pudding

This recipe is actually Tina O'Grady's – my mother. I have some wonderful memories, watching and helping her make this pudding each year. My brother John, sisters Fiona and Shelley and I loved placing a silver coin wrapped in tin foil into the pudding and making a wish as we stirred it. It's a lovely rich, dark, pudding that my family adores. I hope you enjoy it too!

Ingredients

4oz flour
2oz breadcrumbs
1 teaspoon mixed spice
1 teaspoon cinnamon
1 teaspoon nutmeg
4oz butter
4oz dark-brown sugar
4oz grated apple
4oz chopped mixed peel
4oz currants
4oz sultanas

8oz raisins

2oz dried apricots

2 eggs

Grated rind and juice of half a lemon

Grated rind of half an orange

1 tablespoon of either golden syrup or black treacle

¼ pint of Guinness

(4oz chopped almonds is optional, but in our house it was preferred without.)

Mix the butter and sugar together until soft. Then beat in the flour, spices and eggs. Stir in the remaining ingredients.

Leave the mixture overnight, then stir again.

Put the mixture into a well-greased pudding basin. Level the top of the pudding and cover with greaseproof paper.

(Mum's tip – grease both sides of the paper to keep the pudding dry on top!)

Pleat a larger piece of greaseproof paper and cover the basin over the edges. Do the same again with the silver foil and put on top.

Then string around the basin to keep this in place, criss-crossing the string to make a handle.

Place the basin in a steamer over simmering water and steam for 6 hours or put the basin in a large pan and pour enough boiling water in to come halfway up the basin. Boil for 6 hours, ensuring that the water does not boil dry!

When the pudding is cooked, allow to cool and remove the foil and greaseproof paper.

Put fresh paper and foil back onto the pudding.

On Christmas Day re-steam for 2 hours.

Turn it onto a plate and stand for 5 minutes as this helps to loosen the pudding from the basin.

Before serving, drizzle the pudding with brandy and light it. Add lashings of cream or custard (or both!) and enjoy.

A Q & A with Carmel Harrington

1. *Every Time a Bell Rings* **is influenced by Frank Capra's** *It's a Wonderful Life.* **What was it about the film that caught your imagination and inspired you to write Belle's story?**

For me, this movie is so much more than just a beloved Christmas movie. I can watch it any time of the year. I love the contrasts between dark and light explored and how they still translate and work all these years later. Throughout the movie there is a beautiful love story between George Bailey and his childhood friend Mary. A scene where they almost kiss, as they both hold a phone between them, makes me sigh every time I watch it. Achingly perfect. This love was the starting point for me as I created the characters of Belle Bailey and Jim Looney. As I wrote *Every Time A Bell Rings*, I kept the themes of the movie at the forefront of my mind, but I used them in different ways. I twisted things up, made the storyline contemporary and relevant. I wanted the readers to get a fresh and different approach to how one person finds out how much he or she can impact the world. I hope I did it justice.

2. Nora plays such a pivotal part in the book, how did you find writing her character?

Clarence in *It's A Wonderful Life* is such a strong character and quite perfect. I didn't want to attempt to copy him, so I decided to create someone very different for my guardian angel. Nora, a child in appearance, has the infinite wisdom of being a guardian angel for 292 years. I loved the mix of both innocence and wisdom she possesses. As a mother, I've realised that children are our teachers. I learn from Amelia and Nate every day. They see the world through different eyes and ultimately that's what Nora does for Belle. She shows her another way to view the world, but always with love and a wicked sense of humour.

3. Do you believe in angels yourself?

Yes, I do. I believe that my grandmother, Margaret O'Grady, is my guardian angel. I feel her watching over me, protecting me, guiding me in life. And I do believe that when your gut tells you to do something, it's actually a whisper from your guardian angel. When I trust my gut I rarely make a mistake, it's when I've ignored it that things go pear-shaped! I also like the idea that babies were all angels before they made their way into our lives. That thought makes me happy.

4. In the book Belle and Jim are huge fans of Christmas, is it a special time of year for you and your family too? Did any of your own traditions make it into the novel?

Christmas is my favourite time of the year. While many bemoan the fact that it starts too early, I am counting down the days all year round! I love everything about it – spending time with family, visiting Santa, choosing the perfect gift for family and friends, singing along to Christmas carols and songs, going to the pantomime, opening the advent calendar, the food, oh the wonderful food, not just on Christmas Day, but throughout the festive season, parties, decorations and the trees, even the adverts on TV! There's nothing about Christmas I don't like. You see? I'm a Christmas nut!

I grew up in a house with parents who made Christmas special for us. Many of my own traditions are ones that started with Mam and Dad and now that I have my own family, we have added some new ones. And yes! You will see a lot of these in *Every Time A Bell Rings!*

On December 1st, our decorations go up. We have two trees, one in our living room and one in the family room. I've been collecting baubles for over twenty-five years now and they are some of my most treasured possessions.

One tree has an angel, the other a star. All the Christmas presents from friends and family go under the tree in the living room. On Christmas Eve, I bake mince pies and sausage rolls. We go to an early children's mass in our village and Santa always makes a surprise visit at the end, to remind the children to go to bed early. Then, before bed, we all get to open just one present each.

Once the children are asleep, with their stockings hung, it's time for a glass of Prosecco for Rog and me as we watch *It's A Wonderful Life*. I've watched this movie at Christmas for over twenty-five years now.

It's an early start on Christmas morning, as the children wake early. We watch Amelia and Nate open their presents from Santa first of all, then have breakfast, before tackling the family gifts! Rog and I both cook dinner together, which is the traditional turkey and a ham, with all the trimmings.

Oh, I can't wait for December 1st. The countdown is on!

5. What was your favourite thing about writing *Every Time a Bell Rings*?

Singing Christmas songs! Every time I wrote part of the book, I played carols and songs in the background and sang along.

I did feel a sense of responsibility to do Frank Capra's beloved movie justice so I spent a long time looking at the themes in *It's A Wonderful Life* and pulling them apart, seeing how I could use them in a contemporary novel. I had a strong sense of Belle Bailey from the very moment I started to work on the plot. The rest fell into place as I went along. Ultimately I wanted to write a love story and every scene with Belle and Jim in it was a joy to work on.

6. If *Every Time a Bell Rings* was made into a film, which actors would you choose to play your main characters?

@HappyMrsH would be extremely happy if this were to happen! I did have some actors in mind, as it happens.

Ruth Negga as Belle, Colin O'Donoghue as Jim, Emma Thompson as Tess (with padding, as she's half the size of the character!)

7. What made you want to set the book in Dublin? Have you had any special moments of your own on Ha'penny Bridge?

This book has a lot of magic sprinkled in it and as Dublin has that in bucketfuls, in particular the iconic Ha'Penny Bridge, it was the perfect location. When I moved to Dublin at eighteen, I can still remember walking across that bridge for the first time, one evening at dusk, on my way out to meet friends. It's such a pretty spot and the lights as they bounced off the water below seemed so magical. I can remember standing in the centre, looking down and pondering how many people had passed over it. I wondered if that bridge could talk, what stories would it share? Now, when I cross it with the children, we always throw a few pennies in and make a wish.

8. Finally, for anyone visiting Dublin over Christmas, what are your top three festive things to do?

Walking around Dublin city in December is like being part of one big, beautiful Christmas card, with Georgian buildings, twisting cobble-stoned streets, twinkling lights and wonderful window displays. I love nothing more than to stroll around the city, preferably at dusk, soaking up the atmosphere. Grafton Street is one of my favourites. I adore the decorations in the department store, Brown Thomas. There are always buskers and choirs lining the street as you go too. And you never know who you might see because Bono has given a free performance near Fusilier's Arch on Christmas Eve since 2009!

Then, when you need to warm up, head into one of Dublin's many vibrant pubs. Blazing fireplaces, a warm welcome, Christmas music and a glass of Prosecco has me smiling every year! Favourites of mine are Neary's, Ron Blacks or The Bank.

Lastly, I'd check out the Christmas markets, scattered around the city. Both the Docklands and St Stephen's Green are worth a look. They are such a great way to find unusual gifts and also try some local artisan food. Last year I had suckling pig and apple sauce, served in a white bap followed by a huge mince pie and an Irish coffee. Delicious.

Whatever you do in Dublin at Christmas, I promise you that you'll be greeted by a wonderful welcome by all you meet.

Merry Christmas!

Turn the page for an exclusive look at Carmel's stunning second novel, *The Life You Left* …

Prologue

Ballyaislinn, Co. Wexford

<Inbox (2)

To: sarahlawlor0902@yahoo.ie

From: paul.lawlor@cgqh.ie

Subject: Sorry

Sarah, I'm not coming home tonight. Don't try to find me or call my office, I'm taking some time out to get my head sorted. If I don't get away, I'm not sure what I'll do.

If you love me, you will give me the space I need.

Tell the children I love them and I'll be in touch when I can.

Paul

Sarah blinked back tears, confused and disorientated by the email she had just opened. She didn't understand. Those meagre sentences made absolutely no sense to her and mocked her by their cruelty.

She struggled to let the words sink in but no matter how many times she re-read the email, she could not fathom what was happening. She quickly hit re-dial on her husband's mobile, knowing that it was a futile exercise. Yes, damn it, still going to voicemail. She checked the time; it was getting close to 10pm. She hadn't worried at first when Paul didn't appear home for dinner. She figured that he had a late meeting and had forgotten to tell her about it. But by 8pm she was worried and started to call him. His phone kept repeating the same infuriating message.

She ran through the mornings events once again in her mind. Paul had gotten up for work at his usual time, showered and dressed himself, whilst she got the children ready for school. Mornings were always frantic in their house with Sarah making the children their breakfast and school lunches and then dressing them in their uniforms. At some point in the mayhem, Paul would leave for the office, with a quick goodbye kiss for them all if they were lucky.

She supposed he had been quiet this morning, she didn't recall him saying one word to her really, but then again he rarely did these days. She felt scared once again. What had she missed? Their lives had become so frantic – Sarah with the three children and Paul with work, it often felt like they were ships that passed in the night.

A flash of guilt overwhelmed her, almost suffocating her. How could she have been so blind to her husband's distress? Had they drifted so far apart that she, his wife, would not notice her husband falling apart at the seams? So bad that he was having a breakdown of such magnitude that he needed to stay away from his family. An image of Paul in a psych ward popped into her head and she reeled from it, as it evoked a memory so painful it pierced her heart. She quickly threw that image from her mind and went back to this morning. Had he seemed any different when he kissed them all goodbye? She tried to be objective but no matter how much analysis she gave to their humdrum movements, she couldn't pinpoint anything that should have alerted her to this email.

Paul had been his usual slightly moody self but nothing new there. Her stomach started to flip again and she started to pace the living room floor, feeling that somehow or other she was to blame for all of this.

She pondered his request that she not try to find him, but decided that it was impossible to obey. She had to at least try to talk to him, so she began ringing likely candidates that he might have confided in. She started with the obvious, his mother Rita.

'Sarah here. Is Paul with you?'

'No, I haven't seen Paul since last Sunday when you all came for lunch.' Rita replied. 'What's wrong?'

Sarah wasn't sure how to answer that. She glanced at the email again and quickly decided it wasn't fair to worry Rita – yet.

'He's not home, that's all.' Sarah replied, trying hard to disguise her anguish. 'Just a bit worried, as he's not normally this late. I thought he might have popped into you on his way home. I'm sure he'll walk in the door any minute.'

She could hear Rita sigh with relief in response. 'Course he will love. Sure, Paul has always been a workaholic. He's probably on his way home right now.'

Sarah doubted that. A feeling of foreboding overcame her and somehow or other she knew life was never going to be the same again.

Chapter One

'Time for the big finale,' James thought to himself. With a dramatic sigh he put his hand over his face and said, 'and as the sun set, I held her in my arms and she died. I just feel honoured that I was with her when she breathed her last breath. And maybe in some small way I gave her some comfort at the end.'

He wiped an imaginary tear from the corner of his eye and sneaked a peak at his date. Had he overdone it this time? Maybe the tears were too much. Nope, hang on; she had bought his story, hook, line and sinker.

'God she is beautiful,' James thought.

She stifled back a sob and leaned in close to James. 'Oh James,' She whispered, 'You were so brave.' She then touched him on his leg and he knew he'd be getting lucky tonight. Result! The hero story never failed him.

His date was clearly mesmerised by him. At 6"2 with blonde wavy hair, worn slightly long, James had always had plenty of attention. His blue eyes normally sparkled with mischief but sometimes would show hints of hidden depths that made women desperate to be the one to unlock their secrets. He was one of those lucky people that were born with a natural charisma that attracted both men and women. Men wanted to be his friend and women in the main had more than friendship on their minds when they met him.

The sound of his mobile phone blaring out Eliza Doolittle's *Pack Up* interrupted his daydream of how the night was likely to end. Glancing at the handset, he saw that it was Sarah. He ignored the phone and said to the blonde, 'Let them leave a message, nothing is more important than this, right now, with you.' She really seemed to like the cheesy lines. She was practically purring – some girls were just too easy to play.

Momentarily he felt a wave of guilt assuage him. He knew that after a few dates he wouldn't be interested in seeing her again. He just wanted some fun and had no intention of settling down with anyone, just yet. He'd grown up in a house with parents who at best were polite to each other, but on a daily basis made it quite obvious that whatever love had drawn them towards each other at the beginning had long since died. In his career as a private detective, he'd also seen more unfaithful marriages than he'd had chicken curries. From his experience there weren't very many happy ever afters anymore, any excuse and one or the other of the couple was jumping into bed with someone else.

And what about his sister, Sarah? Sure he'd watched her fall apart these past few weeks since Paul had done his vanishing act.

What he wouldn't give for five minutes with that man!

A hand gently touching his shoulder brought him back to his present situation and the hot blonde seated in front of him. He brushed aside any guilt he may have felt; after all they were both adults and he never promised any of the girls he dated anything more than they got. He had a firm rule that he always detangled himself before the fourth date. In his experience it was after this dating milestone that most girls started humming the wedding march.

He could see Sarah's disapproving face in his mind's eye and once again felt a slight twinge of guilt. But one look at his date's long bronzed legs and that guilt disappeared. He was just about to make a suggestion of a nightcap back at his house when his phone beeped with a new text message. It was Sarah again. He clicked open the message on his phone. Two words glared back at him.

Edward's back.

This was bad. Even though Sarah had not mentioned Edward in years, James knew immediately to whom she was referring. The aftermath of Edwardgate still left a mark on both of them.

'Sorry, I've got to go.' James leaned in with genuine regret and kissed the blonde on the cheek, slightly amused by the look of astonishment on her face.

James could see his date beginning to panic at the sudden realisation that James really was leaving. He smiled at her with genuine regret, she did seem like a nice girl, but he was needed at Sarah's and that came first.

'What's wrong?' She asked.

'Edward's back.' James replied.

'Edward?' She asked puzzled. 'Who's Edward?'

'Trouble, that's who Edward is, a whole lot of trouble.' James replied and with that ran to his car, texting Sarah as he went that he was on his way.